DISORDERLY CONDUCT

THE ANNA ALBERTINI FILES # 1

REBECCA ZANETTI

RAZ INK LLC

ACKNOWLEDGMENTS

Thank you to everyone who helped to make this book a reality!

Thank you to Tony, Gabe, and Karlina for being an understanding and fun family who let me bounce ideas (often odd ones) off them constantly;

Thank you to Asha Hossain of Asha Hossain Designs, LLC for the fantastic cover;

Thank you to Debra Stewart of Dragonfly Media Ink for the wonderful edits;

Thank you to Jillian Stein for being the best social media guru in the history of the world;

Thank you to Stella Bloom for the fabulous narration for the audio book;

Thank you to Liz Berry, Asa Maria Bradley, and Boone Brux for the advice with the concepts for this new series;

Thank you to my incredibly hard working agent, Caitlin Blasdell;

Thank you to Jenn Watson from Social Butterfly and M.J. Rose from AuthorBuzz for helping get the word out about this new series;

Thank you to Rebecca's Rebels (my FB street team) and their

hard working leaders, Anissa Beatty, Margarita Coale, and Minga Portillo;

Thank you to my constant support system: Gail and Jim English, Kathy and Herbie Zanetti, Debbie and Travis Smith, Stephanie and Don West, and Jessica and Jonah Namson.

NOTE FROM THE AUTHOR

Howdy everyone! Thank you for picking up a copy of this first Anna Albertini Book. Sometimes, as an author, you have to write something a little different. This series is that for me.

Oh, it has romance in it (of course). Yes, there's a bit of suspense as well - in addition to small town family life and a lot of relatives. The book is written in first person POV, which is different from my other books, and it's from the point of view of the heroine for the entire series. Anna Albertini is an interesting person to me, and not just because she gets burned by a bullet once in a while.

Also, I am a lawyer, and I might live in a small town, but this is in **no way** autobiographical. It turns out that the name Albertini is a distant family name of my relatives, which is pretty cool. However, the story is all made up. The characters are all fictional and so are the towns and counties (like usual). Also, the law is correct. :)

I hope you like Anna's world as much as I do!

XO

Rebecca

CHAPTER 1

*M*y latte tasted like it was missing the flavor. It might be because I had less than a week until I received an anniversary card from a sociopath, and the waiting was painful. Sighing, I took another sip. Well, the brew wasn't so bad, and the prosecuting attorney's office was fairly quiet this morning, so I could get caught up on paperwork.

The outside doors burst open, slamming loudly against the traditional oak paneling. What in the world? I jumped up and ran around my desk, skidding to a stop at my doorway to see a cluster of men stalk inside. Weapons were strapped to their thighs. Big ones.

It felt like a blitz attack.

The receptionist in the waiting area yelled, and a paralegal walking while reading a stack of papers stopped cold in spiked pumps, dropping the papers. Her name was Juliet, and I'd just met her last month but didn't know much about her except she liked to use colored paperclips when handing over case files.

She sidled closer to me; her eyes wide. Even though I wore thick wedges, she towered over me by about a head.

Six agents strode inside, all big and broad, all wearing blue jackets with yellow DEA letters across their backs. There should be a woman or three among them. Why just men? More importantly, why was the DEA invading the prosecuting attorney's offices?

The shortest agent slapped a piece of paper on the reception desk, and the other five stomped around her, prowling down the long hallways and past my office which was the nearest to the reception area. Being the most junior of all the deputy prosecutors, I was lucky to have an office, if it could be called such. I waited until the grim looking agents had passed before walking across the scattered papers to read what predictably turned out to be a warrant.

An arrest warrant.

I tried to digest that reality when the tallest agent, a guy with light blond hair and light-refracting glasses that concealed the color of his eyes, escorted Scot Peterson, the prosecuting attorney, out of the office in handcuffs. My boss was around sixty-something years old with thick salt and pepper hair, bright blue eyes, and a sharp intelligence that had won him cases at the Idaho Supreme Court on more occasions that I could count.

He didn't look right cuffed. I finally burst out of the fuzz of shock, and heat slammed through me. What was happening? Scot was a decent guy. He helped people and even taught for free at the local community college. The agent led him out the door, and then he was gone without having said a word.

The office went deadly silent for about ten seconds. Then pandemonium exploded. The remaining DEA agents started gathering manila files, case files, and random pieces of paper.

I cleared my throat and read the warrant again. It was for Scot's arrest and any documents pertaining to...the distribution of narcotics? "Wait a minute." I interrupted a tug of war between the nearest agent and the receptionist over a picture of her with Stan Lee at a Comic Con. She was in her early twenties, blonde, and very chipper. Right now, she had tears in her usually sparkling brown eyes. "That's outside the scope of this warrant," I protested. No doubt any warrant. Come on.

The agent paused. He sighed, his lips turning down, as if he'd just been waiting for an argument.

I nodded. "Yeah. You've just raided an area ripe with attorneys." Yet in looking around, I was it. The only attorney on the floor. A pit dropped into my stomach, and I struggled to keep a calm facade. I'd only been a lawyer for a month. What did I know? The other attorneys were elsewhere, including my boss, who'd just been arrested.

I swallowed.

"Do something," Juliet muttered, her teeth clenched.

I blinked. "What?" There wasn't much I could do at the moment. While there should be a sense of comfort with that realization, it felt like I *should* do something.

"Anna." Clarice Jones, the head paralegal, rushed toward me with two case files in her hands. She shoved them my way.

I took them instinctively and tried to keep from falling backward. "What's going on?" If anybody knew what was up with Scot, it'd be her. They'd worked together for decades.

"I don't know." Clarice's white hair had escaped its usually too-tight bun to soften her face with tendrils. She'd gnawed away half of the red lipstick customarily blanketing her thin lips. "Worry about it later. You have to take these felony arraignment hearings. Right now."

I coughed as surprised amusement bubbled through me. "You have got to be kidding." I'd been an attorney for a month and had only covered misdemeanor plea bargains to date. Plus, my boss had just been arrested. "Get a continuance. On both of them." I tried to hand the files back.

"No." She shoved harder than I did. Her strength was impressive. "These cases are before Judge Hallenback, and he'll just dismiss if we don't show. He's not playing with a full deck lately, but he's still the judge. You have to take the hearings while Scot gets this mess figured out." She tapped the top folder, which seemed rather light in my hands. "Just follow the notes on the first page. Scot sets out a strategy for each case. The defendant will either plead guilty, in which case you ask for a sentencing hearing sometime in the next couple of weeks. Or they plead not-guilty, and you argue for bond—just read the notes."

District Court? I was so not ready for district court. I looked frantically around the mayhem surrounding me. How could I possibly go to court right now? "Where is everyone else?"

Clarice grabbed my arm and tugged me toward the door. "Frank and Alice are up in Boundary County prosecuting that timber trespass case. Melanie went into labor last night and is still pushing another one of her devil children out. Matt is with the police investigating that missing kid case. And Scot was just dragged out of here in cuffs." Reaching the doorway, which was still open, she tried to shove me through it. "That leaves you."

I dug my heels in.

The agent who'd been so determined to get his hands on the Stan Lee photo rushed my way. "You can't take documents out of here."

Relief swept me so quickly I didn't have time to feel guilty about it.

Clarice turned and glared. "These are just two case files, and the judge is waiting for the arraignment hearings." Flipping open the top one while it settled precariously in my hands, she tapped the first page with her finger. Hard. "Feel free to take a look."

Ah, darn it. The agent scrutinized the first page and then the too few other pages before looking at the second file folder. I should've protested the entire situation, but my knees froze in place. So did my brain. I really didn't want to go to district court. Finally, the agent grimaced. "All right. You can take those." He moved back to the reception area like a bull about to charge.

I leaned in toward the paralegal. "Call everyone back here.

Now." I needed somebody with a lot more legal experience than I had to deal with this.

Clarice nodded. "You got it." Then she shoved me—pretty hard —out the door. "Go to court."

The flower-scented air attacked me as I turned and strode down the steps into the nice spring day just as news vans from the adjacent city screeched to a halt in front of my building, which housed the prosecuting attorney's offices, the public defender's offices, and the DMV. The brick structure formed a horseshoe around a wide and very green park with the courthouse, police station, and county commissioner offices set perpendicular to my building. Directly across sat Timber City Community College, which stretched a far distance to the north as well. The final side held the beach and Lilac Lake.

Ducking my head, I took a sharp right, hit the end of the street, and turned for the courthouse. The building had been erected when the timber companies and the mines had been prosperous in the area and was made of deep mahogany and real marble brought in from Italy. Instead of walking downstairs like I had the last two weeks, I climbed up a floor to the district court level. It even smelled different than the lower floors. More like lemon polish and something serious. Oh yeah. Life and death and felonies. My knees wobbled, so I straightened my blue pencil skirt and did a quick check of my white blouse to make sure I hadn't pitted out.

Nope. Good. I shouldn't be too scared, because the pseudo-metropolis of Timber City had only 49,000 residents, roughly the same as a large state college. But compared to my hometown of Silverville, which was about fifty miles east through a mountain pass, this was the big city.

My wedges squeaked on the gleaming floor, and I pushed open the heavy door and made my way past the pews to the desk to the right, facing the judge's tall bench. My temples started to thrum. I remained standing at the table and set down the case files before flipping open the first one.

A commotion sounded, and two men strode in from the back, both wearing fancy gray suits. I recognized the first man, and an odd relief took me again, even though he was clearly there as the defendant's attorney and on the opposite side of the aisle as me. "Mr. O'Malley," I murmured.

He held out his hand. "Call me Chuck, Anna." He was a fishing buddy of my dad's and had been for years. "They've thrown you into District Court already?"

I shifted my feet. "It's a long story." That would be public shortly. "The DEA took Scot away in handcuffs," I said.

Chuck straightened, his gray eyebrows shooting up. "Charges?"

"The warrant said something about narcotics." We were on different sides right now, and Chuck was a phenomenal criminal defense attorney, but the truth was the truth and would be out anyway. "He probably needs a good lawyer."

"I'll check it out after this hearing." Chuck's eyes gleamed the same way they did when my Nonna Albertini brought her apple pie to a community picnic. He nodded at his client, a guy in his late twenties with a trimmed goatee and thinning hair. "This is Ralph Ceranio. He's pleading not guilty today."

Thank goodness. That just meant we would set things for trial.

Chuck smiled. "Unless you agree to dismiss."

I smiled back. "I'd like to keep my job for another week." Probably. "So, no."

Chuck turned as the bailiff entered through a side door by the bench and told everyone to stand, even though we were already standing. Then Judge Hallenback swept in.

Oh my. My mouth dropped open, and I quickly snapped it shut. It was rumored the judge had been going downhill for some time, and I was thinking that for once, rumors were right. While he had to only be in his mid-sixties, maybe he had early dementia?

Today he wore a customary black robe with a charming red bow tie visible above the fold. It contrasted oddly with the bright purple hat with tassels hanging down on top of his head. A bunch of colorful drawn dots covered his left hand while a grey and white striped kitten was cradled in his right, and he hummed the anthem to *Baby Got Back* as he walked.

He set the cat down and banged his gavel, opening a manila file already on his desk. "Elk County vs Ralph Ceranio for felony counts of fraud, theft, and burglary."

I swallowed.

"My client pleads not guilty and requests a jury trial, your honor," Chuck said, concern glowing in his eyes. He and the judge had probably been friends for years, too.

"Bail?" the judge asked, yanking open his robe to reveal a Hallenback's Used Car Lot T-shirt. Oh yeah. The judge and his brother owned a couple of car dealerships in the area. If he retired now, he'd be just fine. "Hello? Prosecuting attorney talk now," he muttered.

I quickly read Scot's notes. "Two hundred thousand dollars. The defendant is a flight risk, your honor. He has access to a private plane and several vehicles."

"Everyone has a private plane. Heck. I even have one." The judge shook his head before Chuck could respond. "Fifty thousand dollars. How many days do you need for trial?"

I had no clue. I didn't even know the case.

"Probably a week, Judge," Chuck said, helping me out.

I could only nod.

"All right." The judge reached for a calendar and announced the date six months away. "See ya then."

Chuck patted my shoulder. "I'll be in touch."

I swallowed again, wanting to beg him to stay with me for the second hearing. But I had to at least act like I had a clue what I was doing. The bailiff, a brawny guy whose nightstick somehow looked thicker than usual, moved for the door he'd emerged from

7

earlier and opened it. He grabbed an arm covered by an orange jumper while I shuffled the files and looked down, trying to read Scot's mangled notes. Hopefully I could get caught up quickly.

The judge slammed down his gavel again. "Elk County vs. Aiden Devlin for narcotics possession and intent to distribute."

I stilled. Everything inside me, from thoughts to feelings to dreams and hard reality, just halted. I slowly turned to face a tall man dressed in an orange jumpsuit. Oh my God. "Aiden," I whispered, the entire world grinding to a harsh stop.

He smiled, his eyes bluer than I remembered, his face much more rugged. "Hi, Angel."

CHAPTER 2

*M*emories flooded in, so hard and so fast my knees wobbled. It couldn't be. But it was. *Him.* My legs wanted to give, so I tightened my muscles to keep from falling. I looked frantically around, needing something to say. "You don't have a lawyer?"

"No." He flashed the same smile he'd had at seventeen. Sweet with a hint of danger. Well, now it was more dangerous with a hint of sweet.

I couldn't breathe.

"Miss Alberto?" the judge intoned. "You should be saying something right now."

"Um." I bent to read the papers in the file.

"Um isn't good enough," the judge bellowed.

"It's Ms. Albertini, Judge." I winced. Scot's notes danced in front of my eyes, blurring into nonsense. This was Aiden. He was in a freaking orange jumpsuit. Focus, damn it. Scot's notes were all over the place, but there wasn't a strategy or bail plan. I cut Aiden a look. "Let's see how he pleads." The file was a bit light for him to have been in lockup.

Aiden stood straight; his stance wide. He'd been tall as a kid, but he'd gained a couple more inches since leaving town at eighteen. He probably topped out at six-four, which was almost an entire foot taller than me. His hair was still thick and black, and those eyes. The deepest blue imaginable. "I plead not guilty and request a jury trial," he said, his barely-there Irish brogue lilting his consonants.

"Albertini?" the judge bellowed.

I gulped. "Um, we need a week for trial." I had no clue if we needed a week or three months. I couldn't think. This was too much. It was Aiden. Where had he been? Had he missed me? Probably not. Didn't matter. He'd saved me. That did matter—period. "No bond, judge. The state agrees the defendant be released on his own recognizance until trial."

Aiden tensed next to me.

The judge lifted one bushy eyebrow and stared me down, his brown eyes hawk-like. "You sure about that?"

I scrambled through the papers, but nothing made sense. My mind was fuzzy, but even so, the arrest warrant wasn't even there. I had nothing to argue that Aiden should remain in custody except the charges that the judge had listed, so even if I had wanted to keep him locked up, I couldn't. Probably. "I'm sure, Judge," I said, my voice as level as I could make it. The moment could be the end of my career, but I didn't see a choice. Not really. Plus, everything inside me wanted to let Aiden Devlin go free. He'd done the same for me years ago, and that wasn't something I'd forget. Ever.

"So be it. Let's get the defendant counsel and then schedule a hearing for a trial date. You're due an attorney, Mr. Devlin." The judge held his gavel midair.

"I'll acquire counsel on my own, your honor," Aiden said quietly.

The back doors opened, and I turned instinctively to see who'd entered. Two men loped inside, both wearing jeans and black T-shirts. The first guy wore one of those motorcycle vests, or cuts,

I'd seen on television. The guys were tattooed, scarred, and tough looking. Aiden glanced over his shoulder and straightened, standing even taller. I gulped, turned, and looked at the judge, my brain fighting to keep working.

"Court dismissed." The judge slammed his gavel down, stood, grabbed the kitten, and swept through his door with the bailiff on his heels.

I coughed. "I'm not sure what you do next. I mean, how you get rid of the orange jumpsuit and get your clothing back." I was babbling, but I couldn't stop.

Aiden pointed to the closed door. "I go that way. The bailiff would've handed me off to the deputy waiting on the other side if I'd been held over for bond. Right now, I'll go meet him."

So he knew more than I did about the process. That probably wasn't good.

"It's nice to see you, *Aingeal*." The Gaelic word for Angel. A nickname he'd given me as a kid that I still heard in my dreams once in a while. His gritty voice was familiar, even though I hadn't heard it since I was twelve years old. "I mean, Anna."

He remembered.

I blinked. Through the years, I'd daydreamed about him. A lot. He'd turned out even better looking in person than in my imagination, which was pretty darn good.

Talk about angels. If fallen angels really existed, one stood in front of me, his gaze searching mine. His black hair curled around his nape. A face sculpted by the gods—on a good day—showcased eyes created with every blue in existence, all melded together into perfection. In a large package.

But the orange jumpsuit cut through me with a harsh reality. "Tell me you're not guilty," I whispered.

"Long story." His chin lifted. He glanced at the two tough guys by the door and gave them one of those tough guy nods before turning even more toward me. Muscles rippled in his arms and chest as he moved; all power, all male.

I knew he'd grow up to be a badass.

But was he bad?

The judge's door opened, and a twenty-something uniformed officer poked his head out. I think he was one of the Carisea kids —maybe one of the younger cousins. "Devlin? Let's get you processed out."

I stepped away from Aiden, instantly feeling cold. "So, good luck." It was doubtful I'd be prosecuting him.

He paused as if he wanted to say something. "You became a lawyer."

It wasn't what I'd expected. I nodded, the memories hitting me so hard my ears rang. So many moments, seconds really. The ones that marked you for life.

"I guess it isn't surprising." He stepped away. "I'm glad to see you."

Was he? Then why hadn't he called? Or written. Suddenly, anger slid though my veins, piercing the veil of numbness I'd had all day. I welcomed it; this return to reality. "I'm sure." Without waiting for him to answer, I turned on my wedge and strode down the aisle, ignoring his friends and not looking back.

As such, I had no clue if he watched me go or not. From the way my butt tingled, I'd bet he had.

* * *

THE DEA CORDONED off our offices but promised we could return the next day, so I headed home after trying to get the gossip in the office, but nobody knew anything about Scot or his arrest. So, why not go home? I probably should've called one of my sisters, but at the moment, I wanted to burrow into a good book and force reality away for a short time. Or maybe forever.

My body felt electrified and oddly numb. So I drove automatically through the quaint town, driving toward the mountains and a much smaller Tamarack Lake, the top of my Fiat down. The black car was circa early eighties and reminded me of one of those old detective shows with the gumshoe and electric blond criminal. It didn't have airbags, a radio, or even effective seatbelts, but I loved it because my Grandpa Enzio had refurbished it for me. I couldn't wait to get it out of storage every spring to drive during our short-lived summer.

I'd been renting a guesthouse situated far away from a main house made of wood and stone. Trees surrounded my bungalow, which faced the sparkling water of Tamarack Lake. By the time I'd parked on my gravel driveway, my hands were shaking.

I took several deep breaths and walked up the stone walk bracketed by yellow and pink tulips to unlock my door. Quiet and peace instantly surrounded me, and I locked the door, heading straight through the comfy living room for the one bedroom. It was a sweats and ratty T-shirt afternoon.

After changing clothes and popping a Xanax, I sacked out on the overstuffed sofa to read a book. Soon the pill took effect, and I dropped off into an uneasy sleep, ready to face my demons.

Demons really existed.

It was a nice June weekend, and the camping season was in full force for the entire Silverville community. I was ten years old again, skipping rocks across the river with my cousin, Lacey O'Shea. She was my best friend in the entire world, but the contest was heated, and I needed a good skip. She had a trick of twisting her wrist at the last second, which gave her at least one—if not two—extra hops each time. We'd walked up a ways from our family's campsite, shoving through the brambles and slipping over moss covered stone.

But we'd reached a place where the river was wide and somewhat calm. The perfect place to skip rocks, away from all the kids on dirt bikes and four-wheelers finally enjoying the semi-decent spring weather.

I twisted my body, aimed, and sent a rock spiraling. It clipped hard the first hit and then went nine more.

"Nice," Lacey breathed, her twin braids bobbing as she acknowledged

my expertise. Her light brown eyes narrowed, and she shrugged her shoulders to loosen them to prepare for a big throw.

I felt a little smug as I watched her toss, but an arm came out of nowhere and wrapped around my waist, jerking me off my feet. My lungs sucked in air, and I screamed. The hand slapped across my mouth. My skin pricked and I started to fight, kicking and hitting back, even though I was off the ground.

Lacey turned, and her eyes widened. She grabbed a rock and ran toward us, screaming so loud the birds scattered across the water.

The man holding me struck out, hitting her in the side of the face. She went down hard, and I stilled, shocked.

Then he was moving. Fast through the weeds until he reached a four-wheeler. The hand at my mouth hurt, and tears flowed down my face. I couldn't fight. He was too strong. My chest ached, and my heart started hitting my ribs. I couldn't see, and my vision went all fuzzy.

He shoved me into the front seat; a rope was already attached to the dash. He tied my hands, and I tried to jump away, but then we were driving wildly over the rocks and up the mountain.

I turned toward him. He was old—probably around twenty-five with brown hair and a big nose. "Don't hurt me," I whispered.

He turned and looked at me, and his hands were dirty on the wheel. "I won't. Just need a bride."

Chilly pins snapped down my spine. "I'm only ten." What was wrong with him?

He shrugged and turned back to the narrow trail.

I gulped, my stomach hurting. Stranger danger. It was true. How was I gonna get free? I twisted against the ropes around my wrists, but I couldn't get them loose. I wanted my dad. Right now. My dad would punch this guy and get me free. "Who are you?" I asked, my voice shaking.

"Jareth Davey," he said. "I live in the mountains."

I didn't know any of his family. Did he have family? How could I get free? We drove for hours up and around the wild hills of Idaho, criss-crossing and going higher and higher.

Was Lacey okay? I hadn't seen if she'd hit her head when she fell. I hoped she was okay and had run for help. My dad would find me.

But what if he didn't? I was almost too scared to even move. Maybe this was a bad dream. It had to be.

I heard motors in the distance. Dirt bikes and four wheelers. Were they looking for me already? If Lacey had gotten to the family, they'd be looking right away. All the campers all up and down the river would be. Then a helicopter finally roared above.

"Shit," the man said, jerking a hard right and heading for an old cabin set against some rocks. I hadn't even seen it until we were almost there. He parked the four-wheeler under a bunch of trees, undid my rope, and picked me up again.

I started fighting him, punching his throat.

He didn't seem to notice.

Then we were inside a one room cabin with a mattress on the floor and a kitchen with hotplate and pans.

I started to shake. I didn't know what was going to happen, but I needed to throw up. I could see through the slats of some of the boards to the forest outside. If I could just get free, I could run.

He set me down.

I backed away, toward the counter with the hotplate.

He shut the door and turned to face me. "We're married now."

No, we weren't. I panicked and grabbed a cast-iron pan to hold in front of me. It was so heavy that my arms shook. Could I lift it high enough to hurt him?

He chuckled and moved toward me, so much bigger than me that I felt really small. But I swung. As hard as I could, I hit him in the ribs.

He jumped back, his face turning red. Then he lunged at me.

The door burst open, and a boy rushed inside, colliding with the man so hard that they hit the opposite wall.

I screamed and dropped the heavy pan. I recognized the boy from seeing him around town, but he was in high school. He hit the man in the face several times so rapidly I could barely see it. It was like he'd gone wild. The man hit back, and blood sprayed. Then the boy grabbed the pan I'd dropped and hit Jareth full in the face. The man slumped once and passed out.

The boy stood, blood on his chin, and looked at me. He had the bluest eyes I'd ever seen. "You okay?"

I couldn't breathe. Tears blocked my vision. "N-no," I said.

"You will be." He reached for my hand, and I took his much bigger one, holding as tight as I could. "My dirt bike is outside. I'll take you home."

Home. I wanted to be home. I sniffed and let him lead me out of the bad place.

"I'm Aiden," he said. "You're safe now. I promise."

Years later, I sat up on my couch, surprised that night had fallen. Jareth Davey had gone to trial and then gotten off with a technicality. It didn't matter why. He was free and had been since that day.

I received an anniversary card every year on the date of my kidnapping and around Christmas, not signed and sent from different postal locations. I couldn't prove they were from Jareth Davey, but they had to be. They were sent to the post office box I'd kept in Silverville all these years, and the next one was due the following Wednesday. Things were coming full circle, and the nightmare was expected.

Now things had changed. Aiden Devlin was back, and now he was in trouble. Could I save him this time?

CHAPTER 3

*Q*uiet chaos ruled the office when I returned the next day, although the DEA had exited the premises with what I heard was boxes and boxes of documents. I had no doubt they didn't need most of the stuff for their case, but I hadn't been there. I was oddly gratified to see that the receptionist's picture with Stan Lee had survived the raid. She smiled widely when I returned, leaning over the desk. "Have you heard anything about Scot?" she whispered.

"No," I whispered back. "Have you heard anything?" How could Scot have been arrested by the DEA? It was crazy, and nobody knew a thing.

She shook her head. While she'd been friendly during my month of tenure, she was usually busy, and I was just a deputy prosecutor. I'd obviously been bumped up a bit in her mind. She handed over a stack of messages. "I sent the interns to clean up your office, and they should be finished soon."

"Thanks." As the fresh and new lawyer, I didn't have a secretary or paralegal of my own, and the interns usually handled things for the more experienced attorneys. "Is anybody else back yet?"

She shook her head, losing the smile. "No, and it's a mess. We can't get any answers from the DEA."

I nodded like it was all okay and turned for my office just as two college students exited. The first was a tall woman with blue hair. "You're good. The DEA agents left your drawers open and some files messed up, but we fixed them."

"Thanks." I smiled and again acted like the world hadn't just started spinning in the opposite direction. Sure, I was thrown off by my boss being arrested. But Aiden Devlin was back in town, and *he'd* been arrested. I sat on my too loose rolling chair, grabbed the phone, and dialed Celeste. As Scot's paralegal, surely she'd know something. Anything.

"Hi," she said, no doubt having seen my extension number come up on her phone from the opposite side of our office. "How was court yesterday?"

"Uneventful," I lied. "Have you heard anything about Scot? It's impossible that he's been dealing drugs."

"I know. Whatever this is, I'm sure Scot will get it sorted out," she said, sounding lost.

Okay. So she didn't know anything. On to my next topic. "Please find any other documents you have on the Aiden Devlin case, so I can pursue this until Scot gets back. The casefile I took to court yesterday was missing most of what I needed."

She sighed. "The DEA took everything Scot had on that case, and it wasn't much. You have the case file."

Too much was missing. What was going on? "Get me everything you can find that they didn't take. As soon as you can."

She promised to do so and then hung up.

I tightened my calves to keep my chair from rolling away. Then I reached to dial out again when my computer dinged a notice. Crap. I glanced at the time. I was due in misdemeanor court in five minutes. It seemed ridiculous that I was still working the day away when the sky was falling, but court was court, and I was scheduled to be there. So I grabbed the stack of casefiles I hadn't had a chance to read through yet, jumped up, and hustled outside and down the street to the courthouse.

This time I descended to the lower floor, where various people shuffled around as they lined up at the parking ticket counter. I passed them for the smaller courtroom where I was somewhat more comfortable and shoved open the much lighter door. This felt more like home.

An air of expectancy, or maybe dread, filled the small courtroom. A wide aisle split the rows of pews up the middle. Up front the judge's maple bench presided over the room with solid bulk, and matching tables sat in front at either side of the aisle. Unlike the upper floor, this part of the courthouse had been added in the eighties, so the benches were a salmon color and the wood a lighter, more industrial style oak. Fluorescent lights cast yellow shadows across the windowless room, turning the salmon color a dingy pink.

The bailiff standing by the bench, a sweet guy named Larry, glanced up from his phone and nodded.

I returned the 'professional hey' with my own nod, sat, and set down my case folders. This was a chance to reach plea bargains before the judge even showed up, and then all we had to do was go on the record with our deals. Or set trial dates. I glanced around. The public defender wasn't there.

That was okay. I could deal with the criminals myself. Life was pretty simple in my view. Usually. I took the top file, opened it, and read, "Thelma Mullen?"

Two elderly women, one thin and one not-so-much, slowly made their way from the last row to sit at my table. "I'm Thelma and this is Georgiana Lambertini. You probably have a file on her, too," the thin one said, smiling.

The ladies didn't appear a day over eighty with pouffed white hair and more wrinkles than a linen skirt on a humid summer day. Thelma perched like a colorful bird in a skinny purple suit, lime green pumps, and a yellow broach in the shape of a black widow spider. Georgiana had covered her impressive bulk with a bright flowered muumuu above beach thongs.

Thelma leaned forward. "We were nailed with a B and E, sweetie," she said with a twinkle in her faded blue eyes.

I held up a hand. "Don't say anything else. I'm the prosecutor, and I'm not on your side here."

Georgiana patted my hand. "Oh, you're a sweetheart. I can tell. Of course, you're on our side."

"No," I protested, looking around, panic grabbing me yet again. This week was too much. At some point, my heart was just going to implode from the pressure. "You should have your own lawyer. If you can't afford one, we'll get one appointed to you."

Thelma waved the suggestion away. "Oh, we don't want him. We met him and didn't like him. We want you."

"You can't have me," I said softly. "I'm here to prosecute you."

"No." Thelma shook her head. "That's not right. I can tell about people. You're one of the good ones."

She reminded me of my grandma, and the familial guilt slid through me like garlic butter. Maybe this was just a misunderstanding. I opened the case file and read it quickly. "You were caught going through the underwear drawer of your neighbor, Melvin Whitaker?"

The women nodded.

"Melvin lives in the adjoining duplex to yours?" I asked.

"Yes. Melvin has disappeared, and we were trying to find the pot," Georgiana stage whispered as I concentrated on the cataracts in her thick eyes. She squinted at me, trying to focus.

Pot? Eesh. "What are you talking about?"

"The good stuff," Thelma whispered.

"Where is Melvin?" I whispered, not sure why.

Thelma shrugged. "Dunno."

This wasn't making a lick of sense. "First of all, don't confess to anything," I warned them, probably against the vow I'd taken for the job. But come on. "If you don't know where Melvin is, then how were you arrested?" Logic had left the conversation.

"Well—" Georgiana flushed a deep red— "I pushed Thelma too hard through the kitchen window, and she knocked over some glasses on the counter. Eunice Johnson lives on the other side of Melvin. She called the police after she saw me climb through."

Thelma sniffed. "That eighty-year-old trollop has never liked us. Always wanted to hook poor Melvin, and we wouldn't let her."

Could an eighty-year-old be a trollop?

Thelma continued. "The police took their time. We managed to search the kitchen, living room, and bathroom before the coppers showed up."

"We had just started on the bedroom," Georgiana said. "Who knew Melvin was a boxer man? I would've guessed briefs."

"I thought he free-balled it," Thelma said thoughtfully.

"All right, ladies." I wanted to laugh, but the day had gotten completely away from me. I had a lot more to worry about than a couple of sweet old ladies wanting to smoke pot, which was legal just thirty minutes away in Washington state. "What would you accept in this case?"

Thelma's red lips trembled. "Well, we figure we're heading to the big house."

No way would I let these sweet ladies go to jail. There had to be some justice in my job. I tilted my head to the side. "If Melvin wasn't home, maybe you were watering his plants?"

Georgiana's cloudy eyes lit up. "Um, yeah. And getting his mail." She was obviously the criminal mastermind between the two.

"But," Thelma started to argue before her friend shushed her.

I nodded. "We'll see what we can do." They ambled back to their seats.

Just then, the side door opened, and the big bailiff bellowed, "All rise as Judge Williams enters."

Everyone stood, and pews creaked behind me.

21

"Be seated." The judge smiled at the courtroom as she walked to sit at the bench. Her skin was a smooth and deep brown, her lips peach colored, and her salt and pepper hair curly above the judge's robe. "Morning, Ms. Albertini. It's good to see you again." Her brown eyes were sharp and seeking, and she tilted her head to the side, inviting silent gossip or even answers.

I shook my head very subtly—because I had no clue what was happening with Scot or the DEA or pretty much anybody at the moment.

"I see," the judge said, turning to the small stack of case files in front of her, clearly disappointed at the lack of gossip. "Let's get to business, then. Georgiana Lambertini," she called out in a clear voice.

I turned as Georgiana and Thelma shuffled up to my table. Georgiana had donned a pirate's black eye patch.

I shifted my attention to the judge. "This is Georgiana and also Thelma Mullen. They were charged together."

The judge raised her eyebrows. "For breaking and entering?"

Georgiana's hands clasped against her chest. "It was a mistake, judge," she said solemnly, her visible brown eye earnest and cloudy. "We were just trying to be good neighbors. We're getting close to heaven's gates, you know."

"But," Thelma started, then, "Ouch!" She grimaced down at her foot.

Georgiana smiled angelically next to her. "Yeah, we were just watering our dear neighbor's plants," she continued, her face beseeching and sad.

Thelma hummed and fluttered mascara-caked eyelashes. "Well, all right then," she said.

The judge nodded at Georgiana's eye patch. "Were you injured?"

"Oh no." Georgiana flipped the eye patch up, revealing a cataract riddled brown eye. "I thought it was a good look for the big house. You know, so the bad bitches don't mess with us."

The judge buried her head in the file, and I couldn't move. The lady had just sworn in court. It was funny, but…I couldn't move.

Judge Williams cleared her throat. "Ah, all right then. Ms. Albertini?"

For the second time that week, I purposefully didn't do my job. Or maybe I did. The bigger picture was that I seek justice, and at the moment, I couldn't find any by hurting these ladies. "Obviously there was a mistake made here, Judge. The state would like to dismiss all charges, so long as the defendants refrain from repeating the conduct." I said the last with a firm nod toward the two women.

"Of course," Thelma uttered breathlessly.

Georgiana pressed her palms together. "Yeah, we won't make so much noise next time."

I shook my head. "Stay out of trouble. Promise me."

They both nodded, and Georgiana grabbed Thelma's arm and tugged her toward the door.

Judge Williams peered into a file. "Next up I have Randy Taylor."

Randy looked around eighteen and was still fighting acne. He ambled up, his arms skinny and his brown hair back in a man bun. I knew there were sexy pictures of guys on Pinterest with man buns. Randy was not one of those guys.

"Where's your attorney?" the judge asked.

"Fired him," the kid muttered.

The judge sighed. "Is there an offer from the state?" she asked.

I read the file. Randy had been caught with marijuana and then had fled arrest after punching a cop. Not good. Really not good. I didn't like that at all. "Three years."

Randy shook his head wildly, and the man bun fell apart as his hair flew around.

The judge sighed. "I take it you plead not guilty and request a jury trial?"

"Yes, your honor." Randy's voice wobbled this time.

"Fair enough. We'll get a calendar going for the case and set the trial date at the next status conference." The judge made a notation. "Ms. Albertini, you're excused. Looks like it was a quick day."

Maybe for her. Mine had given me a migraine. I grabbed my files and all but fled the courtroom. I pushed the door open and headed into the hallway, winding through bodies and ending up outside. The sun had disappeared, and clouds had begun to gather. I increased my speed toward the office.

Randy ran behind me. "Hey, lady. Come on, give me a better deal."

Irritation almost dropped me cold. I kept violence at bay and squinted at the sky, balancing myself with calves I'd earned by running every day and trying to outdistance stress in law school. If a total klutz and shy geek girl with issues could be athletic, I'd given it my best to be athletic once in a while. "Get a lawyer," I said.

He allowed a kid on a skateboard to fly by and then returned to walk by my side. "When do you think the trial will be?"

I glanced to my left at the perfectly square park with its winding walking trails, new benches, and freshly cut grass. Flowers and bushes ringed the entire area, adding a splash of color. "The misdemeanor criminal cases are probably a few months out."

"Good. Um, do I have to stay in Idaho?" His voice cracked as we skirted perfectly tended purple pansies.

"I am not your attorney. But take some advice and go into Washington state for pot from now on. At least it's kind of legal there." According to the state, pot was legal, although the federal government disagreed but seemed content to turn a blind eye.

"Okay." Randy blew out air in a sigh only an eighteen-year-old caught with pot could muster. We headed toward the crosswalk at the corner, and I breathed in the clean scent of cut grass from the center park. "You seem cool to me. How old are you?"

"Old enough to prosecute you," I said.

He chuckled. The kid needed to leave me alone. My job was to put him in jail, and he wanted to make friends.

He pushed a folded piece of paper in my hand.

"What—" I started to ask.

"Here's my contact information in case you need to find me. I'm not at the address on the arrest warrant anymore 'cause I'm staying with my uncle." A dark flush wandered over his face, and he shuffled his feet before shoving his hands in his pockets.

"Thanks." I slid the paper into his file. He'd just helped the opposition.

He tensed next to me, his eyes darting around.

I scanned the area. A few cars drove by near the corner, the only place they could drive close before turning along the parking area behind my building, but nothing interesting was going on. "What?"

"Just thought I saw someone." He hunched his shoulders.

A screech of tires echoed around the corner, and a brown SUV sped near with the window rolled down. A long, black barrel poked out, and a weird pattering filled the air. What the heck?

Out of nowhere, a large body tackled me to the ground and tumbled me toward the bushes, covering me. The wind whooshed out of my lungs. Fear and panic ripped through me. I struggled to breathe; my face pressed sideways into the grass. "Hey!" Dirt filled my nose. The guy over me was hard as January ice over the lake.

Then silence.

He shifted, rolled me over, and tugged me to my feet. Clumps of dirty grass dropped from my suit. I still clutched my files in trembling hands. Paper cut into my thumb. What had just happened?

The world narrowed in focus. I stared up into the deepest, bluest eyes I had ever seen. I knew those eyes. "Aiden," I whispered. He'd just saved me.

Again.

CHAPTER 4

"*Aingeal*," Aiden murmured. After being free for a day, he looked even better out of the orange jumpsuit. Faded jeans hung low over tight hips under a black T-shirt, giving him even more of a badass look.

"What are you doing here?" I sputtered, trying to regain some sense of reality.

"I was looking for you. Figured we should talk." His gaze narrowed when I swayed. The world seemed to be spinning oddly again. "Anna, are you all right?" he asked urgently as the sound of sirens trilled through the air. His sensuous lips and lilting speech brought goose bumps to my skin.

"Um, yes. I, ah, well. I have anxiety and night terrors still." I gulped, trying to breathe. My skin tingled. Panic attack? Probably on its way.

He studied me.

Realization hit, and heat flashed into my face. "Oh. You mean *this time.*"

He smiled then, and I swear, the sun parted through the clouds. Seriously. "Yeah. I mean this time." His voice was so gentle, I wanted to cry.

That quickly, I returned to reality. This disaster and danger. My stomach heaved, and my knees buckled. Someone had shot at me. I started to fall.

Strong arms swooped me into the air. "I've got you."

Aidan Devlin had just saved me. Again.

His dark eyebrows lifted as several police vehicles barreled to a stop in their side parking lot. Befuddled, I took stock. My wide gaze landed on Randy, who leaped to his feet, his eyes wild with fear.

"What the fuck?" he bellowed.

I tried to spit out a piece of grass and remember that I was a lawyer, all grown up, and not a terrified ten-year-old kid who'd been kidnapped by a psychopath. "Are you all right, Mr. Taylor?"

Uniformed cops spilled out of the police station. Emergency vehicle doors opened from the parking area, and boots hit the ground.

Randy glared. "Who shot at you?"

Aiden tightened his arms. "I think they were shooting at you, sport." His voice still hinted of Ireland, the lilting tone sounding like my Mom's and grounding me for a moment. I leaned my face into the strong cords of his neck and breathed in salt, musk, and man, trying to calm my stomach. Trying to ignore the nerves firing all over my body. He held me easily, securely in his solid arms as I regained my equilibrium. I so didn't want to puke in front of him.

"It's all right, Angel." He pulled me closer, dipping his head to cradle my face in comfort. To shield me on all fronts—from any more hurts. It was the same way he'd held me when he'd saved me before.

Did he remember doing so?

This was crazy. I should stand on my own feet like some modern-day lady of justice. But I didn't. I burrowed deeper. Into strength and safety. It's where I had wanted to be for well over a decade. I'm not sure what that says about me, but it's probably not something to put on a headstone.

"Deep breaths. They're long gone. No more shooting." His voice crooned from a magical place, and I concentrated on it, sucking in air, trying to keep from falling into a panic attack. "You control your own mind. Take it somewhere else. Just for a moment."

My concentration shot straight to the hardness holding me. His breathing remained steady, his stance secure. Man, he was strong. And I liked the way we fit. I shook my head—this was insane, and I needed some space. No matter how many times I'd dreamed of him through the years, I had to pull it together. He was a criminal defendant facing trial, for Pete's sake. People changed.

The sound of running feet as people barreled out the courthouse doors brought me back to the present. I surveyed the fancy suit I'd borrowed from my sister, Donna. Two jagged rips marred the skirt, but no bullet holes. Thank God. No wounds.

"I'm okay now." I leaned to look up into his face. "You can put me down." My arms remained around his neck, and I fought the urge to play with the thick hair curling over his nape. Feeling safe was almost an aphrodisiac. Who knew?

"I think I'll keep you for a while." His gaze ran over my face, his jaw tight. Sounded good. Then he took a quick inventory and blew out a breath. "Ah, sweetheart. You're bleeding."

I followed his gaze to my right shoulder. Holy crap. Blood welled, and suddenly my shoulder hurt. A lot.

"Jesus. You got shot," Randy yelled.

Shot. Bullets and blood. Oh God.

Aiden stalked forward several paces to place me on the stone ledge that cornered the park. Quick movements had my sister's jacket removed, and him leaning forward to peer at my wound.

Randy sniffed next to us, and I fought the urge to keep from screaming. Panic would only make things worse. My vision hazed. Wasn't there an artery somewhere close to the bullet hole? Oh no. There was an artery.

"I'm bleeding out," I sniffed.

Aiden bit back a quick grin. I knew he did, because a dimple flashed in his left cheek for just a second. "You're okay," he murmured.

"Hey Devlin." The other man dressed in black that didn't hide his intricate neck tattoos jogged up to hand my savior a smartphone. He was one of the guys who'd come into the courthouse the day before.

I blinked to keep conscious. Yep. I could feel the blood just draining out of me.

Aiden straightened and slid the phone into his back pocket. "The bullet burned you, Angel. A Band-Aid will suffice." He partially turned toward the other man. "Get a first aid kit."

I glanced down at a bad scrape. Oh. Just a scratch. No artery or spurting blood. Hmm. So much for worrying about my Last Will and Testament.

A spring breeze scattered pine needles across my shoes. I shivered in my light blue camisole, heat rising in my face when I remembered I hadn't worn a bra. I mean, why would I since I'd kept the jacket on all day? "Ah, er…" My nipples pebbled against the silk.

Aiden grinned, shifting his weight to block me from the arriving police and bystanders gathering on the sidewalk. "Seriously. I've wondered. How are you?"

"You could've written. Emailed. Called." I tried to hold back another shiver as well as the hurt I had no business feeling. "I mean, if you really wanted to know."

"I had to leave, sweetheart. You know that." His gaze ran over my skirt, somehow heating my legs.

"You could've called." I sounded sad, and I didn't want that. He'd left when he had turned eighteen. His grandma had died, and he'd been a person of interest in a felony car-stealing ring. So he'd just left. "I missed you."

He sighed. "I was told you needed to move on without me."

I blinked. I'd only been twelve years old when he'd left, and I'd thought he'd created the moon. He was sweet and kind and he'd saved my life. He was my friend, and I'd followed him around like a lost puppy for two years. He'd treated me like a kid sister, and I'd liked it. "Who told you to leave me alone?" My voice shook, I was so angry.

"Your shrink." He lifted one very broad shoulder. "Dr. Petrolche said you were too attached and needed to heal on your own after...everything."

That stupid shrink. He was crazier than I'd ever been. "They arrested him for having an affair with an underage patient." I had known he wasn't a very good psychologist, even as a kid.

Aidan's dark eyebrows rose. "I hadn't expected that."

Randy coughed several times. "You were in therapy? Are you crazy? You can't prosecute me if you're nuts."

"Shut up," Aiden said mildly, looking at my legs again.

The other man jogged back up and handed Aiden a red box. Aiden grabbed Bactine out of the box to spray my shoulder before placing a wide bandage just above my bicep. For such a giant, he had a gentle touch.

I blinked, concentrating on his warm fingers and not the fact that I'd been shot.

"You'll be okay." He gently tugged my arms back through my jacket sleeves. Or rather, Donna's jacket sleeves. The intimacy in his helping me re-dress made my thighs tingle and my heart thump. I wasn't feeling like his little sister any longer. The six-year age difference didn't seem that much now. "We'll just put this back on before you talk to the police," he said.

"Police?" Randy took a step back. "I think I'll—"

His voice squawked at the end when Aiden grabbed him by the scruff of the neck. "You'll give a report."

A much gentler hand grasped my good arm and tugged me to my feet. The shield Aiden provided made me feel special in a way I wouldn't want to describe, considering I needed to be a tough lawyer and not some fragile woman from the fifties.

Aiden nodded to a swiftly moving man emerging from the dusty door of the police station. "That's Detective Pierce. He's a total dick, but you need to make a statement too, *Aingeal*."

Although the sweet nickname warmed me throughout, when I tried to settle my stance, I swayed. Shock, fear, I don't know. I was such a wimp.

Aiden pushed me back down to sit on the stone ledge and gestured toward the detective. "Pierce can come to you, Anna."

"How do you know his name?" I asked, the day taking on a surreal haze.

"Long story."

Aiden seemed to have a few of those. The detective strode over, hawk-like gaze belying the casual gait. "I thought you were in jail."

"I got out. That happens for the good guys, Detective Pierce. This is Anna Albertini and a witness, Mr. Taylor," Aiden said.

Pierce was probably in his early forties with just a hint of gray at his otherwise dark blond temples. His eyes were a light green that all but sizzled with intelligence, and his lanky form nicely filled out a dark brown suit. He looked at me and then back at Aiden, and his jaw tightened hard enough that it had to hurt. "Who shot at you this time?" he snapped.

I blinked. He was talking to Aiden. "What's going on?" I asked.

Aiden tilted his head to Randy. "Shooter aimed for him."

"Randy. Randy Taylor," Randy said, sniffing loudly. Uniformed cops spilled around, marking off spaces, and Randy seemed to wilt.

"What happened?" Pierce yanked out a battered notepad that looked like it had floated the river more than once and tapped a shiny Silverville Cross pen on the paper.

"There was a pattering sound from a car, and I was tackled," I said, my voice trembling.

"What kind of car?" Pierce scribbled a couple of notes.

"It was brown." My memory was blank. Completely. I drew the sides of my ruined jacket together with shaking hands.

Pierce lifted his head and turned toward Aiden; his gaze accusatory.

Aiden rested a heavy hand on my shoulder, and I realized I'd swayed forward. He tightened his hold. "Brown Range Rover, 2005 model, no plates. Two men inside. Driver about forty, pocked skin, faded black leather jacket. Shooter was thin, twenties, goatee and blond wearing a jean jacket and shooting an AK-47. Crappy shot." He tilted his head toward Randy. "The possible target."

Pierce scribbled some more, lifting his head to pin Randy with a hard gaze. "Who wants you dead, kid?"

"Nobody. I mean, nobody." Randy's Adam's apple bobbed up and down as if it too, wanted to make a run for it. "This is just a possession charge. It was just some pot, man." He wiped his nose on the sleeve of his white shirt. "I got the drugs from my Uncle Melvin. Melvin Whitaker."

I gasped, my wide gaze slashing to Randy. Melvin *Whitaker*? The same neighbor the elderly ladies had tried to rob? Did the guy supply the whole town, or what? "Tell me more," I said quietly.

Randy took a step back, obviously realizing he shouldn't be confessing to us. "Uh, sorry. Oops."

Pierce grinned, making him look more like an older male model than a cop. He glanced back at Randy. "How much pot?"

"Just a joint—one tiny little joint. Misdemeanor charge." Randy sank down next to me, running a shaking hand through his hair. The kid smelled like smoke and had quite smartly forgotten to report that he'd hit a cop. I stayed quiet for now.

"Any chance Uncle Melvin is pissed you stole his pot?" Pierce asked.

"No." Randy shook his head. "It was just a joint—the guy's like a total nerd. He wouldn't shoot at me."

"Where does Uncle Melvin get his pot?" Pierce's voice remained casual, but those eyes narrowed in like a coyote spotting dinner.

I listened carefully. If Randy was dumb enough to talk, I wasn't going to stop him.

Randy shrugged. "Dunno. He works out at that seed company on the border, and his stuff is always the best." He turned red, his gaze shifting to me. "At least, that's what I've heard. I mean, this was my first joint."

Aiden didn't even attempt to hide his chuckle at that.

I struggled to unfreeze my brain.

Pierce had to be an inch shorter than Aiden, which still made him tall. "Did you recognize the shooters?"

"No." Randy shook his head. "I saw the gun, and then this guy shoved me to the ground before landing on top of this lady lawyer." He flipped his shaggy hair toward Aiden.

I glared. "I think you mean to say thanks for saving my life." Ugh. I sounded like a mom correcting a toddler.

"Oh. Yeah. Thanks, man." Randy stood. "Can I go now?"

"No." Pierce curled his lip. "I need a list of who'd want to kill you."

"Nobody, man. Really." Randy eyed the cops swarming the grounds and taking witness statements. "If I think of anyone, I'll call you."

Pierce exhaled slowly and turned his focus on Aiden. "We all know you were the target. Too bad they missed."

Randy's head swung around, his mouth dropping open. "Hey—yeah. You were right in the line of fire." He brushed dirt off his skinny jeans. "Maybe this had nothin' to do with me, dude. It's all about the big man in black."

Aiden crossed his arms. "I can't be sure." His eyes darkened.

Tension spiraled through the already hectic afternoon. Pierce's lids half-lowered. "What are you involved in now?"

Now? I squinted to read Aiden's suddenly unreadable face.

"Nothing." Aiden peered down, his tone remaining level.

"We'll see." Pierce tapped his pen again.

Aiden's smile held more warning than humor, and my breath caught all funny in my chest. "If I am up to something, then no doubt you're the guy to figure it out," he said softly.

Red spiraled across Pierce's sharp cheekbones. "That cocky attitude is gonna finally bring you down." He eyed both Randy and me. "You're all coming into the office right now for an interview." He nodded at Aiden. "Devlin—I'm looking forward to it."

"I hope you're well rested, then." Aiden's expression didn't change.

Okay. Where had Aiden been the last twelve years, and what the heck had he been doing? Besides being arrested for dealing drugs. Sure, he'd been a wild youth, but there had been a sweetness in him I'd never forgotten. And he had saved my life.

"Five minutes. My office." The detective hurried off to speak with a couple of uniformed officers by the door.

Randy cleared his throat. "I, uh, have to go call my work and let them know I'll be late. Meet you in the sheriff's office." Without waiting for an answer, he pivoted and made a fast exit toward the parking lot.

"He'd better come right back," I muttered.

Aiden dropped into a crouch at my eye level. "Feeling better?"

No. "Sure. Um, why does a police officer want to take you down?" I asked. Aiden just couldn't be the bad guy. There had to be some mistake, right? He'd saved me from being shot, and he'd saved me from a fate worse than death when I was only ten years old.

Aiden lifted one muscled shoulder. "Cops have never liked me. It's that simple."

No, it wasn't. "Aiden—"

"Pierce is the asshole who arrested me, and we might've gotten in a bit of a scuffle. Not your problem." Aiden tugged a small stick from my hair to toss to the grass. "I'm fine, though."

Fair enough. I tried to straighten my spine and look tough. Good manners won out. "Thanks for rolling me to the ground."

His eyes lit, and that amazing mouth threatened a smile. "Any time, Angel. Any time."

CHAPTER 5

Three hours after learning that a bullet can burn, I drove away from the courthouse toward my small bungalow on a nearby lake. No way was I returning to work for the day. I was done. The police had separated Aiden, Randy, and me for the interviews. I should've wanted to know about Randy's information, but truth be told, it had been Aiden who'd filled my mind.

The questioning had been exhausting, but I really didn't remember much other than the brown vehicle.

Detective Pierce had been very intent that the shooter had been aiming at Aiden.

Just where had he been the last twelve years?

My phone buzzed in a reminder, and I looked down to see I'd missed twenty-two calls. I winced. My mom was from a big Irish family, and my dad a huge Italian family, and when they'd combined into marriage, they'd created enough family members to fill a small stadium. My folks tried to be true to both sides of my heritage, even giving all three of us girls both Italian and Irish names. For a time in my teens, I'd punch anybody who called me Annabella Fiona Albertini, but I was fine with it now.

My phone rang, and I lifted it to my ear. "Hello."

"Oh my God, are you okay?" My sister, Tessa, was the first to reach me. "We just heard you'd been shot."

"I'm fine, Tessa Carmelina—" I said her full name to throw her off. Unlike me, she still really disliked it. "How did you hear?" Dumb question. Seriously. Even though I was in the big city, everybody knew everybody, especially if that everybody was from Silverville. "Forget it. I don't want to know."

Tess exhaled. "So you weren't shot?"

"Not really. Just clipped." Yeah, I kind of sounded like a badass. "But that's not the big news."

Tess was quiet for a second. "Seriously? What's the big news?"

"Aiden Devlin is back." I lowered my voice to a whisper even as I took a corner a bit too fast. "He's *here*."

"Whoa. Wait a minute. He didn't shoot you?" Tess's voice quieted.

I snorted. "Of course not. He may have been the target."

"How does he look?" Tess's voice rose in a weird hush. As usual, she got right to the point.

"Like Aquaman, Jared Padelecki, Angel, the Arrow, and your best wet dream combined," I affirmed. "Seriously. The guy is like airbrushed in real life."

Tess breathed out. "Wow. Okay. So. What now?"

What now? Huh. Good question. "Probably nothing. I mean, we talked, but then we were interviewed separately, and he didn't ask for my number or anything."

"Did you ask for his?" Tess asked.

"No. I was a little shaken after the whole shooting issue." I rubbed my eyes. Should I have asked for his number? "He also sidestepped any question I asked about where he's been and why he's back. The cop on the scene really didn't like him." Not that Detective Pierce was anybody I knew or trusted. But still. "I don't know, Tessa. A lot of stuff came up the second I saw him." Including my libido.

My other line rang, and I glanced at the face of my phone. "Oh.

That's mom. Gotta go." I clicked off and answered the other line. "I'm fine, *Mathair*," I said, using the Gaelic translation for 'mother' to calm her down.

"You were shot. Right? Did the bullet hit an artery?" my mom asked urgently.

If the bullet had hit an artery, I wouldn't be on the phone. I took a deep breath. "No, no, not at all. Honest. It just scratched me. Won't even scar." My mom took scars as a personal affront to her mothering skills. "I'm fine."

"I have a call to your father. He's down in the mine looking at that new vein. Should I get him up right now? I have the emergency number." Stress clipped her voice.

"No. I really am fine, Mom." I gentled my voice. "Honest."

She was silent for a couple of moments, and then she exhaled. "Thank Mother Mary. That's wonderful." Something rustled. "I'd heard that you walked away, so I was fairly certain your arteries were spared, but a mother needs to hear confirmation."

I took another turn, this one away from the lake and more toward town. "I understand."

"So your body is all right, and now we must deal with your head." More papers rustled.

I sat straighter, my heart kicking back into gear. "My head is fine."

"You were just shot at," she countered. "I already called. You have an appointment with Wanda Versaccio tomorrow afternoon. You know? Your fourth cousin twice removed on your Uncle Sebbachi's side? She's Italian, but that's okay. We don't have any Irish psychologists in the family. Wanda divorced a woman who was not treating her right and just opened a practice in the city. She's taking patients."

No, no, no, no, no. "I don't need a shrink, *Mathair*." Sure, I'd seen a psychologist while in school to become a shrink, because it was part of the gig. But I'd left therapy in my past when I'd changed my mind and decided to become a lawyer. "I'm fine."

"No. You must go and, ah, work through it? Yes. That's it. You'll have night terrors, and maybe Wanda can help you keep them at bay." My mother's voice softened into the pure ability to cause guilt. "Or I can come and stay with you. You know I won't sleep a wink if I'm worried, anyway."

I closed my eyes and then quickly reopened them when I remembered I was driving down the main street in town. My Italian grandmother could place a guilt trip with the precision of a sonic drill bit, but even she was no match for my mother. There was something about guilt placed with the soft lilt of an Irish accent that could cut deep. "Mom."

"I'm texting you her office address. Go after work tomorrow, or I'll be on your doorstep." She clicked off.

Two seconds later, my phone trilled with a text. I glanced down to see the map of Disneyland beneath it. Mom was still figuring out texting. I sighed. It probably wouldn't hurt to talk things through. Sometimes current events brought the past back up, and it'd be nice not to have a bunch of panic attacks this week, especially since work was so chaotic.

Even so, that was yet one more thing to worry about the next day.

For today, the spring sun shone down as I drove through my quaint town and toward my much smaller lake. I pulled into my small drive and parked next to a convertible Bug and a gleaming white Escalade.

My sisters were there.

Surprising tears choked in my throat as I jumped out of my car and headed toward the front door, taking a couple of precious moments to compose myself as I strode past the tulips to the cottage door. The scent of fresh gnocchi hit me first as I pushed inside my cozy living room.

Tess took one look at me from her perch on a stool and reached for a bottle of Cabernet to pour a second glass. I smiled, dropped my laptop bag near the door, and headed for comfort. "Hey." She nudged the glass down the bar.

I sat and reached for the glass, taking a big swallow and warming my stomach. "Hey."

We both faced the kitchen over the granite bar where Donna, AKA Donatella Tiffany, was stirring a red sauce in a pot. She also had a glass of wine in front of her. While she inherited our father's Italian genes with her black hair and brown eyes, Tessa had inherited our mom's Irish genes with her red hair and green eyes. Nobody had figured out where my coloring of light brown hair and grayish green eyes had come from. It was a family joke that we should look back at mailmen through the years.

Donna partially turned, a purple apron covering her black business suit. "How badly were you shot?"

"Not at all," I said, warmth flushing me. "It's honestly just a scratch. How did you keep mom away?"

"Mah Jong night," Tessa said, twirling her drink around in her glass. "Told her to go play and that we'd be here, which we'd be here anyway."

Yeah. That was the truth. "I also promised to see the new shrink in town," I admitted.

Donna grinned; the wooden spoon half-lifted in the pot. "She's a very distant relative, a lesbian and is now single, and Grandma Fiona really wants a shrink closer in the family circle and not so distant. Just a warning. She'll try to fix you up."

I snorted. "I like men." Always had, and if my response to Aiden earlier was any indication, I always would. "She'll have to find somebody else to bring a shrink closer into the family circle." Grandma Fiona had been thrilled when cousin Jakob had married a medical doctor from Philadelphia. Now we apparently needed a dentist, shrink, and last I heard, she really wanted a forensic pathologist, too. Sometimes it was better not to ask why. "At least one of the Staperelli kids finally became a priest." Every Italian family needed a priest. That was almost a law.

Tess nodded. "That did take the pressure off the Rasetini boys." They were cousins a few times removed.

Donna turned down the gas and then moved to toss a spinach salad. "We thought you'd need comfort food."

"I do," I said softly. "Between the DEA raid and then the bullets, it was bad enough today. But…"

Tess turned toward me, her glass up in the air. "Aiden Devlin."

I clinked with her. "Aiden Devlin," I breathed, my stomach doing a somersault.

Donna paused with the tossing and turned to study me over her slim shoulder. "How does he look?"

"Amazing," I said, sipping now. "Better than I'd imagined. All tough and muscly, and his eyes are somehow even bluer than they were before." He'd been a cute kid. There was nothing cute about him now. It was all so much better.

Donna leaned back against the counter. "Aiden has been arrested and charged, though?"

I nodded and took a deeper drink.

She sighed. "He was a troublemaker, even back when, and he had to leave town. It makes sense that he's still breaking the law."

I frowned. "He wasn't part of that theft ring." He'd been accused of stealing cars, but there hadn't been proof, and he'd taken off. "You know the sheriff didn't like him."

"For good cause," Donna argued, her eyes flashing. "I know he saved you, and that matters. But even so, it doesn't mean he was a good guy or turned out good today." She rubbed her hands down the apron, her normally smooth brow furrowing. "You don't owe him anything."

That was so untrue the air heated in my throat. "Yes, I do." I would've been raped or killed or both if he hadn't shown up when he had. "I do owe him, Donna." In ways I couldn't even explain. Wasn't sure I wanted to find the words. "Some things are fundamental, and that's one of them."

Tessa usually stayed out of any family strife, which had earned her the nickname of Switzerland. Yet this time, she shook her head. "I agree with Donna. The entire community was out looking for you, and anybody who'd found that cabin would've entered to find you. Aiden just happened to be the one who did."

He'd been sixteen years old, and he'd charged inside the cabin and fought with a man twice his age and size without hesitating.

In my head, in my heart, Aiden Devlin had been my knight in shining denim from that very second.

Whether or not he now wore an orange jumpsuit. What I was going to do with that information, I had no idea. "I understand you're worried," I said, wanting to placate my sisters.

Donna eyed me. "But?"

Yeah. But. "I don't know," I said honestly. First thing the next day, I was absolutely going to figure everything I could out about his case and the charges against him. Whether or not I was the person supposed to put him away.

CHAPTER 6

*F*riday morning dawned slightly gray and misty, but
the nightmares had left me alone the entire night. It
might be because Tessa had stayed over, and she kicked like a
purple belt. Tess had always been a kicker. I left her lightly
snoring in my bed after dressing in a flowered skirt with white
dress shirt and navy-blue jacket, also known as my 'facing the
world' outfit. The yellow, red, and navy shoes added even more
spunk, and by the time I'd driven across town and parked, I was
more than ready to face the day.

I couldn't decide anything about Aiden until I read the
complete case file on him, so at least I had a plan of attack. Since
Scot was no doubt out of the office and probably still in DEA
custody, there wasn't anybody to prevent me from investigating.

I walked into my office and ran smack dab into a seriously
hard male body dressed in a way too fancy suit for Timber City.
He grasped my arms to keep me from falling, and I looked up into
deep brown eyes.

He released me and took my hand in his. "Nick Basanelli."

Yeah. I knew his name. My Italian heritage sat up and sang *O
Sole Mio.* I had to clear my throat to speak. "Hi. Anna Albertini."

"Anna Albertini, the youngest of the Albertini three." His gaze seemed to delve right past my designer armor and into the floundering lawyer I was. I remembered him. He was my sister Donna's age and had been the biggest football star to ever come out of our small high school.

I cleared my throat. "Are you looking for me?" Why was Nick Basanelli in my office?

"Absolutely." His tone held a warmth that was contagious. He kept my hand in his much larger one as we studied each other. He had true Italian black hair over tawny brown eyes that more than hinted at strength and ambition. His face was strong and straight, his jawline formidable, even with the sweet dimple in the middle of his chin. He filled out his expertly cut suit with a muscled edginess. Yeah. Basanelli had grown up nice. Really nice. "I've already talked to the other attorneys and will speak with staff at a meeting later."

I frowned and edged around my desk, feeling somewhat more in control with the heavy oak between us. "About what?"

He gestured toward my seat, and I sat. Then he sat. Ah, his mama would be happy with his manners. "The governor appointed me as the county's prosecuting attorney while Scot Peterson is on...leave."

I blinked. "You're a lawyer?"

"Yes. Was in the JAG Corps and then private practice in Boise. Now it looks like I practice criminal law on the state level." He smiled, small lines crinkling at the corners of his intelligent eyes.

Man, I bet juries loved this guy. He'd been in the military? Interesting choice for one of the wild Basanelli boys. Yet our small department seemed like a step down for him. Unless—it was just another step. Military experience, private practice experience, and now criminal law with what looked to be a big case? "Planning to run for office, are you?" I blurted out. Our state attorney general was definitely getting up there in age, and a high-profile drug case could make or break a career.

Nick's eyebrows rose. Those bourbon colored eyes narrowed and then twinkled. "I'd heard you were smart."

Pleasure filtered through me, and I bashed it away. Smart girls weren't so easily charmed. "I haven't heard much about you."

His smile was full-on this time. "I'm sure you can change that fact with one phone call."

I couldn't help but return the grin, because he was correct. One call to one of my grandmothers, and I'd know everything about Nick Basanelli to the point of his favorite ice-cream. When you're from Silverville, you're from Silverville. "What's going on with Scot's case?" I asked, trying to sound professional and not like the entire world had gone crazy.

Nick studied me for several moments, heating parts of me that should so not be heated at work. "Scot has been trafficking drugs, including meth, for the last five years, according to the DEA. He's going to be charged federally, and we're going to take him down for possession and distribution on the state level—for starters."

For starters? What else had Scot been doing? "Are you sure?" I whispered. While I had only known Scot for a little over a month, he seemed like an okay guy to me. Dedicated to the job and all of that.

"Yes," Nick said. He sat back in the chair, looking like he owned the room, even though it was my office.

"Since Scot is being tried federally, why not save the state taxpayers money and just let the *federal* prosecutor deal with him?" It seemed unnecessary to have both federal and state investigations and trials.

"The case is related to Aidan Devlin's, which is a state case. I want them both."

Out of pure instinct, I settled into poker mode the second Nick said Aiden's name. My expression smoothed out, and I forced myself to breath naturally. Then I watched him watch me for a reaction. The silence drew out until he stopped smiling and looked at me as if finally seeing me. With contemplation and something else. Something heated. Scalding hot. Interested.

"You let Devlin go free yesterday," he said softly.

My chin lifted just enough to show he'd hit nerve. "There was nothing in the case file I received to argue otherwise." Which was the absolute truth. "Do you have the complete case file?"

"Not yet."

Well then. Ha.

He exhaled slowly. "Here's the deal. You're the only attorney here without a long-time connection with Scot. That makes you the only person I trust and the second chair on both cases. If you have a problem with that, speak up now."

My mouth dried up. I'd won the match, but the war was in his hands, and we both knew it. He was talking about a felony case. A serious one. "I don't even have *misdemeanor* trial experience." Any trial experience. Heck. Any real motion practice experience. "I'm green as green gets, Nick."

"I'm a good mentor," he said smoothly, his tone licking right across my skin, not hiding the innuendo in the slightest. Great. He'd gone from flirty to intent. Apparently, the guy liked smart girls.

I'd worked hard to banish 'um' from my vocabulary in preparation for trials, but one slipped out anyway.

He pounced on the weakness like a hawk spotting a field mouse. "I know your history with Devlin, but the past is in the past. He's a criminal, Anna. Your job is to put criminals away, and we both know why you went into this area of law."

"Do we?" I murmured, lowering my chin just enough.

He nodded, deadly serious. "You didn't get justice, so you're seeking it for others. I've seen it before." He stood and loomed over the desk. "What you don't know, is that I take very good care of my friends. Of my colleagues. I'll get you what you want."

I frowned. Was that a come on? A promise for a job in Boise at some point? "What exactly do I want?"

His gaze was fierce but his tone oddly gentle. "I have connections all across the world. You want to know where the guy who got away with kidnapping you is and what he's doing this very day? I can find Jareth Davey for you. I promise." He turned and walked out of the room, not waiting for a response.

Which was a good thing, because I couldn't speak. Not a word.

* * *

MY MIND COULDN'T LET GO of Nick's remarks for the remainder of the morning. Jareth Davey was a lingering shadow in my life from the second he'd kidnapped me. After the trial, he'd disappeared, but even now, I looked over my shoulder sometimes. He'd be around forty years old and probably was as crazy as ever. Considering he still sent me cards every year for the anniversary and for Christmas, he hadn't forgotten about me. I shivered.

Enough. I had to get out of the office, and I kept my head down as I hurried past the receptionist and into the spring day. For an early lunch, I bought a turkey sandwich at McQuirk's Deli next to the courthouse and wandered around the park, past several of the college buildings, and down to the weathered picnic tables skirting the lake. Clouds gathered above and turned the water a deep gray, but the breeze was still somewhat warm.

As planned, I found my cousin Pauley O'Shea perched on a table, slightly hunched over, a bag of breadcrumbs in his hand as he faced a gaggle of ducks at the water's edge. Nobody else was around yet. Gingerly, I sat my butt on the table, careful not to slide on the rough wood and rip my skirt. "Hey."

"Hey." His long fingers slid into the bag, and he tossed crumbs at the squawking birds. The breeze lifted his thick brown hair, and I glanced at his thin shirt and pants. He should have on a coat, but I didn't mention that yet.

Instead, I nodded toward a sign pounded into a nearby tree that said, 'Don't Feed the Birds.' "You're breaking the rules."

He threw another handful, rocking slightly, not looking at the sign or at me. "Nobody will yell at me."

Probably true. "How was your first week of summer classes?"

"Same as last semester, which was my first semester in college." He watched the birds for a few more minutes. "Everyone is old, and it's boring." He rocked back and then forward. "I am smarter than the teacher."

"You're smarter than almost everybody," I said absently. At sixteen years old, in college, he was probably the youngest in the classes. Was that going to be a problem?

"Are you checking on me?" he asked, his neck rolling fractionally.

I nodded. "Sure. I also like talking to you, which you know." He was Lacey O'Shea's younger brother, and the closest person I had to a brother. I reached for the bag.

"No." He pulled it away. "You will get in trouble."

I snorted. "Because I'm not autistic?"

"Yes. I get away with stuff." His lips twitched with almost a smile.

That was true. Pauley was autistic with savant qualities, and he used it to his advantage once in a while. "Well, I'm pretty," I said slowly. "I could charm my way out of trouble."

"You are not charming." Pauley tilted his head a fraction, his expression thoughtful, even as he stared straight ahead. Then he held the bag out to me, barely shifting his weight to do so. "Though you are pretty."

I grinned and took a handful. "Why aren't I charming?"

"How should I know?" He moved the bag to his other side. "Charming people are smooth. You are not smooth. You are fun and lively and goofy. I like you better than charming."

Everything inside me went gooey and warm. "Thank you."

He almost shrugged. "Just telling the truth." Then he paused. "Lacey was in a shootout in Detroit yesterday."

I blinked. "What? I hadn't heard that yet. Is she okay?" My heart kicked up several notches.

"Yes. I think she shot the other guy, but she is not giving full details yet." Pauley shook out the bag so the bread bounced around.

While I'd become a lawyer to fight the bad guys, Lacey had gone ahead and become a cop. A pint sized one with a tough attitude. We video-conferenced at least once a week. I swallowed. "I wish she'd come home and get a job somewhere around here." For some reason, she wanted big city experience first.

"Me too," Pauley murmured. "Heard you got shot, too."

"Barely," I said, leaning cautiously back on my hands. The tabletop scraped my palms, but the wood was cool. "Aiden Devlin saved me."

Pauley nodded. "I heard. No secrets if you're from Silverville, even though it's fifty miles away. Fifty miles. Fifty is a gold wedding anniversary. Fifty." He quickly looked at me sideways for the first time since I sat down. Then he focused at something across the lake. "Is he good or bad now?"

So apparently news of Aiden's incarceration had hit the streets. "I don't know. In fact, I'm not sure what to do. I want to help him, but it might be my job to put him back in jail." The words poured out of me before I could stop them, and I cut off abruptly. This was too intense for a sixteen-year-old to listen to. "Sorry. That sounded like a confession."

Pauley threw more bread, his arm movement jerky. "I am not a priest," he agreed.

Humor took me. "True. What do you think Father Hamlet would say?"

Pauley scratched his head, his profile pale. "Probably to follow the law. Though laws, like the bible, were written and interpreted by men. Good and bad go deeper than words on paper. Any paper."

I stilled. Sometimes Pauley's genius took me off guard, even though I'd known him his entire life. I had no doubt he'd do another year at the local college and then head off to Harvard or MIT or somewhere for geniuses. His social interactions were becoming pretty good, too. Sometimes I wished I could just get into his head and see how it all worked. From day one, Pauley had fascinated me. "Maybe I should help Aiden." How? I just wasn't sure.

Pauley flipped his wrist over to check his watch and then returned his focus to the birds. "If you do not know if Aiden is good or bad, you do not know whether to help him or not. Find out."

I bit my lip. Clarice still hadn't gotten back to me with any answers or more records, but there was one place I could go and try to get answers. It was probably a bad idea—definitely a bad idea—but when had that stopped me? "You're right." I hoped off the table. Everything inside me wanted to hug my cousin or at least give him a peck on the cheek, but that's what I wanted and not what he needed. Like many folks on the spectrum, Pauley didn't like being touched. "Thanks, P."

He nodded, still not looking at me. "Thank you for checking on me. After class my mom is picking me up to go shopping for shoes before going home. Tell my sister that I am fine."

I grinned. "You've got it. Have a nice rest of the day."

He frowned. "History class is next. I already know what happened before now."

Yeah. He probably did. "Well, if nothing else, you'll learn that history repeats itself," I joked.

He didn't smile. Then he turned and looked at me, full on. Sometimes I forgot how deep and dark his brown eyes were since he rarely made eye contact. "Does it?" He broke his gaze free and looked back at the far shoreline.

The chill that swept over me had nothing to do with the breeze off the lake. "Apparently." Because like it or not, Aiden Devlin was back, and danger was all around. Again.

CHAPTER 7

I left Pauley to his ducks, knowing he needed solitude before tackling a classroom with other people, but my walk to the courthouse was slow, my heels clipping softly on the sidewalk skirting the grassy park. Little green sprouts poked up between the cement, and the smell of both oncoming rain and spring flowers hinted on the breeze. Even though I'd been shot at the other day, those shooters had been after Aiden or Randy, so I couldn't find it in me to be worried that it'd happen again. I had enough to be concerned about. I reached the outside of my building and looked up the flights of stairs to the heavy door.

The wind picked up. My phone dinged, and I answered it. "Albertini."

"Hi, Anna, it's Clarice." Even through the phone, the head paralegal's voice was dignified. "I can't find any other records of the Devlin case in Scot's office, which is now Nick's office, by the way." She sniffed.

I winced. How long had Clarice and Scot worked together? "Thanks for trying."

Her voice lowered to a whisper, and it sounded like she cupped a hand around the receiver. "I heard that Scot was

51

released on bond about an hour ago. Maybe you should go talk to him?"

He was out on bond? How had that happened? "Good idea. Would you give me his address?"

"Sure." She read off his address. "He lives around Lilac Lake toward Boomerang Bay."

"Thanks. I'll check in with you later." I clicked off. Making a mental decision with no debate whatsoever, I turned and walked around the corner, away from the park, and toward the parking lot on the other side of the building. Rose bushes lined the building, just starting to bud. Somebody had placed hay around them for winter survival, which was lazily blowing across the lot now that the snow had dried from it.

I should probably check in with Nick about this, but I really needed to talk to Scot alone. Just once. So I jumped into my Fiat and fought with the ancient seatbelt before giving up and driving onto Justice Road toward Main Street. Even though it was still June, the summer crowd had arrived in town, and I dealt with minor traffic until reaching Lilac Lake Road. Lilac Lake was much larger than my quiet Tamarack Lake, and I wound around it, hoping Scot was home.

The clouds darkened the sky, deepening the color of the lake, which threw up a series of whitecaps. The top was still down on my car, and I ducked lower in the seat to stay warm with the heat blasting.

The homes along the lake were a blend of hand-built cabins that had been in families for decades and mansions of the newly arrived millionaires from other states, mostly California, standing side by side. Scot lived in one of the new gated communities cut into the hillside. Impressive houses stood past the gate, placed on half-acres leading down to the lake. My engine protested a little loudly as I idled near the keypad keeping the gate shut.

Now what? Biting my lip, I pressed the directory, checked out the numbers, and started pushing all of them. It worked on television, so why not?

Nothing happened.

I found Scot's name and pressed his button.

"What?" he snapped.

"Hey, boss," I said, my breath coming faster. "It's Anna. Can I come in? Really need to talk to you."

"Damn it. Fine." The speaker crackled, and the gate slowly swung open.

I drove through before he could change his mind. The homes were dark stone, wood doors, and shingled roofed with perfect green landscaping and sprouting purple flowers. I read the uniform numbers on each front post until reaching Scot's house. The log home was two stories and close to the lake with what had to be a spectacular view. Sucking in fresh spring air for courage, I parked and made my way past cheerful tulips to his heavy wood door.

He opened it before I could knock.

I stepped back. Scot was usually a little grizzly, but the arrest had obviously been tough on him. His normally cleanly shaven face showed white stubble that contrasted eerily with his blood-red eyes. Dark circles stamped hard beneath them. Instead of his usual suit with stained tie, he wore wrinkled jeans and a threadbare T-shirt with a drunk mouse on it. "What could you possibly want, Albertini?"

"Explanations." I pushed past him, my mind spinning too much for caution. Then I stopped cold in his entry way at the expansive view of the lake outside. This place had to have cost a fortune. Slowly, I turned.

He shut the door. It was then that I noticed the glass in his hand. Auburn liquid in fancy crystal. "Already drinking, huh?" I asked.

"Sit." He gestured toward a brown leather sofa facing a tall stone fireplace that was currently dark and silent.

I swallowed and moved around the sofa table to sit, my heels echoing on the wide wooden slats of the floor that somehow looked exotic. Original oil paintings of stunning sunsets as well as winter scenes adorned the walls.

He followed and dropped his bulk into a matching chair. "I can't talk to you without my attorney present."

Then asking him if he was guilty was probably a mistake, and no doubt he was much too smart to say anything that would incriminate himself. "The DEA took the files on Aiden Devlin's case. Tell me you have a copy here," I said.

He blanched. "Stay out of Devlin's case. You're way out of your league." The words were curt, but the tone weary. Exhausted.

"I know," I whispered. "There doesn't seem to be much of a choice. Nick Basanelli just made me second chair, and I'm worried he's more concerned about adding a notch to his trial record than finding out the truth. Than seeking justice."

A hint of a smile crossed Scot's face, lifting the thick wrinkles for a moment. "Second chair. Big promotion."

Didn't feel that way. "All the other attorneys have worked with you for some time, and considering that..."

Scot's chin lifted, and regret filled his eyes. "Right. I guess they'll all be investigated pretty thoroughly."

"Have you been selling drugs?" I blurted out, unable to stop myself. It just didn't track. Scot was a prosecutor who had spent twenty years putting bad guys away. He'd hired me and had given me my first chance to pursue justice. To do what I needed to do. "Tell me you haven't been breaking the law."

"I can't talk about my case, Anna," he said, turning to look out the window at the stormy lake. "Also, I'm represented by counsel, and you're not supposed to talk to me without him here."

None of this seemed possible. I followed his gaze to see a boat cutting across the waves, heading by the docks, no doubt seeking a fishing hole around the bend. "I understand, but I do need any records, research, or documents you have on Aiden's case." Of course, if Aiden's case and Scot's case were related as Nick suspected, I wouldn't be able to trust anything I read. But something was better than nothing at this point.

"I don't have any other records or documents here," Scot said quietly.

"Then why arrest and charge Aiden Devlin? Where are the case files?" Sure, I could get the arrest warrant from the police station, but Scot had decided to charge Aiden, and there had to be enough documents to uphold that decision somewhere. None of this was making a bit of sense.

Scot frowned, his grizzly eyebrows dancing with the movement. "What do you mean? The trial folder has all of that information in it."

I slowly shook my head. "No, it doesn't. I couldn't even find enough to ask that Aiden, I mean Devlin, be held over for bond." If I was going to think of Aiden as a defendant, I should use his last name. At least around other people until I figured out what was going on.

Scot rubbed his whiskered chin. "That's odd. I put together a complete trial notebook just to make sure."

My blood started to thrum faster through my veins. "To make sure? Of what?"

For the first time, he drew back. He lost the overwhelmed look, his gaze sharpening and making him appear more like the guy who'd hired me. The one who'd made Supreme Court Justices sit up and take notice. "Anna, get out of this case. Mine and definitely Devlin's. Trust me." He leaned forward and grabbed my arm, his grip digging deep and causing pain. "If you have to quit the prosecutor's office, then do it. This is too big for all of us."

Chills clacked down my back. "Scot. You're scaring me."

"Good. The day is really done here."

What did that mean? I opened my mouth to answer, to ask more questions, when the entire wall of windows facing the lake crashed in, jagged shards of glass exploding in every direction.

Scott yanked me toward him and to the plush carpet as a booming pattering cut through more glass from the lake. The only thing out there was that boat I'd seen. Bullets shot from the boat lodged into the wall and front door, splintering the wood into jagged pieces. My throat closed, and I covered my head, crying out.

I didn't know much about automatic gunfire, but this sounded deeper than the other day. Glass fell all around me, and I stiffened head to toe, trying to stay as low as possible on the ground.

Would they beach the boat and run up the hill?

I hadn't looked to see how many people were on the boat. How many people were shooting at us? Could we get free? The front door seemed so far away.

Cotton from the furniture puffed all around, dropping gently onto my hands as they protected my head.

The cacophony of bullets continued, and framed paintings dropped to the ground. A frame hit my thigh, and I yelped, scrambling away from the windows and over glass. Something slippery caught my hands, and I slid, falling flat on my face. I managed to turn my head at the last second, and my cheekbone took the impact instead of my nose. Pain rippled along the entire side of my face and lodged behind my eye socket.

The sound was deafening, and even so, I could hear the blood rushing between my ears. Clutching my head, I rolled as close as I could to the demolished sofa, trying to stay low.

Then quiet.

Deadly silence pounded into my very bones. A picture near the front door crashed to the floor, and I cried out.

Were they coming? I turned my head. "Scot?"

No answer.

Hot needles pricked my skin from inside my body, adrenaline let loose. "Scot." Staying on my belly, I turned to see him near the fireplace. It took a second for the sight to register. "S-Scot?" My voice wavered. He lay on his stomach, his left arm bent at an unnatural angle, and his face covered in blood. So much blood that it blanketed the floor.

I gagged. A second ago, I'd slipped in his blood. "Scot?" I tried again, but his eyes were open, staring at me blankly. A sob caught in my aching throat, and I used my elbows to pull myself toward him through the already sticky mess, my legs dragging behind me. The smell, coppery and rusty, made my stomach lurch.

I reached him and felt for a pulse, even though I knew I wouldn't find one. Catching my breath, I shoved him over to perform CPR, trying to keep as low as possible. The second I began compressions, blood squirted from several holes in his chest and abdomen.

Scot was dead. There was no way to bring him back.

Safety. I had to get to safety and call for help. Swallowing down bile, I turned and crawled toward the window. If they were coming, I would need to stand and run. Holding my breath, I grasped the edge of the sill with my bloody hands and lifted enough to look down at the lake.

The beach was empty, and the lakefront clear. The boat had taken off.

My entire body shook. Wind blasted inside the broken windows, and more glass dropped. I dodged out of the way and dropped to my butt, surveying the destruction. Then I did a quick survey of my arms and legs. Everything hurt, but I couldn't find any bullet holes.

Tears blurred my vision, and I wiped them away, a sense of urgency grabbing me by the throat. Unable to force myself to stand, I crawled toward the bullet-riddled front door and opened it, tracking blood onto the wide cement porch. There I dialed 911 and gave a report, my voice both shrill and shaking. The officer told me to stay put if the shooters were gone.

I couldn't move, anyway. I leaned back against the closed door as the wind battered against me. The blood on my skin and clothes got stickier and my nausea stronger.

Sirens sounded in the distance. Instead of reassuring me, my anxiety pricked up again. My central nervous system misfired in a million directions as the adrenaline rush began to dissipate, leaving me cold and terrified—taken instantly back to that horrible few hours in my childhood. I gulped in air, trying to breathe. I'd survived that time, and I'd survive this one, too. Tears streamed down my face, but I let them fall. I was alive. That said something.

A persistent pain in my right ankle caught my attention, and I leaned to the side to see a bleeding and now familiar injury. A hysterical laugh coughed out of me, high pitched and odd—carried away by the wind.

Another bullet had burned me.

CHAPTER 8

$\mathcal{U}$niformed police officers arrived first, followed by Detective Pierce. Even though I was pretty sure he didn't like me, I was relieved to see a friendly face. Okay. Make that a familiar face. He surveyed the scene and disappeared into the house for about thirty minutes. By the time he came to question me in the front of the house, I'd already talked to a uniformed officer, given a statement, and found a safe spot to sit on a swing at the far edge of the porch. Somebody had brought me a rough blue police blanket that smelled like wet dog, and I gratefully huddled inside it.

"Miss Albertini." Pierce strode toward me and past the potted flowers that had somehow escaped the carnage, his world-weary eyes sharp. A pretty brunette lab tech did a double take at him and then quickly turned back to work. I guess he was handsome in a too intense fortyish year old way.

I swallowed, holding the blanket around my shivering body like a shield. Blood had dried on my hands and beneath my nails, although the lab tech had scraped beneath each one. Even so, I wanted to get into a shower so badly I itched. For the moment, I tried to put on what my Grandma Fiona would call a lady warrior's expression. "Long time no see," I said quietly.

He didn't appreciate my humor if the tightening of his jaw provided any indication. He wore a darker brown but just as fitted suit as he had the day before. His tie this time was Christmas green instead of the gold stripe last time. "Do you require medical attention?"

The kind question caught me off guard. "No," I whispered, huddling down. An officer had given me a Band-Aid for my ankle, and the bleeding had stopped.

Pierce's gaze softened a fraction, even as he drew out his battered notebook. "All right. Tell me exactly what happened, and we'll get you out of here." He smelled like something deep and salty—the distant part of the ocean?

I'd already told the other officer, but I knew this was part of the process. Pierce no doubt needed to hear the timeline himself, and he'd also want to compare this statement with the other one, just to make sure I was telling the truth. So I told the truth the best that I recollected it. Everything had happened so quickly.

Just as he was finished asking questions, a shiny black Jeep Cherokee barreled down the road and lurched to a stop. Dust was still settling when Nick Basanelli jumped out, slammed the door, and made a beeline for me. His brown eyes were sharp, his shoulders back, and his stride very quick for a guy that big. He looked like a guy intent on rescue, and everything inside me perked up as much as possible, under the circumstances. Reaching us, he dropped to his haunches to face me. "You okay?"

Tears pricked my eyes again. He'd come for me. "No."

He turned to look up at Pierce, staying at my level of sight. "Any leads?"

Oh. Yeah. Nick was the head prosecuting attorney, and this was a murder scene involving one of his employees. I worked for Nick. That's why he was there. Not out of some totally unrealistic need to make sure I was okay after meeting me once for a few minutes. Geez. I really needed to find a date or two. My face flushed. I also needed to stop looking at big strong men to cuddle into. I was a prosecutor, darn it. That made me a badass, whether I felt it or not.

Pierce stared evenly at Nick. "Not yet. Just processing the scene now," he said. "I have the lake deputies out looking for the boat, but we didn't get much of a description." No judgment lay in his tone.

"Okay." Nick grasped my arm and assisted me up. "If she's done, I'm getting her out of here. Let me know when you're finished with the scene. I want to walk through." Without waiting for Pierce's agreement, Nick led me around the Jeep, his arm around me. A camera flashed, and we ducked. "Nosy press," he muttered, helping me into the seat. The vehicle smelled like smooth cologne and male.

I settled into the leather seat, my head still spinning as he shut the door, crossed around the front, and stretched inside next to me. My mind ran through the entire scenario again, and the sound of bullets hitting wood echoed through my head. I shivered. "Thank you for getting me out of there." No way could I drive right now.

"Of course." He started the engine and pulled away from the lake house. From this angle, it looked like a paradise and not a bloody disaster. "Tell me what happened."

I couldn't. Not one more time. It was just too much. "Read the reports." I hugged the blanket closer around my body and stared out the windows at the beautiful homes with the incredible lake views. Neighbors stood out on their stoops, some at the edge of their driveways, watching the swirling lights at Scot's place. Nobody ventured close, as if unwilling to leave their slices of paradise for the darker side of life, hoping they'd never be touched by it.

Nick remained silent for several miles as he drove away from the houses and down the twisting and turning lake road. The sun finally broke through the clouds, sparkling the water into a glimmering blue instead of the depressing gray. "I need to know what happened from your perspective." His voice was low and calm. Somehow reassuring.

He was right. He was now the head prosecutor for the county, and he'd end up prosecuting whoever had done this. I was a witness, so at least I'd probably disqualified myself as an attorney on this one. So I ran through the events again, this time closing my eyes to make sure I got it all. I couldn't think of anything I'd missed, but something felt just out of my reach. Something I'd noticed or heard. What was it?

Nick asked questions similar to the ones asked by Pierce, his voice calm, his mind obviously quick. He spent a little more time asking me about Scot Peterson in general. My impressions, what I'd noticed while working for the office, any guesses I might have. His questions had a logical connection to the case and each other, and the way his brain drew those parallels was impressive.

I finished answering and opened my eyes to see we were closer to town. "Why did you really take this job?" I surprised myself by asking. There were tons of ways for him to reach the point of running for office; returning to northern Idaho and taking over a shitstorm of a disaster seemed too risky.

"Family," he said simply, not expanding.

Ah. That I could understand. Family meant everything. I turned to study his strong profile. His grandparents and his mom still lived in Silverville, that much I knew. His mom was an accountant for pretty much everybody besides the larger companies and knew most of the miners in town by name. "How is your mom doing?"

"She's doing well but facing a knee replacement probably in a month or so. Busted it snowmobiling last season, and it hasn't healed well enough. Both of my brothers have moved home. Ricky is working with mom in accounting, and Dominick left the

SEALs and is now a cop in Silverville. Gets a lot of cats out of a lot of trees." Amusement tilted his lips.

I warmed again. Just enough to be uncomfortable. "Um, did you ever hear anything from your dad?" Darn my curiosity, but we were talking, and it was the type of gossip that had lasted through the years, still brought up by old men fishing by the side of the river. His dad had been a foreman at the Independence Mine, and he'd taken off without a word with his secretary when Nick had to be, what? Maybe fifteen?

"Nope." Nick's hands remained relaxed on the steering wheel, but even so, a tension seemed to spiral from him.

"I'm sorry to pry," I said, meaning it. I'd had no right to ask. He'd been so nice to me, and now I'd overstepped. This was all so odd, but I wanted him to like me—especially professionally. Maybe on a friend level. Man.

He glanced at me; his bourbon colored eyes soft. "We were talking about family, and it's a logical question. Don't worry about offending me. If you ever do, which I doubt, I'll let you know." His smile released the worry I'd been holding.

I nodded, oddly grateful. He probably could level somebody with a reprimand. Even so, Nick Basanelli was hard to pin down. He was definitely ambitious, but his kindness at the moment helped. Juries probably really did love him. I suddenly wanted to know everything about him, including where he'd been and what he'd been doing besides practicing law. Did he have a girlfriend? My face heated again, and I turned to watch the lake out the window. He was my boss, and I had to keep him in that category.

Being a female attorney in a small town was one thing, and it came with certain advantages, but it could all be tanked by sleeping with the boss. With anyone in the legal community, actually. I had to be careful, and I knew it. Not that Nick was sending those vibes, anyway.

My mind flashed to Aiden and his sizzling blue eyes. Talk about vibes. All sorts of heated and wild ones. Just the thought of him finally banished the chill with a heated flush. What a disaster. I had to get over the childhood crush I'd held for him and do my job. Hopefully I could clear him or help him in the process, but I had to stop thinking about him as my hero. Same with Nick. They were both strong men, intriguing men, but I had enough on my plate.

It was time to be my own hero.

Maybe I should get a cat or something that would be warm and furry and love me. With that thought, I sighed and rested my head against the window. It was so hard being a grownup.

CHAPTER 9

The sun set across the lake in hues of bright pink and yellow when Nick and I returned to the office and walked from the parking lot and along the rose bushes to turn the corner. My mother was waiting on the front steps of the Justice Building.

Nick's cheek creased. "Looks like word has spread," he whispered.

I sighed and moved in for a hug, trying to keep my composure as my mom's rose scent surrounded me. "I'm fine." I stepped back, studying her.

My mom bore a striking resemblance to Maureen O'Hara from her *The Parent Trap* Days. Red hair cut in a bob, soft green eyes, and a jaw of pure Irish rock. She wore pressed white pants with a light blue sweater nipped at the waist, and her shiny gold cross matched her gold stud earrings. Her pink lips were pursed, and those eyes held familiar worry. Raising three girls, three very-different-from-each-other girls, had given my mother lines at her eyes that were a perfect combination of laughter and worry. Today they were all worry. "You must stop getting shot at."

I couldn't stop my chuckle that unfortunately held a hint of hysteria. I couldn't lose it in front of both my mother and Nick. My nerves felt like they'd been scraped raw by an old handsaw, and holding myself together caused my arms to tremble just enough that my mom tightened her hold, making me want to cry like a toddler who'd scraped her knee. I bit my lip hard enough to taste blood, instead.

Nick stepped in. "Mrs. Albertini. It's very nice to see you." He held out his hand like his mama no doubt had taught him to do.

My mom's eyebrow arched, and she released me to extend her hand for what appeared to be a gentle shake. "I've heard you were back in town, Nick. Please tell me you're going to put a stop to all of this drug nonsense and shootouts." Her soft lilt was iron strong with the demand.

Although I was a little miffed that she expected the big, strong man to handle the problems, I did understand. He was, after all, now the head prosecutor and my boss. Even so, I spoke up. "We're working on it, Mom. It's a couple of cases, and don't worry. The shooting is over." Scot was dead, so the killers unfortunately had been successful. But were they the same shooters from the other day? Those had been aiming at Aiden or at Randy Taylor, so my churning gut told me there was still danger out there, and somehow, I kept ending up in the middle of it.

"All the shooters are done?" My mother kept her attention on Nick, apparently following the same train of thought.

His smile was charming with a boatload of respect. "I don't know, Mrs. Albertini."

My mom's nod was all approval. She did like the truth. "Thank you for the honesty." She removed her hand and then patted his arm right above the monogrammed cuffs. "However, you're in charge now, Nicolo."

I tried not to wince.

She leaned in, the Irish in her voice now out in full force. "That means that the shooting must stop, and it's your job to make it happen. Your duty requires protecting the people working for you. I'm speaking to you as a mother. Do we understand each other?"

There was only one answer, and Nick gave it, his eyes sparkling. "Yes, ma'am."

"Good boy." She patted him again and then linked her arm through mine, gently turning us both. "Now Anna, I'll give you a ride to Wanda's. You didn't forget your appointment, did you?"

My stomach dropped. I had forgotten. Completely. "Mom, I don't think—"

"I figured." For a woman two inches shorter and probably twenty pounds lighter than me, she moved like a good wind, within seconds having me at her Ford Taurus, circa two thousand and five. People from Silverville bought and kept American, trading vehicles only when they fell apart. Fords rarely did.

I slipped inside, and the smell of the lavender air freshener somehow eased through me, relaxing my shoulders from down around my ears. It had been a tough couple of days. Maybe speaking with a shrink wasn't a bad idea, although dredging up all the emotions from the past didn't seem necessary. I had enough of a disaster going on in real time that maybe we could just concentrate on that.

"That Basanelli boy grew into his ears," my mom mused, handing over a plain T-shirt for me to change into. Then she started the engine and drove out of the lot at a too rapid speed.

I gratefully changed my shirt and then yanked on my seatbelt. "Um."

She ripped around the corner onto the main street. "I've heard he's single. Was engaged."

I perked up. "Nick was engaged?" I didn't want to be interested, but engaged? "What happened?"

She sniffed and drove through an intersection as the light turned from yellow to red. "Apparently they were both lawyers in Boise, and things went south. I don't have all the details." *Yet.* She didn't need to say the word. She would know the entire story within a week, and hopefully she'd tell me without my having to ask for it. "Dating somebody you work with would be a disaster."

I stilled. Was my mother, the woman who was still waiting impatiently for one of her daughters to marry and give her grandchildren, warning me off Nick? "True."

She nodded emphatically, whipping the car into a parking space on the main road through town, near a series of older and well-kept brick buildings. "Yes. If you went to work with your Uncle Gino, then you'd be free to date Nicolo. Prosecuting criminals, seeing the bad side of life, can't be good for your spirit. It certainly isn't good for my piece of mind, which is rapidly dwindling."

Right. My mom was the sharpest person in any room every time. I bit my lip. From my first day of law school, my mom had tried to get me to work with Uncle Gino, who, as far as I could trace, was a seventh cousin three times removed on my dad's side of the family. Gino was about sixty years old, did more transactional law than litigation, and thought a fax machine was too new-fangled to deal with. "I am not going to work for Gino," I said for the thousandth time. At least.

"Just think about it." She craned her head to look out the front window at the nearest building. "Wanda is on the third floor. There's a public restroom on the first floor where you can wash off your hands."

I'd forgotten about the blood. A chill skittered down my back faster than a firefly trapped in a T-shirt, which happened all too often while camping. How had I forgotten the blood, even for a second? I swallowed and opened the door, stepping out into the breezy dusk. "All right. I can catch a ride home."

"Don't be silly. Tessa is working, and I'll go check on her. If you're not interested in Nicolo, then maybe she should see if he has eaten dinner." She started the car again.

I sighed and shut the door. Tess worked as a waitress at Smiley's Diner, just down the street, and she'd probably love to take Nick a steak sandwich. Turning, I made my way into the building, which smelled like furniture polish over dusty wood. It took several pumps of gritty soap to get rid of the blood, and I tried not to watch the red swirl down the drain of the old porcelain sink. Scot's blood. My stomach lurched and I coughed down bile.

After drying my hands, I made my way up the wide and squeaky steps to the third floor, which held three offices, all with closed doors. The doors were worn oak with square windows made of frosted glass, and not one had a sign. Light illuminated the window of the far-left door, so I headed that way and knocked, poking my head in. "Dr. Versaccio?"

A woman wearing dusty jeans and flannel looked up from across a smattering of boxes across the narrow wooden slats of the floor. She stood near a cushion top green built-in desk by the window. Her black hair was swept up in a messy bun, her wire-rimmed glasses were askew, and her lipstick half chewed off. "Hello?" She didn't sound like she'd been expecting anybody.

I stepped inside. "I'm sorry. I'm Anna Albertini, and my mom..."

Wanda sighed and dusted off her hands. "My grandma, also." She wiped a smudge of dirt on her cheek and spread it nearly to her eye, making her look like a boxer after a rough fight. "I said I'd love to see you next week."

I forced a smile. "That sounds better, anyway." I slowly edged backward in case a sudden movement changed her mind.

Her gaze sharpened. She looked younger than what had to be mid-thirties, and she had that 'just got divorced and in shape and I'm feeling good' look that was universal. "Well. I could use some company. Especially family." Reaching down past a box, she drew out two Wallace Brewery Pale Ales. "Have a beer with me?"

My throat was suddenly parched but my suspicions up.

She gestured me toward her with one of the bottles, which had dew drops sliding down to the floor. It was fresh, probably bought just a few hours before. "You're going to talk to me anyway, and we both know it, so why not do it over a beer?"

That was fair. I shut the door and wound around boxes to accept the brew before looking around.

She kicked a box my way. "There are books in there. You won't fall through." She leaned over and dragged an even bigger box close and sat, her sigh full of relief.

I twisted my cap off and took a seat, wincing as my ankle protested. I leaned down and readjusted the bandage.

Her eyebrows lifted as she tipped back her bottle.

"Burned by a bullet," I explained before taking a big drink. The smooth brew washed down my throat and settled, warming and easing me more than it should. Alcoholics ran in my family, and I never wanted to be dependent on alcohol. On anything, really. "Second time this week."

Her throat moved as she swallowed. "You sound like a badass."

"Right?" I agreed, settling more comfortably on the cardboard. "That's what I was thinking."

"Do you feel like a badass?"

Such a shrink question. "No," I said honestly. I liked her. She reminded me of Donna. "I feel scared and lost and like there's a monster coming for me out of the darkness."

"Well." She set her beer down. "I guess that gives us a good starting place."

I sighed. "Yeah. Okay."

CHAPTER 10

*B*oth of my sisters stayed the night, probably figuring that my getting shot at required double protection. Tess kicked me at various intervals, mumbling about dogs and men, and Donna shifted restlessly on the sofa outside the bedroom, so none of us got much sleep. Escaping to the office early on Saturday was almost a relief. While my talk with the shrink had been necessary, I was still feeling a little raw from it, and escaping into work probably wasn't the way to deal with stress.

But as I entered my office, the quiet of the empty building surrounding me, I finally took a full and deep breath. Okay. I might not be able to steer much in life right now, but I could investigate Aiden's case. This, at least, was under my control.

I grabbed a newspaper off the floor, wincing at the front-page picture of Nick with his arm around me at Scot's house. We looked pretty friendly.

Wonderful. All I needed was that type of gossip.

I started with some misdemeanor case files just to get into the flow of litigation. Two minor burglaries, several drug charges, and a trespass case. All pretty easy to schedule and plan. My guess was that only the trespass case defendant would go to trial and the others would plea out.

Then I opened the too thin case file for Aiden Devlin, and my heart rate automatically quickened. I'm not sure what I was magically hoping to find, but the only documents secured inside were the arrest warrant and the Notice of Arraignment sent from the court. No notes on why or how Aiden was arrested, no trial plan, no evidentiary documents. Only ineligible notes on one piece of yellow legal paper that had been ripped unevenly off the pad. No wonder I hadn't been able to decipher it in the stressful situation of District Court. Swirls and clouds all attached by jagged lines from a pen that had apparently lost most of its ink.

And now Scot was dead.

I bit my lip and squinted, trying to understand the odd diagram.

It looked like 'ice cream' was in the center cloud. What legal words looked like 'ice cream?' I couldn't think of any, and now I was hungry.

Scot had scrawled Aiden's name and phone number at the top left corner. Since it appeared that Aiden hadn't hired an attorney as of yet, that made sense. Scot could speak directly with Aiden.

As could I.

At the realization, I leaned back in my chair. It made no sense for Aiden to talk to me, and in fact was an incredibly bad idea for him to do so, but that didn't mean I couldn't ask. First, I had to figure out what was going on. They taught us in law school to never ask a question in court that we didn't know the answer to, and this wasn't court, but I still needed some sort of background before I could talk to the defendant. Or maybe I just wasn't ready to see him again.

I leaned over and studied the paper closer. A barely legible scrawl on the bottom right corner caught my attention. I frowned and partially turned the paper, squinting to read better. The name took shape, coming together like a Captiva Code on a website. *Melvin Whitaker.*

Wait a minute. I lifted my head and shut my eyes, trying to attach facts in my brain. Why would Melvin Whitaker's name be on notes in Aiden's case file? Whitaker supposedly had supplied the pot that Randy Taylor had been caught with and that the elderly ladies had been trying to find.

Just who was this guy? The connection for every drug case in the darn county?

The DEA had gone through my computer, and having found nothing, they'd left it in place, unlike Scot's. Leaning over to type on my keyboard that unfortunately was missing the S, I conducted a criminal defendant search for Melvin Whitaker. Nothing. No arrests, no records whatsoever. Not even a parking ticket. Huh. Well.

Then I went through the database to find investigators who contracted with the prosecuting attorney's office. While we worked with the police on every case, I wouldn't mind an outside source on this one. I found the number for one of the Lugi uncles, who were distant cousins on my dad's side and had been PI's for years. I left a message asking for investigations into Melvin Whitaker, Randy Taylor, and Aiden Devlin.

Then I sat back in my chair and tried to reason through the last couple of days.

Indecision didn't feel good, so I shifted through the case files on my desk and found Thelma Mullen's folder and took a quick note of her address. Melvin lived right next door, so maybe I should actually do my job and start investigating these drug cases. The very least I could do would be a drive-by, and since the sun was finally not hiding behind June cloud cover, why the heck not?

Then, taking a deep breath, I called the one person I really didn't want to talk to.

"Pierce." Even the detective's phone answering voice sounded cranky.

"Um, Hi. It's Anna Albertini." My voice sounded way too hesitant. "The DEA took most of our records, and I don't have a casefile on Aiden Devlin. I don't have even one document to use in prosecuting him."

Detective Pierce was quiet for all of two beats. "Don't you talk to each other over there?"

I blinked. "Excuse me?"

"Basanelli already called earlier this morning, and I put him in contact with the DEA drug task force. He should have everything we have by mid-day, including all of the information on the Lordes."

Oh. I closed my eyes and winced hard enough my nose hurt. Of course. "Lords? Who are they?"

Pierce's sigh was forceful enough, I swear my ear burned. "Lordes with an e. They're a motorcycle gang located north of Spokane that deals in drugs, guns, and everything else. Aiden is a Defender."

A Defender? Episodes from *Sons of Anarchy* ran through my mind. "Motorcycle Gang or Club?" I asked, my voice shaking again. Darn it.

"What's the difference?" Pierce snapped.

The difference was that one has sexy tough guys with muscles and hot bikes. The other killed people. "How long has Aiden been in this, ah, group?" I asked.

"Long enough, Ms. Albertini. It's your job to put him away, and you should remember that. He's a bad guy among really bad guys."

The condescension in the tone made my teeth ache. "I know my job, Detective. Thank you for your help, and I hope you have a fantastic day." It wasn't a 'bless your heart,' but for northern Idaho, it meant the same thing. When all else fails, fall back on manners, which was a lesson I'd learned from every woman in my family. Even so, I hung up before he could say anything else. I thought it over. Nick was already on Aiden's case. It didn't surprise me. Nick wasn't in the office, so he must be working from home. I needed to get my hands on that information.

For now, I grabbed my purse and headed for the door. It was time to get to work.

* * *

SUMMER HINTED on the Chokecherry breeze as I drove through the retirement community. The flowering trees would only last a couple of weeks, but they were a welcome sight after months of grey sky and winter. Even so, in a northern Idaho spring, clouds could come rushing in any second to settle in for the week. For now, I lifted my face to the meager sun and enjoyed the drive.

Beyond a brick monument declaring the place 'Sunnyside Retirement Community,' perfectly tended lawns spread from single homes to duplexes, all green and bordered by flowering shrubs. The houses ranged from white to purple to an electric blue. Did older people go color blind? Or did they just have better senses of humor than the rest of us?

Double checking the address on my phone, I pulled into the driveway of a white duplex. The left side had wild pink trim along the edges and windowpanes, while the right had a muted tan.

I went for the pink side. Thelma opened the door before I could knock, wearing a short orange jumpsuit with lime green polka dots. "Anna. Oh, my. Come in out of the cold." Her bony fingers wrapped around my arm to tug me inside to the small tiled area next to contractor grade beige carpet.

"It's seventy degrees," I protested. The woman might be skin and bones, but she had a heck of a lot of strength.

"Exactly." She shut the door. "Would you like some hot chocolate?" She squinted up at me through bottle thick glasses, her brown eyes huge and concerned.

Everything in me softened, and I concentrated just on her for a moment. "I'm fine. But I wanted to ask you some questions about Melvin, if that would be okay."

Delight lifted the wrinkles across her pink dusted cheeks. "Oh. How lovely. Am I a witness?"

I stumbled. "Um, more like a source."

She clapped her hands together, the smell of her vanilla lotion wafting up. "Like an informant?"

"Sure."

She gestured toward the adjacent living room and its matching floral sofa and chair set. "Well. Then please have a seat."

I grinned. "Thanks." The carpet was sturdy beneath my tennis shoes—definitely not soft. I took a seat on one of the chairs. "Where's Georgiana?"

Thelma perched on the edge of the other chair, her little body vibrating like a Chihuahua seeing a treat. "She and a couple members of the bridge playing group drove over to Spokane for the day. When we couldn't get the pot from Melvin, we found out where the best dispensaries are—"

I held up my hand. "I think it'd be better if you didn't tell me about any crimes you ladies might want to commit." If they brought the marijuana over the state line, they were breaking the law. Again.

"Oh." She straightened her knobby shoulders. "Of course. It's just that it helps with the cataracts, you know?"

I didn't know, but I nodded anyway. "So. Let's just start at the beginning. Tell me about Melvin. What do you know about him?" I could use her thoughts to supplement whatever the Lugi brothers found.

"Well." She fluttered her hands together. "Melvin is quite hand-some and probably the youngest single male in the community. He's in his sixties, I think."

That was young for the area. "Okay." I smiled, letting her talk.

She leaned toward me. "He works across the border at Greenley Seed Company."

I frowned. The seed company owned acres and acres across the prairie and researched, grew, and sold grass seed—the kind you put on your lawn but did not smoke—countrywide. Were they growing pot now, too? The industry was closely regulated, so those records should be easy to find, if so. But if Melvin was bringing his work home with him, into Idaho, he was breaking several laws. "What does Melvin do?"

She shrugged. "I think he said something about research and development. Once in a while, he's still wearing a white lab coat when he gets home." Her penciled eyebrows wiggled. "He's quite handsome in the coat. Have you ever played doctor?"

I jerked at the question and then coughed. "Not since I was a kid." I grinned. "With one of the McDonnell brothers from St. Regis." Up camping on a good weekend, actually.

Her eyes twinkled. "Yes, well, it's a good pastime."

I shook myself back to the present. "How do you know that Melvin keeps pot at his home?"

She snorted. "He smokes it out back, and a lot of people drop by to visit him, you know?"

As if on cue, a car pulled up outside. We both turned and moved in unison for the sofa to peer through the thick chintz curtains and spy. I'd love to get a visual on Melvin.

A cute blonde female in her late teens or early twenties popped out of a white convertible to move toward the door. Thelma dug her elbow into my side in an effort to crane her neck to see, but the entry way to Melvin's was around the side of the garage.

Then the girl came back into sight, holding a backpack, followed closely by...Randy Taylor?

I straightened; my heart rate speeding up. "Randy is living with his uncle?"

"He stays over a lot," Thelma confirmed, clutching the edge of the sofa, her weight barely leaving a dent in the sofa cushions. "The kid doesn't talk much." She sniffed.

The blonde opened her door, and I caught sight of a logo on it.

"Tranquility Spa," I read out loud. Interesting. I'd read about the new spa down by the river in the local paper. As we watched, Randy looked around and then accepted an envelope from the blonde.

I sucked in air. Had that just been a drug deal? Just how much pot could fit in that backpack? "Do you know the girl?" I whispered, even though the windows were closed, and we remained nicely hidden behind the heavy material.

"Not really," Thelma whispered back. "She and that kid smoked out back a few times last week, and he called her 'Cheryl.' That's all I know."

All right. Good enough. I pulled out my phone and had Siri call the Tranquility Spa.

"Tranquility Spa, this is Felicity," came a very chipper voice.

"Great. I'd like to make an appointment with Cheryl on Monday?" I said, watching the blonde zip out of the driveway.

"She has appointments open in the afternoon. Would you like to do the 'Bring a friend' promotion for the Spring Special with first Mandy and then Cheryl?"

I blinked. That would probably seem less suspicious than just seeing Cheryl. "That would be wonderful," I said.

"Great. Let me get your information," Felicity said.

"Anna Simms and, ah, Tessa North," I said smoothly as if I'd gone undercover a million times before.

"Nice." Thelma elbowed me again.

I shared a grin with her. Yeah. I could do this. My sister would have a lot of fun being somebody else for a day, too. After disconnecting the call, I was feeling a bit triumphant. Maybe I should take this investigatory work across the border and just check out Aiden Devlin and the Lordes.

Why not?

CHAPTER 11

J left Thelma's after giving in and having a turkey sandwich on rye, side of potato salad, and hot chocolate. My belly was full, and my body relaxed as I drove from Idaho into Washington and headed north. I'd conducted a quick google search on my phone and found that the Lordes owned a garage north of Spokane that worked on vehicles.

My Fiat was in pretty good shape, so I didn't really have an excuse for stopping by. But I'd think of something before I arrived. How tough could it be?

Aiden had said he'd wanted to talk to me before he'd rolled me to the ground, so it was kind of an invitation.

Traffic was a pain, but I made my way north and let the phone's navigation system guide me. Would Aiden be there? My hands grew damp on the steering wheel, and I rolled my eyes before wiping them off. Even if we didn't have a past, he was a guy who'd draw my attention on looks alone, much less with the intensity flowing from him. Of course, that could've been because he'd been in court stuck in an orange jumpsuit and possibly headed back to prison. Maybe he'd seem more mellow on a spring afternoon in June.

Right.

I drove past a mall and then several businesses, continuing north until the commercial buildings became less polished and more ramshackle with barbed wire and barred windows becoming frequent. On a bright note, the traffic thinned out.

Lordes' Business Garage wasn't what I expected. A chain link fence, topped with barbed wire, was open wide to reveal a four-stall garage covered in rusting sheet metal. Men worked inside on various trucks. Different vehicles were lined over to the right, including two B&B delivery trucks, one with its hood up.

There was no clubhouse, no apartments, no cool office like in the movies.

The sign above the garage looked newer with a logo for Lordes on it along with a lion wearing a crown. A lion with sharp and blood-stained teeth.

I shivered but drove inside the perimeter. Oh, this was such a complete mistake. I pulled to a stop near a small door to the far left, which must be the office. A man the size of a bull moose stepped outside, his blond hair and beard bushy and long. He wore grease-stained jeans beneath a light blue T-shirt with leather cut. I knew what a cut was from television.

I didn't have a window to roll down since the top was off. "Hi."

His gaze raked me as he wiped his hands on a filthy looking rag. He opened my door. "What's the problem?"

With the car. What was the problem with the car? I felt frozen in place but instinctively stood up and sidled away from him. Lie, damn it. Say there's a funny sound from the engine. Act like an airhead. "I'm looking for Aiden Devlin," I blurted out, heat rushing into my face. Crap. There went my cover.

The giant looked me over and then rolled his eyes. "Of course, you are. Bitches are always looking for Devlin." He said it casually, naturally, as if using any old adjective.

The bastard had called me a bitch and didn't even realize he was insulting me. I opened my mouth to let him have it when reality smacked me. Wait a minute. He accepted my reason for being there. Oh. So many women sought out Aiden, it was normal. I should've felt relief. Not so much.

"Devlin," the guy bellowed. "Get out here."

Wait. Did I really want to see Aiden? I tried to keep my expression calm. What had I been thinking? I'd just wanted to do a drive-by. That's all. What was wrong with me?

"What?" Aiden snapped, appearing out of the farthest garage. He wore ripped jeans and a dark T-shirt, sans the cut. His thick hair curled around his ears, a smudge of grease decorated his very muscled left bicep, and a dented wrench looked at home in his hand. He turned his head and stopped short, his blue eyes blazing through the day.

A couple of guys inside the other garages looked up from their various vehicles.

"Company," the guy next to me said, amusement heavy in his tone. "Not your usual type."

Usual type? What did that mean?

Aiden's expression didn't change, but he muttered something that didn't sound complimentary. Then he turned and moved toward me. A lot of guys strutted, or walked, or just ambled. Not Aiden. He prowled. Everything inside me wanted to jump back in the Fiat and peel out. But his gaze, that hot and deep ocean blue gaze, pinned me in place.

Butterflies on meth crackled through my abdomen with a shocking heat.

By the tense angle of his jaw, he wasn't happy to see me. He arrived, and the scent of male, oil, and leather came with him.

"Gonna introduce us?" the first guy asked.

"Anna, Spider. Spider, Anna," Aiden said shortly, his gaze not leaving mine. "Somethin' wrong with your car?"

Numbly, I shook my head.

"Good. Get in." He gestured toward the open door and crossed back around to slide into the passenger seat. The entire car lowered with his bulk. He tossed the wrench to Spider, who easily caught it. "This might take an hour." Then his gaze raked me, but unlike with his buddy, tingles exploded all over my body. "Or maybe two," he said lazily.

Fire slashed into my cheeks, but I settled into the car and drove quickly out of the lot, ignoring his friend's chuckle behind us.

It took me several miles to find my voice as I drove even further north, not sure where I was heading. "Was that really necessary?"

Aiden remained silent, taking up too much room in the small car, his gaze on the old buildings turning to wheat fields. I drove for about a half an hour, my mind spinning. The stalks soon blanketed us on both sides, waving softly in the slight wind.

I swallowed. Was silence a good thing? Probably not. I cut a glance at him sideways. In profile, he looked just as tough as face on, but the angles were sharper. More defined and somehow deadly. He was the best-looking guy I'd ever seen in real life, and part of that was a danger stamped across his features that went beyond roguish. A fierceness that was hard to quantify and uncomfortable to feel but too intriguing to ignore. "Aiden?"

He nodded toward a dirt cutout. "Pull over."

My lungs compressed fast and hard. I didn't know this guy. It had been twelve years since we'd breathed the same air, and there was a lifetime of experiences we hadn't shared. All I knew about him was that he'd been charged with a felony and was a member in a drug-running motorcycle club. But that couldn't be right. I pulled the car over, and dust blew up behind us.

"Jesus." He was out of the car in one smooth motion of pure maleness, slamming the door.

I had less than a second to pull away and leave him, but I shut off the ignition instead.

"What the holy fuck are you doing?" he bellowed, throwing

both arms out. He'd been sitting there stewing for the entire drive?

I blinked. Frightened by my week so far and now faced with his temper, mine just up and exploded. "My fucking job," I yelled back, jumping out of the car and shoving the door closed. This was all just too much. "You have a problem with that?"

He stared at me across the convertible, wheat behind him and an empty road behind me. "Your job?" His voice lowered, deepened. "You've been a prosecutor for a lousy month, Anna. You shouldn't have anything to do with a felony drug case, and you know it."

He'd checked up on me? That thought shouldn't be as pleasing as it was. "I'm second chair," I countered quietly.

His chin lifted, his eyes darkening to a hue that would take me forever to name. "Second chair?" His eyes closed and he rubbed the back of his neck. "Jesus Christ. Claim a conflict of interest and get off the case."

"Why?" I whispered. That's why he'd wanted to see me the day before? To get me off the case? "Are you guilty?"

"You owe me," he countered, his raw toughness such a contrast to the cheery wheat behind him that I wanted to take a picture.

Yet his words penetrated. My stomach rolled over and not in a good way this time. "Yeah. I do," I said softly. "What do you want?" I asked out of more curiosity than anything else.

"You off the case. Nothing else." He hooked his thumbs in his threadbare jeans. "Tell me yes."

Now my chin lifted. "You've gotten pretty bossy, Aiden."

His eyes glimmered for a moment. "Yeah. I don't suppose you've gotten pretty obedient?"

I slowly shook my head.

"Didn't think so." He sighed, and a light of what might be admiration glimmered in his eyes. "You were a tough little thing, even way back when. For now, get off my case, and we'll call it even. Deal?"

"Why?" I whispered.

His jaw clenched. "Because people are ending up dead, and I don't want anything to happen to you." For the first time, I caught a glimpse of the angry and vulnerable boy he'd been at sixteen. "You're the only good thing I've ever done in my life. You have to stay safe."

The sweetness behind the plea caught me hard and fast. "I can help you. Whatever you've done, I can help you find a way out." It was my turn to save him. "Tell me everything, and I'll go to bat for you." Maybe he wasn't really guilty. Maybe he was just an accomplice who could get immunity. Or at least a reduced sentence. "Please."

He was around the car before I could blink, towering over me. "I don't want your help. Got it?"

I looked up, way up into his face, reminded once again of his size. An energy cascaded from him, angry and tense. Oddly sexy. "No." I'd do my job within the law, but if there was a way to help him, I'd find it. "Tell me your side of the story."

"My side?" His left eyebrow rose. "There's nothing I can say that makes my life all right for you to fix, so stop. You honestly have no idea what you've walked into." His jaw clenched hard enough I could see it.

"Really?" I countered, poking him in the chest. "My boss was just shot right in front of me. I think I have a clue."

"You don't." In a shift of muscle, he plucked me right off the ground to sit on the hood of my car.

The air sliced all funny in my chest, and I gaped at him. "What are you doing?"

He leaned in; his hands planted on either side of my hips. "Showing you that you're totally out of your depth. You're in the middle of nowhere with a guy out on felony bond after having left a club business where fifteen guys would provide an alibi if I needed one." His head jerked slightly toward the car. "Do you even have a gun in there?"

"Always." I probably should've been scared, because every word he'd said was true. But I wasn't. Oh, my entire central nervous system misfired like a supernova, but none of that was fear. Maybe a dollop of caution with a whole boatload of curiosity. "You won't hurt me."

His nostrils flared and he straightened. "Damn it." This close, his eyes were a myriad of different blue hues. "I won't hurt you, but I can't keep you from being hurt. What we do—this is too big to protect anyone as nosy as you are from. Just trust me."

I couldn't answer him, because I was going to try and save him if possible. First, I needed facts. "Tell me the whole story."

"No." He looked me over, head to toe, his gaze penetrating.

I tried not to squirm and looked back, knowing I was totally losing this staring contest.

Then he shocked me by running both hands through my hair and messing it up more. His touch was slightly rough with a whole lot of heat.

"What are you doing?" I swatted his hands away.

He leaned back and studied me again before twisting the neckline of my T-shirt. His calloused fingers brushed the bare skin of my chest, and I couldn't help a shiver. The caress danced down my skin with a wave of heat.

I slapped him again. "What the hell?"

"The guys don't know who you are, but if they ever do, I'd rather they think we were out here fuckin' and not talking," he muttered, checking over the rest of me.

Heat blazed into my cheeks. "Oh, for goodness sakes." The idea of sex with Aiden was one I'd had over the years. That was imaginary Aiden and not this real-life devil. Truth be told, I wasn't sure I could handle him. I glanced down at my twisted shirt. "Happy now?"

He stepped back and looked me over, his mouth pursing. "No."

Then, against all possibilities, he moved back in, his rough palm skimming along my jaw. I started to argue, and his mouth covered mine.

Shock blasted through me followed by a wave of heat. His thumb pressed against my jaw, and I opened my mouth. He swept in, kissing me, pushing me so I had to struggle to keep from falling back onto the hood. Every kiss I'd ever had, even in law school, pooled into memories of a girl kissing a boy.

This moment was all man kissing woman.

I groaned low, kissing him back, arousal zinging through me faster than I would've ever thought possible. He went even deeper, and I completely lost myself in him.

Then he released me.

I gasped for air, my mind fuzzing, my body wide awake and ready to go.

He ran a thumb over my still tingling and no doubt swollen bottom lip. "Now I'm happy," he murmured, his eyes an unfathomable blue and his expression unreadable. "You can drive me back now."

CHAPTER 12

*I*n Silverville, for my family, the first Sunday of every month meant a barbecue. I usually caught a ride over the pass from Timber City to Silverville with one of my sisters, but Donna had gone over early to help Grandma Fiona cook polenta, and Tessa was coming late after a dinner shift she'd covered for a sick co-worker. So I drove alone, my thoughts still jumbled after my impromptu meeting with Aiden the day before.

I'd spent Saturday night and all of Sunday trying to ignore the fact that he'd given me the best kiss of my life while just trying to make a point. Or trying to make it look like we'd been kissing.

Had he felt a thing?

Why did I even care about that? First of all, he hadn't even asked to kiss me. He'd just done it. That wasn't okay, no matter how good it had felt. And second, I wasn't looking to date Aiden Devlin, regardless of my silly fantasies through the years. I was, however, going to help him as much as I could within the law. Whether he liked it or not.

My parents lived in a sprawling log home fronting a river usually full of trout. Acres of fields and then trees spread in every direction, giving them about twenty acres of solitude, which was good because often our family barbecues numbered at least fifty people.

Home to me meant fragrant food, lots of voices, and a smattering of English, Italian, and Gaelic often rattled about together. I guess chaos felt right.

I found a spot to park to the side of the long driveway and made my way to the house, finding Pauley sitting on one of the large rocks creating a wall of flowers below the front yard. He twirled a white daisy in his hand, while the sound of people out back carried over the house. "Hi," I said, balancing the fruit salad I'd managed to put together before leaving home.

He looked up, his dark eyes focusing from behind his thick glasses. His hair was smoothed back. "I heard you got shot again."

I shook my head and perched precariously on the adjacent rock. A Koi pond wandered from the other side, and the fish sparkled bright orange in the sun, no doubt happy to be out of hibernation. "Not really. The second bullet just nicked my ankle."

He tapped on the rock with his free hand. Three times. Two times. Three times. Two times. Three times.

I let him tap.

He looked toward the pine trees. "Maybe you should find an occupation where you do not get shot." It was his way of expressing affection—logic and reason.

"It's an idea," I agreed. "I appreciate you worrying about me."

His gaze turned to the fish. "You seem to get in danger statistically more than most people, and now your job adds possibilities. Maybe you should be a stay-at-home mom."

I grinned. He'd gone through the safest scenarios to find a better alternative for me. "I'm not married, and I don't have kids."

He jerked his head. "True. You could get married and have kids. It would please your Grandma Fiona greatly. This country is a somewhat safe place to have healthy pregnancies and births." He frowned and rocked back and forth for a while. "Though there is still danger, and you would have to drive them places. Car accidents happen frequently."

"True." I set the bowl on my lap and relaxed, letting the sun warm me.

"Artists usually are safe," he mused. "Though I have seen you draw, and you will not make any money."

I nodded. "Starving to death doesn't appeal to me."

He twirled the daisy again. "Gardener?"

"I don't really like dirt," I said, closing my eyes.

He was quiet for a moment.

"I like to cook," I said.

"You always use too much salt. You should not be a cook," he said.

Amusement and love took me. "Once. At the family picnic in the park two summers ago, I may have used too much salt in the potato dish."

Two taps. Three taps. Two taps. "Twenty-seven times through the years," he said, his focus moving to the trees. "I can list them all for you."

And he could. I snorted. It was too bad I couldn't use his statistical brilliance to help me with my cases—at least not at the moment. Maybe someday I'd have enough information to know what to ask, perhaps as soon as the next day, once I got my hands on the DEA files. "No, thanks. I'll take your word for it."

"People usually do," he mused. He smoothed down his ironed jeans. "You should stop avoiding going inside now."

I started. "I'm not."

"You are."

I bit my lip. "Why would I avoid going inside?" Even as I said the words, I wanted to wince at the stupidity of them.

He sighed. "You got shot. There are grandmothers inside. It's that simple."

Yeah, it was. Not that being fussed over by grandmothers was a bad thing. But when it came with lots of other attention, sometimes it was too much. "Is that why you're out here?" I asked.

He shrugged. "I'm out here because I am me."

I smiled again. Yeah. That nailed it. People gave small towns a hard time, but truth be told, we've always accepted everyone. If someone's uncle only ate purple food, you tossed in some purple food coloring for your mashed potatoes at the picnic. If a person saw ghosts, you let them have their moment. If kids had trouble concentrating, you figured out how to help them, even if the answer was unconventional. Even before diagnoses such as autism became the norm, we treated our 'eccentric' folks just like everyone else. "Did Aunt Jenny bake you red potatoes again?" Pauley had gone through a red only eating phase about three years ago, but he was back to eating all colors now, and Jenny couldn't seem to let go of the red phase.

"Jenny is on a date, busy, seeing a dirt-bag asshole of a wife cheater from Bozeman," Pauley said, his features still pale in profile.

I jumped. "Where in the world did you hear that?"

"Your dad," Pauley said.

I smacked my head. My dad was one of the greatest guys in the world, but he really had no filter. None. Why hadn't I heard that Aunt Jenny was dating someone from Montana? When had this started? "Well, I should get in there." And find some answers.

Pauley smirked. "Yes. Also, Nick Basanelli was invited tonight."

My stomach dropped. "What? Why?"

"Well, we have a lawyer in the family, so that's not it." Pauley blinked. "Though your mother has no grandchildren."

Oh, man. I sighed and turned for the deep steps leading up to the door. "I'll save a seat for you by the river swing."

"You always do."

* * *

AFTER TOO MANY hugs and kisses to count, and a quick greeting to Nick, I helped set out food before heading for the small barrel table by the river. It fit three people, and Pauley had already somehow gotten a plate and sat. I joined him, followed by my sister Tessa. It was very often the three of us at the table. I thought of it as Pauley's table, away from too much commotion.

Yet, no one had ever tried to take my place. Maybe it was my table, too. How often did the family oddball know they were the oddball? Hmmm. "Am I weird?"

"Yes," Pauley said, separating his corn and salad with a knife.

I chuckled and dug into my macaroni salad. It was Nana O'Shea's recipe, and she still thought her several tablespoons of sweet pickle juice was a secret, so we let her have that one.

"Man, he's hot," Tessa said over her glass of tea.

I didn't need to look, but I did anyway. Nick stood over by the barbecue talking with my dad. He was just as spectacular out of his suit, wearing dark jeans and a black golf shirt with a logo from a Palm Desert course. It stretched nicely across his chest, and the hand holding a beer bottle looked strong. Masculine. "You'd make a nice couple," I said, ignoring the stress that would put on me since I worked for the guy.

She coughed. "I was talking about you. Geez. Can you see me with a guy like that?"

I paused and turned to stare at her. "Yes." Tess was smart and kind and wild. Truly beautiful with red-blonde hair and green eyes. "Why not?"

She shrugged and took a bite of her burger. "He's a lawyer."

I rolled my eyes. "So am I. It's not that hard." Then I sighed. Tess had a hang-up because she hadn't gone to college, and I just didn't get it. "You're really smart."

"I know." She set the burger down.

But she didn't. Not really. It was weird to be in the position of trying to encourage my older sister. She'd always been my protector, just as fierce as Donna. "Tess. If you're having a hang-up about college, go get a degree. If not, then don't confuse education with intelligence. Some of the dumbest people I know are lawyers."

"Like you," Pauley snorted.

I shared a smile with Tessa. A joke from Pauley, a real joke, was a rare and special treat. "I'll think about it," Tessa said. "Though I'm not sure I want to spend four years learning about business. I might want to just start one."

"Really?" I chewed thoughtfully. "That's awesome. What kind of business?"

"I'll let you know when I decide," she said.

I nodded. "Fair enough. For now, make sure you have tomorrow afternoon off. I got us spa appointments—on me."

She frowned. "On you?"

"Yeah. Part of a case." I filled her in on what I could, and her eyes glimmered with the excitement of going undercover. Kind of, anyway. I had just finished when a shadow crossed our table, and I looked up to see Nick. I swallowed and introduced him to Tessa and Pauley.

He finished shaking hands with Tessa. "I have to get going but thought you could walk me out. Have a couple of thoughts about our cases."

Our cases. I liked the sound of that way too much and had to remind myself that one of the cases was about Aiden, who'd just kissed me the day before. Really well.

"Sure." I stood and took my paper plate over to the garbage. My legs were a little tingly. There were a zillion good-looking guys in the world, but this one was smack dab in the middle of mine. And I didn't know a thing about him—not really. "Good idea."

You'd think leaving a family barbecue, one held every Sunday, would be easy and quick to do. You'd be wrong. It took nearly twenty minutes for Nick to make it from my table, across the lawn, and finally through the house, saying goodbyes and coming up with plans. Finally, we stepped outside and walked toward the Koi pond.

"It was nice of your family to invite me," he said.

"I work for you and you're single," I said easily, dodging over the rocks.

He chuckled. "Yeah. That's what I figured. Silverville really never changes."

No. It didn't. I turned and shielded my eyes from the sun with one hand. "You wanted to talk about the Devlin case?"

"First thing tomorrow," Nick said, the sun behind him creating a fit outline of his muscled body. "We'll set up a war-room and go over the information I received from the county police about Scot Peterson as well as Aiden Devlin, since I believe the cases are related. I've also called in a couple of favors with the DEA for any of their surveillance on Devlin and the Lordes."

The net was definitely tightening around Aiden. Considering Scot had been killed, was Aiden in danger as well? Was it possible the cases weren't somehow connected? "I'll be in at eight," I murmured.

Nick paused and ran a hand through his dark hair, ruffling the thick mass. "I requested your harassment casefile regarding Jareth Davey from the Silverville police force."

I paused. My current casefile? "Why?"

Even with the sun behind him, his eyes glowed a low amber. "I told you I'd find Jareth Davey for you. I'm surprised you didn't tell me about the cards he sends to you."

My stomach cramped, and I lifted my chin. "I haven't asked you to find Jareth Davey. I don't want to know where he is." His location didn't make one bit of a difference in my life, so long as he didn't live in Idaho. "Why do you even care?"

For the first time, something flickered in Nick Basanelli's eyes. Something uncertain. "I want to help."

I didn't need help. "How did you even discover that there is a current investigation?"

Nick rolled his eyes. "Seriously?"

Good point. Silverville. No secrets. "I don't care about the cards." I couldn't prove that each anniversary and Christmas card came from Jareth Davey, and since he'd never made a move, I wasn't going to spend my life letting him scare me. That was his plan, and he wouldn't win. I passed each card on to the small police department in Silverville, and they fingerprinted them, with no luck. Then I ignored them, breathing easier from June until December because there would be no cards. "Drop this, Nick."

"He still contacts you. You need to know where he is," Nick said quietly.

"Why?" My voice rose just enough to give me caution. There was no reason Nick wanted to get involved with this. If he wanted to manipulate or control me with the promise of finding Jareth, he was dead wrong. "We can't prove the cards are from him, and even so, that barely rises to harassment."

"Maybe not," Nick said. "But the cards prove he hasn't forgotten about you."

I thought about the well-kept Lady Smith & Wesson nine-millimeter handgun secured in my glovebox, even now. "That's good. I haven't forgotten about him, either." Then I forced a smile. "I'll see you tomorrow at work." With a polite nod, I turned to head back to my family, my heart beating way too fast for me to keep the smile on my face.

CHAPTER 13

I went for a black skirt with a taupe silk shirt for Monday morning. Red kitten-heeled pumps and garnet jewelry added some color, and by the time I'd sucked down a double latte and entered my building, I was ready for the day. The office had been put to rights, but a cloud still hung over the premises. The entire floor seemed muted and subdued.

"You're here." Nick came out of his office and straight for me, dressed today in a dark blue suit with red power tie. Was he already running for office, or what?

"Yeah." I dropped my purse inside my door.

"Good." He grasped my arm and escorted me past the receptionist and back into the entryway for the building, his hold firm and his stride long.

I pulled free. "What are you doing?"

He paused near the stairwell and looked down at me. Finally seeing me. "Oh. Sorry." He shook his head, but each hair remained perfectly in place. Why that was sexy to me, I'd never know. "I get on a roll and forget to take a moment." His brows drew down, giving him a slightly clueless look.

"I bet juries love that expression," I murmured.

His eyes sharpened, and a slow smile crossed his face. "Yeah. They do."

I shook my left arm out so my bracelets fell where they should be. "How about you stop trying to manipulate me and just play it straight?" This guy had more angles than a geometry textbook, and I was getting tired of it.

His chin lifted. His nicely sculpted, cleanly shaven, dent in the middle chin. "That's fair."

I waited, forcing my feet to remain still and not tap. "Why are we outside the offices?"

"I set up the war room downstairs." Gesturing me toward the marble stairway, now he waited.

Clipping carefully in the heels, I started down the stairs, acutely aware of him at my back. The lawyer let off some heat. "Why downstairs and not in our conference room?" My brain rushed to catch up. "Wait a minute. You don't trust anybody there." I turned on the bottom landing to face him.

He nodded. "They're all still being investigated. We have no idea if anybody was working with Scot or not." He moved past me and shoved open a thick oak door. "Except you, of course."

Of course. Because I was so new. I followed him down a dingy hallway rarely used. A doorway to the left showed some mats, a couple of punching bags, and mismatched heavy looking free weights. A few of the lawyers in the building still worked out there, but I liked the nice and well-lit gym across town. Finally, we reached the third locked wooden door to the right, and Nick opened it with a key. "Here we go." He flipped on a light that flickered a few times before strengthening.

I followed him into a windowless square shaped conference room with wooden table and seventies-style metal chairs. The floor was cracked tile that might've been white at one point, the walls were a dingy yellow, and the light cover a beautiful stained glass of green and blue. I studied it.

"Pretty, right?" Nick asked. "I bet there's a history with it." He moved for a stack of manila files and a couple of notebooks already sitting on the table next to several yellow legal pads, pens, and markers. He'd already attached a whiteboard to cover the entire far wall, and right in the center was Aiden Devlin's picture, with Scot's over to the right. Then Nick kicked out a chair. "Have a seat."

The seat wasn't too dusty, so I smoothed my skirt and sat, reaching for a legal pad. "What have you learned?"

He drew out the chair at the head of the table and dug through the stack next to him for a legal pad to read a thick stack of notes. "All right. Aiden Devlin became a Defender, AKA an Enforcer, in the Lorde's Motorcycle Club about two years ago."

I started taking notes. "Just two years?" While what I knew about clubs came from television, I still knew something. "That's enough time to be a Defender?" We'd get to what he enforced and defended later.

"Good question." Nick flipped over the top page. "The Lordes patched over a motorcycle club in Portland called the Diablo Riders two years ago, and it looks like Devlin was with the Riders for a decade. It was a small club, and apparently he rose quickly with this new Lordes group to a position of Defender." Nick looked up; his gaze somber. "With a group like this, he had to deal some tough shit to rise so quickly. You get that, right?"

No. None of this made a bit of sense to me. "Why does one club patch over another?"

Nick exhaled. "The Diablo Riders got caught trafficking drugs and guns, and the DEA put away who they could. There was no evidence on at least five of the members, and the Lordes patched them over quick, meaning they assimilated the remaining Riders into the Lordes."

I rubbed my chin. "So the DEA followed the former Riders to the Lordes?"

"No. The DEA was already watching the Lordes as well as the

Riders. The two clubs worked in tandem, which explains the bloodless patch over."

Heat spiraled down my throat. "You're saying that Aiden has been trafficking drugs and maybe guns for more than ten years."

"That's exactly what I'm saying," Nick said, his voice low and calm. "The Lordes own an apartment complex in Idaho, near the Washington border, on the prairie close to the freeway, where many of the members live, and the DEA raided it a week ago, finding guns and drugs ranging from heroin to marijuana."

"That's how Aiden ended up in our jail," I murmured.

"Yeah," Nick said. "They had enough to distribute—especially meth. The DEA lab will break it down and find out where it came from. The guns included several sawed-offs, Mk 14s, and handguns with the registrations filed off." He leaned back in his chair, his voice softening just enough to provide warning. "And you let Devlin go free."

There he was. The trial shark. Finally, I could see it. Frankly, it was a good look on Nick. Sexy, strong, and sharp. "I was pretty much frisked by the DEA on my way to court, and there was nothing in the case file." My voice remained clear and surprisingly steady. "If you're doubting my abilities, I'm more than happy to step down."

He steepled his fingers together beneath his chin, his expression smoothing right into thoughtful. "This case, taking down the entire Lordes organization, could be a career maker for you." He leaned forward. "Come on, Anna. I've read your entire personnel file. You're as ambitious as I am."

Yeah, I was. But my fight was for justice and maybe a bit of revenge against predators. His was for, what? Power and prestige? Or was there more to Nick Basanelli? "Why did you become a prosecutor?" I asked.

One corner of his mouth ticked up. "That's a conversation we'll have over drinks. Several."

I tilted my head, my attention grabbed. Was Nick asking me

out? Or was it a colleague type of comment? Tons of colleagues went for drinks after a trial. What did I want it to be? "Every time I ask you a question, you evade," I murmured.

"Yeah." He looked back at the stack of case files and research sheets. "I probably do. Have a drink with me tonight after work, and we'll talk."

That wouldn't do. I had a spa appointment, and for what, I hadn't even asked. Probably a facial or a massage. I'd be mellow and greasy and probably not prepared for drinks. Or I'd be pumped up with more intel on Melvin Whitaker, the drug trade, and how Aiden was involved. "I'll have to take a raincheck on that," I said.

Surprise flashed across Nick's face to be quickly banished. "Sure."

Triumph filtered through me, and I hid the accompanying amusement. Most women probably didn't turn down an invitation from the handsome attorney. I cleared my throat and got back down to business. "What's the connection between my former boss and the Lordes?"

Nick dragged a case file from the bottom of the stack. "Aiden was pinched in an effort to answer that very question." Nick handed over several eight by ten photographs.

I pulled the first one closer to see Aiden and Scot meeting in a red booth in a darkened room. "Where is this?"

"Dunphey's Bar over on Oakwood," Nick said, sliding that picture out of the way. "This is down at the marina." The second picture had Aiden on a sailboat at the lake and Scot leaning over the rail, their expressions intent.

I fought the urge to run my finger over Aiden's angled face. "Who was under surveillance?"

"Devlin and the Lordes," Nick said, showing yet another picture of my dead boss and Aiden together—this one at the park. "The DEA caught sight of these pictures and had Devlin taken in the drug raid with the hope of getting him to talk and implicate

Scot Peterson. They asked for assistance from the local cops, so they wouldn't tip their hand and show they were making a federal case. The local cops practically coerced your former boss to charge Devlin, hoping it would force a situation."

I shook my head. "Why did the DEA raid our offices and arrest Scot? Aiden hadn't had a chance to talk, or it looks like he didn't, so why tip their hand?"

Nick tapped a pen on the table. "Because Scot was going to rabbit. He'd purchased a first-class ticket to Jamaica and was leaving first thing Saturday."

I just couldn't see Scot being part of anything illegal. He'd been the prosecuting attorney for years, winning the election every time he came up. I tried not to stare at Aiden's mugshot on the wall. All right. "Does the name Melvin Whitaker mean anything to you?"

"No. Why?" Nick leaned toward me.

I told him about the elderly ladies, Randy Taylor possibly selling drugs to the blonde girl from the spa, and the scribbled note in Scott's case file for Aiden that had Melvin's name written down.

Nick listened intently and took notes. "When the private investigators you hired get back to you, let's chat. The county will pay their fee. I think you might be on to something here."

Maybe. "I have an appointment at the spa."

He paused and leaned back, his eyes thoughtful. "I'm not sure that's a good idea."

I shrugged. "I'll be careful. If Randy's blonde friend gives me an opening, I'll just ask about drugs." I gave up and looked at the mugshot. In it, Aiden's hair was mussed and needed a cut, his jaw was whiskered, and his blue eyes pissed, even in the black and white photo. "You and Aiden are the same age, and both grew up in Silverville. Were you friends?"

"I'm a year younger," Nick said. "And no. I was the golden boy, and he was the rebel." Pure fact leveled out his tone.

"It looks like things haven't changed," I said, my heart hurting a little.

Nick followed my gaze. "Tell you what. Assist on this case, give it your all, including your connections, and I'll help you help Devlin if I can."

I swung toward Nick. He'd finally zeroed in on how to motivate me. "I owe him."

Nick grimaced. "I'll be here when you learn the painful lesson about blind loyalty and how destructive it can be." He held out his hand. "Deal?"

I slid my smaller hand into his, surprised by his warmth. "Deal." The satisfaction that filled his eyes should've given me pause.

It was too late for that.

CHAPTER 14

A spring storm hit late morning. Tessa picked me up right after lunch, and we drove through town and around the south end of the lake to a brand-new building covered in sleek river rock. As we entered the copper accented lobby, the sounds of flutes in the rainforest filled the air. Did anybody really ever play the flute in the jungle?

"What do I do?" Tessa whispered in the elevator as we lifted to the third floor.

"Just be Tessa North and keep your eyes open," I whispered back. "If there's a way to talk about pot, do it."

She nodded; her eyes alight. I grinned. This going undercover was kind of fun.

We checked in, donned thick white robes, and headed into the Zen room, which had more flutes playing. Frogs croaked, and birds chirped along. Tess poured us some ice-water colored with lemons and cucumbers, and we burrowed into thick, fabric-covered chairs. A wall of glass showcased rain battering the dark grey lake outside. I sunk deeper into the silk cushions, slowly exhaling. My breathing evened out and I sighed.

A small blonde named Mandy silently entered the lounge and

then asked me to follow her. She wore a tidy cream outfit that looked like hospital scrubs.

Hopefully she gave massages. I still hadn't asked about my appointments when we checked in.

We entered a tiny room with a table draped with crisp white sheets. The walls were smooth stone, and a copper fountain gurgled on the granite counter. Flutes tinkling around us, I turned around to face her, feeling a little vulnerable in my robe.

"Have you had a Brazilian before?" Mandy asked.

I coughed. "What?" That couldn't be right. No way.

She nodded her head to the table. "A Brazilian. The 'Summer Special' promotion? Have you had one before?" She stirred something in a small pressure cooker held on a narrow metal tray.

"God, no." She was between me and the door. "Um."

"It's no biggie, you'll love it," she said with a smile. "Have a seat."

Okay. It was almost bikini season. But a Brazilian? "I, ah, just thought I had an appointment with Cheryl." I sat gingerly on the table.

"You do, after this. She does a wonderful pedicure. Now just lay back and relax."

Famous last words. I lay back on the plush table. Mandy pulled the bottom of my robe apart. What had I been thinking? I recited exceptions to the hearsay rule in my head. Some woman was now looking at my hoo-hoo.

Going undercover wasn't as fun as I'd thought, but I'd better get to it. "So. This is going to be painful. I don't suppose you have a sedative or anything?" I croaked.

"There are numbing agents in the wax." She used a tongue depressor to spread warm wax across my private area. The heat irritated but didn't quite sting. Her hands were steady as she covered the wax with a piece of paper and pushed down.

All right, that was no big deal.

"Take a deep breath," she chirped. Then she yanked, and pain ripped into me.

"*Holy Mary Mother of God!*" I leaped off the table, away from her and into the wall. My foot tangled in my flapping robe. I struggled to regain my balance before going down on all fours to hit the cold floor with the hard slap of skin on stone. The healing scrapes on my hands from the other day screamed in reaction. With a gurgle, I lurched to my feet and backed against the smooth wall, clutching my robe together with trembling hands. Forget going undercover.

Mandy stumbled back in shock, steadying herself and the metal tray. I stared at her, the table between us. She gave a high-pitched giggle and eyed the door. I eyed the door, too.

"Okay," she said softly, soothingly. She stretched both hands out at me, much like she would to a rabid animal. "It's all right. The first pull is always the worst."

I whimpered, and a bit of drool slid out of my mouth. I kept my gaze glued to her, my heart pounding beneath the robe. Fire lit my hoo-hoo, and adrenaline flowed freely through my veins. I didn't care about being a lawyer any longer.

"Um," she blurted out, "you probably don't want to leave it like it is."

Biting my lips, I leaned forward and opened my robe. Oh no. There was one huge strip missing. It looked like I was wearing half of a toupee. A minor one. I wasn't all that hairy to start with, but it really didn't look good. I thought quickly for a moment. This pain had to lead to something. "This would be easier with a pot brownie, if you know what I mean. Have one?"

She blinked. "Um, no. That's kind of illegal."

I looked back down. There was a good chance no one would be near the area before the missing hair could regrow. "How long can it take to grow back?" I wiped my nose on my sleeve, my hoarse voice echoing around the peaceful room.

"Up to eight weeks." She glanced again at the door.

Yeah, lady. Freedom was on the other side—for both of us. "Eight weeks?" There was a good chance, a really good chance, that nobody would be anywhere near this area of my body. But still. "Do you know where I could get something to mellow me out?" I tried again.

"No." She gestured to the table.

Fine. I barely kept from glaring at her as I climbed back onto the table. My head hit the pillow, my hands covering my face. I had to find some sort of information on drugs, or this was so not worth it.

"Though I'm sure you can find brownies across the state border." Her deep breath echoed around the room as she moved back into place. Warm wax blanketed me again. Then the paper. She yanked.

"*Holy crap!*" I kicked out a leg. The metal tray shot across the room. Mandy leapt into action, grabbing the crockpot before it could hit the floor. Her elbow flew out, knocking into the light switch by the door.

I reached forward to help just as the room plunged into darkness. Startled, I tumbled in a heap to the hard floor, and Mandy's legs tangled with mine. She landed on top of me with a muffled 'oomph.' The breath whooshed out of my lungs as pain flared along my chest.

We sat motionless in the darkness for a couple of beats.

Her sigh filled the silence. Then she scrambled to her feet, and light flooded the room again. I climbed back onto the table, my robe parting in the middle.

I leaned up, taking a good look. I wasn't done yet. "Sorry," I mumbled as I lay back down.

Mandy's giggle was full of nerves as she pulled the tray back into place. She made quick work of the remaining areas. While I swore quite a bit, I managed to stay still and not kick anything else. When she had transformed me to billiard ball smoothness, she sighed, her relief apparently greater than mine. Hard to imagine.

I stumbled bowlegged back to the Zen room, wanting to kill somebody—pretty much every man I knew. There I sipped ice water, waiting in the plush chair. My nether regions smarted painfully.

Going undercover was for the birds. I closed my eyes and concentrated on quieting the noise in my head.

* * *

"Anna?" The voice was soft and came from far away.

I jerked awake, instantly surrounded by flutes and a frog. Ah, crap. Blinking, I turned to see Randy Taylor's blonde friend in the doorway, wearing the standard spa uniform. "I'm Anna."

She smiled. "I'm Cheryl. Would you like to follow me?"

Last time I'd followed somebody out of the Zen lounge, I'd ended up naked and waxed. "Sure." Gingerly holding my robe together, I stood and followed her, passing Tessa just heading in.

She limped; her knuckles white as she clutched her robe together. "I'm going to freaking kill you," she hissed in my ear as she staggered into the lounge.

I snorted and followed Cheryl; my mood lifted. Now that was funny. She led me into a quiet room with a pedicure chair, and I gingerly sat, plopping my feet in the warmly delicious water. I groaned. "I could use a good joint right now."

Cheryl chuckled and took her chair, leaning over to scrub an exfoliant over my calves. "Just relax. I heard you yelling a little while ago, and now you're fine." She looked up, her eyes dancing. "I know it's a pain, but think how happy your boyfriend will be."

I let the water soothe me. She'd given me the perfect opening. "Yeah, no kidding. Do you have a boyfriend?"

"I do." She ducked her head to splash water over my leg. "We've been dating for six months."

"He's a good guy?" I asked. How could I ask about drugs? About Melvin's possible connection to Aiden?

"Yeah." She wiped off her chin. "How about you?"

I swallowed as an idea hit me. Just how much did she know? "Um, yeah. I'm dating Aiden Devlin. He's one of the Lordes."

She blinked. "No kidding? You're dating a Lordes Defender?"

My heart kicked it up, and I forced myself to stay calm. "You've heard of Aiden?"

Pink dusted her cheeks. "Yeah. I mean, I've been to a couple of parties out at their apartment complex. He's so hot, but I thought he was dating a redhead."

Jealousy, totally unwarranted and unwanted, shot through me. "Nope. Not anymore. Just me." I bit my lip, my brain clicking rapidly. "Is your boyfriend a Lorde?"

She chuckled. "He wishes. But no, he's just done some business with them."

"Oh." I lowered my voice to a whisper. "The drugs?"

She stiffened and moved to my other leg. "A Lordes old lady wouldn't ask that question."

Crap. I sucked at this and was losing her. "I know." Drowning in my own stupidity, I let her pull my foot out to dry. "It's just that Aiden is pissed and took away my pot, and of course, nobody else will give me any. I knew about you and Randy, and I just thought…" Man, I was full of it. Seriously full of it.

"Oh." She filed my toenails. "I guess that makes sense, but I'd hate to get Randy in trouble with the Lordes. Those guys don't mess around."

Suddenly, I kind of felt like a jerk. She seemed really nice. "Forget it." Plus, what kind of latitude did I have as a prosecutor? It was okay to investigate, but at some point, it was the police's job and not mine. "I'm sorry to have made you uncomfortable."

She shrugged. "You obviously know what we do here for the Lordes. I could get you a couple of joints out of the stash, but you can't tell your old man."

The idea of Aiden as an old man was ridiculous, but I'd watched Sons of Anarchy and knew all the lingo. All right. Some of the lingo. "Not in a million years." Just how involved was Aiden in this drug business? Did he have a drug problem, or was he in it for the money? What did the spa do for the Lordes? There wasn't a cool way to ask. Although, since she'd used the word 'stash,' they must be selling drugs out of the new spa?

She continued the pedicure, and I picked out bright pink polish. What the heck was I going to do with two joints? It was illegal to possess them, but how could I tell her no now? She finished up, and I went to take a shower in the large locker room. There were two joints in my locker when I opened it for my bag, in which I'd tossed jeans and a T-shirt earlier.

Feeling like a criminal, I shoved the marijuana in my purse and put on makeup, meeting Tessa in the lobby. We paid, and I took her to dinner at a local pizza shop, letting her snipe at me about the Brazilian she hadn't intended to have. By the end of dinner, we were both laughing, although the pot in my purse created a cloud of doubt around me.

Finally, she dropped me at my car, and I headed home. I'd turn the drugs over to Nick the next day and report everything I had learned. He'd promised to help me with Aiden, and I believed him.

Sighing, my head and privates aching, I parked and walked toward my door, stopping short at seeing a large form sprawled on my porch swing.

I gulped.

"Hi, Angel," Aiden said, his sapphire colored eyes layering through the soft dusk, his voice low and husky with a hint of pissed. "Rumor has it my old lady had a Brazilian today. Wanna show me?"

CHAPTER 15

*M*y lungs stopped working. They didn't hitch, and they didn't stutter. They just up and froze. So did my feet. I stared at him across the stone walkway, acutely aware of the absence of distance between us. My girlhood fantasies about Aiden Devlin hadn't prepared me for the reality of his focus as a man. He was predatory and did nothing to hide it.

For the first time, I saw him clearly. And I didn't know a thing about him. Not really. "You're trespassing," I said.

His smile was slow and sure. "Turnabout, fair play, and all o' that."

I shivered, and my gaze caught on his mouth. Tingles pricked inside my chest and right down to my abdomen. Butterfly wings of both intrigue and warning. "Rumors fly fast. Are the Lordes running drugs out of the Tranquility Spa?"

He didn't so much as twitch. "If we were, you'd never find the proof."

That wasn't informative in the slightest. Since he was obviously irritated with me, I wasn't sure how to read into his bravado. Or maybe he was being perfectly honest. "I find it interesting that you've already been called with information about your old lady." Man, I hoped I was using the biker gang lingo correctly. "Especially since there's an obvious drug connection between the spa and the Lordes."

"If it were obvious, I'd be in handcuffs," he rumbled easily. "When somebody asks questions about my boys, claiming to be mine, then anybody with half a brain would give me a call. The chick at the spa has more than half a brain, even if her man doesn't. Now. We gonna talk about you being mine?"

The archaic language ticked me off. Completely. I told myself that nothing inside me went a little bit gooey and warm at the possessive claim. Nope. I was not that woman and the caveman act didn't work with me. Regardless of his hard-cut jaw and way too tough-guy body. My slightly quickened breath and weakened knees had everything to do with the disintegrating weather conditions and not the biker defender. Geez. I needed to talk to the shrink again, because lying to other people was understandable. Lying to myself was a huge mistake.

Thunder cracked in the distance, and I jumped. The clouds would be rolling in soon, and as if in warning, the air began to cool. Kicking myself into gear, I strode down the path, up my stairs, and to my door. "I'm investigating a case, Aiden." I unlocked the door, barely sounding breathless. "If you don't like it, then start cooperating with me."

I didn't hear him move. One second I had the key in the lock, and the next, I was flipped around and pressed against the door, a giant of a man towering over me.

My head snapped back, and I looked up, meeting his gaze directly, even though my heart thundered. "This is not cooperating." For some reason, I'd always had the ability to think and feel two different things, and often my mouth had a mind of its own, which came in handy when my body was rioting like this. "Back up."

He moved in. Both hands flattened on the door, and he leaned down, his angled jaw close to mine. "I don't give a warning twice,

Angel. Step off of my case." The Irish was out full force in his deep voice this time. Intriguing and definitely sexy.

I'm not sure what a Lordes Defender expected when giving a threat, or an order, but he wasn't going to get it. I levered up on my toes and leaned in closer, my nose nearly touching his. His pupils dilated, and I enjoyed the surprise there. "I'm trying to help you, and if you don't knock it off, I'll stop." Then I planted both hands on his very hard chest. "You don't want me for an enemy." I pushed.

To my surprise, he stepped back. Then he studied me, his gaze probing and oh-so-damn blue. "You don't know me anymore."

The words, although they'd been said by my sisters as well as myself, still pierced with a truth that shattered the make-believe world I'd created years ago about him. *Starring* him. "You don't know me, either," I whispered. "I don't need saving now. You do."

"You keep investigating this case, and you *will* need saving," he said evenly, the Irish lilt disappearing again.

"From you?"

"No." He exhaled, frustration drawing his brows together as he ducked his head and studied his boots. "How can I get through to you?"

I held up a hand. "I get it. You want me to stay away from you." Even though he was barely more than a stranger now, the idea still hurt.

His head snapped up. "Oh, baby. I'd like you to get as close as you can to me. Just drop your investigation. Let somebody else take those chances, and you stay safe." Those eyes deepened along with his voice, which now held the low seduction of an Irish brogue. Full and thick with promises of stormy nights and raw passion.

Warmth spread through me like a heated port. There was nothing sexier than a bad boy bent on seduction, and I knew it. "I'm sure sleeping with the prosecutor would help your case. Nice try." My voice remained shockingly steady.

His cheek creased. "Who said anything about sex?"

"Sweetheart," I murmured, "I've dreamed of sex with you since I was sixteen years old."

He blinked.

Yeah. I'd learned early on that the truth, the real truth, was often more surprising than the best crafted lie. "Same with Dean Winchester, who also doesn't exist in real life." My imagination didn't keep me warm at night, but it was still a heck of a lot better than reality, apparently.

"Oh, I exist." Aiden stepped in again, his hand clasping my waist and resting heavily on my hip. He smelled of leather and man, and the warmth he brought covered me head to toe. His hold was gentle but his strength obvious, and my breath shallowed out.

Touching him, being this close to him, was a mistake beyond simple words. But something in me, maybe the whole of me, didn't care. I should have. I know it. But finally, after all of these years, Aiden Devlin was close enough to kiss.

As if reading my mind, he drew even closer. "I've thought a lot about that kiss the other day. You?"

I lifted my head to meet his gaze. "Yeah. I think you should've asked first." My voice was throaty. Husky. My chest felt heavy, my breasts alive.

This was a new feeling. Completely.

Challenge crossed his high cheekbones, as obvious as an oncoming storm over the mountains. And his drawl. Well, now. That was all male. "I see. Can I kiss you now?" His lips were close enough that his minty breath brushed my mouth.

I'd never backed down from a challenge my entire life. Yet finally, a threat of caution ticked through me. Oh, not enough. But I did hesitate, and the wind brushed my hair across my chin to fall back to my shoulders. "Yes." Then I held my breath, expecting him to move.

He didn't. Not at first.

His lids lowered to half-mast, and his gaze ran leisurely across my face. The wind blew in from the side, against us, but I couldn't move.

His hand slid down the door and then cupped my jaw, his palm warm and calloused. "I wondered about you. Through the years," he rumbled.

I breathed out, the nerves in my torso, just beneath my skin, all but vibrating. His thumb brushed across my bottom lip; his touch soft. His chin lifted just a fraction as he watched his finger on my mouth, his eyes flaring, his shoulders squared and blocking the rising moon. "Aiden," I whispered, wanting him with a depth that should've scared me.

"Yeah," he said, as if talking to himself.

I jerked my head, dislodging his hand, and then levered up and took his mouth in a kiss, my hands curling over his broad shoulders and into his T-shirt.

He drew air in, from my mouth. His broad hands on my back pressed me up and closer to him.

Then he took over, going deeper. My eyelids shut as sensations rippled through me, so hard and fast and deep I stopped thinking. Gravity pulled me down, and he lifted me back up, kissing me deeper, all but surrounding me with male power and strength.

He shoved me back against the door, one hand planting next to my head, his mouth driving against mine in a way that was all pleasure.

I forgot that Aiden Devlin was kissing me and just felt. Hot and needy and somehow powerful. So many feelings rioted through me, and I chased each one. He moved against me, his mouth dropping to my neck to place hot kisses along my throat and then farther down, his lips warm along my collarbone and lower.

The second he hit upper breast, I gasped, my eyelids flying open.

More. I wanted more. I grasped his jaw and jerked him back up to me, and he kissed me hard.

We both panted when he drew back, his eyes dark pools of blue. "You gonna ask me in?" he rumbled.

I blinked. Kissing Aiden on my porch was one thing, asking him inside for the night another. A big thing. Not just because he was a defendant out on bond. I was in over my head, big time, and I was smart enough to know it. When had that ever stopped me?

I took a deep breath, not sure what was about to come out of my mouth. My phone buzzed, and I tugged it out of my back pocket, my gaze still trapped by his. "Albertini," I said, my voice beyond husky.

"Did you go to the spa to see Cheryl?" Nick Basanelli's voice held an urgency that drew me up short.

Aiden's expression smoothed out, but he didn't move away from me.

I gulped. "Yeah, why?"

"Because I'm looking at a dead kid we just identified as Randy Taylor," Nick muttered. "I'm on the dike road off Tamarack Lake. You'd better come down here." He clicked off.

I froze in place, the phone still held to my ear.

Aiden eyed me, wiping my lip-gloss off his bottom lip with his thumb. "I take it I'm not staying the night."

I shivered. Had I gotten Randy Taylor killed? Was Aiden a murderer? The dike road was only a couple of miles around the lake from my bungalow. There was no way Aiden dropped a body and then showed up on my porch to kiss me, right? Emotion clutched me, and I plastered both hands against his chest, the phone still in one. Then I shoved. "Did you kill Randy?" If he did, I was in danger, and right now, I didn't care. This was too much. All of it. Way too much.

Aiden straightened to his full height, and all lazy lust disappeared from his eyes, sharpening the blue so brilliantly they cut. "What are you talking about?"

"Randy Taylor is dead down by the dike road. Two miles from here." I punctuated each word with a smack of my phone against his chest. "Did you kill him?"

Aiden's brows drew down. "No."

"Did the Lordes?" I snapped.

His face lost all expression and somehow hardened at the same time. "I have to go." He turned and strode down the steps and across the walk, moving quickly past my car toward the road.

My mouth gaped open, and my chest hurt. Bad. He'd walked? Seriously? He reached the end of the drive and disappeared behind a couple of trees. The roar of a motorcycle engine pierced the night, a flash of taillights pierced the darkness, and then he was gone.

I hadn't seen his bike, but I hadn't been looking.

Why had he hidden it? The wind whipped up, snapping into me, and the chill that shook me had nothing to do with the weather.

CHAPTER 16

*I*t was the first crime scene I'd visited where I hadn't been shot at, and it looked just like the ones on television. Red and blue lights flashed from different emergency vehicles, shining through sweeping tree branches, yellow tape cordoned off the area, and techs milled around, searching for evidence. It had taken me a little while to attach the top to my car, so I'd probably missed a lot of the activity. Detective Pierce snapped orders near the water's edge where two uniformed officers tripped over the rocks to finish setting up a white tent that glowed eerily in the dark.

As if even the sky feared Pierce, it waited until the tent was in place before opening up with a crash of thunder and a pummeling of rain. He caught sight of me where I'd pulled my car over at the beginning of the dike road, where many people usually fished or swam, and I swear, even from that distance, his gaze narrowed.

I lifted my hand through the rain as if in a wave, but he didn't return the gesture.

Nick came around the tent, said something to Pierce, and then headed my way. His shorter hair was mussy from the rain, and his whiskered jaw gave him the look of a pirate. He wore long athletic-type sweats, a matching sweatshirt, and tennis shoes. Basanelli after-hours wasn't bad to look at. The rain smashed my hair to my face, and I pushed it away, trying not to shiver. He reached me, already shrugging out of the dark blue zip-up sweatshirt to reveal a tight gray T-shirt. "Where were you when I called?" He threw the sweatshirt over my shoulders.

"Home." With Aiden, my mouth still tingling from his. I shook my head and tried to hand the thick material back, noticing Detective Pierce still watching us.

"Jesus." Nick shoved my arm through one sleeve, and I let him, not wanting the cop to see us struggle.

The jacket smelled like foresty cologne and something else. A wood fireplace? I settled into it. "Thanks."

Nick wiped rain off his forehead, looking more Italian than ever with his olive-colored skin and sharp angled face. "You ever see a murder scene, besides Scot's?"

I gulped. "No."

"You're going to see this one." He pivoted and held up the yellow crime tape for me to duck under, waiting patiently until I'd done so. Even though he was about a foot taller than me, he was much more graceful as he moved under the tape. How many times had Nick done this?

Did I really want to be a prosecuting attorney? Maybe I should consider doing civil work with Uncle Gino.

Thank goodness I'd changed into tennis shoes and jeans at the spa. I walked over the uneven ground toward the tent, my head hurting and my hands shaking. Questions should've been ripping through my head, but I couldn't concentrate. Finally, we reached the tent and Nick opened the flap facing the lake.

My stomach rolled. I swallowed down bile and leaned to see inside, which was lit by several camping lanterns. Randy Taylor lay partially on his side and stomach, his jeans and white shirt muddy. His left arm was bent at an odd angle, his chin was purple, and his one visible eye was closed with the remainder of his face hidden by the rocks. His hair was still in a man-bun, and he looked young. Very. "How did he die?" I asked, unable to look away.

"Somebody bashed his head in," Nick said, dropping the flap and turning me away. "My guess is rock but could be bat or brick."

My stomach lurched and I gagged.

"Whoa." He pulled me away from the body with an urgency that had my feet slipping on rocks, so he grasped my arm to steady me. I let him.

Detective Pierce snapped from the other side of the tent. "Get her away from the crime scene."

Man, I wanted to flip him off. Instead, I took several deep breaths and stumbled back toward the yellow tape, Nick's hand on my arm somehow reassuring. "Dick."

"Yeah," Nick agreed, holding the tape up again and letting me through, seemingly oblivious to the rain molding his gray T-shirt to what looked like very cut muscles. "You needed to see that. No more covering for Devlin or the Lordes, and no more investigating on your own."

I couldn't exactly argue with him, considering my dinner was about to come up. I regained my balance and turned, looking up at his implacable face. "Is this my fault?"

"No." Nick sighed. "It's the fault of whoever killed him. They're starting to tie up loose ends."

Aiden couldn't have done this. Randy Taylor and Scot Peterson had been killed, and both were being investigated for drugs. Sure, Randy was dealing with pot, and who knows what Scot had been in to—if he had been guilty. "So, the shooters in the brown car outside the courthouse the other day were aiming for Randy." At least they weren't trying to shoot Aiden.

"Maybe. We keep racking up bodies, so who knows," Nick said grimly. "The connections are weak. Pictures of Aiden having a drink with Scot Peterson, probably representing the Lordes.

Randy Taylor selling drugs—maybe for the Lordes. This is all conjecture, and I can't prove a bit of it."

I shuddered. My peaceful town was becoming a different place all of a sudden. "Why here and why now?" I murmured.

Nick's gaze sharpened. "What do you mean?"

I gestured toward the lake I'd played in for decades. "Here in northern Idaho. Why are we all of a sudden having drug deaths? We're not a big city, and it's not easy to get here." Seattle was the closest big city at about a six-hour drive, and Canada was two hours away. "We're not exactly a great route to anywhere else."

Nick coughed, his gaze warming. "You're more than a pretty face, Albertini."

Something heated inside my chest. "Um, thanks?" So he figured out I wasn't a moron. That was nice. He thought I was pretty. "Want to continue that line of thought?" What did he mean? What wasn't he telling me?

"Not really." He looked back toward the innocuous white tent. "Though you're right. The answer to why here is easy. The answer to why now—I haven't figured that out yet."

My mind mulled it all over, and I didn't like the answer I found. The Lordes were here. That's the why of the place—maybe. But why *now*?

Nick let me work it out. "Yeah. The Lordes are here, so that explains the location. But why now?"

I squinted up at him. "Why do I get the impression you're not telling me everything you know?"

"Because I'm not telling you everything I know," he said, shifting until the lights were behind him and I couldn't see his face. "I have suspicions, but I don't have facts yet."

"You don't trust me." For some reason, that hurt a little. How crazy was that?

"I don't trust anybody, Anna."

The use of my first name caught me by surprise and made him

seem more approachable than normal. "What's your agenda?" The words blurted out before I thought them through.

He leaned over, trapping me against my car. "Just to catch and put away the bad guys. Like always."

I looked up at his handsome face. Oh, he'd make a great senator someday, and I thought he was looking at me a little differently than he had. As if he was finally seeing me. I coughed and covered my confusion with more questions about the case. "When did Randy die?" I asked, moving toward my car.

"Don't know, but the body was discovered an hour ago, and considering this road is pretty busy with folks heading home after work, I'd say the body was dumped about two hours ago, or somebody would've seen it." Nick opened my car door, and I dropped into the driver's seat.

I scrubbed rain off my face. "Aiden was at my house tonight, waiting for me."

"When?" Nick snapped.

Shuddering, I told him about my trip to the spa, talk with Cheryl, and finally meeting with Aiden. I left out the kiss, but I did hand over the two joints that had been in my jockybox.

"Christ." Steam actually rose from Nick's soaked shirt as he shoved the marijuana in his pocket. "Have you lost your mind?"

Geez. What would he think about the kiss? "Possibly, but think about it. Randy might have been selling drugs through Cheryl at the spa—drugs he had acquired from his Uncle Melvin. There's probably a connection to the Lordes, but I don't see it yet."

Nick looked at me like I was crazy.

I cleared my throat. "Also, I can't imagine Aiden dumped a body here and just headed up to my house to talk to me." To kiss me and ask to stay the night. That would take a sociopath, who didn't have feelings, and I knew Aiden did. Pretty deep feelings. I'd known him as a kid, and he wasn't a monster.

"People change," Nick said shortly, as if reading my every thought.

Heat climbed into my face.

"Hey." Detective Pierce strode over the ground toward us, ducking beneath the yellow crime tape. "Uniforms brought in the girlfriend. I may need you there to sign off on a deal if I can get her to talk."

"Cheryl Smythers?" I sat up.

Pierce paused in turning. "You know her?"

"We'll meet you at the station." Nick slammed my door before I could speak, crossing around my car to settle his bulk inside. "You okay to drive?"

Ignoring the still-staring detective outside my window, I nodded. "Yeah. Why? Where's your car?"

"I was out running when I got the call," Nick said.

I ignited the engine and cut him a look. "Where?"

"On the lake road," he said, buckling his seatbelt. "Where else?"

I backed the car away from the crime scene. Yeah. Where else? Aiden wasn't the only one who could've dumped a body, but...I shook my head. Now I was seeing killers in everybody. "I'm not sure I like my job," I muttered, turning on the windshield wipers.

"Amen," Nick said grimly, his gaze on the storm. "I hate to tell you this, but it's going to get worse before it gets better." He sighed, not looking my way. "It always does."

CHAPTER 17

"There's really a two-way mirror," I murmured, sipping the worst coffee I'd ever tasted while watching Cheryl fidget through the glass, well past midnight. We stood in a small and dark room at the police station watching her, while she sat facing us in a metal chair, her hair a wild mess and her eyes bloodshot. Was she high? Her hands shook on the smooth wooden table, and she kept picking at her cuticles. "Looks scared."

"Should be," Nick retorted from my side, his wet jacket back in place. "I told Detective Pierce about your interaction with her at the spa while you were finding us coffee."

I winced. "Bet he didn't like that."

"That's an understatement," Nick said, studying the blonde.

"I could've told him," I said, the thought giving me a headache already. I didn't need Nick Basanelli covering for me.

Nick shook his head, and his wet hair sprayed a little water. "You work for me, Albertini. If there's a problem with the police, I deal with it first."

I hated the relief that filled me at that statement. "Um, thanks."

"Then I'll probably fire you," he said, not so mildly. "From now on, let the detectives investigate, or your butt will be out on the

street so fast you won't have time to call your grandmas with the news before they hear it from the grapevine. Got it?"

Why did I get the feeling that Nick had been somewhat gentle with me so far? I wanted to get irritated or protest, but I was just so tired—and wet. And kind of scared in general. "Fine." It was a sucky answer. I was saved from having to redeem myself when Detective Pierce strode into the interrogation room and slapped a case file down on the table. I jumped as high as Cheryl did at the sound.

He didn't go easy on her, but she held tight to a story of not knowing a thing about drugs running through the spa. Finally, when Pierce confronted her about the two joints she'd left for me in the locker, she turned and glared at the window. I barely kept from stepping back. "You bitch," she said, looking so different from the smiling woman who'd given me a pedicure that my toes started to ache.

I sipped more of my coffee.

"Fine," she muttered. "I had a couple of joints, and this bitch was hurting so much after having her entire pubic area waxed smooth, that I felt sorry for her. I gave them to her, so it wasn't a sale or a distribution. It was one woman helping another." She glared harder, focusing somehow close to where I stood. "I hope you get ingrown hairs."

I winced. Was that a possibility?

"There's a lotion called 'Smooth Lava' that will make sure you don't," Nick said matter-of-factly by my side.

Heat ripped into my face, which only got hotter when Pierce turned and looked over his shoulder at me, his gaze both interested and irritated. Great. Now everybody knew I was clean shaven. "How does he know where I'm standing?" I whispered.

Nick shrugged. "Good guess?" He started to say something else and caught himself, snapping his mouth shut. Probably something about my smooth bikini area, which as my boss, he couldn't say.

I didn't ask what comment he'd held back.

Through the glass, Detective Pierce flipped open the top of a manila file and pushed a photograph toward Cheryl. "We found Randy a couple of hours ago," he said. "This is what he looks like now."

She froze, her gaze on the photo. All the color faded from her already pale face. Then she lifted her head, her face hardening, and sat farther back in her chair with her arms crossed. "I'm done."

"Tell me everything, and we'll protect you," Detective Pierce urged, leaning toward her.

"Like you protected Randy?" she asked, her shoulders hunching. "Not in a million years." Tears gathered in her eyes, and she wiped them away as if in slow motion. "You idiots have no idea what's going on."

"Then tell us," Pierce said. He worked Cheryl hard for another hour, but she didn't give a thing up.

Nick finally entered the room, his gait casual and his position obvious, even in the sweatsuit. "I'm the prosecuting attorney, and I'll get you a deal. Protect you."

She eyed him head to toe. "Right. You can do that?"

"Yeah. Work with me." His voice was low and sure, his manner comforting. At least it would be to me, but I wasn't in the hot seat right now. Not really.

She blinked. "Wh-what do you want to know? I've just seen the pot. Honest."

Man, Nick was good. The woman was already opening up to him. He didn't look at Pierce. "Ah, sweetheart. You already know I don't give a shit about marijuana," he murmured.

Pierce's head swiveled, and his brows drew down as he studied Nick. But he didn't say anything. What the heck was happening? I moved closer to the glass; my heart kicking awake even though I was clueless. Why was Pierce looking irritated and curious at the same time?

Cheryl scowled, her pink lips drawing back. "It's all about pot. That's what I have. What do you mean?"

"Let's just say I want to bake a nice loaf of bread," Nick drawled.

I wouldn't have thought it was possible, but Cheryl paled even further. Fine blue lines showed beneath the thin skin on her forehead. "I want a lawyer," she blurted out, her voice shaking.

What the heck?

Nick cocked his head. "I know what you know, lady. Tell me everything, and I'll protect you. It's too late to play dumb."

"Law-eeee-er," she spat, the terror in her eyes obvious.

"Get out," Pierce snapped at Nick, scooping up his documents. He strode out of the interrogation room and into my room with Nick on his heels. They'd barely entered when Pierce turned and shoved Nick up against the wall. Pictures of a dead Randy Taylor fell out of the case file to land on the floor. "What the fuck is going on?"

I instinctively backed away from the mass of testosterone.

Nick didn't so much as blink. "I have what you have, detective."

"Bullshit," Pierce muttered, right into Nick's face. "This is my case, and I want to know what the hell is going on in my city. What has the DEA told you about the drug trade that I obviously don't know?"

"Nothing." Nick shoved Pierce back a step. "You're the investigator, Grant. Figure it out."

Huh. Pierce had a first name. Grant Pierce. The name even sounded like a cop's name. Though none of this made sense. The county prosecutor should be working with the county and state police, not the federal DEA. Just who was Nick Basanelli, and what the heck was he doing in Timber City?

Pierce turned and pinned me with that hard green glare. "What about you? What would you use to bake bread?"

Flour? Sugar? Were those synonyms for drugs I didn't know about? I kept my expression smooth and didn't answer.

Nick leaned in toward Pierce, and my breath caught all funny in my chest. If they started punching, I needed to get out of the way. But he kept his hands at his sides. "Listen. The county prosecuting attorney was arrested before being murdered, and I have no idea who he was friends with in your shop. I don't trust you."

"You don't trust anyone, asshole," Pierce said, his voice just as level as Nick's. "If you think I'm not investigating you, you're crazy."

Nick's eyes darkened to a deep brown. "Bring it on, detective."

"Plan to." Pierce took several steps back, and the atmosphere calmed a miniscule. "We have to work together on this case, so now is when you tell me everything. If you're withholding information, I'll arrest your ass for obstruction."

Hmm. Good threat.

Nick just smiled. "Yeah. You try that."

I had the oddest sense they were about to whip them out and compare. Nick should definitely tell the detective whatever lead he had, but I wasn't going to suggest it right now. Contradicting my boss in front of the angry cop would be a huge mistake.

Finally, Nick turned to look at Cheryl through the glass. "Cut her loose. Let's see where she goes."

Pierce shook his head. "Why? I can arrest her on the possession charge and threaten her with distribution of the two joints at the spa, but that's just to keep her here temporarily." His gaze slashed toward me. "I could arrest you, too."

Nick stepped partially between us. "Deputy Prosecutor Albertini was acting on my orders in an investigative capacity when she accepted the two very minor joints. Then she reported it to me immediately and turned over the drugs. Try and arrest her, Pierce. Give me something fun to do while I figure out who I can trust."

Pierce rolled his eyes. "You have one day to start cooperating before I arrest you. For now, get me a search warrant for Cheryl's home and one for where Randy Taylor was staying—with his uncle, Melvin Whitaker. I want both within the hour."

"You'll get the warrants when we get them," Nick returned, heading for the door. "For now, cut Cheryl Smythers loose."

"Fine, but I'm putting a man on her, and when we have the warrant, I'm executing it immediately. If she's home and in possession of drugs, I'm bringing her in again," Pierce said.

I paused in following Nick and faced the detective. "Are you doing the notification to Randy's uncle?"

Pierce's jaw tightened. "As soon as I have the warrant to search his place. How about you go get that?" Man, he was a cranky bastard. Or maybe murder just ticked him off. Though, it was obvious my office wasn't sharing information with the police, and that had to be a new one for him, and maybe he had a right to be pissed.

Even so, I gave him my sweetest smile and followed Nick out of the room, catching up with him on the sidewalk to our offices. The rain had calmed, dropping in soft plops through the cloudy night. "What the heck was that about baking a loaf of bread?" I gasped, trying to match his long strides.

"Maybe I was just hungry." His tennis shoes had dirt, mud, and pine needles on them. From the crime scene?

"Right." So he didn't trust me any more than he did the detective. "If I'm second chair on this, shouldn't you at least level with me?" I hated not being in the loop. My gut told me that a lot more was going on than drug and gun running, but what could it be?

"I'm sure I will. For now, let's get the warrants." The breeze lifted his now dry hair.

I shrugged against the increasing wind, more than a little irritated that he wasn't sharing information. "Fine. What's the plan for that?"

"With the meager evidence we have?" He slowed down just a little. "Judge Hallenback. He's the only one crazy enough to give us warrants on these facts."

Wonderful. Just wonderful.

127

$\mathcal{J}$udge Hallenback lived in one of the stately mansions downtown, built by timber magnates over a hundred years ago, directly across a street and private beach on Lilac Lake. The road was private with a gate, which had been open for once. Nick and I stood on his wide and darkened porch with round and stately columns bracketing us. The moon tried to glow through the clouds, barely showing.

Rain continued to patter down as Nick knocked for the third time on the thick door, trying to peer past the inlaid glass at eye level.

A ruckus sounded inside. "Maybe we should've waited until morning," I whispered, clutching the warrant request against my chest.

"Ouch," came loudly from inside followed by several bangs.

The porch light flicked on and flooded us, and I shut my eyes in protest. Then I blinked several times just as the door was yanked open. "What the holy hell are you doing on my porch at one in the morning?" the judge boomed, standing there bucked-ass naked, save for the purple tasseled hat.

"Uh." I took a step back.

"Whoa." Nick stared intently at a place over the judge's right shoulder. "Ah, Judge? We need you to sign a warrant."

"Crazy people out late at night." The judge moved back and grabbed a white woven blanket off what looked like a Damask decorated sofa. He wrapped it around his waist. "Who in tarnation are you?"

Nick looked up. "Nicolo Basanelli, and I'm the current prosecutor for Elk County."

The judge looked at me and scratched the salt and pepper whiskers on his sagging chin. "You, I know. Alberto, right?"

"Albertini," I murmured, trying not to stare at his bare chest, which was covered with pink flowers from a marker that smelled like blueberries. They were upside down as if he'd drawn them himself, which he must have. "Anna Albertini, Judge."

"Huh." The judge shook his head, and the tassels danced around him. "Whatta you want?"

"Warrant. Two, actually." Nick took the papers from my chest and handed them over. "Sorry to awaken you."

The judge squinted down at the first document. "You want to search the residence of Melvin Whitaker." He read through the application, hummed a bit, and handed it back. "Nope."

It was the first time I'd seen Nick speechless. So, I stepped in. "Excuse us, Judge?"

The judge shook his head again, and the wild tassels caught my gaze. "You don't have enough. Some kid who's dead might or might not live there? What proof do you have that the deceased lived with his uncle?"

I cleared my throat. "The deceased gave me a piece of paper to find him at his new address, which is Melvin Whitaker's address. We also have the statement of Melvin's neighbor, Thelma Mullens, who said that Randy lived with his uncle."

The judge narrowed his faded blue eyes. "Where's the affidavit of the neighbor attesting to that fact?"

Geez. Come on. I sighed. "We don't have an affidavit."

Although Thelma would probably love to be part of the case. "I talked to her, and I've sworn to it in my affidavit. I am an officer of the court, Judge."

"I know who you are, Alberto!" he thundered. "Get me the affidavit, and I'll sign the warrant. If that's all—" He clutched the door.

"No." Nick wedged his foot in and then winced as the judge pushed. "We have another warrant application, Judge." He handed over the other papers and managed to kick the door open a little more, pushing the judge back a couple of feet.

The judge frowned and read over the papers, drawing them up to his face. "Cheryl Smythers." He glanced up. "What kind of name is Smythers? It's not even spelled right. There should be an 'i' instead of 'y.' Who spells their name like this?"

I couldn't find an answer. The judge was really losing it. "She was in possession of drugs, Judge."

The judge rubbed his whiskers again, reading the papers. "At her place of work. Where's your proof that she has drugs at her personal abode?"

Okay. The guy did know the law, even though he was crackers. "It just seems likely," I said, not sounding sure.

The judge slapped the papers back at Nick. "Get me probable cause, Basanelli, and I'll give you a warrant. If you come here at night again, this late, bring me a fuckin' ice cream cone." Then he slammed the door.

I gulped.

Nick let loose with an impressive litany of swear words strung together in Italian, reminding me of my dad trying to fix his carburetor. There was nothing like a string of fierce Italian expletives. He ended with a nice 'fucking tassels.'

I glanced his way. "You know, he wasn't wrong."

"I know," Nick said grimly, turning to go back to my car. "We'll get that affidavit from your witness tomorrow, or rather, later today, so the police can at least search Whitaker's house. For now, you'll have to drop me off at home on your way."

I paused at the base of the steps as the night grabbed hold of me. I'd seen a dead body. What if Aiden was at my cottage again? While I didn't fear him, whether I should or not, I didn't want to see him right now. "How about you drop me off at my sister's and just bring my car to work tomorrow?"

He paused and looked over his shoulder at me. "You okay?"

"Yeah." This time of year, I rarely stayed alone, anyway. I glanced at my watch, seeing it was now the next day. Tuesday. One day before I'd receive the anniversary note. My stomach lurched, and my head began to hurt. The note would arrive, I'd deal with it, and then the gate would open for six months more of breathing easily. Until the next note. "She lives over Smiley's Diner on Main Street." I tossed him the keys; my hands suddenly too shaky to drive.

He caught them in one hand, cool guy style. "All right. Let's go."

* * *

I'D CALLED Tessa on my way up her stairs so she wouldn't shoot me when I used my key. The smell of the diner, eggs and bacon, wafted through the ceiling, and I took a deep breath. When was the last time I'd eaten? Was it only the night before? So much had happened. My stomach rumbled.

Worse yet, it was now Tuesday. Only one day left before the anniversary of my kidnapping. I shivered and unwelcomed fingers clacked down my spine. Life was not fair sometimes.

Tess's apartment was quiet, and I knew my way in the dark, reaching her bedroom and shucking my jeans for a T-shirt I found on our Nana's fainting couch at the base of Tess's bed. Dawn was finally breaking outside, barely lighting the room from her open window. She rolled over to face me, her voice muffled as she threw the covers open to reveal flowered sheets that had probably been our mom's. "Why so late? Or rather, early?"

I slid inside and faced her, much like we had as little girls. Then I told her about the entire night, not leaving anything out.

Finally, I wound down, snuggling beneath the hand-quilted comforter.

"Wow." Tessa yawned; her wild hair spread out on the pillow. "The dead body sucks, and let's not talk about that again. But you kissed Aiden."

I nodded, catching my hair on the pillowcase. "Yeah." I'd already gone into too much detail about how great of a kiss it was. Finally. "I just can't believe he's a killer. I mean, I know he's with the Lordes, and they don't seem to be great guys, but it's Aiden."

She snorted. "Believe me, it's easy to be fooled by a guy."

I already knew that. In fact, I'd dated a jackass in law school for quite a while, but nobody compared to a couple of Tess's exes. She had horrible taste in men. Truly terrible. Or perhaps she just had bad luck. I wasn't sure. "What do you think?"

She shrugged beneath the covers. "Heck if I know. It's really easy to mix up who you want somebody to be and who they really are. You've been dreaming about this guy for years, and you've created an image in your head. What if you can't see past that to the Lordes Defender?" Her voice was sleepy but her mind clear in the way that Tess had of getting to the meat of a fact. "Just because you want him to still be your hero doesn't mean he is."

That was true. "Do I owe him?" I whispered.

"Doesn't matter what I think because you believe you owe him," she whispered back, like we had as kids. "Let's start there. Do you think you owe him?"

"Yes," I said.

"If you can save him, are you going to?" she asked.

I nodded.

"Okay. Are you willing to lose your job or break the law to help him?" she asked.

I thought about it. "No. I'll help him within the law." If I broke it, then I was as bad as the people I wanted to put away. He'd gotten hurt helping me, and I was willing to get hurt paying him back, but I wouldn't break the law. I had to believe in something after what had happened to me, and the law was it. Even though Jareth Davey had perverted it. I sighed. "This is hard."

"I know," she whispered. "Tomorrow is the day. Are you okay?"

"Yeah." My eyelids started to droop, even though my anxiety was up and would be until I received the anniversary letter from Davey tomorrow. "Maybe he's dead and won't send the card this year."

"We can always hope," she said. Then she was quiet for a few moments. "I've thought about going after him through the years. Just taking him out so he couldn't send any more cards."

I nodded. "Me, too."

She reached out and held my hand. "Did you know that Dad had the Lugi uncles try and find him a couple of times?"

I swallowed. "No." It did sound like our dad. Sometimes I thought my family considered me fragile and damaged. Scared. Helpless. One of the reasons I'd become a lawyer was to prove how strong I could be. Now I enforced the law and tried to find justice. "Why didn't they say something?" I asked.

"They've never found him," she said, sounding more awake now. "That's kind of scary."

"He lived off the grid here, so he's probably doing the same thing elsewhere." I sounded way too logical, while I felt like a scared kid again. I shook it off. The cards were sent from all over the States, and sometimes from other countries. I figured he had friends send them or something. It didn't matter. Someday, and I had no clue when, he'd come for me.

I was armed—and I was ready.

$\mathcal{I}$ borrowed black pants and a cream-colored blouse from Tessa and was late to work on Tuesday, skidding in barely with enough time to head to misdemeanor court that morning. It wasn't until lunch that I had time to call Thelma and ask her to come in and sign an affidavit. She was delighted to do so and said she'd bring brownies after her appointment with an eye doctor.

I really wanted those brownies.

When she showed up, I ate two before anybody else could get to them. Nick was absent most of the day, and for some reason, Celeste wasn't inclined to share his location. Maybe she was starting to like being his paralegal. He'd left my car in the lot and my keys at the front desk before I'd even made it to work. So I finished up the day and called him to ask if he wanted me to take the new paperwork to the judge, having to leave a message on his cell.

I stared at the finished paperwork on my desk, which had only a smudge of brownie frosting on the corner.

My phone buzzed. "This is Anna," I said.

"Hey. It's Nick. Let's see the judge tomorrow. I'm on to something today." He sounded distracted. "Let's grab breakfast at Smiley's. Seven in the morning." He clicked off without waiting for an answer. Humph. That was mildly annoying.

On the bright side, I had some free time. So I headed home and went for a run, careful to stay on the path and keep my surroundings in sight. A murder had occurred on the dike road, and the world seemed even less safe than it had a week before. I breathed heavily as I finished and returned home to make a simple chicken and rice dish. I wondered what Aiden was doing.

Was Tessa right about him? Of course, she was. There was no way any man could live up to the guy I'd created in my head through the years. After reading for a while, I headed to bed, more than a little exhausted after the night before. Breakfast with Nick. A business meeting and not a date.

The phone buzzed me awake sometime after midnight. I fumbled for it on the dresser. "Wh-what?" I mumbled into it.

"She's dead." A loud crash sounded. "Damn it. My foot."

I blinked awake, my mind clearing. "Nick?"

"Yeah," he mumbled; his voice slurred. "She's dead. My fault. So young."

I sat up and flipped on the bedside table lamp. "Who's dead?"

"Cheryl Smythers," he hiccuped. Something crashed.

Cheryl was dead? What? What was wrong with him? "Are you okay?"

He sighed, the sound loud through the phone. "No, Albertini, I am not fine. I am totally and completely bombed." He hiccuped again.

I pushed from the bed. "Where are you?"

"In my condo," he mumbled. "Didn't I tell you where I live?"

"No." I reached for a pair of jeans I'd tossed over a chair, my hands shaking. "What condo?"

"Blueridge Condos above the marina. Lucky number seven, baby," he slurred. "Shoot." More banging sounded, he grunted, and a loud crash echoed. Several, actually, followed by a hard grunt. "Stupid stairs." Then he clicked off.

I wiped a hand across my face. What the heck? Was it part of my job description to help out a drunk Nick Basanelli? He had called me, and he was living in the condos right above the Tamarack Lake Marina and only about five minutes from my cozy cabin. How was Cheryl dead? The bodies were piling up, and I wanted some answers. So I tossed on a shirt, brushed my teeth, yanked my hair into a ponytail, and headed out to my car.

The night was cool but not raining as I drove around the lake road to the luxury condos. It figured Nick would live there. I parked next to his Jeep and strode up the stairs to knock loudly on his door.

He opened the door dressed in faded jeans and nothing else. What was it with bare male flesh these days? Although, unlike the judge, Nick was something to look at. Hard muscles with a tattoo over his bicep that surprised the heck out of me. Some sort of military designation? His jeans were unbuttoned and his feet bare. A bunch of boxes were stacked behind him. "Albertini," he murmured, weaving in front of my eyes. "What are you doing here?"

I tore my gaze from his nice chest to see a bleeding wound above his eyebrow. "What did you do?" I moved toward him, reaching for it.

He slapped my hand away and staggered back. "Fell down the stairs. Gravity wins every time."

I peered closer but didn't try to touch again. "You might need stitches."

He scoffed. "Stitches are for wimps." Then he grinned, making him look more boyish than I could've imagined.

My chest warmed. Whoa. I had to keep myself in check here. "Let me at least put a bandage on you."

He shut the door and leaned toward me, bringing the scent of whiskey with him. "We gonna play doctor?" His eyes glimmered a soft amber, and with his five-o-clock shadow, he looked like a guy who knew all about anatomy.

"No." I pushed past him to walk beyond the stairway toward a great room overlooking the lake. More boxes were stacked on a leather sofa and chair. The kitchen was to the left with high-end appliances, and no doubt his bedroom was upstairs. I was not going up there. "Where's your first aid kit?"

He followed me, picking up a half-full crystal tumbler holding an amber liquid that matched his eyes. "I'm a bachelor. There's no first aid kit." He lifted the glass to his mouth.

I grabbed it, yanking it from him.

"Hey." His lip pouted out. I swear it did. "Give that back."

"No." I moved for the kitchen and dumped the contents in the sink. "You've had enough."

He tucked his thumbs in his jean's pockets, not seeming bothered by the blood sliding down his face. "You're kinda mean late at night."

"You have no idea." I stepped over several more unopened boxes and started pulling out drawers. "You need to unpack."

He sighed and reached above the fridge, bringing down a box of bandages. "Here." Taking my hand, he drew me toward the round kitchen table and sat. "You wanna fix me, feel free." Then he tipped back his head and shut his eyes. "Then I get to fix you."

A drunk Nick was a huge flirt. And he was good at it. I gingerly cleaned his wound and did the best I could with the bandages, having to step between his legs to get close enough to do so. No doubt he'd done that on purpose. "You're my boss, you know," I reminded him, throwing the bloody paper towels in the garbage.

He opened his eyes, and his pupils dilated. "Yeah." His hands settled on my hips. "Right now, I don't care."

"I do." Even though those hands felt pretty good, I grasped them and stepped away. Oh, I wasn't dating Aiden, but his mouth had been all over mine just the night before, and messing around with my boss was a mistake, anyway. "Tell me about Cheryl."

With another exaggerated sigh, Nick pushed from the chair and headed for the living room, knocking boxes off the sofa so we could sit. Then, giving me a look, he went and poured two full tumblers of bourbon.

I took the drink and sat, waiting for him to do the same. Then I turned to face him on the sofa. "Talk."

He took a deep drink, and his throat moved nicely. "Cheryl is dead. Probable overdose." He shook his head. "Shouldn't have cut her loose." He partially turned to face me, bending his knee on the sofa. "She was only eighteen. A kid."

I sipped the drink, and warmth exploded down my esophagus. This was the good stuff. Even so, familiar anxiety tingled through me. "Overdose? What's your gut feeling about that? Deliberate or accidental?"

He tipped back more of his drink. "She didn't seem suicidal." With the bandage over his eye, he looked like a tough guy—the kind a nice girl wanted to tame. "There wasn't a sign of struggle at the scene."

He'd visited the scene and studied another dead kid. No wonder he was drinking.

"Was there a needle in her arm?" I asked, thinking through television shows and overdoses.

"No." His gaze caught on the liquid swirling in his glass. "My guess is pills, but we won't know until after the autopsy, which the coroner is doing as we speak."

That was fast. Seriously, although it isn't like our county had a lot of homicides or suspicious deaths. Even so.

"The coroner is my uncle on my mom's side," Nick said, looking up.

Yeah, that figured. The Basanelli family was as big as mine. Unlike Aiden's family, of which he was it. Why he kept popping in my head while I was staring at a half-dressed and very sexy lawyer with whom I had a lot in common, I didn't want to examine. Must've been that kiss. Or the million fantasies I'd had through the years. "Nick? How about you level with me?" Maybe I could get more out of him in his current drunken state.

He sighed and took another big drink. "As soon as I know something, I'll share." His chin dropped, and his eyes darkened. "My source on Jareth Davey came back empty. The guy is in the wind. No clue where he is."

The switch in topics threw me, and I covered by taking another drink of the potent brew. "I've never known where he is," I admitted. "Don't care. There will be another card from him that arrives sometime today in my post office box, from somewhere different than before, and then I won't hear from him until Christmas." I forced a smile, one I hoped looked brave. "So I breathe easy until then."

Nick shook his head and then winced as his wound no doubt hurt. "No. We have to know where he is."

Awareness pricked through me, and my hand tightened on the glass. "Why do you care?" He was way too invested, and it wasn't because I worked for him now.

He exhaled, and his shoulders drew down. "I was there," he said softly, his gaze back on the glass.

I blinked. Once and twice. "You were where?"

"At the river." He met my gaze evenly. "We were working on new dirt bikes, and I saw him on his four-wheeler. Knew he didn't belong on our property, but I didn't do anything. Didn't say anything. I thought about it and went back to my bike."

The words registered and I picked through them. "Before he took me."

"Yeah." Self-disgust twisted Nick's lip.

Oh. Man. One day screwed up so many people. "Nick. You had no clue he was going to kidnap somebody. He could've just been a tourist out for a ride. It was camping season."

Nick shrugged. "Yeah, but he didn't look right. Maybe if I

would've confronted him, maybe if I would've said something to my dad about the guy trespassing, then it wouldn't have happened."

I drank down the rest of my glass. This was one of my least favorite subjects in the entire world, but the guy couldn't blame himself for something he had nothing to do with. "Listen, Basanelli." I moved closer to him and poked his knee on the sofa. "You're looking at this like a scared fifteen-year-old kid and not a grown and educated man of what, thirty-one?"

"Thirty," he said, looking affronted.

I bit back a laugh. "All right. I've learned, through a whole lot of therapy, that you can't look at things like that kid anymore. Step back and pretend it wasn't you. Would you still be mad at that child?"

"I don't know." He set his glass down. "Regardless, I've wanted to apologize for over a decade, so I'm sorry, Anna."

There was a sweetness in Nick that caught me off guard and was way too appealing. "You're forgiven," I said softly. Sometimes that's all a person needed.

"Thank you." Now his smile was charming and boyish. He slid a hand into my hair. "You really turned out beautiful."

That was the booze talking, for sure. I had good genes, odd ones that didn't identify with either side of my family, but pretty was on my best day. Both Donna and Tessa were beautiful in totally different ways from each other. I should've backed away from him, but I felt all warm and gooey, and his hand was strong. Not as calloused as Aiden's, but close. "What are you doing?" I asked, my gaze dropping to his mouth.

"This." He leaned in and brushed his lips across mine.

Desire danced through me right before warning. Oh, man, he felt good. He slowly kissed me, his mouth coaxing, his lips firm. My head swam, and I kissed him back, just for a second. Well, I meant for it to be a second. Nick Basanelli, not surprisingly, knew how to kiss.

He tasted like whiskey. The good kind.

But he was my boss.

I drew back, almost in slow motion. "We can't do this." For one thing, he was drunk. For the other, I couldn't be the woman who slept with her boss. There were no secrets in my life. But it would probably be totally worth it in the short term.

He released me; his gaze slumberous. "You're right. Completely." He moved back, still graceful after drinking so much. "Now you have to sober up before driving home. How about we put in a movie?"

The switch caught me off guard, and now my body was all on fire. "Good idea." I didn't care which movie he chose.

He turned on the television and pivoted to kick his feet out onto a couple of boxes. "Just so you know, I'm not always going to be the prosecutor and your boss."

I blinked. Was that a promise or a threat? "I'm aware," I murmured.

And boy, was I.

CHAPTER 20

*W*orking hungover sucked, and Nick hadn't kept his promise to treat me to breakfast, instead opting to take warrants to the judge again. Worse yet, it was Wednesday. The anniversary. So I sat in my office chair, my head aching, waiting to hear from Nick about work.

Donna popped her head in the door. "Hey."

"Hey." Everything inside me perked up at the twin lattes in her hands. "God bless you."

She chuckled, a light tinkling sound. Then she moved inside, shut the door, and handed over the coffee.

I took it gratefully and drank several gulps. Hazelnut—my favorite. Then I studied my oldest sister. Donna looked a little like a young Isabella Rossellini with her black hair and intelligent eyes. Her hair was in a bob and her lipstick a muted mauve, and she wore a pretty pink suit with to-die-for purple pumps. "Are you showing a house today?" I asked.

She nodded. "Three of them. Two are big commission houses on the lake." She'd been a realtor for about five years and kicked ass.

Since it was the day of the dreaded oncoming letter, I'd see a lot of my family just dropping by to make sure I was okay. It was awesome when they brought treats. "I'm sure you'll sell both," I said, meaning it.

She nodded. "If your boss is staying in town, he should look at a couple."

Heat flared into my face.

Donna took notice, daintily sipping her drink. "That's a pretty blush."

I drew in a deep breath and let it out slowly. "I accidentally kissed Nick last night."

"Accidentally?" As usual, Donna took a moment to think through her response. "Did you trip and fall on his face?"

A laugh burst out of me, followed by amusement that lifted the cloud that had been pressing down on me all morning. "Well, that's one way to get a promotion." Then I sobered and told her the entire story.

She wiped lipstick off the lid of her cup. "You know, that does sound rather romantic. Those Basanelli boys are known to be good kissers—along with everything else that comes after the kissing. Well, except for the commitment part."

I nodded. "Yeah."

"Plus, he's probably a lot safer than Aiden Devlin, even though he is your boss." Donna's voice remained casual, but I could tell she'd been worrying about it.

I drank more of the fragrant brew. "I love you, Donna. Stop worrying."

Her dark eyebrows rose. "That's my job. I'm the oldest."

"Barely. By four years," I retorted. She was still in her twenties, having been a realtor after taking a couple years off after high school. I still didn't know the full extent of where she'd traveled. "We're not kids anymore."

"No, we are not." Her eyes twinkled. "Tess told me about your spa appointments."

I chuckled and leaned toward her. "It still hurts a little. What was I thinking not asking about the type of appointment?" Then I lost my smile as I remembered that Cheryl was dead. As in actually dead. What were the chances her overdose was accidental? Considering Randy had been murdered, not so great. I sighed. "Maybe I should work with Uncle Gino."

Donna shrugged. "That's up to you, but don't let fear keep you from doing what you want." She eyed her delicate watch and stood. "I have to go. You okay?"

"I'm fine." I forced a smile.

"Good, because mom said to tell you that you have another appointment with cousin Wanda the shrink tomorrow at four." With that great news and a big smile, Donna stood and all but ran off before I could argue.

I sighed. My phone buzzed and I lifted it to my ear. "Anna Albertini."

"Hi, sweet girl." My dad's voice boomed through the line, echoing off walls. "It's Wednesday."

I grinned. "Yeah, I know." My dad always started work late in the silver mine once a week and took the time to call all three of his girls, even though he'd more than likely just seen us at Sunday barbecue. "I'm at work and Donna was just here. She brought me a latte."

"Good. There's a new study out that coffee increases life expectancy," he boomed, no doubt having been told that by my mother.

"That's good to know," I said. "Did you get the core results on the new samples back yet?"

"Nope, but I'm telling you, it's a good vein," he said. "A real good vein. Silver is back."

My dad was the best at what he did. He didn't have a geology degree, but he saw veins where nobody else did, which was why he'd been the mine foreman for about forever. Plus, he was really good with people. "I'm sure it's a good vein," I said, meaning every word.

"Yep. Also, I'll get your mail from the PO Box today and will call you tonight with what I find. I might just come over and take you to dinner."

I stared at the now empty coffee cup. My dad had taken over my Silverville post office box for a week in June and in December since Jareth Davey had started sending me cards. I'd kept the box through the years, changing it once, but Davey had found the new box number, anyway. Plus, Silverville was so small, you could just write a person's name on it without a box, and it'd end up in the right box. "I can do it," I said.

"No need. The sheriff and I have it down," my dad said, his voice unrelenting.

Truth be told, I didn't want to see the card from Davey. I hadn't actually held or seen one for years. They went from my dad, wearing gloves, to the sheriff, also wearing gloves. Every year they fingerprinted the cards and envelopes, and every year didn't find Jareth Davey's prints. But still. There wasn't much else to do. "Okay, Dad. Just let me know that a card arrived." Maybe this would be the year Jareth moved on. One could always hope.

"No problem. All right. Gotta call Tessa. Is she still dating that moron from the bank?" he asked.

"I don't think so," I murmured. "I think they only went to one dinner, anyway. She said he was boring."

"Good. You're all too young to settle down. Bye, sweetheart."

My mood lifted again. My dad wanted us in convents, and my mom wanted grandchildren. "Bye, dad."

"Oh, don't forget your appointment with Wanda the shrink tomorrow afternoon. Your mom wanted me to remind you. Bye." He clicked off.

My dad was a giant of a man, towering at well over six feet, but my mom ruled the roost. Always had. I sighed and clicked off, only to have my phone buzz immediately. Man, I was popular today. "Albertini," I answered.

"It's Nick. We can get into Cheryl Smyther's home now since

she's dead, so I obtained the warrants for her place and Whitaker's duplex, based on Thelma's affidavit. Do you want to execute the searches with the police?"

I immediately stood. Anything to take my mind off that fact that a card would be arriving in Silverville around three in the afternoon today. A card from a sociopath. "Absolutely. Where do you want to meet first?"

* * *

MELVIN WHITAKER HAD the same eyes as his nephew. Brown and deep. At the thought, standing on his front porch, I immediately forgot about the warrant. "I'm so sorry for your loss," I murmured.

He nodded, reading over the warrant while Detective Pierce, Nick, and two officers had already moved inside. "Thanks. He was a good kid just finding himself."

That was probably true. "Do you have any idea who could've killed him?" I asked.

Melvin shook his head. "No." He refolded the paper and focused on me. He was probably in his mid-sixties with silver-gray hair, dressed in black slacks and a blue polo shirt. We'd obviously caught him on his way to work.

"What exactly do you do at the seed company?" I asked.

He leaned against the doorjamb, not blocking my way but obviously trying to ignore the men behind him going through his stuff. "I'm a plant geneticist, trying to splice new generations of grass."

"Just the lawn kind or also the marijuana kind?" I asked.

His gaze sharpened behind metal-rimmed glasses. "Both. Our labs are on the Idaho-Washington border, so we can do both." He smiled, revealing nice dentures. "We actually had to extend the building farther into Washington state to make sure the marijuana research was only in that state. How weird is that?"

I nodded. "That really is. Randy was caught with pot. Was that from you?"

Melvin's smile slid away. "I won't discuss my nephew's case."

That was fair and probably smart. "Why do you live in Idaho?" I asked quietly. If Melvin researched pot and used it recreationally once in a while, why not live in Washington state to start with?

"I'm moving in two months," Melvin affirmed. "I rented this place with my girlfriend for a twelve-month lease because she works in Timber City. Then she dumped me, and I'm on the hook for another two months. I let Randy move in since he was out of work, like usual."

All of that added up nicely. I thought through the last week, since he seemed willing to talk to me. "Did you know Cheryl? Randy's girlfriend?"

Melvin shook his head. "Not really. I mean, I met her a couple of times when she picked up Randy, but I never talked to her. Why?"

I shrugged. Her death hadn't been reported in the news yet, so he probably didn't even know she was dead. "Just curious. She had some pot from Randy, and I wasn't sure how much."

"I'm not talking about that," Melvin said quietly.

Yeah. So, Melvin created species of marijuana, brought some home, and possibly sold it for extra money through Randy and Cheryl, or for the Lordes. That made sense, but proving it would be tough, especially since Randy and Cheryl were dead. I studied the geeky man in front of me. He didn't seem like a murderer, but who knew.

He studied me right back.

I was almost out of questions, so I hit him with the one I wasn't sure how to ask. "You know anything about baking bread?" If Nick wasn't going to tell me what he'd really been asking Cheryl the other night, I'd try here.

Melvin's chin lifted, and his narrow nostrils flared. "I'm done talking to you." He turned on his heel and moved back into his house, already pulling a phone out of his back pocket. No doubt to call a lawyer.

What the holy heck was going on?

Going on instinct, I walked across the shared driveway and up Thelma's sidewalk, passing the vibrant flowers. Pierce and Nick could handle the search at Melvin's. Something told me they wouldn't find a thing, anyway. Georgiana yanked the door open before I could reach it, and the scrumptious scent of chocolate chip muffins hit me before I'd even walked up the two small steps. "Come in, come in," she gestured, craning her neck to see behind me at the police car at the curb.

I smiled and moved past her. Today she wore a set of big faded overalls over a shirt covered in bluebirds. Pink tennis shoes with matching pink scarf over her gray hair completed the outfit.

Thelma bounced from the sofa, silver hoops at her ears dancing. "What's going on next door?" She was dressed in Daisy Duke jean shorts and crop top, showing the sagging skin of her stomach. "I changed into my hot-stuff outfit when I saw the officers. Who's the lead guy with the dark blond hair?"

"Detective Grant Pierce," I answered easily as Georgiana shut the door. "He's in his early forties, and he doesn't wear a wedding ring. I don't know if he's married or not."

She fluttered her heavily mascaraed eyelashes. "Would you introduce me?"

"I'd love nothing better," I said, meaning every syllable. "How about we let them finish tossing Melvin's place first?"

She clapped her hands, her myriad of rings flashing different colors. "Lovely. I have always wanted to be a cougar." Then she squinted. "Unless you're saving him for you, of course. There's nothing wrong with a daddy complex."

"He's not that much older than me," I said thoughtfully, taking a seat on a chair when Thelma waved me that way. "Too young for somebody looking for a daddy complex."

Georgiana rolled her eyes. "Would you like a muffin?"

"More than anything in the world." I smiled.

Thelma settled back on the sofa. "I won't take him if you're interested."

I shook my head. "Nope. I've caught my limit on men lately." Not that I'd really caught either Aiden or Nick, but the last thing I needed was a detective in my personal business. "Grant Pierce is all yours."

"Oh, goody." Thelma bounced on the cushions, sending her earrings clanking. "Now, tell us what's going on next door."

Georgiana returned and handed over a muffin and milk, and it took me several minutes to chew in absolute heavenly bliss before I answered. "We have a warrant to search Melvin's place because of the pot exchange I saw between Randy and Cheryl the other day." Then I took another big bite of warm, gooey chocolate muffin.

"It is so sad about Randy," Thelma said, her eyes clouding.

I finished my muffin. "I agree. Hey, did either of you ever see Randy with anybody else besides her?"

"Nope," Thelma said.

Georgiana sat. "Not really. The only visitor I've ever seen is one of those hot biker guys like you see on television, and he was there to see Melvin and not the kid."

Bits of muffin caught in my throat, and I coughed, reaching to down the milk in one gulp. I wiped off my lips. "Biker guy? Like a Lorde's member?"

"Lord? No crowns or anything like that. His leather jacket had a shield with a bleeding lion on it," Thelma said.

Holy crap. It was the Lordes. There were a lot of Lordes members, probably. That didn't mean anything. Yet, I had to ask. "Tell me about this guy. Is there any chance he had black hair that's a little too long but is still sexy, a big torso, and is tough-guy handsome?" I could barely breathe.

"Yes, and he had the most spectacular blue eyes," Thelma said, her voice dreamy. "So blue it's hard to describe. Have you ever seen anybody like that?"

"Yeah," I said slowly.

Thelma nodded. "I heard Melvin say goodbye, and he called the guy 'Devlin." Isn't that the best name ever?

Not at the moment. Aiden knew Melvin. It was time to confront my old friend—after we served the warrant on Cheryl's home.

CHAPTER 21

*a*fter leaving Thelma and Georgina's, I glanced at the navigation directions on my phone to find Cheryl's place. Or what had been Cheryl's place.

How could the young blonde be dead?

I took a left turn toward the bad side of town when my phone buzzed with a video call. Pulling the car over into a deserted parking lot that no longer held a building, I accepted the call. "Hello?"

"Hey." Lacey O'Shea's pretty face came into view. She was still blonde with freckles and deep topaz eyes, which were dark with concern, and she was in her cop uniform, looking tough. "Today is suck it day, and I thought I'd check in."

We always called each other on this day, considering it had shaped both of us. "I kissed Aiden Devlin," I blurted out.

Her chin dropped and her eyes widened. "What? Whoa. How? I mean, when? Well?"

I laughed. "Yes, to all of that. He's in town, he's in trouble, I may have to prosecute him, and he's as good as a kisser as I dreamed."

She shook her head like a kitten that couldn't sneeze. "Okay.

There's way too much to unpack there. I only have a minute here and just wanted to check with you. Promise you'll call later and tell me everything. I mean *everything*."

I laughed, feeling better than I had in days. "I promise. For now, I'm fine. You?"

She shrugged. "I'm okay. We survived this day years ago, and I keep reminding myself of that. Is Pauley okay?"

"Yes," I said. "I'm keeping an eye on him and will report back. When are you coming home?"

She sighed. "I'm not sure. Probably sooner rather than later."

Oh, there was something to unpack in that statement, too. I nodded. "We're definitely going to talk later. Love you."

"Love you, too." She clicked off.

I pulled the car back onto the road and headed to my destination.

Cheryl had rented a dilapidated single-wide outside of town surrounded by other run-down trailers. The owner of the park, a huge guy with a potbelly not constrained by his stained wife-beater T-shirt, had taken one look at the warrant and handed over the key. A few neighbors lifted their plastic blinds to peer at me as I stood on the rickety steps waiting for the lead officer to open the door.

An older black SUV pulled to a stop in the mud, and Detective Pierce jumped out, his gaze hot. "That was not very nice."

I bit back a smile. "I thought they might have information." Yeah. I'd called Pierce over to meet Thelma and Georgiana before I'd left. As the detective approached me now, I let the smile loose. "You have chocolate at the corner of your mouth."

He wiped off his mouth. "She pinched my thigh. I'm gonna have a bruise for at least a week."

"Toughen up, copper," I murmured, enjoying his discomfort way too much. Then I caught sight of Nick in the passenger side of Pierce's vehicle, on his phone. His gaze met mine, and heat tried to climb into my face. We hadn't had a chance to talk yet, and that kiss was still on my mind. Plus, watching a movie with him had been way too comfortable, even though it had been an old action movie starring Sylvester Stallone. I turned just as the uniformed officer finished clearing the place.

"We didn't find a thing at Whitaker's earlier. Let's hope we do better here." Pierce yanked blue gloves from his back pocket and handed them over. "Try not to disturb anything."

I wasn't a moron. "Thanks." I pulled them on and waited for him to proceed me. It was my first search, and while prosecutors didn't usually participate, I was glad to be there. A part of me was fearful I'd brought danger to Cheryl and Randy, and I hoped I hadn't contributed to their deaths. Plus, I was a little curious. Having the right to go through somebody else's secrets was a little intriguing, and that was probably bad.

But still. I walked into the small living area and tried to pretend like I knew what I was doing. There was no sign of emergency personnel or life-saving devices. "Wait a minute. Where was Cheryl found?" I hadn't thought to ask.

"In the park not too far from your office," Pierce said, moving toward the dirty dishes piled in the minuscule kitchen.

I turned to the twin chairs next to shelves, which also had crap scattered across them. Apparently, Cheryl hadn't been much of a housekeeper. The place smelled faintly of burned noodles and moldy carpet. I moved for the shelves to see framed pictures of Cheryl and an older woman next to one of Cheryl and Randy. They were smiling at the lake, the sun on their faces, looking young and free.

A pang hit me. How could they both be dead? Here one second and just gone the next. "Did Cheryl have family?"

"Sister in Los Angeles. They weren't close. I'm not sure she's coming out for the body," Nick said, stepping into the room.

I swallowed and turned to take a stack of photos off the shelf to go through. Most were of Randy at the lake, river, and park. Several were of people at the spa, friends of Cheryl's. In so many of them, she looked happy. There was one of her and Randy smoking what looked like an e-cigarette in the park by my building. "I read somewhere that people put pot in these cigarettes."

"Yeah," Nick said, black gloves on his hands as he went through the bottom shelves. "They use a hash oil in the vape pen."

I shook my head at the kids. What had they gotten involved in? I flipped through the pictures, stopping short at one at the bottom. Randy and Cheryl sat in some sort of booth with an obvious party going on around them. Somebody to Randy's left wore a Lorde's leather cut. In fact, there were several in the background. I squinted, my breath catching as I looked closer.

"What?" Nick straightened and looked over my shoulder.

I tapped my finger at two figures behind Cheryl. "Recognize anybody?"

Nick dropped his chin, nearly hitting my arm. "Yeah."

I swallowed. It was Aiden Devlin, Melvin Whitaker, and Scot Peterson, obviously talking next to the bar, their faces leaning toward each other as if whispering, all three with intense expressions. My stomach dropped hard. The connection between all three of them was right there.

Nick straightened. "It's time to interview Aiden Devlin." He looked toward Pierce, who was watching from the kitchen. "Bring him in, would you?"

Pierce smiled; his expression grim. "Gladly."

* * *

AIDEN DEVLIN OVERWHELMED the interrogation room. Dressed in his leather cut, black T-shirt, and faded jeans, he looked like the dangerous man I suspected him to be. He also looked bored.

I stood safely on my side of the one-way glass next to Nick. It had only taken Detective Pierce an hour to track down Aiden and bring him in, and apparently Aiden had come willingly with no fuss. Even so, the cops were letting him cool his heels for a while in the room.

Nick cleared his throat, staring straight ahead. "I should apologize for last night."

I didn't take my gaze off Aiden. "No need. I'll just use it to blackmail you at some point."

Nick snorted. "Hey. To the best of my recollection, you tried to kiss me, Deputy Prosecutor Albertini."

I grinned. "Your word against mine, and I win every time." Turning, I fluttered my eyelashes even while noting the fresh bandage above his eye.

His gaze ran over my face, those amber eyes warm. "Yeah. I see that."

Heat moved into my cheeks, so I turned back to the glass.

As if he knew, Aiden looked up, his gaze meeting mine directly. My breath caught. There was no way he could see me, but I swear, he looked right at me. Heat, the super lava hot kind, exploded in my abdomen.

The door opened, and Detective Pierce strode inside the interrogation room with a lumbering, square-shaped guy the size of a small tree wearing a DEA jacket. I straightened.

"This is interesting," Nick murmured.

Pierce slapped a case file down on the table and drew out a chair while his buddy did the same. "This is DEA Agent Frank Zimmerman, and he's pretty interested in talking to you, Devlin."

Aiden smirked and looked from Pierce to Zimmerman and back. "So the state and feds are working together for once. I feel like I'm bringing people together here."

"Yeah. You're a real unifier," Zimmerman muttered, sounding like he smoked three packs a day.

"I am trying to get into heaven one day," Aiden agreed, drumming the fingers of one hand on the table.

Pierce quickly read through Aiden's rights. "Understand?"

"Yep," Aiden said, not requesting a lawyer.

Why the heck wasn't he asking for a lawyer? I chewed on my bottom lip.

"How did you know Scot Peterson?" Pierce asked.

Aiden kept drumming. "Scot Peterson was the prosecuting attorney of the county, and he filed charges against me for drug possession and intent to distribute." Aiden's chin lowered. "Drugs and guns were found in an apartment complex owned by the Lordes but not in my personal space there. However, truth and facts didn't seem to matter to your prosecuting attorney. Rumor has it that he is now deceased."

I shivered.

Pierce's head lifted. "You knew Scot outside of your criminal case."

Aiden's eyebrows lifted. "I did?"

"Yes." Pierce flipped open the cover of the file and slid several pictures across the wooden table. "You and Scot at the marina. Here at the park. And here...at what looks like a Lorde's party."

If Aiden was surprised by the pictures, he didn't show it. Not a bit. His brows drew down. "Yeah. I think he was following me. Stalking me, maybe." One by one, Aiden slid the photos back with his index finger. "It's too bad you don't have recordings. Then you'd know what he wanted from me." He shrugged. "Guess you'll have to take my word for it."

Nick shifted his weight next to me. "He's not fazed in the slightest."

No. The hot-headed kid I'd known had grown into an ice-cold adult. Aiden glanced at Zimmerman. "That all you got?"

Pierce leaned forward, drawing his attention. "Not even close. We have a very pretty grey-eyed deputy prosecutor who found this picture." He pushed one across again. "Of you with Melvin Whitaker, behind two kids who are now dead. The sweet lawyer also talked to Whitaker's neighbors and discovered you'd visited a few times."

"Damn it," Nick snapped.

I blinked. "What?"

"He just put your neck out there." Fury vibrated low in Nick's tone. "I'm going to kick his ass."

Pierce went for the kill. "I believe you know my deputy prosecutor."

Aiden's smile didn't reach his eyes. Not even close. His fingers stopped tapping, and he leaned forward this time. "She's nowhere near yours, Pierce. She never will be."

I blinked. What was happening?

"Ah, crap," Nick muttered.

I turned toward him. "I don't understand."

Nick glanced down and snorted, rolling his eyes. "Jesus."

There was a whole lot of subtext going on here, and I was missing all of it. "I've just been doing my job," I said, trying to make sense of the conversation. Was Pierce trying to get a rise out of Aiden by using me? If so, why would that make Aiden mad? Sure, he'd kissed me, but we hadn't been friends for twelve years. "This is befuddling," I muttered.

Nick coughed out a laugh.

Aiden glanced at where I stood, somehow, and turned back to Pierce. "Does she know why you left LAPD?"

I perked up.

Pierce didn't so much as twitch. "I don't believe we've had that conversation yet. Although, considering she spent the night with prosecuting attorney Nicolo Basanelli last night, I don't know that she wants to understand my life."

Nick's indrawn breath coincided with my gasp.

I swiveled toward him. "I did not stay the night."

"I know," he said dryly. "I'm sorry. Detective Pierce made a comment about my bandage today, and I retorted that it wasn't nearly as bad as the one you'd done for me. Apparently, he's running with the innuendo. Probably just to see if he can get beneath Devlin's skin. I'll set him straight after this. I promise."

Great. That's all I needed. Then I stared back into the room.

157

Aiden's expression remained the same, so Pierce's gamble hadn't worked. Then he looked up again. Directly at me.

Fire burned in those blue eyes. All sorts of different hues of blue flames. I took an involuntary step back.

"Well then," Nick breathed. "Guess that answers that."

CHAPTER 22

*W*ednesday had been one of the longest days of my life, and I drove down my long driveway, sighing in relief at having the day almost done. Of course, my dad would probably be calling within the hour with the news that I'd received an anniversary card.

I loved June eighth through December twenty-first. I truly did.

For now, I was going to relax. Until I saw Aiden's black and shiny chrome motorcycle right up against my garage door. Come on. He'd only been let loose an hour before, and he'd headed right to my place? I stopped my car and rested my head on the steering wheel.

I ran through my options of leaving, calling the police, or facing him.

He came around the garage, no doubt having heard my car. He was still wearing the jeans and motorcycle jacket, and as he leaned against the siding, he was quite the sight. Bad boy behind his bike. I should've taken a picture and sold it for calendars.

Instead, I exited my car and slammed the door. "What are you doing here?"

"I'm not sure." His *oh shucks* shrug was kind of appealing, although the dangerous glint in his eye negated any cuteness. "I had a shitty day, and chances are, so did you." He ran a rough hand through his thick hair, leaving it ruffled and too sexy. "You know what today is."

Yeah. So, he did remember. I glanced at my watch. It was surprising my dad hadn't called yet. "What do you want, Aiden?"

His gaze ran from my boots to my face. Then he cocked his head at the bike. "Wanna go for a ride?"

I stilled. A ride? My gaze slid from him to the big bike. Sure, I'd ridden dirt bikes my entire life, but a motorcycle on the open road was another story. I couldn't just go for a ride with him. The guy had just been in police custody for questioning, although he obviously hadn't been arrested. This time.

"Come on, Anna," he coaxed, pushing off the side of the garage. "Let's go for a ride. Feel the wind in your hair and the rush of power between your thighs. We can just forget everything for a few minutes."

Between my thighs. Surprisingly enough, I don't think he meant it as a come-on or an innuendo. The idea of being free and away from life for a short time was beyond enticing. Just to not think.

He gave that smirk that had ticked me off earlier and straddled the bike, kicking it free. Then he shrugged out of his jacket and held it out to me, his face full of dare. How many times through the years had I dreamed of him asking me for a ride on a motorcycle? Would it be as good as I fantasized?

I've never claimed to be anything other than human.

Without a word, I tossed my purse back into my car and strode to him, taking the jacket and putting my arms through the sleeves. It was way too big and smelled like him. Wild and free. Then I took his hand and hopped up behind him. The feel of the hard leather against my legs caught me first, and then I slid my hands around his waist. His abdomen was flat with ripped muscles that made me bite back a groan. He levered up and then down, starting the bike, and it came to life with a fierce roar that vibrated throughout my entire body.

"This is such a mistake," I muttered, wrapping my arms more securely around him. Around Aiden Devlin.

He laughed, the sound low and masculine. "Hold on, Angel." He flipped around and drove down the drive.

Exhilaration rushed through me and I held on tight, throwing my head back to feel the rush. It felt beyond amazing. We reached the end of my drive, surrounded by trees, and he slowed. I settled my chin on his T-shirt.

He spoke over his shoulder, his mouth close to mine. "Hold on tight, go loose against me, and just enjoy the ride. Trust me to take care of you." Then he turned the powerful beast, opened the throttle, and let loose.

I tightened my hold and relaxed against him at the same time, letting his body steer the bike around the twisty turns of Tamarack Lake road. Trust him? I did. It was probably a mistake, but with the roar of the bike and rush of the wind, I really didn't care right now. I was free and safe and wild and all me. There were no cases, no anniversary cards, no stress.

Just the wind and the incredibly hard body I was holding.

I turned my head to rest my cheek against his muscled back, closing my eyes just to feel. I'd be lying if I said the danger inherent in both the man and the ride didn't call to me on some level. My shrink could worry about that tomorrow.

It took about half an hour to reach the opposite side of the lake, and Aiden pulled off into an empty camping area. I looked around, spotting the tire swing hanging from an old pine tree that had been there forever. He cut the engine. I slowly released him and sat back.

In a move that was as fast as it was smooth, he twisted, hooked an arm around my waist, and pulled me around to face him on the bike with the handlebars cradling my back. His thighs bracketed mine, and his hands on the bar bracketed, well, me.

I gave a surprised yip. Then I grinned. "You have used that move before."

His eyes twinkled the darker shades of the blue spectrum as the sun went down. Birds came back to life around us, but other than that, we were alone. "Not with you."

Charming. Definitely charming. With his hair mussed and his face more relaxed than I'd seen it so far, he drew me in a way I couldn't explain. Wouldn't want to. Yet, I had questions. "Did you kill Randy Taylor?"

He drew back slightly, his brows rising. "No. Did you sleep with Nick Basanelli?"

Surprise caught me, but I hid it. "No. Did you kill Cheryl Smythers?"

His face softened a fraction, and he looked me right in the eye. "Absolutely not. Even if I had killed her numbnuts of a boyfriend —which I did not—I could never kill an eighteen-year-old girl. Not in a million years."

I believed him. Right or wrong, smart or beyond stupid, I did believe him. "All right."

He cocked his head to the side. "Why does the detective think you slept with Basanelli?"

Why did Aiden care? I shrugged. "Seeing Cheryl's body hit Nick hard last night, and he got drunk and called me. I kept him company and bandaged his head."

Aiden's chin lifted in that way tough guys' did. "Basanelli got drunk and then called you."

I blinked. "Well, yeah." It didn't sound great the way Aiden said it.

"Right, and I suppose he didn't make a move." Aiden's faint Irish brogue lifted his consonants.

Well, kind of but not really but maybe a little? I wasn't sure how to answer that.

"Exactly," Aiden said. He shook his head. "Basanelli was a jerk in high school and isn't better now. He's all ambition, and he doesn't care who gets hurt in his climb to the top. Watch your back, Angel."

"I think you've pegged him wrong," I said, not sure why I was sticking up for Nick. Sure, he was ambitious, but he seemed like a good guy. "You're the one out on bond. Speaking of which. Do you run drugs?" Would he be as honest about this?

He leaned in, making my breath catch all funny. "You know I can't talk about an ongoing case with you."

"You don't have a lawyer," I reminded him. "You can talk all you want."

"Yeah. I'm not going to."

That was legally fair, and I couldn't let go of this opportunity. "When you were talking to Detective Pierce, what did you mean that he left his old job for a reason?"

Aiden's gaze landed on my mouth. He was definitely losing interest in the conversation. "Pierce had an affair with a coworker and was pretty much forced out of the LAPD. Came up here for a fresh start, although there were rumors of other misconduct that couldn't be proven." Aiden threaded his hand through my hair and pulled me away from the handlebars and toward his mouth.

Oh man, I wanted that kiss. What was up with me kissing people I shouldn't lately? However, this was an opportunity, and I was going to take advantage and hopefully catch him off guard. I was almost to his mouth. "What do you know about baking and drugs, Aiden?"

He paused, his mouth just a breath from mine. "Excuse me?"

Oh, shoot. I couldn't help myself. I bit his bottom lip just hard enough to leave an indent. "You heard me."

His hand moved and then twisted in my hair, pulling my head back. I jerked in surprise but couldn't move my head. "Did you just bite me?" Curiosity and something darker lingered in those eyes.

"Yes," I whispered. "I also asked you a question."

His nostrils flared. "What do you know about baking and drugs?"

Not enough. Nothing, actually. "Just that nobody will tell me what's going on. Nick won't tell me," I said in a clear attempt to manipulate him that probably didn't make sense on any rational level. "Will you?"

"No." Aiden said the word with a slight yank to my hair. "I will tell you that I bite back."

I blinked.

"Oh, not now." He released me and smoothly moved me back behind him on the bike. "And it sure as shit won't be on your mouth." Without waiting for a response, he levered up and started the bike, forcing me to grab on as he peeled out of the camping area.

Okay. Everybody I talked to got all cranky when I mentioned baking and drugs. I held on, my mind spinning, as he took me back to my cabin.

Then, with a surprising gentleness, he assisted me from his bike. My knees wobbled for a moment. A buzzing from the car caught my attention. Oh, crap. If I didn't answer, my dad would go nuts. It had to be him. "Just a sec." I reached over the closed door and tugged my phone from my purse. "Hi, Dad. Have news?"

"No, honey." My dad's voice boomed, but he sounded a little uncertain. "There was no card in the box. Maybe he's finally given up."

I couldn't move. All right. No card? That was almost as frightening as the cards. At least there had been consistency there. "Maybe he's dead," I offered.

"I'm hoping. Do you need me to come get you?" my dad asked.

Tears pricked my eyes and I turned to keep Aiden from seeing. "No, Daddy. I'm fine. I promise I'll call you tomorrow." We said our goodbyes, and I hurried over to hand Aiden his jacket.

He grasped my chin. "Anna? What's wrong?"

"Nothing." I swallowed. Okay. I needed to process this. Then my gaze caught on the narrow silver mailbox next to the garage. "No." Almost in a daze, I moved for it. It was impossible. For years, Jareth Davey had sent cards to the post office box. Not once, not in college or law school or my summer camps had he found me. My hand shook as I opened the box and drew out my mail. Several bills and a big pink envelope. I swayed.

Aiden was off the bike in a second. "What is that?"

I let everything but the pink envelope drop to the ground. My legs shook harder than my hands as I flipped it over. My name with no return address. It was stamped as being processed in Spokane, which was our closest processing center. "Oh, God."

Aiden took the envelope to open. I let him. "What is this?" He flipped open a card with flowers and a Happy Anniversary on it. Then he opened the card. Nothing was written inside. "I don't understand." But an awareness sparked in his eyes as he put the pieces together. "Anniversary?"

"Yes." Tears clogged my throat, and I looked wildly around at the peaceful trees on either side of us. "He sends one every year and then also a Christmas card, always postmarked from different places. He sends them to my post office box in Silverville. Never to wherever I'm living at the time."

Aiden's jaw hardened, and his eyes drew down. "Are you serious?"

Numbly, I nodded. "Yeah." Jareth Davey knew where I lived. He'd mailed the card from either Timber City, Spokane, or one of the numerous smaller towns around the area that had its mail processed in Spokane.

What was I going to do now?

Aiden shook his head. "Your family hasn't taken him out?"

I coughed out a laugh. "We can't find him. The cards have come from Austin, New York, Los Angeles, Denver, Paris, and even Nantucket Island."

Aiden froze. "Are you kidding?" He turned the envelope over in his hands.

I shook my head.

He looked around as well. "When did the one from Nantucket come?"

I frowned. That was a freaking weird question. "I don't know. Maybe three years ago?"

Aiden handed over the envelope, his expression harder than iron. "Guess I'm not done saving you, am I?"

CHAPTER 23

With one phone call, my family descended upon my cottage like the wrath of the Irish and Italian mobs. My sisters arrived first, followed by my parents. The Silverville sheriff came with a tech and took the envelope, promising to get the envelope processed as soon as possible. It didn't matter. Although both Aiden and I had touched the envelope, Davey had never left a fingerprint, and I was sure he hadn't started now.

There was no way to trace the cards to him. Not legally, anyway.

Aiden had taken off the second Tessa had arrived, still oddly quiet about the entire situation. It probably did seem weird.

My family and I ate a bunch of food, and we talked about everything except Jareth Davey. While my uncles had tried to find the guy through the years, no doubt Nick had contacts they didn't. He'd made the offer, and it was time he came through. I wasn't sure what I'd do with the information, but I needed it.

My parents went home around ten, having to drive fifty miles across the mountain pass, and my sisters stayed the night. We watched old movies and ate too much popcorn, and I only got a couple hours of sleep before I had to go to work.

Thursday was a light day for me with no court, so I dressed in nice jeans and a blue blazer, not really caring what anybody thought. After a cursory check in my office, I left and headed down to the war-room, where I found Nick drawing connecting lines between Aiden Devlin, the Lordes, Melvin Whitaker, and Scot Peterson. Pictures of Randy Taylor and Cheryl Smythers remained to the side.

He finished drawing his last line as I walked in. "I talked to my brother in Silverville and heard about the anniversary card sent to your house." He looked over his shoulder, his eyes clear and bright. Definitely more awake than I was. "I've already reached out to contacts in the military and will have a location for you as soon as possible."

I opened my mouth, but no sound came out until I cleared my throat. "Thank you."

Nick turned to face me, also wearing jeans and a blazer. Apparently he didn't have court today, either. "I think you can create a harassment case based on the years involved, but proving Davey has been sending cards is going to be difficult since he hasn't left prints."

"I know," I whispered. "I'll figure that out once we find him."

Nick nodded. His phone dinged from the table, and he read a text. "The autopsy is finished on Cheryl Smythers. Do you want to come with me to talk to the coroner?"

I swallowed. "Yes." No. Definitely no. I'd never been to the morgue, and I was more than happy with that, but it was time to put on my big girl pants and go to work. "You're driving." I still wasn't all that steady after receiving the letter at my home the night before.

We'd already reached his vehicle and driven through town toward the hospital area when he hit me with his next bomb. "I'm thinking of firing all of the attorneys and paralegals in the office."

As if discussing the weather, his voice remained calm and thoughtful.

I jerked. "You can't fire six lawyers and what? Ten paralegals?"

"Five. There are only five paralegals." He glanced my way. "You'll have to help hire new ones."

I shook my head. "There's no way we can cover everything in the meantime. Come on."

He pulled into the back lot of the morgue, which was set away from the brick hospital. "We can push off work to other counties until we're up and running. Yeah. That's the plan."

It was a rotten plan. Especially for the hard-working people who probably had nothing to do with running drugs or whatever else Scot had been involved with. "Fine, but you have to give the existing employees a chance to apply, interview, and possibly be rehired."

"I can do that." He tossed his sunglasses on the dash and stepped out into the dewy morning.

Sometimes he was such a butthead. Grumbling to myself, I followed suit, trying to appear okay with the fact that we were about to visit dead people. Or rather, where dead people got cut up. My stomach lurched. I sucked it up and followed Nick through the back door, which he opened by using the weathered keypad next to it.

We walked into a hallway, and he silently led the way to an elevator at the end, passing several closed doors. "You ever been to the morgue?"

"No." The elevator door opened, and I fought the very real urge to turn and run.

"This is a small one, so it won't be like you're in the big city," he said, pressing the button for LL2. "In other words, there won't be tons of bodies around. So take a deep breath, and you'll be fine." Then he glanced at me, his brown eyes shrewd. "Take a deep breath now. Not down in the morgue."

I gave him a half-hearted grin at the lame attempt at humor.

When the elevator door opened, I let him take the lead. A clean and rather dark hallway led to a light blue door, which he opened to reveal a locker room. There were cubby holes filled with materials, and he turned and tossed me plastic shoe covers and a mask, which I quickly donned. Then he moved to another blue door and opened it.

The smell of formaldehyde and death hit me instantly. Bleach, too.

In the room, there were three gurneys, all shining and free of bodies. My gaze tore past the counter with scales and other medical equipment to the refrigerators with their square boxes.

Nick tore off his mask, and slowly, I removed mine. "Guess we're late." He pointed to another blue door to the north. "That's where the dead are processed by being fingerprinted, and the x-ray room is beyond that."

A final blue door opened, and a grizzly man of about eighty limped in, manila files in his hand. He had short white hair and clear brown eyes. "Hey, Nicolo."

Nick nodded. "Hi, Uncle Bay. This is Anna Albertini. Anna, this is Dr. Bayson Mandi, the county coroner and my uncle."

"Nice to meet you, Dr. Mandi," I said, feeling weird with the plastic covers over my flats.

"Call me Bay," the coroner said. "Everyone else does."

Nick jerked his head toward the refrigerators. "Who do you have in there?"

Bay glanced down at his files. "Cheryl Smythers and an unknown old guy pulled out of the river. Apparent drowning." He rolled his neck, and it cracked. "Randy Taylor and Scot Peterson have both been released to the mortuary." He scratched the pale and wrinkled skin next to his big ear. "Not used to this many bodies at one time. Miss the old days."

"The old days were filled with injured lumbers, miners, and hookers," Nick returned.

"Yeah, but for some reason, it's getting harder." Bay sighed. "Kids look so young now that I'm so old."

"Kids look young regardless," Nick said soberly. "What do you have?"

It felt odd having this conversation in the lab, but nobody else seemed to mind, so I tried to roll with it.

Bay rocked back on very white tennis shoes. "Scot was shot, Randy Taylor suffered blunt force trauma to the head, and Cheryl Smythers overdosed."

"Labs on any of them?" Nick asked.

Bay shook his head. "It'll be another week, and I've even put a rush on it. The lab in Boise is busy." He shrugged.

Nick's gaze narrowed. "Tell me you tested Cheryl like I asked."

Bay glanced at me and then at Nick. "Yep. Definite opioid, and a whole lot of yeast, as you suggested." He focused on his nephew. "Want to tell me how you knew that?"

"Chasing a lead," Nick said. "By the way, where are the cops?"

"Detective Pierce was here an hour ago," Bay said easily. "And yes, before you ask, I gave him my full report. He's aware of the yeast, although he might not know what it means."

I wanted to ask what it meant, but I kept quiet for the moment. Oh, Nick was going to talk once we were in the car, whether he liked it or not.

"Is that it?" Nick asked.

"Nope." Bay leaned back against the door he'd just used. "Cheryl Smythers had defensive wounds on her arms and bruised knuckles from fighting somebody. There were bruises down her esophagus and along her mouth and jaw, in addition to hematomas on her upper arms and ribcage."

I frowned. "What does that mean?"

Nick ran a hand through his hair. "It means somebody pinned her and shoved drugs down her throat to kill her."

The poor girl. Who would've killed her? "Drugs? Wouldn't it have been easier just to strangle her?" I asked. If her killer was strong enough to hold her down, wouldn't he or she have been strong enough to just kill her?

"Definitely," Bay said. "This is a message, without question."

"Or an experiment," Nick returned. "It's new product. Untested. Just how much did it take for her brain to stop telling her heart to beat and her lungs to draw in air?"

Bay's papery skin paled a bit more. "She would've been unconscious within the hour, and probably dead within another hour."

The poor girl.

Nick shook his head. "Thanks, Bay."

"Yeah." Bay sighed. "It's only June, and this is my third homicide. I didn't have any last year. Not one." His sharp gaze raked Nick. "Is it a coincidence you're here now?"

"There are no coincidences. You know that." Nick turned for the door. "Send over the reports when you get the chance, would you?"

"Sure. Just as soon as I fill out the Smyther's death certificate to mark it as a homicide," Bay said wearily.

I glanced at Nick as we walked out of the room and ditched the plastic shoe covers. How terrible it must've been for Cheryl to die that way. "I don't believe in coincidences either, Nick. It's time you told me the full truth."

He nodded. "All right, but it's gonna be over pancakes. I have been promising you breakfast."

I nodded, keeping my composure. He meant that as a working breakfast. Right?

CHAPTER 24

$\mathcal{W}$hen you wanted milkshakes in Timber City, you went to Pete's. When you wanted burgers, you went to Ralph's Burgers. And when you wanted pancakes, you went to Smiley's Diner. I'd like to say that my sister wasn't delighted to see me accompanied by Nick as we seated ourselves at a booth near the windows, but I'd be lying. She all but danced our way with menus.

I started to introduce them when I remembered they probably knew each other from high school, even though Nick was Donna's age, which was two years older than Tess.

"How's it hangin', Basanelli?" She grinned and handed over a menu.

"Pretty good since I'm finally home." His return smile held a boatload of charm.

She pushed her reddish-blonde hair away from her stunning face. "My sister tells me you might have contacts good enough to find Jareth Davey. That true?"

Of course, she'd go right there. Family. I mean. Just…family. I sighed.

"I'm sure going to try." He sobered, handing back the menus. "I've already reached out but haven't heard anything."

"Good enough. I take it you both want pancakes?" She reclaimed the menu.

"What else?" he asked.

Giving me a wink, she turned and headed back to the kitchen, her jean-clad butt swaying. I rolled my eyes. "She's single, you know."

"No kidding." He shrugged out of his blazer, revealing a nice white button-down shirt. When he rolled up the sleeves to reveal strong forearms, my hardly dormant libido flared awake.

I shoved it away. Between Aiden and Nick, I just needed to stay single. "Tell me about the drugs," I said.

Nick waited until Tess had delivered cups of coffee and sweating water glasses before he cleared his throat. "Okay. You know how opioids and prescription drugs are the new problem on the streets?"

I nodded. "Yep." Everyone who watched the news was aware of the epidemic.

"Well, apparently somebody finally figured out how to cheaply mass produce opioids that are twice as strong as hydrocodone. It hasn't been a problem up to now because of the difficulty in doing so." He took a big drink of his coffee. "It's called Beast as kind of a joke. Baking and yeast."

I frowned. "I don't get it."

"There's a new drug on the street called Beast. A lab in Portland was able to synthesize opioids from yeast cultures grown in a lab instead of using poppy flowers. It's like when all of a sudden everyone could cook meth in baby bottles in microwaves. It's a disaster." He shook his head. "The yeast had to be engineered as well. They have a hell of a lab somewhere."

I blinked. "Portland?" Why was that significant? Something hinted at my consciousness.

"Yeah. Where the Diablo Riders were located before being patched over by the Lordes," Nick said.

Ah, crap. Aiden again. "Okay?"

Nick sighed. "The DEA shut down the Portland lab and arrested two scientists, but a lot of product had already been produced, and we believe there's a brand-new lab somewhere around here. The Riders, and now the Lordes, are the key component in the distribution, we think, along with Scot Peterson, your former boss."

"Melvin Whitaker is a chemist," I said slowly. "You think he's making more of the drug?"

Frustration drew down Nick's brows. "Whitaker has the pedigree to do so, but the only reason we're even looking at him is because of his location—that the Lordes are here. And we've been through his entire lab on the border, while the cops have been keeping an eye on him. He might just be dealing pot to the Lordes as a side job. I'm not sure."

I took a drink of my coffee. "You think Cheryl was killed with this Beast drug."

Nick nodded. "The DEA and the state police are working together, and I was brought in from Boise to coordinate trial strategy—pending arrests. The DEA can take down the manufacturers, and we get the distributors and dealers, so everybody has a piece of the pie."

That made for a good election strategy, now didn't it? "You were working on this case in Boise?"

"No." He took another drink of coffee. "I've had a couple high-profile drug convictions and was brought in the loop right before the DEA arrested Scot Peterson. It didn't hurt that I have connections in the area, as do you."

"All right." I played with my napkin. "Here it is. Say Melvin Whitaker is somehow and somewhere manufacturing more, ah, Beast." What a stupid name for a drug. "And the Lordes are distributing it along the drug pipeline. How are they doing it?"

"Dunno." Nick sat back. "Both the DEA and the state police are investigating, and so far, we've got nothing. There's a definite puzzle piece missing."

Tessa brought our pancakes, and I snorted at seeing a smiley face drawn with huckleberry syrup on mine. She was the best. After she'd flounced away, and after I'd taken two big bites, I mulled over the case again. "When the Lorde's apartment building was raided, I assume you found Beast?"

"Yep. Not a lot, but enough." Nick shuddered in pleasure at his first taste of huckleberry pancake. "God, I missed these. Serving in DC and then Boise, I really missed these."

Yeah. To think most of the world thought a huckleberry and a blueberry were the same thing. Sad. Truly sad. "Why arrest Aiden? There have to be many members of the Lordes. Why him?"

Nick flushed and focused on his rapidly dwindling pancakes.

I chewed thoughtfully, and as the reason hit me, I choked. Nick gingerly nudged my water glass toward me, and I grabbed for it, sucking down half the liquid. Then I set it down and wiped my eyes. "No. Come on. Because of me?" How was that even possible?

Nick winced. "Did you honestly think it was a coincidence you were in court for his arraignment?"

Yes. I shook my head, pinpricks of awareness springing up along my arms. "You did that?"

He rolled his neck, not quite meeting my eyes. "Yes. I was part of the investigation before the police raided the Lorde's complex, and I suggested they bring in Aiden." Nick held up a hand. "Saving you on that one day is the only good thing he's done in his entire life."

My mouth gaped open. Aiden had said almost those exact words to me. "Nick," I breathed. What could I say?

He met my gaze evenly now, his serious. "I need every advantage I can get in the case, and if you being a part of it throws Devlin off his game, I have to take it. In fact, I already took it."

I lost my appetite and pushed my plate away. Heck. It was nearly cleaned off, anyway. "I haven't talked to Aiden Devlin for twelve years. If he has been living a life of crime, it's ridiculous to even think he'd stop for me. Or because of me."

Nick shrugged. "Every guy wants to be a hero, and on a day in June years ago, he was yours. There's something to manipulate there, even if I can't articulate it."

My stomach rolled, and I stood.

"Where are you going?" Nick asked, no give on his face.

"I don't like you right now," I said, turning to head for the door.

"I get that a lot," he said quietly behind me.

Yeah. I'd just bet he did.

* * *

I'D PARKED my car and almost made it to the office when a thought hit me, and I veered right, walking across the park, past campus, and down to the water where Pauley was throwing crackers to the ducks. There were a couple of people down the beach having a picnic, but as usual in early June, the place was mostly deserted. That would change soon enough as summer roared in. For today, clouds blanketed the sky, turning the day a deep gray, but there was no wind. So, hey. Life didn't totally suck.

Pauley sat on one of the wooden tables, and Wanda Versaccio, my new shrink, sat on the sand a short distance away, looking at the water.

I paused. "Are you guys having a session?" If so, I'd get out of there. Plus, if Pauley was gathering himself for class, he wouldn't want a lot of people around, and to him, two could be a lot.

"No." Pauley tossed a cracker toward a bored looking duck who ambled over and sniffed at it. "Distant cousin Wanda the shrink is just visiting."

Wanda looked over her shoulder and gave me a nod.

177

I stepped on the worn bench and sat on the far end of the table from Pauley. "I think that's how shrinks have sessions."

Pauley thought it over, his profile steady. "Maybe. We didn't talk about my feelings or deep childhood trauma, so I do not believe it is a session."

Wanda stiffened and partially turned to face him from her perch on the sand. "You have deep childhood trauma?"

Pauley's lips twitched, and he tossed another cracker. "I stand corrected."

I glanced at him, delight bubbling through me. A joke from Pauley was one of the most precious gifts in this entire life, and even though my head was still reeling from Nick's revelations, I took a moment to bask. "You are so funny sometimes."

"I am funny all the times." Pauley rocked back and forth. "You just do not always understand."

That was probably true. I took in his striped shirt, dark jeans, and blue shoes. "I like the new tennis shoes."

"They have good arches." Pauley folded up his now empty paper bag into precise squares, his gaze watching his hands work. "Your voice is higher than normal. Are you angry or upset?"

"Both," I admitted. "And kind of confused."

He stood. "It is good that cousin Wanda the shrink is here. I have class." He'd walked up the sand to the tree line before he paused. "It was nice to see you. Have a good day." With the niceties properly given, he straightened his shoulders and climbed the stairs toward the college.

"I like him, a lot," Wanda said, standing and wiping sand off her jeans.

"Me too," I murmured, lifting my face to the wind as it blew back my hair. "Were you having a session with him?"

"No. If I were, I would've told him," she said, walking forward and claiming Pauley's seat on the tabletop. "I was walking by the beach and saw him, and he knew who I was instantly, so I sat, and we chatted. He doesn't seem to need therapy."

178

"Unlike me?"

"Oh, you definitely need therapy," Wanda said, her eyes sparkling. "Rumor has it the anniversary card from Jareth Davey this year came to your home address and not the post office box."

I blew out air. Why couldn't there be one secret in my life? "Yeah. Which means he knows where I live." I held up a hand before she could talk. "Yes, that scares me. And yet? It also fills me with a sense of anticipation. I've been waiting for him to make a move for too many years. Isn't it about time?"

"I'm not sure about that." She leaned to the side to study me.

"I am so tired of just reacting to whatever some man is doing in my life," I muttered. Every year I waited for that blasted card. Now I was trying to fight Aiden on saving himself, and apparently, I'd been expertly manipulated to do just that by Nick Basanelli. "I really have to stop kissing men I shouldn't. No matter how sexy they are."

Wanda turned all the way and crossed her legs beneath her on the table. "Now that sounds more interesting. Let's talk."

The shrink fit right in with my family, and I kind of liked her. Well, I totally liked her. For now, I needed to handle my own problems. My spine straightened. "No. It's time to stop talking." I jumped off the table. I had to figure out the Lorde's involvement in the Beast trade, and there was only one place for me to go for that—Melvin's. But first, reconnaissance with Thelma and Georgina to get some more background information and maybe brownies or muffins. "This has been good. You're a decent shrink, Cousin Wanda, and I think this counts for our meeting today, so please cancel my afternoon appointment. I'll see you later."

Yeah. I was done waiting.

CHAPTER 25

I listened to a hard rock station on the way to the retirement community, trying to pump myself up. Melvin Whitaker hadn't exactly asked for a lawyer the other day, so I could talk with him unless he said he was represented by counsel. If I got any answers from him, I would track down Aiden next. Rain splashed down as if in disagreement.

Thank goodness I'd left the top of my car attached.

For now, I wondered if Thelma had any more of those chocolate chip muffins as I parked in the driveway and walked to their door to get a little more information before I confronted Melvin. The area was quiet, and no sounds came from the attached duplex. Was Melvin even home? I rang Thelma's doorbell, peering around the calm community. Peace and quiet thrummed through the neighborhood. No answer. Darn it. My stomach growled, even though I'd eaten plenty of pancakes earlier. Well, I might as well try Melvin's place. Maybe he'd talk to me. Wondering if I should call Nick with an update, even though he was an ass, I walked past the bright flowers to the driveway.

I made it past my car and was half-way up Melvin's walkway when the door caught my eye. It had been smashed open.

Just then, a huge guy with pocked skin walked out.

I froze, staring at him. Oh God. I knew him. He was one of the shooters from the brown van the other day. I hadn't been able to describe him, but now facing him...there he was. He'd been shooting at either Randy or Aiden. Probably Randy, considering he was dead. The guy's eyes widened as he stilled, too.

His buddy came out behind him.

There wasn't time to get in my car and start it. Totally going on instinct, I pivoted, ran around my car, and barreled up to Thelma's door to frantically twist the knob. Shockingly, the door opened. They hadn't locked it? Gasping, my head reeling, I lunged inside to slam and lock the door. Running boots echoed their way up the driveway. I yanked my phone from my back pocket and called 911. "Um, I think I'm in trouble," I whispered as the operator answered.

"Your name and what trouble?" the very calm woman asked.

"Well, these two guys shot at me the other day, and now they're trying to get into this house." I gave the address, my heart beating so hard it hurt. "Tell Detective Pierce that it's Anna Albertini, the deputy prosecutor."

"Sending assistance now. Can you get to a safe place?" the woman asked.

One of the men banged against the door. My breath panted out in short gasps. Holy crap. A buzzing started in my ears. They were coming for me. They knocked on the door, and something heavy slammed against it. The door wouldn't hold for long.

"I have to run," I said, shoving the phone back into my pocket. This couldn't be happening. But it was. I dashed straight to the sliding glass door and out to a tiny back yard. A furious pounding erupted from the front of the house. I slid across the wet grass to a tall wooden fence that had shards of rough wood scattering along its face. The forest land spread out behind it with glorious hiding places. I sucked in air and clambered up the boards. Slivers ripped into my pants and skin. I perched on the top, scanning the dark trees for safety until the world tilted. I yelped, plunging to the marshy grass on the other side.

Mud caked my clothes and hands. I struggled to my feet, barreling for the forest. Behind me, someone's ragged breathing cut through the humidity like a buzz saw. One shoe ripped from my foot, stuck in the mud. I darted between mature pine trees and through prickly bushes. These guys had probably killed Randy. Why were they in Melvin's house? My lungs seized and I almost threw up.

The rain drizzled between the branches. Someone cleared the fence behind me, and heavy feet splashed in puddles. "She went north," a hard, male voice hissed.

I needed to get back to my car. Shuddering, I searched for the right tree. It was directly ahead of me. An older pine with sturdy branches and plenty of needles. I leapt for the lowest branch, grabbing on with both hands. Thick bark dug into my palms. My feet swung, caught purchase, and I pulled myself into a seated position. Muffling a sob, I reached for the next branch and scrambled to stand.

Then I scampered up into the dark depths of my haven. My remaining sandal scraped and slipped against sharp bark. My fingernails shredded with each foot I climbed, pain lanced through my fingertips, and growling noises came from my throat. Finally, I pulled myself onto a thick branch, about thirty feet off the ground.

I prayed they hadn't expected me to climb a tree. The rain pelted harder, frizzing my hair around my face. I wiped my running nose with the back of a muddy hand. I wanted to cry but was too scared to make a sound. Where were the police? My heart galloped as the adrenaline continued to pump through my system. My hands screamed in pain.

Footsteps echoed below me.

"I saw her head this way." It was the same voice. I leaned a bit, peering down at him. A large bald spot showed through sparse brown hair. He glanced around. His round face showcased a nose that had been flattened by something strong. Thick shoulders in a blue slicker led to wide hips in black Levi's, and one dark, hairy hand pointed with a silver handgun.

"Who is she?" The other man was a slim blonde. Probably in his late twenties. I glimpsed pocked skin and a thick goatee. The muted black of his gun contrasted with his pale fingers.

"She was Taylor's lawyer. Who knows what he told her."

No, I wasn't. Geez. I had been on the opposite side of Randy. Sometimes I wondered about our school system.

"Fuck. Where is she?" The pocked guy asked.

I needed to get that gun if they found me. How? My mind spun. Then, blessed sirens sounded in the distance. Finally.

"Get back to the car!" Flat Face bellowed the order to Pocked Face. They took off for Thelma's fence at a dead run.

The rain beat down on me while I waited to make sure they were gone. I winced at the blood mixed with fresh mud on my hands. Then I slowly descended, the bark digging into my legs. Suddenly, my hands slipped on a branch, and I tumbled to the ground. I hit with a thud. The air whooshed painfully out of my lungs. I lay in the mud and let the rain splatter me for a second. Nothing felt broken.

A flurry of activity sounded, coming from the duplex and around the fence. "Anna!" Detective Pierce bellowed.

"Here." I started to sit up.

He reached me in a second, his gaze worried and running over me. "What the hell?"

I probably did look like a mess. "I swear to God, Pierce, if you kiss me, I'm just done," I muttered. First Aiden, then Nick, and now the hottie detective. What was it with the enormous amount of testosterone in my life right now?

He straightened up. "What?"

Yeah. That probably didn't make any sense. I flopped back down and planted an arm over my eyes, more than happy to stay in the mud if everyone would go away. "Between the Brazilian from hell and falling from the tree, everything I have just hurts." Yeah, I sounded a little pathetic.

Pierce sighed. Rather loudly. "There's a cream called Lupo that can help with the Brazilian."

It took a second for his words to register. I slowly moved my arm down so I could blink into the rain and see him. What was up with these guys all knowing about those type of creams? "Are you serious?"

He nodded, his eyes twinkling. Who knew the detective even had a sense of humor? For once, he actually looked approachable. "You can order it online. I have a first aid kit in the car if you need bandages anywhere else. For now, how about we get you out of the rain?"

I needed to start thinking before speaking. Seriously. "Tell me Melvin Whitaker isn't dead in there." I couldn't take another dead body. Not a chance.

"Nope. The place looked tossed as I ran through it, but no dead body."

Thank goodness. "Okay." Well, that was something.

"Come on, Anna. Let's get you into the car." While his voice was gentle, it held that clear command he always seemed to have. The cop was kind of bossy. Maybe it was the approximate fifteen-year age difference between us that gave him that tone.

"Fine." I accepted his proffered hand as uniformed officers began to mill around. "I don't need a bandage, although tweezers would be nice to get the splinters from my palms." Now that I was somewhat safe, all sorts of aches and pains roared to life. My right leg really hurt from where I scraped it on the rough bark.

"You need a doctor?" he asked, whipping out of his light jacket to drape over my shoulders. Pierce smelled like the ocean breeze —salty and fresh.

I shook my head and surveyed my destroyed clothing. "No. I'm okay."

"Good." He steered me around, his touch surprisingly gentle. "Let's get you to the station to make a statement. We have tweezers there."

CHAPTER 26

*A*fter a grueling session with Detective Pierce, one Nick Basanelli interrupted half-way through to conduct his own set of questioning, I went home absolutely exhausted. At least I'd been able to pick all the slivers and bark out of my hands before spraying them with antibacterial stuff the police kept available.

Nick's newest lecture on staying out of the investigative side of my job had only irritated me. Part of my job was helping to investigate.

My day just got worse when I saw the motorcycle parked in front of my garage. Come on. Wincing, I got out of my car and headed for the porch.

"What the hell happened to you?" Aiden stood from his position on the porch swing.

"What the hell are you doing here?" I snapped.

His frown darkened as he caught sight of my filthy foot. "I'm not sure. Just wanted to check on you."

Wasn't that sweet? I felt like punching him right in the face. I shrugged, my teeth started to chatter; whether from wet clothes or delayed shock, I wasn't sure. His eyebrows lifted, and he grasped my arm to propel me forward. We walked into the warm kitchen. The aroma of stew from the crockpot hit me instantly. Man, I was hungry.

Aiden sniffed the air like a wolf with a scent. "What is that?"

"Tuscan Soup." I had thrown the ingredients into the crockpot before heading to work earlier. Man, what if Nick was right? What if I could get through to Aiden for answers? I didn't like myself very much for thinking that way, but I had just been chased through the woods by a couple of killers. So, why not? "Would you like to stay for dinner?"

"Hell, yes."

"Why don't you open a bottle of wine while I change?" I nodded at my wine rack—I needed a drink. I started limping forward with my decrepit sandal. My other foot left a brown squishy trail in my wake.

A hand on my arm stopped me, and I looked up into concerned blue eyes. "Are you injured anywhere?"

The sweetness threatened to shake my resolve, and the temptation to snuggle into his big chest caught me hard. I shook my head. "No, just cold."

A frown settled between his brows as he pulled a stick out of my hair. "Where does it hurt?"

Everywhere. "Um, I may have a couple of bruises."

He grasped my wrists with the lightest of touches, turning over my hands. Raw, red scrapes slashed across both palms, even though they'd been treated at the police station.

Everything around him stilled. Even the air. I gulped.

He lifted his gaze, a muscle spasming in his jaw. "Where else?"

I shrugged. Aiden angled his head to the side, staring at my legs. My knees started to tremble.

His eyes fired. "Do I need to kill somebody?"

I huffed out a laugh. He didn't even smile.

"Um, no." He had to be joking. Didn't he? It figured his time of being my hero was long past. The hint that he'd like to be one again gave proof to Nick's analysis of him. Just great.

"What happened, Angel?" Aiden asked.

The trembling moved north until even my shoulders shook. "I don't think I can talk about it." Yeah, I wanted to trust him. At this point, I couldn't trust anybody. Except maybe Detective Pierce, and we didn't even like each other.

Aiden nodded once. Not like he was agreeing; more like he was having an internal conversation. "We'll see. Are you in danger now?"

"Right this second?" Not if Aiden wasn't a threat.

"Yes," he said, his voice low and smooth.

"No. The police arrived in time." I didn't like this conversation. "Of course, maybe you know the guys who chased me. They were the men from the brown van who shot at us the other day." Then I watched him closely.

Just surprise and then something darker crossed his face. "I don't know them." His thumb ran through the mud on my chin. "You weren't followed home?"

"No."

"Are you sure?"

"Positive." Kind of. If they'd wanted to stop me from identifying them or saying they were at Melvin's today, it was too late. There was no reason to seek me out now. "Are you sure you don't know them? I mean, you described them well, and maybe they were shooting at you?"

He straightened. "No. They were shooting at Randy Taylor."

"Either Randy or you, Aiden." I studied his face for any hint of a lie. "They were at Melvin Whitaker's house today. You know him, right?"

"Why were you at his house?" A muscle ticked in Aiden's jaw as he didn't answer my question.

Wrong place and wrong time? "Just doing my job."

"That ain't your job, and you need to stick to the courtroom. For now, I'll find out who they are," he said.

"Not your job. Bad guys are bad guys. I can handle it." I just didn't have the energy to question him right now. "Aiden, I'm freezing. Pour the wine, I'll be right back."

He paused. "People aren't all good or all bad, Anna. Ever." He released my hands.

"We'll have to agree to disagree on that one." My job depended on it. I hobbled through the great room, my bedroom, and into the bathroom. I gasped in dismay at my bathroom mirror. It was even worse than I'd feared.

My hair frizzed around my face in frightening angles, loaded with sticks and bark. Mud smeared across one of my cheeks and down my windbreaker. A jagged rip ran through my jeans, and my remaining sandal was filthy. Bark and clumps of bushes stuck haphazardly throughout the mud, completing the disastrous look. My eyes were wide, frightened in my pale face.

I shimmied out of my wet clothes, and hopped in the shower, moaning as hot water cascaded over my battered body. My shoulder and hip already sported deep purple bruises, and one leg held raised red abrasions. Scratches and long cuts stung my knees and hands. But the water balmed some of the hurt.

I hurriedly washed the mud out of my hair before turning the shower off. Then I let myself turn the shower back on, sit on the floor, and then bawl. Everything hurt, people were trying to kill me, and I just couldn't handle it.

Finally, I wound down, feeling somewhat better. Lifting my face to the cooling spray, I settled my shoulders. All right. I'd been kidnapped at ten and had survived that.

I could survive this.

Turning off the cool water, I stepped out of the shower and dried off with a fluffy white towel. Then I wrapped it around me while walking into the bedroom. There I threw on panties and eyed clean jeans. But my blue striped pajama pants beckoned from the bed, and my body just hurt. I quickly donned them, the matching tank top and some thick comfy socks. To complete the look, I wrapped a thick sweatshirt around my torso like a fuzzy knitted hug.

I dodged back into the bathroom and ran a comb through my curls, figuring I'd rather eat dinner than dry my hair. I swallowed three Advil dry and then put a couple of bandages on my palms, noting the scrapes weren't so bad with all of the bark and dirt gone. A swipe of gloss didn't help my face enough. With a shrug, I headed out to face Aiden.

How many times through the years had I fantasized about domestic bliss with him? Man, I really was crazy.

He had set the table, and a bottle of Shiraz breathed on the counter. Leaning against the wall, he crossed his arms and watched me walk into the kitchen, his eyes sharp and his face thoughtful. He seemed solid and somewhat safe in his black shirt, dark jeans, and flak boots. My mind reeled; I wasn't sure what questions to ask him. Maybe he'd feel pity and just roll over and confess everything. I hoped he didn't have much to confess.

He just couldn't be bad.

I tried for a reassuring smile, reaching into the freezer for a bag of homemade rolls, liking the feel of the cold bag on my aching palms. They went into the microwave before I stirred the stew. It was my Nana's recipe. Gravied beef, roasted carrots, and puffy potatoes scented the air, and I ladled two big bowls and handed them to Aiden to put on the table. He poured the wine, and I placed the heated rolls onto a large plate before crossing to the table and sitting down. He followed suit.

We ate in silence for a few minutes, and the stew warmed me.

He grinned. "This is delicious."

"Thanks."

"It's actually homemade," he murmured.

"Yep. I like to cook, Aiden."

He took a sip of his wine, his eyes focused on me. "So."

"What do you know about a drug called Beast?" I asked, too tired to worry if I was going to tick him off.

He jerked and then lost all expression.

"That much, huh?" I muttered. "You were arrested for possessing it, and I have to assume the Lordes are distributing it. How about you do the right thing and become an informant?" That way we could get the bad guys, and hopefully I could help Aiden out.

"I'm not an informant, sweetheart." He poured more wine for us both. "The drugs they found on the raid weren't in my room."

"You're a Lorde, a Defender, and you're responsible for the entire complex." I hadn't even had a trial yet, and even I could make that stick in court. I set my fork down. "Seriously, Aiden. How did you end up in a motorcycle gang that's running drugs? Why?" It hurt somehow. To think the guy I'd dreamed about for so long had turned out to be a criminal doing something that would hurt people.

He sighed. "You don't know anything about me."

"I know you lived in Ireland until you were fourteen and came to live with your grandma in Silverville when your parents died," I said. "You were quiet and kind of rebellious, and you saved my life. That's as much as I know."

"My parents didn't die," he said, sipping his wine. "Well, my mom died when I was a toddler, but as far as I know, my dad is still alive. He beat the crap out of me to the point that my Grams got custody." Setting down his glass, he shrugged, his eyes harder than I'd ever seen them. "I came here, made a few friends, got in a little bit of trouble, and then left when Grams died."

I leaned forward, my heart hurting for him. But he was finally answering some questions. "Before you left town so suddenly, were you boosting cars in the city?" I'd never believed it.

His grin showed the charm he seemed to try and hide. "Listen, counselor."

I shook my head. "That was years and years ago. If you had

been boosting cars, the statute of limitations has run." Curiosity finally perked me up.

"Huh." He sat back, studying me. "Then, yeah. I was boosting cars."

My mouth dropped open, and I quickly shut it. Trying to remain composed, I breathed out. "So, it was true? The sheriff was right?"

Aiden chuckled. "Yeah. That old asshole wanted to put me away regardless, but in that case, he was right. My mistake was in stealing a car out of Silverville. It was the sheriff's aunt's car, actually." He snorted. "I was part of a group out of Spokane stealing cars. We were paid a set amount, depending on the car, when we delivered them to a chop shop in the Tri-Cities. I'm sure the place closed down eons ago."

"I, uh—" I didn't have any words. My temples started to hurt.

He kind of ducked his head. "Yeah, sorry. I know that's not what you wanted to hear."

No. It really wasn't. "I defended you. To everybody," I murmured, trying to be angry but just not finding the energy at the moment. Tomorrow, I'd get pissed. That was a good plan.

"Thanks for the defense." He set his napkin down. "I don't suppose you'll be kissing me goodnight?"

Man, he was sexy. He really was. "Maybe," I said.

His eyes darkened to the color the lake got once a year right before winter. "Really?"

I was tired, I was hurting, and I was done. For years, I'd dreamed of him, and now he was here and right in front of me. The past was coming back, too fast to stop. He was the only good thing from a day that wouldn't leave me alone.

Maybe I didn't want *him* to leave me alone. "You know, Aiden? I'm going to keep drinking. You should, too." I filled our glasses again.

He shrugged, looking big and dangerous and distant. "As much as I'd love to find your g-spot, baby, this is a bad idea."

Maybe I just didn't want to stay alone with danger out there. No. It was Aiden. I didn't want him to leave. "Suck it up, Devlin. Either take a drink or get out." Man, I was tough all of a sudden.

He took a big drink. "I'm not gonna let anything happen to you, Angel. No way will you be in danger. You can trust me to take care of it, but you're gonna want me to do that distantly. Stay smart and stay away from me."

Being smart wasn't getting me anywhere. "No." I tipped back the glass and let the heated wine explode down my throat.

Consequences could screw off. For now.

CHAPTER 27

J awoke comfortably warm in my bed. The last thing I remembered was swigging more wine with Aiden the night before. Awareness filtered through my haze. A large male body wrapped around me from behind, hence, the warmth. One strong hand cupped my breast, spreading heat through me *everywhere*.

I stretched a bit against the hardness behind me, and then froze, at the *hardness* behind me. Morning wood at its finest.

My movements awoke him. He pulled me closer, murmuring drowsily against the back of my neck, the fingers on my breast seeking and easily finding my nipple. Liquid heat shot straight south from his hand as his lips moved leisurely across my ear.

I took a moment and tried to think. A large t-shirt covered me, my underwear was on, and Aiden wore briefs that did nothing to conceal his impressive length. His chest felt hot and bare against my back. Mine ached heavy and full.

In a smooth motion, he pulled me onto my back and rolled on top of me. His dark hair fell rakishly over his forehead. Even in the early hour, his eyes were the clear blue of the purest sea.

"Um, did we..." I tried to ignore the hard body over me. It was impossible to ignore.

"Not yet," he grinned, the dimples flashing in his strong face. I figured they were a rare sight and thought it safer for womankind that way.

He pressed into me, and my eyes rolled back into my head. Then he leaned down and kissed me gently. One broad hand slid down the side of my body before cupping my rear to pull me even closer against him. Heat met heat. You couldn't get more direct than that.

I fought the whimper wanting loose and tried to focus my eyes on his.

"If you want to stop me, say it now," he said softly against my mouth as his hand started to knead. "I didn't take advantage of you last night because you were toasted, but you're sober now, and this is your decision."

My mind questioned what I should do. My body told my mind to shut the hell up. There were some experiences a girl shouldn't miss.

I don't know if it was the good night's sleep from the wine, or the fact that I hadn't had an orgasm with someone else in the room for far too long, but I leaned up to nip his full bottom lip. "You said something about a g-spot?"

His eyes turned a predatory blue, and he showed his teeth in a slow grin. "Let's see what we can do."

His lips dropped to mine. Now, I thought he had kissed me before. I was wrong. Those were mere hints, mere tantalizing peeks at what he could really do.

He wasn't gentle. He wasn't soft. He was all heat, depth, and fire. I think I heard Gaelic angels singing in the background, but that could've been the blood rushing through my veins. His free hand reached up to tangle in my curls, pulling my head to the side, angling my face. He was hard and dominant, and I was surprised by how much I liked it. How much it ignited the already glowing fire within me. I'd have to figure that one out later. Right now, my hands were full.

The hand on my rear moved to slide teasingly across my front; the small silk thong no match for the heat of his hand. His mouth, now on my neck, stilled. "I forgot about the Brazilian."

I figured he would be familiar with the concept. "I don't see the big deal."

He nipped the soft area between my neck and shoulder before his tongue soothed the sizzling skin. "You will."

He ripped my shirt over my head, and I gasped. His mouth traced a hot, insistent trail from my neck to my breasts. His warm mouth engulfed one nipple as he pulled my aching bud into his mouth, and I pushed up against him, my hands clutching the solid muscles of his shoulders. He chuckled against my skin. I moaned.

He moved further south, kissing and nipping along the way. My thong was quickly ripped in two. In the back of my head, I knew I shouldn't like that. The good Catholic-girl in there balked, but I forgot all about her when his mouth found me, and my body started singing 'hallelujah'.

Though I did pray loudly to God at least three more times during the morning.

AFTER PLAYING WITH AIDEN, I was very late for work. I wore a white shirt, black skirt with matching jacket, and muted pumps in preparation for Scot Peterson's funeral set for that afternoon, even though it was a Friday. My mattress hockey with Aiden had taken longer than any girl had a right to expect, and I had to admit, I was a bit, well, *tender*. It had been a long time, and Aiden was nothing if not thorough. Very thorough. I can truthfully say that not only did I have a g-spot, but it had never been truly discovered before. I wondered if he had some sort of squatter's right to it now. I frowned at the thought.

Carefully balancing two lattes while walking down the steps, I found Nick in his war room already taping pictures of the guys who'd chased me up into a tree to the big board. Would he be able to tell I'd had sex with a suspect the night before? I should probably admit it, but I just couldn't. Then I looked at the big board.

Just seeing their faces made me trip, and the heated liquid splashed over my hand. I winced.

Nick rescued the coffees and set them down. His dark hair was almost long enough to curl around his ears, but not quite. "Meet Bert McLeroy—" he pointed to the guy with the acne scars "—and Chris Mayers." He tapped the balding blond guy. "Low life thugs with known connections to the Third Street Boys gang out of Portland."

I wiped the coffee off with my other hand. "How did you identify them?"

"Morons left their prints at Melvin Whitaker's. We have BOLO's out on both of them and should have them in custody soon." Nick said, stepping back to study the board. Then he looked over his shoulder at me. "Holy shit." Turning, his chin dropped. "Pierce didn't tell me it was that bad."

I gingerly poked at the scrape along my cheekbone, which had somehow extended up in a nice purple arc around my eye. So much for the concealer I'd plied on so generously. "Well, I did fall out of a tree," I said, trying not to sound too defensive. Then I'd had spectacular sex with a bad boy.

Nick leaned back against the table and reached for his coffee, his gaze not leaving my face. "I thought I told you to stop investigating outside of legal theory and online databases?"

I really didn't like being told what to do. My hackles rose, and I had to shove them back down, considering this was my boss. At least for the moment. "Because I'm a woman?" Yep. I went right there.

To my surprise, he paused as if thinking it over. "No. That's not it." He took another deep drink. "It's a couple of things. One, we have both the DEA and the state police on this investigating, and our jobs don't come into play yet. Two, you're green, Anna. Brand new at this. You shouldn't even be in the deep end of the pool right now."

When his pause went on for too long, I lifted my chin. "And three?"

"You're a magnet for trouble." He handed my coffee back to me. "I've been a prosecutor for almost a decade, and not once have I had to climb a tree to escape a guy with a gun."

Well. Since he put it that way. I took another drink of my coffee, enjoying the extra hit of vanilla flavor Tessa had given me. I hadn't even told her about my sleeping with Aiden yet. Then I looked at the board, and at Aiden's picture right in the middle. "Who are Bert, Chris, and the Third Street Boys? Another motorcycle club?"

"No. Street gang with connections up and down the west coast. They run drugs and guns and everything else." He took a drink of the coffee. "My guess is that they're competing for Beast, and the best way to do that is to kidnap the chemist. Why they shot at either Randy or Devlin outside the courthouse, I don't know."

My eyebrows lifted. "You think they were at Melvin's to kidnap him because he's the chemist?"

"Don't see why else they would've been there."

My face hurt, and I tried not to mess with the bruise. "Melvin is probably in hiding."

"Wouldn't you be?" Nick asked.

I wanted to be right now. Instead, I squared my shoulders and studied the board. "Have you found a stronger connection or any more proof of criminal activity between the Lordes, Scot Peterson, and Melvin Whitaker?"

Nick gave a low grunt. "No. Closest I've gotten is that those two morons shot at Randy Taylor, or at Aiden Devlin, and then they showed up at Melvin's house to chase you into a tree."

I rolled my eyes. "Whatever."

"We have a possible manufacturer of Beast in Melvin, dealers and money guys in the Lordes and Devlin, and what in Scot Peterson? What's his connection as the former and now dead prosecutor?" Nick shook his head. "I've gone through his finances with everything I have, and there's nothing amiss."

"Maybe Scot was innocent," I said, looking at his picture. "Just because he met with both Melvin Whitaker and Aiden Devlin doesn't mean he was a co-conspirator in the drug trade."

"There's no other explanation," Nick countered.

Well. If there was one, I hadn't found it. "Maybe."

"Do you still think Devlin is innocent?" Nick drawled.

After the revelations of the previous night? That he had been stealing cars as a kid? "I'm not saying he's a perfect citizen," I murmured. "But drug dealers are bad, and I can't see him being bad." What was it Aiden had said? Nobody was all good or all bad. "I don't think he could've killed anybody."

Nick shook his head and then glanced at his watch. "I have felony arraignments in ten minutes. You?"

"Misdemeanor first appearances in half an hour." It seemed odd to be going through the motions of my job when so much more was at stake right now.

Nick turned just as I licked extra syrup off my bottom lip. He blinked. Then his gaze dropped to my mouth, and I swear, my upper lip tingled. What was wrong with me? Aiden's lips had just been on me.

"I'm your boss," Nick murmured.

Heat spiraled through me. "Yeah. You've told me that quite a few times."

"I don't even think I like you," he said, his eyes a very intriguing amber color.

Some of the heat dissipated. "Ditto." And I meant it. Okay, kind of. He was likable in an intense, ambitious, possibly narcissistic way.

He shook his head and focused on my eyes. "Good ole Detective Grant Pierce asked me if you're seeing anybody."

I jerked, my brain spinning. "You're kidding."

"Nope. Seemed really unhappy to be asking the question, but he did it anyway." Amusement lifted the corners of Nick's mouth. "He's way too old for you."

"Huh," I said, lacking any other brainpower for a response.

Nick shook his head. "There's just something about you."

"What?" I asked, meaning it. What could it possibly be?

"I have no idea," Nick said thoughtfully.

Amusement grabbed me, and I laughed. That was just funny.

"Maybe it's the laugh." Nick grinned. "You have a great one."

Okay. "Well—"

"You also have the cute girl-next-door thing going on."

All righty. I didn't need any more scrutiny from Nick. Plus, no woman wanted to look like somebody's little sister. We all wanted, at least at my age, to be a bombshell. A dangerous one. "I have no intention of dating anybody in this business. No cops, no lawyers, no judges."

"Just criminals, huh?" Nick asked, his eyes gleaming.

"Low blow, Basanelli," I returned, even though it was a great hit. Yeah, I wanted to help out Aiden, and he'd been spectacular in bed. Right now, my only interest in him should be solving my case and putting bad guys in jail. If there was a way to help him turn his life around in the process, I'd take it for old time's sake, since I really did owe him. Maybe I should forget all of these hot men and just get a cat. "I'm not dating criminals, either." It wasn't really a lie. I hadn't been on a date with Aiden.

"You've just listed everyone you're likely to come across in the next five years," Nick said.

It was so crappy of him to point that out. "Maybe I'll join one of those dating apps." Why was I talking out loud? If all else fails, deflect. "What about you? Don't you need a silent, pretty, and supportive spouse for your run for office? One who smiles duti-fully when you open your mouth, just to hear the brilliance?"

He blanched. "Ouch. You're cranky in the morning."

"You started it," I said, sounding like any kid on the playground.

He snorted. "Yeah, yeah I did. I'll know better next time." His smile warmed.

I didn't have the energy to deal with Basanelli in a charming mood, and he was swiftly heading that way. "Don't you have to be in court?"

"Yep. I'm going. Also, keep in mind that Detective Pierce is at least a decade and a half older than you. Like I said, he's way too old for you," Nick said.

I sighed. Enough about my dating life. "Get going. I'll study the murder board and then head up to the office."

"Take a couple of minutes to look at these." Nick gave a short shake of his head that somehow looked regretful and then pulled out a dark brown file folder from the bottom of the stack. "The DEA finally gave up the rest of Aiden Devlin's rap sheet, and it's interesting information." He glanced down at his watch. "I'll leave you to your reading." Giving me an awkward pat on the shoulder, he strode from the room, looking like an upcoming senator in his black suit with black tie.

My gaze glued to the case file. Swallowing, I pulled out a chair and sat. My hand shook as I flipped open the file to see a mugshot of Aiden taken at least ten years ago. One of several mugshots.

I slid the coffee away and read quickly. Through the years, Aiden had been arrested for armed robbery, grand theft auto, drug dealing, and distribution. There were numerous assault charges along with a couple of pretty violent looking batteries, and he'd managed to avoid serious prison time more than once.

That was nothing compared to being a person of interest in several drug-related homicides as an Enforcer for the Diablos—of which he had been three times before being patched over into the Lordes.

I'd slept with him the night before.

I flipped over the last page to a picture of Aiden in his cut, his jaw covered with a beard, his eyes hard and unrecognizable. My stomach cramped. His face swam, and I realized my eyes had filled. I angrily blinked tears away.

Was it too late to save him? More importantly, what had I done?

CHAPTER 28

J grabbed case files from my office on the way to misdemeanor court, once again not having had time to look them over before arriving. Once there, I met a cute and even greener deputy public defender named Clark Bunne, who had to be around twenty-five and fidgeted nervously. His skin was a warm beige and his head bald, and he had that earnest look that juries would love once he got the hang of the courtroom. Even his smile was sweet. He was the exact opposite of the men I'd been dealing with lately, and I warmed to him immediately, even though we were on opposite sides.

A uniformed officer sat at the back of the courtroom, and I felt a bit better having him there, even though I didn't know which hearing he was attending.

My mouth almost dropped open when Judge Hallenback swept into the courtroom wearing his judge's robe, red cowboy boots, and that stupid hat with the tassels. He was sucking a purple popsicle. He nodded at me. "Alberto. Good to see you again."

"Um, thanks Judge." I quickly introduced Clark and tried to appear normal.

The judge sighed. "Everyone is getting ready for the funeral, so I said I'd cover these hearings. Haven't been to misdemeanor court in years. Years and years. Smells funny in here." He glanced down at his case files. "Let's do this." Then he started humming 'Can't Touch This' loudly.

I coughed and read my files, motioning for Clark to do the same. Most of my cases involved either pot or meth, and I guess the news stories about the current drug epidemic were true. We pled most of them out with only two going to trial, and Clark was a quick learner, even though the judge went from talking about the law to *I Love Lucy*.

Finally, Clark was finished with his files, and he fled the courtroom with an apologetic smile. People had already filtered in for the next hour of civil hearings, which I wasn't involved in. I only had one case file left when the judge called for Charles Monroe to come up.

I turned as the defendant loped his way to the front. He was in his late seventies with thinning grey hair. Folds of skin down his neck made him look like a hungry chicken.

"Hiya hot stuff," he whispered in my ear as he sat down at the table Clark had vacated. A large olive trench coat encased Monroe's skinny body, and furry brown slippers with beaver heads covered his feet. Maybe he and the judge would get along fine.

I lifted an eyebrow and opened his file to read the charges while the judge did the same thing. I tried not to giggle as I read about the charge and the rather hilarious witness statements. Most of them were in support of the guy and asked that he not be charged. I glanced at Monroe. "Do you have an attorney?"

"Don't need one." He grinned.

It was his choice. "You were arrested for indecent exposure at the Elk's Lodge during bingo?"

"Yep." His chicken neck bobbed up and down. "I wanted to give them Lady Elks something to talk about. You know, not many of them are getting any now." His small brown eyes gleamed with conviction.

"Is this your first offense?" I whispered back.

"Offense?" His voice rose. "Are you kidding? I gave them a freakin' gift." He leaned toward me, across the aisle, and lowered his voice. "I got me some of them blue pills, and boy do they work."

Oh God.

The judge cleared his throat. "Alberto, is there a plea offer from the state?"

I didn't have time for this. "The state offers two months' probation conditioned upon Mr. Monroe keeping his clothes on from now on."

"Two months?" Charles jumped to his feet before I could respond. "Those old birds should be paying me for the show. Two months? No freakin' way."

The judge gave me a firm nod. "Alberto, please control your client."

"He's not my client, Judge. I'm the prosecution." I stood to my feet and leaned toward Charles. "Um, probation is not a big deal. You won't have to do anything."

He turned sharp eyes on me. "Maybe you don't understand what I'm saying! I have blue and white pills. I'm the Beast—it's all about Beast now. Let me show you." He reached down and unbuckled the coat, shucking it to the ground. He was suddenly and completely naked.

The Beast? I yelped in surprise at the sight of his shriveled wanker, sunken chest, and bony knees. His skin was as close to waxy chalk as I'd ever seen. I never wanted to get old. Ever. The courtroom erupted into surprised gasps and some laughter as Charles jumped across the aisle and up onto the prosecution table. He turned toward the crowd, shaking his floppy penis and singing, "Lookie here, praise the blue pill, lookie here..."

The judge pounded his gavel on the desk.

I leaned down and grabbed the fallen trench coat before holding it up to Charles and averting my eyes. "Put this back on," I hissed as the bailiff reached for him from the other side of the table. Charles jumped down to my empty chair, grabbed my shoulder, levered himself to the ground, and quickly dodged behind me. He sure was spry for an old guy.

The bailiff rounded the table and reached over my shoulder to grab at Charles, who used me as a shield. His gnarled hands dug into my shoulders. *Please, God, don't let his penis touch my funeral suit.* I'd have to burn it.

With a happy yelp, Charles leapt over the short wooden divider between the gallery and my table. He quickly jumped up and ran along the empty front pew. He stopped for a moment and wiggled his skinny butt my way, treating the gallery to his waving Johnson. The uniform cop sitting in the back stood and stalked down the aisle. The bailiff ran into the row. Between them, they tried to herd Charles toward the aisle. He reached the end of the pew, and the bailiff had him until Charles kicked out and knocked the bailiff into the cop.

With a howl, Charles jumped back over the divider and rammed into me.

My hip slammed against the wooden table, and my skirt snagged on the worn ledge. "The Beast? Is that a pill?" I gasped. How did the old guy know about the illegal drug?

"Yeah, baby." Charles scaled up to the tabletop again. He did his earlier dance, this time singing that they couldn't catch the magic penis.

Darn it, my leg would bruise from that. "Tell me about Beast."

"Got it from a friend because friends are friends forever and also have blue pills," Charles sang loudly.

What the heck? My adrenaline pumped faster. Was Beast on the streets? "Who is your friend?"

"Can't tell ya."

"Enough!" I yelled at Charles and lifted his coat to him. His fuzzy slippers grinned evilly from the table. With a growl, the bailiff made a leap for Charles, who tried to scramble away, but his legs tangled in the coat. His arms windmilled around, and he fell onto me. My face bounced off the edge of the table, and sharp pain lanced through my cheek. I hit the ground, and the wind burst from my lungs. The old naked guy landed atop me, his skinny arms and legs flying in different directions. His coat rested between his penis and my suit, thank goodness.

Charles grabbed my white blouse. A tearing sound filled the air as it ripped down the middle. The bailiff hauled him off me. Then I was free. The bailiff threw the coat over Charles and gave him a good shake. The cop reached two hands under my armpits and lifted me to my feet. I tried to regain my balance only to discover that I'd lost a shoe.

"I'm Bud," he said in a deep growl as he waited for me to let go of his arms. "Detective Pierce has me on you during work hours."

On me? "Because of yesterday? The two guys in the van?" I squinted my one good eye up into deep black eyes set in a hard-boned face with a nose that had been broken more than once.

"Yep," Bud said. "We have a man on you during work and one on your house. Until we catch those guys."

That was actually sweet. I smiled, and he smiled back. He had a short buzz cut and was basically built like a Mack Truck. "I appreciate the protection. Do you see my shoe?" I stepped back.

Bud nodded and leaned down to grasp my black pump.

I took the shoe. "Thanks."

He raised an eyebrow the size of a lime. "That's going to be quite the shiner. Another one."

At least it was the same side of my face as the other bruise. I leaned down and placed my foot in the shoe. No doubt, I looked terrible. My hair had escaped the braid to frizz wildly around my head, my right eye was closed in pain, and my stockings, skirt, and shirt were ripped. I turned and glared at Charles. He folded his hands in front of him and gave the judge an angelic smile.

"Quite the show, huh?" Charles whispered out the corner of his mouth.

The judge ordered Charles into three-day observation at the county psychiatric hospital. I might have had a duty to argue that he deserved a criminal charge, but my mind still reeled with the images of an old man penis, and I couldn't make the effort. Plus, maybe I could interview him at the crisis center about Beast. The bailiff handed Charles off to Bud, who looked me up and down before leaving, probably so he could report full details to Pierce and the rest of the police force in Timber City. Great.

I limped back to the office and wondered again why I hadn't studied business in school. A quick trip to the ladies' room revealed I was too kind in my earlier assumption of how I looked. It was beyond terrible. Catastrophic maybe. My hair stuck out in frizzy spirals, and a deep purple bruise spread over my right cheekbone under my squinty, bloodshot eye. In movies the heroine always looked so sexy with a bruise marring her perfect face; somehow the bruise always accentuated high cheekbones. My bruise looked splotchy and painful and kind of grotesque. The only thing the shiner accented was my now uneven skin tone.

I threw the blouse and nylons in the trash. At this rate I wouldn't have anything to wear to work but jeans and a workout bra. The rip in my skirt was up the side and not too bad so long as I didn't move. I tugged my hair out of the braid and put my hands under the faucet before running them through my hair—when all else fails, curls will do. Finally, I buttoned up my jacket. While the material plunged further than I'd like at work, it was the best I could do.

It was time for Scot's funeral, which should be packed considering he'd been the prosecutor in the area for so many years.

I wasn't ready to face that many people with all of my bruises...and whisker burn down my neck from Aiden. It was time for more concealer.

CHAPTER 29

*T*he funeral was a somber gathering of law enforcement, judges, lawyers, and general townspeople in a nondenominational church in town. No family. Scot had worked as the prosecuting attorney for at least a decade, and as a deputy prosecutor before that, but he wasn't an Idahoan native. Most of us had family going back generations. If not, you were new to town, even after decades.

It looked like Scot had been well liked, and apparently, he'd attended one of the summer camps on the far side of Timber Lake as a child. That's how he became aware of the area in the first place. The preacher spoke quietly and reverently, mostly about Scot's success in the courtroom.

The fact that Scot had been gun-downed after being arrested by the DEA was off limits for the day, and I was fine with that.

I stood between Nick Basanelli and Detective Pierce, feeling bracketed by maleness and guilty about my liaison with Aiden. They'd both given my new bruises a once-over but had quite smartly not said a word. Now they scanned the crowd in a way that made me feel like I should be doing something besides feeling sad that Scot hadn't had any family. What would it be like to be alone in the world?

I truly couldn't imagine.

"Ex-wife number one." Nick dipped his head toward a forty-something-year-old platinum blonde standing up by Celeste near the casket. How was the paralegal doing? I should check in with Celeste after the service.

I couldn't see the face of the first wife, but her suit looked like Chanel.

"Number two," Pierce added, lifting his chin to the adjacent pew. This woman was a brunette with liberal gray through her hair. She was trim, almost dainty…also in Chanel.

"Paid a fortune in alimony," Nick whispered.

Geez. They were like two gossipy old men who should be sitting on porch swings. Somebody clapped up front, and I jumped, craning my neck to see who'd interrupt the preacher.

"Ah, great," Pierce muttered.

I elbowed him in the ribs, so he'd move over, and then I caught sight of what he'd seen. I winced. Judge Hallenback was dressed in a neon green suit jacket with the logo for Hallenback's Used Car Lots somehow emblazoned across the back. He wore a striped clown wig. His brother stood next to him in a muted brown suit that also held the logo.

"They give car dealerships a bad name," Nick said.

The judge clapped again, and his brother shushed him.

"We need to do something about that guy," Pierce said. "It's time for retirement."

A slight ruckus at the rear of the church had me turning to see Pauley pushing away from a crowd gathered near a series of white pedestals covered in flowers. I froze for a minute. Then I launched into motion, every protective instinct I had on full alert. The crowd was too much for him. "Excuse me." I pushed by Pierce in the pew and accidentally stepped on his shoe with my heel.

He hissed out a breath.

"Sorry." I gingerly made my way past bodies to the aisle and then hurried toward the back.

Pauley was fidgeting, his face pale, his body contorting in a buttoned-down white shirt. He yanked at the collar. "No."

I reached him, careful not to touch. "Pauley? I need some air. Would you please come outside with me?"

He pulled harder on the collar, his eyes darting around.

"Pauley. Outside." Without touching him, I pushed open the heavy door and walked outside into the drizzly day. It had been a long time since I'd seen one of Pauley's episodes, partly because his medicinal regimen was good and partly because Pauley was amazing. Even so, anxiety twittered through me. Then I felt guilty about that.

My shoulders relaxed fractionally as I walked down the concrete steps to the cracked sidewalk. Since I'd been surrounded by law enforcement, my bodyguard had been given the rest of the day off, and I was glad there wasn't another person around to agitate my cousin.

Pauley exited the church and immediately clasped his hands together, his gaze on his brown loafers, his steps a little jerky.

I drew air in, not caring that light rain drizzled over my aching face. In fact, the coolness felt good. "You okay?"

"Yes." He walked past me and then turned to follow the sidewalk away from the church.

I followed him, avoiding weeds through the concrete, appreciating the older homes and fully-grown trees down the quiet street. Finally, we reached a small park with a couple of swing sets and slides. Pauley moved for a brightly painted green picnic table off to the side and took a seat on the wet top to rock slightly.

I slowed my steps and approached slowly, angling up to sit next to him.

We both looked at an older brick home across the street. Vibrant purple lilac trees decorated the entire left side and around the corner, smelling delicious at a distance and even in the rain.

I cleared my throat.

Pauley looked at me and then back at the house. "The crowd bothers you."

I blinked. "Yeah. You?"

"Yes." Rain drizzled down, splotching his brown pants. But he didn't seem to mind, which was good.

"Why did you attend Scot's funeral, Pauley?" I set my heels on the bench and curled my fingers around the table. The heavy paint had smoothed the wood enough that it didn't scratch my still aching palms.

"Scot was my friend." Pauley tilted his head to the side. "Scot died. Blood stopped pumping to his heart and to his head and he died. My dog died two years ago on a Thursday. He was hit by a car. Scot died on a Friday. He was hit by a bullet. *Your* dog died on a Monday. He was just old. Everyone dies."

I tried to keep track of the conversation, but the first statement kept my attention. "You and Scot were friends?" How was this possible?

"Yes. Scot was my friend. Lacey is your best friend, even though you are cousins. She told me you were best friends. But you do not live in the same town." He rocked slightly. "Lacey is my sister. She is also my friend. But not best."

I let him talk in his way as he dealt with life. Maybe with death. "Okay. Let's talk about you and Scot."

"Scot was my friend." Pauley clasped his hands together on his pants.

Okay. That truly was news. "How did you and Scot meet?"

"On a Wednesday in February at school. Scot talked to my class, and then Scot talked to me."

I didn't like Pauley having a friend unknown to me. I really disliked the fact that the friend had never said a word to me about my cousin. I hated the fact that said friend had been murdered. "What did you and Scot do?" I asked softly.

"Worked on equations. Good work. Smart work." Pauley said, pushing off the table. "Want to see?"

Yes. Without a doubt. "I'd like that, Pauley. Show me. My car is over there."

* * *

APPARENTLY, attorneys weren't the only folks with war rooms. Pauley led me through a dusty smelling college library to another hall hosting offices for visiting professors. He had a key to the last dingy maroon-colored door at the far end.

I walked inside to see one entire wall covered by a map of the western half of the United States. Lines were drawn from city to city along with equations neatly transcribed on sticky notes throughout. Timber City was circled in dark black ink, and the lines all followed from there. "Las Vegas, Missoula, Portland...". I moved closer, reading aloud as I walked over the industrial maroon and brown carpet. "Rexburg? Louisville?" Both very small towns. "What is all of this, Pauley?" I had a feeling I already knew. Well, kind of. The smaller towns didn't make sense.

Pauley stood over by a desk covered in various papers, which he quickly began straightening into stacks. "Scot must have come in here. These are not organized."

Since he was distracted, I took out my phone and snapped several photographs of the map. "Who drew on the map?"

"Scot drew the lines, and I wrote the equations." With the papers in neat stacks, Pauley turned back around to face me.

Warning ticked through me followed by a healthy dose of anger at Scot for getting Pauley involved. How dare he take advantage of my cousin's great intelligence and innocence? "These look like distribution routes."

Pauley looked over the map. "That is exactly what they are with calculations for time and distance." He moved closer to me, careful not to touch his shoulder to mine. "It makes more sense to take a big shipment to Las Vegas and then go from Vegas to Los Angeles and Vegas to Denver." He scratched his elbow. "In comparison to going directly from Timber City to Los Angeles."

My throat went dry and I cleared it. "What are you distributing, P?"

His smile flashed for the briefest of seconds. "I am not distributing anything. Since you meant to ask what was being distributed, I will tell you. Handlebars."

I jerked, heat flushing down my esophagus. "Handlebars?" Was that some new name for a drug? I'd thought Beast was a stupid name.

He nodded. "Yes. With a manufacturing plant outside of town, making handlebars for motorcycles, these would be good distribution paths." Then he tapped the smaller towns on the map. "These places have a lot of motorcycle clubs, so they would be a good place to distribute and sell."

Stupid Scot Peterson. He'd found the best way to distribute drugs by using Pauley. At least Pauley had no idea. "What else could you distribute this way?" I asked.

Pauley shrugged. "Anything, but the smaller motorcycle towns wouldn't factor in."

Those towns weren't really known for motorcycles. More for horse auctions and rodeos. I frowned and studied the map. Pauley hadn't traveled much yet, and he probably wouldn't know that. "Scot told you that these towns have a large number of motorcycle clubs?"

Pauley scratched his chin. "Scot? No."

I couldn't breathe. So, I swallowed rapidly to get my system back working. "Pauley? Who told you about the motorcycle towns?"

He must've caught something in my voice, because he straightened and moved back to the desk, tapping errant pieces of paper into strict lines.

"Pauley?" I struggled to keep my voice level.

Finally, the papers perfect, he turned back around. "It was a secret because nobody wants to upset you. You are fragile, still."

"Baloney," I burst out, wincing as he blanched. "I'm sorry, but I am not fragile, and you don't need to keep secrets from me." I wish Scot were still alive so I could punch him in the face. "You need to tell me what's going on. Who told you about the motorcycles?"

Pauley looked up to meet my gaze and then just as fast looked away. "The Lordes motorcycle club is building the motorcycle handle-bar factory. They were working with Scot to bring jobs to the area and make money." Pauley clasped his hands together. "Aiden Devlin is in charge, and he is staying home now." Finally, Pauley smiled again. "I thought that would make you happy, which is why I helped them with the math. Does that make you happy?"

"No." I tried to make sense of it all. "Is there any chance you've met a Melvin Whitaker?" There had to be a connection.

"No. No Melvin. I met a Meryl once, but she was a woman. Friends with our grandma. Good lady."

It was then I noticed a blinking light in the far upper right corner of the ceiling. "What's that?"

Pauley looked up. "That's Scot's."

Was it a camera? Motion activated when we entered? Panic clawed through me, although I was just being paranoid. "Let's go, Pauley." I grasped his arm and all but ran us both outside

A motorcycle was parked next to my car along with Spider standing next to it. Tattoos covered his neck, and he looked big against the bike. Two trucks were behind him. "Spider," I said quietly, edging in front of Pauley. "You're away from your garage."

Spider smiled, revealing a gold front tooth that was brand new. "Pauley? I need some help with your equations. Get in the front truck."

CHAPTER 30

*I*t might've been my Irish blood, or maybe my Italian, but sometimes righteous fury felt good. Proper. Energizing. Especially if somebody was doing something rather stupid, which I was in challenging Spider. Pauley was more important than anything. This late on a Friday, the parking area of the college was mainly deserted as darkness fell quickly, but even so, I planned how to get to the gun in my car. "He's not going anywhere with you."

Spider crossed huge arms. "Get out of the way."

"It is okay." Pauley moved around my car for the truck before I could stop him. "I will be home soon, although I am supposed to meet my mother and go home."

"No." I made a move.

Spider ended up in my space, smelling like motor oil and oddly enough, soap. He towered over me by at least a foot, and he was broader than I remembered. Muscle combined with a bit of fat, but he looked really tough. Strong. His eyes were dark and his features blunt. "I'm the president of this club. How about you and I go for a ride? Devlin ain't interested."

"You take my cousin anywhere, Spider, and I'm calling the cops." I levered up as close to his face as I could get. "It'd be kidnapping and child endangerment charges, for sure."

If I'd hoped to scare Spider, I failed. He didn't even twitch. Instead, he poked at one of the many bruises on my face.

Pain echoed behind my left eye. I slapped his hand away. "Knock it off."

He grinned. "You need some protection, sweet thing. Anybody who'd hurt you like that should have a nice hole in his head."

My stomach dropped. "In exchange for what?" Yeah, sometimes curiosity was a killer.

"Sex. A lot of it." He dropped his hand. "You need a new man. Devlin ain't interested for some reason."

"Not true." Aiden stepped out of the passenger side of the farthest truck, winding around to prowl toward us in the darkness. He wore faded and ripped jeans and a leather jacket over a light T-shirt. His boots were black and big, and they made an ominous sound over the still wet asphalt.

I hadn't seen he was there. Everything inside me halted and then a rush of feelings hit me so hard I almost doubled over. Relief and gratitude were first. Maybe a slight tingle where he'd bitten my left buttock the night before. Then I doubled down on the fury. He was there to get Pauley? Definitely not.

"Hi, Aiden," Pauley said almost cheerfully as he levered up into the truck, which was driven by another huge guy wearing leather. This one was bald with an interesting skull-shaped ring taking up half of his substantial left nostril.

"Hi, Pauley," Aiden returned, his gaze remaining on me as he reached us.

Spider sighed. "You said she was fair game."

Hurt hit me through the fury. Why, I don't know. But still.

Aiden shook his head. "Not fair game. Just said I didn't want her."

Ouch. Even though I wanted to kill him, that kinda hurt.

"That makes her fair game," Spider said reasonably.

Lava boiled through me. "I'm not a pet, you assholes."

"She's spunky and cute. I like her," Spider said, completely ignoring me.

My fingers curled into a fist, and Aiden quickly wrapped his entire hand around it. "Claimed."

One word. Just one word.

A shiver took me, and it wasn't fear.

Spider sighed and his shoulders went down. "Fine. Geez." He shifted slightly to the right, and sliver glinted near his hip. A gun. He had a gun tucked in there. "Stop changing your mind, would you?" He nodded at my aching face. "You're not taking very good care of her."

"I plan to," Aiden said grimly.

I tried rather uselessly to tug my hand free. "Pauley? Get out of that truck," I yelled.

Spider went from playful to deadly in a second. "He's coming with us, but you have my word he'll be safe. We'll get him home before dark."

I grit my teeth. "You drive one inch out of this parking lot with him, and I'm calling the police." I vibrated I was so angry.

Spider looked at Aiden. "You claimed her. Control her."

Aiden's hold was too firm to break, so I shifted my weight to take out his knee.

"I wouldn't, Angel." His voice was calm but his gaze a heated blue. He turned his head toward the truck. "Pauley, get out of the truck, please."

I blinked.

Spider grunted. "We need him."

"No, we don't." Aiden faced the club president, looking almost bored. "He's a minor, and we don't need that kind of trouble right now. We have the numbers and can work it out from there. This isn't worth the risk."

Spider scowled. "You're whipped, Devlin."

Aiden partially turned and put me behind him while keeping my hand. "Have I let you down? Even once?"

Spider faltered. "No."

"Well then, trust me." Aiden waited until Pauley had walked back to my car. "Get in, Pauley." Once he had, Aiden switched his hold on my hand and then began moving toward the school. "Pauley? You and Spider stay here. Anna and I will be right back."

"No." I protested and dug in my heels.

Aiden barely pivoted while ducking to the side, and less than a heartbeat later, I found myself over his shoulder, looking down at the ground as his strides ate up the distance toward the door.

"That's better," Spider yelled.

"Hey!" Rage ripped through me so fast my skin burned. I punched Aiden as hard as I could in the lower back. "Put me down."

He ignored me, and pretty much the few patrons in the library, as he stomped through toward the office in the back. Then he unlocked it and dodged inside, flipping me over to sit on the desk. He had his own key. I opened my mouth to scream, and he planted his palm directly over it.

I sucked in air.

He leaned in; his eyes so blue they were hard to stare at. "Pauley is outside with Spider. We have about five minutes before Spider decides to fuck it and takes your cousin away from here to work on some math we're struggling with. Yeah, you can call the cops. Yeah, it'd probably be kidnapping. If you find Pauley again."

As a threat, it was good. Tears threatened to prick my eyes, and I shoved them away as he removed his hand. "You'd hurt Pauley?" I didn't believe it. I couldn't.

"No. I'm trying to help him and you right now." Lines etched into the sides of Aiden's mouth. "Work with me." Turning, he ripped the map off the wall and gathered the stacks of paper in one arm. "Then get your cousin out of the way and you stay there, too. I don't like your face bruised."

My face bruised? Seriously? "Fuck you, Aiden."

He quickly went through the desk drawers, which were empty. "Let's go."

I jumped in front of him. "You're not taking that evidence out of here." Stumbling, I started dialing my phone to call the police.

A motorcycle roared to life outside.

I gasped and turned to run through the stacks of books and out into the day. Spider was on his bike, and Pauley was still in my car. Okay. My legs trembled. I walked toward the car as fast as my black funeral pumps would allow.

Aiden followed and shoved the papers at the guy with the nose ring, who took them to the vacated passenger side seat. The truck roared away followed by Spider, who gave a short wave as he left. The remaining truck idled quietly with an older man at the wheel who stared straight ahead.

I furiously turned on Aiden as he walked back around my car toward me. "You just stole evidence in a homicide, dumbass. Might as well follow me to the police station."

He opened my door. "All I took was my own documents. No stealing. There's no proof of a homicide in those papers, which probably won't exist much longer."

"No, but you have no right to a key to an office at this college." I shoved him as hard as I could in the gut, and he took a step away from me. "In fact, I think that alone is probable cause to arrest you." Oh, I was bluffing a mile a minute now, but I was too pissed to stop. "Got it?"

He grasped my arm and flipped me around, pushing with just enough strength to land my ass in my seat. "Scot gave me the key because we were working on a project together."

"Handlebars," Pauley said helpfully, staring straight out of the windshield.

Aiden's jaw firmed. "Yeah. Handlebars."

I slapped his hand away and reached to slam my door shut, flipping on my headlights. "I can't believe you got my cousin involved." Betrayal scalded through me, and suddenly, every bruise I had ached. Bad.

Aiden curled his big hands over the side of my door since I'd left off the top. "Would you just stay away from me and this situation? Don't go anywhere without the police guard they have on you."

I sucked in air. How did he know that? "You just tied yourself to Scot in a way that corroborates those pictures we have of the two of you." Every time I tried to convince myself that Aiden wasn't involved with the drugs, something new popped up and slapped me in the head. Now I'd slept with him. So much for my career. "You're running Beast, aren't you? Nick is right."

He sighed. "I told you not to trust Basanelli. Jesus. You want to solve an old crime? Find out what happened to his dad. The guy didn't just disappear."

I blinked. "Sure, he did."

"Yeah. The wife-beater with three kids, three tough boys, just took off and left." Aiden shook his head as he dropped the bombshell.

That was ridiculous. He was just trying to throw me off. "As far as I can see, you're the only one breaking the law. The only one with a record. You and Scot are tied together, and I've found your drug plan."

His gaze hardened even more. "You have no idea what Scot and I were working on, Anna. I would like to start a motorcycle business, and specialized handlebars is a good and economical place to start. Pauley is a witness to our intent, and I'm sure he'd be fine testifying to that fact."

Was that a threat? I swung my head toward him. He was such a liar. My chest hurt. "You're in too deep for me to help you," I whispered.

He leaned in and brushed a soft kiss across the newest bruise on my cheekbone. The touch feathered through me, somehow bringing a sadness I hadn't expected. Then he stood, studying me with that blue gaze that still haunted my dreams. "I always was, Angel."

CHAPTER 31

*N*ight had completely fallen as I dropped Pauley off at his mom's office. Then I called Nick and filled him in on the events of the afternoon.

"You have pictures of the map?" he asked.

"Yes. I'm heading to the office to get them printed out right now. I think we can show that Aiden and Spider took evidence in Scot's homicide since it was all from his college office. Is that enough to get us another warrant?" I asked, my stomach growling, having missed dinner. In fact, when was the last time I'd eaten?

"Yes. To search the Lordes' apartment complex in Idaho, at least. We don't have jurisdiction in Washington. We need to get our hands on those other papers Devlin took." It sounded like Nick was swirling ice in a glass. "I'll put a uniform on Pauley to keep him safe."

I breathed out finally. "Thank you."

"Of course. We're not going to get anything tonight—it's too flimsy. Let's meet first thing in the morning and find a wide-awake judge for a warrant who doesn't mind working on a Saturday. Get some sleep, Albertini." He disengaged the call.

It was good advice, and I did just that, once again staying the night with Tessa. She had to work extra late, so I had the bed to myself until she dropped into it, immediately falling sound asleep.

The next morning, I borrowed a flowered skirt and matching sweater from her before heading to the office, once again not minding that I was working on a Saturday.

I tried to center myself in my car on the way to work, grateful the night had been void of nightmares. Or of dreams in general, especially of Aiden. There was a chance we could arrest him for taking the documents from the college, but the evidence was flimsy unless we could prove the drug connection. Not that I wanted to arrest him. What was in those papers that had been on the desk? I should've fought him over those, but everything had happened so quickly. He was definitely in the thick of this mess.

Yet, I felt in my heart that Aiden would never hurt me. Even my brain told me that. But did that matter? Those drugs did hurt other people, so he had to be stopped.

I reached the office and printed out a copy of the map from my phone just as Nick ran in with a signed warrant.

"Detective Pierce is executing right now on the Idaho apartment complex, and hopefully we'll find enough there to get a Washington warrant for the garage," Nick said. He shook out of his black jacket, leaving just dark jeans and a perfectly pressed blue shirt. "I'll drive."

Sounded good. I grabbed the printout and followed him outside. Fluffy clouds had moved in and were starting to cover the sun as I jumped into the front seat of the jeep, studying the printed-out map as he drove away. "It doesn't make sense," I murmured.

Nick glanced over; his hands sure on the steering wheel. "Those are clear interstates with certain cities mapped. Las Vegas, Reno, San Jose…"

I leaned back to study. "Clear distribution channels." I pointed to the math off to the side. "These smaller towns don't make sense."

Nick frowned. "Agreed. Rexburg, Idaho? Newcomb, Utah? What's the deal?"

"Maybe it's in the how of the distribution," I murmured as rain began to splatter down and hit the windshield. "Those towns are in farmland. Maybe rodeo?" What could it be?

"There's a connection. We just haven't figured it out." He pressed the gas once on I-90. "I didn't ask. Are you all right?"

"Yeah," I said softly. "Mad as hell that they involved Pauley."

"Don't blame you."

I cleared my throat. "So, um, Aiden had a few things to say about you." The paper crumpled on my lap, and I gingerly smoothed it out.

Nick snorted. "I'll just bet. What? I was a rich kid from the other side of town who is so ambitious I'd risk your life?"

Well, that actually did sound familiar. The hair stood up on my neck. It felt odd to be talking to Nick about Aiden without admitting what had happened between them. "No. That you and your brothers took care of your dad. In a bad way."

Nick stiffened, and tension poured from him. "Really? I'd thought that rumor had finally died."

So, it had been a rumor.

"What else did the career criminal say?" Nick growled.

I tried to breathe normally. "Just that your dad hit your mom and then disappeared one day when you three brothers were teenagers. He made it sound bad." How odd was it that both Aiden and Nick had rough childhoods? "Was it true?"

A muscle worked in Nick's jaw. In profile, his features were so straight and Italian, he could be part of a sculpture. "Yeah. It's true. Our dad was a total dick who liked to hit. When he skipped town with his latest side piece of ass, we were all better off."

"You were how old?" I asked.

"Fifteen. My brothers were both fourteen." That's right. The other two were twins. I'd forgotten. "And no, we didn't kill the bastard." Nick rolled his neck, and his knuckles whitened on the steering wheel. "Although, I'm not sure I wouldn't have at some point. I'd finally hit a growth spurt and was almost as tall as him. Not as broad or strong, though. It would've been a good fight."

My arms chilled, and I rubbed hands together. "I'm sorry, Nick."

He shrugged. "Small towns thrive on gossip, and that was a juicy piece. It just so happened he got in a few good hits before leaving town, and we all were bruised that week. Rumors and gossip, you know."

Yeah. I did know. "Is that why you went into law?"

"Maybe. It's supposed to help people who can't help themselves." Now he sounded thoughtful. "I believe in justice. Maybe in vengeance." He turned and pinned me with his amber gaze. "What would you do to Jareth Davey if you could?"

That was a question I truly didn't know how to answer. "Depends which day you catch me on."

He nodded, turning back to the road. "I get that. I really do."

After about fifteen minutes, he exited the Interstate for a residential area near the Idaho-Washington border. Single-story brick homes with manicured lawns led to nice apartment buildings, a few businesses, and then some run-down homes with burned lawns and a lot of weeds. Finally, we reached a series of apartment complexes, each more depressing than the last.

The clouds finally disappeared, letting the moon shine down. At the end of a winding dirt road, a Lorde's shield hung in the middle of a three-story apartment complex with peeling paint, dented doors, and cracked windows. In contrast, a series of garages lay to the east against forest land, all open and sporting impressive looking motorcycles. Their bikes were obviously more important than anything else.

Uniformed police officers, all wearing body armor, tossed the multitude of apartments as well as the garage. Several Lorde's members, inducing Spider, lounged near the garages, watching impassively.

He gave me a head nod as I stepped out of the Jeep, careful of a half-smashed milk carton on the ground. Nick soon joined me, putting his body between me and the club members.

I swallowed and turned toward the building, my gaze searching. No Aiden, and I didn't see the truck he'd been in earlier.

Detective Pierce strode out of a lower level apartment and straight at us. My stomach wobbled just a little. Pierce in a bullet-proof vest over pressed black slacks was something to look at. Big and broad and suddenly looking more appealing than I'd noticed. The rain darkened his already dark blond hair, and he yanked off his refractive glasses as he reached us. "No Devlin and no printout of a map or anything else," he confirmed.

Nick sighed. "Drugs or guns or anything?"

"Nope," Pierce confirmed. "They've cleaned the place up real nice since our last raid. The dogs haven't even gotten a hit." He glanced down at me. "Want to go through Devlin's apartment with me? See if there's anything that gives you a clue to where he's gone?"

"Sure." I shivered in the rain; glad I'd worn Tessa's sweater. "What about the Lordes' place of business at the garage in Washington?"

"Already called the DEA, and they were able to obtain a federal search warrant based on the information in your Idaho warrant," Pierce confirmed, turning and ducking his head as the rain increased in force. "I've also requested the other DEA case files of Devlin's earlier arrests before he joined the Diablo Riders."

I followed, letting the rain cool my face, which heated way too fast at the mention of Aiden's name. Oh, I'd screwed up, that was for sure. Yet something in me didn't quite regret the morning with him. Maybe I was the one screwed up. We walked up worn concrete stairs to the second floor and entered the first door on the left.

The place smelled like Aiden. Wild, free, and leather. "What do you hope the additional DEA files will tell you?" I asked, looking around.

Pierce shrugged. "For one thing, how did Devlin escape arrest when most of the Diablo's were hauled in?"

Good question. Of course, it seemed that Aiden was smarter than the average drug dealer. For sure. I breathed in his scent, wishing I didn't know it so well. His living area was sparse with an old green sofa and gold chair. One lone framed picture sat on the sofa table of him and his Grams, probably taken when he was around sixteen. I picked it up, noting his genuine smile and too serious eyes.

He'd had that look from the beginning. "I understand his childhood was traumatic before he left Ireland," I murmured.

"A lot of people have crappy childhoods," Pierce said, taking the picture and sliding the back off to look for evidence. Just the photo was in there. "Most of them don't sell drugs or commit assaults." He tossed the entire bundle on the sofa, where it bounced.

I couldn't help myself. I picked it up and set the picture to rights, securing it inside the frame before setting it back down. Then I looked some more. Aiden's kitchen held an old toaster and microwave with no dishes in the sink. The fridge revealed a couple of takeout cartons and a six-pack of beer.

Then I turned for his bedroom, which was also neat. Clothes were folded nicely in the drawers.

A male tech shimmied from beneath the bed, tugging out a red lace bra. "Thirty-Six D," he said, bagging it before drawing out two thongs, one black and one a hot pink. "Size four and size six. This guy gets around," the tech murmured.

"There are club bunnies," Pierce muttered. "They think motor-cycle gangs are sexy."

I wasn't sure about the club, but Aiden Devlin was definitely sexy. Chances were he didn't have trouble finding female companionship. The guy could really kiss. Jealousy tried to rear inside me, and I slapped that bitch down. Not now.

Pierce's phone buzzed and he lifted it to his ear. "Pierce." Then his face cleared, and his eyes blazed. "Excellent. Thank you for the speed."

I paused. "What?"

"Based on the information you provided, I finally got a warrant to dump Devlin's phone. Guess who he has been in contact with a lot the last few months?"

I held my breath. "Who?"

"Melvin Whitaker." Pierce smiled, and the sight was less than pleasant. "It's time to drag them both in." The dark amusement slid from his face like a PowerPoint animation. "That is, if we can find them."

CHAPTER 32

$\mathcal{T}$hunder woke me out of a dead sleep, and I sat straight up in bed to turn on the bed table lamp. Breathing deep, I leaned back against the headboard and listened to the storm. Harsh rain splattered down, pinging off the roof while the angry wind threw pine needles against the windows.

I exhaled and calmed my body. Truth be told, I loved spring storms. There was something about being safe and cozy inside while nature roared a protest to the end of winter.

Even so, I grasped the .380 auto off my bed table and padded barefoot through the bungalow to peer through the window by my front door. My relief was complete at seeing the squad car still parked by the garage.

Having a police guard really did lead to a decent night's sleep. The unregistered weapon in my hand that I'd purchased at a garage sale years ago didn't hurt, either. Yeah, I had a registered gun in my car and a concealed permit to carry. But I had a few more around for protection. Someday Jareth Davey was coming for me, and I wanted to be ready.

I kept the gun at my thigh while walking back to bed just as my cell phone rang. My chest compressed. Phone calls in the middle of the night were always bad.

"Hello?" I answered.

"Hey. It's Detective Pierce." The sound of rain echoed all around him.

"This can't be good," I muttered, setting the gun in my drawer and reaching for the discarded jeans on the chair.

"Nope. Not at all." Indiscernible voices came across the line. "Meet me at the morgue in fifteen minutes."

I paused in pulling my jeans up. "No way. Uh, uh. I am *not* going to the morgue in the middle of the night."

He sighed. "Just wait in your car for me. I promise I won't let the ghosts get you."

"Wait—" But he'd hung up. Who was in the morgue? It wasn't family or anybody I was close with, or he would've done the notification in person. But why me? Or had he called Nick, too? Grumbling, I zipped my jeans and threw on a blue sweater before brushing my teeth and yanking my mass of hair into a ponytail.

I ran out to my car, somewhat mollified that the cop car followed me all the way to town and to the morgue, where Pierce was already waiting, leaning against the wall by the back door and smoking a cigarette. The sight of him doing so caught me off guard. Pierce had a vice? My tennis shoes splashed up water, but it had stopped raining, so I didn't bother with a jacket. "Those things will kill you," I said when I approached him.

He dropped the butt into a puddle of water. "I know. I quit months ago, but this case…"

It was oddly gratifying to see that the cranky detective wasn't so perfect. Even now, in the middle of the night, his dark blond hair was perfectly in place, the gray at his temples giving him a look of sophistication. Or maybe experience. I followed him inside the silent building. "Who is dead, Pierce?"

"How about you call me Grant after midnight?" He pressed the button for the elevator.

Right. Was he flirting? If so, he sucked at it. I lifted an eyebrow.

He lifted his right back.

Okay. Now he was getting annoying. With a huff, I followed him onto the elevator, down a floor, and onto the morgue level. Sheets covered two bodies on the examination tables. Bile rose in my throat.

Dr. Bay Mandi looked up, his eyes huge through goggles and his frame wiry beneath the white lab coat. He lifted the goggles. "Hi, Anna. Detective Pierce."

We both said hi.

Pierce tugged a sheet off the face of the first body, showing a huge flat nose. A clear bullet hole was visible in the center of his forehead. "Know this guy?"

I gulped. "Yes," I croaked. "He's one of the two guys who shot at us the other day in front of the courthouse and then chased me away from Melvin's and up into that tree." When Pierce pulled the other sheet free, the room swam around me. Another bullet hole in the middle of the forehead. "That's the other guy. The one with acne."

My knees buckled, and Pierce grabbed my arm, steering me out into the hallway. I took several deep breaths.

Pierce pushed me onto one of several plastic orange chairs lining the hallway. "I need to know. Did you tell Aiden Devlin about these two men?"

I needed to put my head between my knees. Oh, boy. Now was the time to confess everything, and yet, maybe I should just answer the question. "Yes. Also, Spider said guys like this needed a hole in the head." Had he been telling me something?

"And Devlin?" Pierce persisted, dropping to his haunches so we were face to face. The breezy scent of salt and ocean wafted near me.

My stomach lurched. I nodded. Aiden would never do anything like this, right? "Yes. I told him about these guys." When

232

we'd been having a nice dinner, and my guard was down. Way down—which ended in excellent morning sex.

"What did he say?" Pierce asked quietly.

My mind spun. "He said—he said that he wouldn't let me be in danger, and that he'd take care of it." It couldn't be. Right?

"Well," Pierce said grimly, "I guess he did."

* * *

AFTER RETURNING HOME from the morgue, I couldn't go back to sleep. So I cooked for a few hours, making meals to store in the freezer. I found comfort in my kitchen, remembering the many times I'd cooked with both of my grandmothers. My mom disliked the kitchen with a passion, but my dad was a great cook. He'd taught me as much as my grandmas put together. I threw together two lasagnas, a dish of cannelloni and some homemade spaghetti sauce before placing them in the freezer. Feeling guilty, I blended the ingredients for a hearty Irish stew before dumping it in two plastic bags, wanting to appease both sides of my heritage. I also made a Bailey's cheesecake. I was covered for dinner for a couple of weeks, at least.

Waiting until an almost decent hour, I called Wanda to see if she could fit me in for an early appointment, even though it was Sunday. If I let myself stop sleeping again, I'd lose too much of what I'd worked hard to do. Talking to her would help.

I quickly got ready and headed out to what actually felt like a warm spring day. Finally.

My hands rested on the steering wheel as I wound through town, dressed down in dark jeans with a sweater for the nice Sunday. Maybe I'd just wear sweats and watch a Supernatural marathon of my own, eating only pizza and ice-cream. Although, I'd have to beg off of the family barbecue that day, saying I had a cold or had to work. It was okay to do so once in a while. Yeah. That was a good plan.

My phone buzzed. "Albertini," I answered.

"Hey, Sunshine. It's Sheriff Franco over in Silverville. Sorry to bug you on a Sunday."

The sheriff was about eighty years old and had coached me in softball for over a decade. Even so, I wanted to smack my head against the steering wheel. "Hey, Sheriff. Dad said you have the newest letter."

"Yeah, that's why I'm calling. I've had requests from a federal agency for the cards, or copies of them, as well as the case files. Do you know what's going on?" The sheriff sounded the same as he had my entire life. Calm, cool, and grumpy. He was like another grandfather to me.

Unfortunately. My temples started to ache just enough to tick me off. "Yeah, I think so. Nick Basanelli has taken over as the prosecuting attorney here, and he promised to call in some favors to find Jareth Davey." Though by all accounts, it wasn't going well. Davey knew how to hide. "My guess is that Nick has friends in several agencies."

The sheriff cleared his throat. "You want to know where Davey is?"

"Yeah," I said softly, pulling into a parking slot on Main street. "I'd like to at least know."

"Okay dokey. I'll send them the info. Bye." He hung up.

I grinned. He'd never been much good on the phone. Thought it was too impersonal for people who really wanted to communicate. Then I stepped out of the car to the sidewalk, wove around a flowerpot and into the building, taking the stairs to Wanda's office.

The place looked much better than before. The boxes were gone, the books were stacked on shelves, and the plants had been placed at strategic points. Wanda gestured me inside and then finished a phone call, pointing toward a sofa near the fireplace and two chairs.

I chose one of the chairs.

She hung up and walked my way, dressed in a pretty floral skirt with white blouse. "I'm glad you called."

"Thanks for fitting me in on a Sunday." I waited until she'd sat and then told her everything that had happened since I'd last seen her, including my trip to the morgue just hours before.

"Bailey's cheesecake?" she asked after I'd wound down.

I started. "Well, yeah. Wait a minute. What about the morgue?"

She grinned. "Sorry. I'm hungry. Any chance you could pay me in food?"

"Gladly," I said, sitting back in the overstuffed chair and finally relaxing for the first time all week. "You don't cook?"

"Nope. My wife did, and I miss that as much as her." Wanda sighed. "So. The morgue. I mean, *Eww*. Right?"

"Right." I leaned forward. "It smells like formaldehyde and death. So gross. Do you think Aiden killed those guys?" The question was haunting me. He couldn't have done that.

She shrugged, and her trio of gold necklaces tinkled delicately against each other. "Dunno. What do you think?"

I set my head back on the chair. "I really don't know. If he did, that scares me." I wasn't ready to tell her that I'd slept with Aiden. I'd talk to Lacey first about it, like usual.

Wanda waited.

Heat climbed into my face. "Then I wonder—"

"If Aiden would take out Jareth Davey for you?" she asked quietly.

My gaze dropped to my hands. When was the last time I'd had a manicure? Way too long ago. Not that I could go to the new spa, since they'd been shut down for running drugs. "Yeah. I know it's wrong."

"Who could blame you?" she asked. "The guy has stalked you your entire life, and you can't find him. How freeing would it be to know he was gone?"

My head jerked up. "You think I should ask Aiden?"

"God, no. Murder is wrong. It's not wrong for you to wish you could feel safe again." She leaned forward. "Don't feel guilty about feelings, Anna. They're all good and right. It's actions that make or break us."

Intellectually, I knew that, but it sure helped to hear it. I glanced at my phone. My hour was half up. "I need you to profile Aiden for me," I said.

She crossed her legs. "I've never met the guy."

"I know, but based on everything I've told you, do you think it's possible he killed those two guys from the van?" I didn't want it to be true.

"Sure." She tilted her head. "Don't you?"

After seeing his rap sheet, it'd be logical to think that, but I didn't. I just didn't think he'd cold-bloodedly murder two men. "Why would he do such a thing?"

"Why do you think?" she asked.

The shrink's questioning was starting to tick me off. "That's what I'm asking you. He wouldn't have killed them just because of me, right? I mean, if he did kill them. They're from a rival gang, so that would put them in the crosshairs of the Lorde's guns." I hoped.

She glanced toward the window, obviously mulling it over. "Well, he saved you when you were kid. Per your words, he thinks that's the only good thing he's ever done. Would he take that further to save you again?"

I held perfectly still. "Yeah. Would he?"

She looked back toward me, her eyes soft. "You know him better than I do. Psychologically? Yes, it is possible. What do you think?"

I really didn't know. My phone dinged, and I glanced down at a text from Nick saying both Melvin and Aiden had been brought in. I guess I was about to find out.

$\mathcal{N}$ ick pulled a table closer to the one-way window in the police station interview room, and I gratefully hopped up on it to watch the interrogation of Melvin Whitaker. I'd already called my mom to tell her I had to work and would miss the Sunday family barbecue this week.

"My grandma cut out the picture of us in the paper from the other day," Nick said, also taking a seat. The wooden table groaned under his weight.

I rolled my eyes. "Figures. I'm sure mine has, too." They'd completely ignored the fact that we'd been on the scene of a homicide at the time. I looked through the glass. "Where did you find Melvin Whitaker?"

"Hotel near the border. He'd used credit cards," Nick said.

Melvin looked even skinnier than last time I saw him. Today he wore wrinkled gray pants, a polo shirt, and a shiny gold watch. His skin sagged at the arms and beneath his chin just enough to show he was in his sixties and not in good shape. Probably spent too much time in a lab creating illegal drugs. He fidgeted on the small chair, scratching his ear once in a while.

Nick leaned back. "He looks nervous already."

I nodded, my mind thinking over the day. "Hey. The sheriff from Silverville called, and I told him to release copies of my ongoing case files about Jareth Davey to your friends."

Nick turned. "What friends?"

I sat up straighter, my spine snapping to attention. "Somebody federal. I figured it was you calling in favors."

"No," Nick said slowly. "I have a couple of private investigators I work with who are the best. I have them hunting down Jareth Davey."

Wait a minute. "Then who asked for my files?"

Nick shook his head. "Don't know, but we're going to find out after this. I promise."

I didn't have time to answer because Detective Pierce strode in, still wearing his tac gear and looking powerful. Probably to intimidate the scientist. Pierce slapped a manila file down on the table, and Melvin jumped. "Do you understand your rights as they've been read to you?" he asked.

Melvin looked up; his eyes sharp. "Yes."

"So you'll be interviewed?" Pierce asked, taking a seat to the left and keeping our view unobstructed.

"Sure." Melvin shrugged a narrow shoulder. "I have done nothing wrong. What is going on?"

Pierce leaned back as if he had all the time in the world. "How do you know Aiden Devlin?"

"Going right for it, is he?" Nick breathed. "Nice."

Melvin fidgeted more. "I've never heard that name."

Pierce pulled the manila file toward him. "You've never met Aiden Devlin?"

"No."

"Ever talked to him on the phone?" Pierce asked.

"No," Melvin breathed, looking toward the door.

"That's interesting." Pierce drew out a piece of paper that had been highlighted across a bunch of rows. "Because these are your phone records, and these highlighted rows show phone calls between you and Aiden Devlin, who is a Lordes Defender and a well-known criminal in the area." He pushed the paper across the table.

Melvin swallowed, his Adam's apple jiggling. His gaze dropped to the paper, but he didn't reach for it. "You didn't have probable cause to search my phone."

Pierce nodded. "Probably not, but Devlin committed a battery and took evidence in an ongoing investigation, so I had plenty of probable cause on him to get a warrant. This is his phone dump... and here you are. Over and over and over again."

Melvin swallowed again. "That doesn't prove anything."

"You just lied to me. That proves something." Pierce drummed his fingers on the tabletop before pulling out two large photographs. "Here are two guys who ticked Devlin off. As you can see, they're both dead."

Melvin paled; his gaze caught on the paper. "Then I shouldn't tick him off."

"Ah, but now you're a loose end. It's my understanding, as a Lorde's Defender, that Devlin takes care of all loose ends. You're a smart guy. What do you think one bullet does to the brain?" Pierce asked.

"I haven't done anything." Melvin shoved the autopsy pictures back. "Period."

"Where's the lab, Melvin? Give me the info, and I'll make sure you get a good deal. A safe deal that keeps you far away from Devlin and his motorcycle gang." Pierce pressed him.

Nick glanced at me. "Pierce is pretty good at this, but I'll bet you twenty Melvin lawyers-up before giving the info."

"I'll take the bet," I murmured, leaning forward. Melvin was starting to sweat, and his thin hair was looking greasy from the extra moisture. "Pierce has him." Where was the Beast lab, and who was the distributor?

Pierce sighed. "All right. Let's go easier. You're obviously a genius, having learned how to cheaply mass produce opioids. You'll be famous if word gets out."

Melvin flattened his hands on the table. "I work for a seed company, splicing all sorts of grass. Legally. No opioids."

"You know how I know?" Pierce leaned forward. "Remember a guy named Mark Channelton? Young guy?"

Melvin paled.

"Yeah. Channelton turned snitch about three months ago because he helped you acquire the yeast. This guy can finger you. The walls are starting to close in," Pierce murmured.

Melvin looked away from the table. "Never heard of him."

Nick cleared his throat. "We have Channelton in Boise on ice as we wait for a trial. Gave the asshole complete immunity and will hand him over to the US Marshals for a new life once this is over."

Pierce pressed Melvin harder. "Tell me about the distribution plans. We have a copy of the map, so we know the routes and times. How are you planning to transport the opioids?"

Melvin looked toward the mirror and then back at Pierce. Red burst across his thin facial skin, highlighting the myriad of early dark spots. He'd definitely spent some time in the sun to have aged his skin so badly so young. "Opiods? What in the world are you talking about?"

I bit my lip. "He's really not a good liar."

"No. A jury will hate him," Nick agreed.

Pierce leaned forward. "Work with me, Melvin. I can protect you from these guys. Tell me about the manufacture of Beast, give me the location of the lab, and fill me in with the distribution plans. For all of that, I'll give you a deal you won't believe."

"Immunity from all," Melvin said evenly, dropping his chin.

Pierce sighed. "Not a chance. Plead guilty to manufacture, and you'll only serve five to ten years. That's a phenomenal deal, but you have to tell me everything."

Melvin studied him. His shoulders dropped.

I held my breath.

"I want a lawyer," Melvin said.

Nick snorted. "You owe me twenty, counselor. Told you."

Darn it. I thought we'd have him. Well. Maybe Pierce would get more out of Aiden. I kicked back to wait for the next show, my heart battering my rib cage.

* * *

AIDEN WALKED IN BEFORE PIERCE; his hands cuffed behind him. Even so, he looked dangerous, and once again, bored. When Pierce uncuffed him, Aiden pulled out a chair and winked toward the window.

My breath caught and my abdomen performed a slow roll.

"What a jerk," Nick muttered.

Pierce sat in the same place as before.

Aiden cocked his head. "The bulletproof vest and gun at the waist don't impress me, Pierce. You might as well get comfortable for this one."

Pierce didn't move. "You ever worn one of these?"

"Nope," Aiden said.

"They're far more comfortable than you think." Pierce dropped a much heavier case file on the table than he'd had for Melvin.

I swallowed. "Double or nothing, Nick? I bet Aiden doesn't give up a thing."

Nick studied Aiden through the glass. "No bet. He's been through this before. He's not gonna talk, and he's not gonna ask for a lawyer. We don't have enough to hold him, and he knows it."

"Then why did we bring him in?" I asked.

"The Lordes are getting nervous. Antsy. They know we have Devlin, and while he's in an important position, he's only been with them for two years. They have to wonder how he escaped being charged with the other Diablos. I have no doubt Pierce will have Spider in here at some time and hint at that very thing." Nick's long legs reached the floor.

Mine dangled in the air. Wouldn't that put Aiden in even more danger? "Pierce is just applying more pressure?"

"Yeah, and he'll put Melvin in hot water. Soon."

Pierce tapped the table. "Melvin Whitaker gave you up, Devlin. Completely."

"See?" Nick said.

Aiden flashed a quick smile, and while I'd like to say it didn't do something funny to my abdomen, I'd be lying. "Not gonna discuss other people with you, Pierce."

"Smart," Nick muttered. "Didn't lie, so we can't cross-examine him on his statement. Man, I hate this guy."

I should, too. In ordinary circumstances, I probably would. But not Aiden.

"What about pretty Anna Albertini?" Pierce asked, his voice lowering. "Want to talk about the spunky lawyer with the green eyes?"

My jaw dropped, and I shut it.

"He's just trying to get into Devlin's head," Nick said quickly.

Aiden looked around Pierce to the window, somehow zeroing in on me again. "Her eyes are more gray than green. Obviously, you haven't been that close to her, or you'd know that."

"Have you been that close to her?" Pierce asked.

"Fourteen years ago, she was all eyes," Aiden rumbled. "Skinny little thing with tons of brunette hair and big eyes. You know what she was doing the first time I saw her? Really saw her?"

I couldn't breathe.

"No, what?" Pierce asked.

Aiden focused back on him. "She was swinging a cast-iron skillet that weighed more than she did at a monster. That's what she was doing." He leaned forward, threat in every line of his body. "She's not somebody you use in an interrogation, in any manner. Say her name again, and I walk. Instantly."

My lungs protested, and I forced myself to exhale. Air in. Air out.

Pierce leaned back. "Those are some strong emotions, Devlin."

"Moments define us," Aiden said softly. "Anna and I shared one. An important one that probably shaped us both in ways you can't imagine. Years later, here we are."

There was something poetic about his words, and his meaning shot right to my heart.

"She's a lawyer and you're a criminal," Pierce snapped. "In fact, she's been put in danger more than once because of you and because of this case. So how about you do the right thing, for the second time in your miserable life, and tell me what I need to know to close this thing? Protect her again, Devlin. It's the only way."

Aiden's chin lifted very slightly. "You gonna protect her? Be her hero, Pierce?" His chuckle lacked humor. "You want it, don't you? Man, she has an effect. One of a kind."

I shifted uneasily on the table. This line of questioning, this back and forth, really sucked.

Pierce's chuckle was just as dark as Aiden's. "Oh, no. She has a hero, buddy. It's all you. Now why don't you prove it?"

That hit so close to home I had to look away. Just for a second.

"It's part of the game, Albertini," Nick said, not looking my way. "Take yourself out of the equation. Pierce knows what he's doing, and it's a good strategy. Devlin's getting worked up."

I turned back to study both men. Nick was wrong. Aiden was as calm as possible, although his eyes blazed that fierce blue they got when he was pissed. "Maybe I should talk to him."

"Not yet," Nick said. "Pierce is going down a good path."

Pierce flipped open the top page of the case file. "You knew her as a kid, when you were almost a man. She was ten, you were sixteen. Got a thing for young girls?"

Aiden rolled his eyes. "No. She was cute and hung around. I

didn't see her as a woman until, well, last week. Now I know she's all woman."

My chest did a funny jumping thing.

Pierce straightened. "Know what I've learned in this job? Criminals, no matter how smart, always make a mistake. We know Whitaker has created a viable Beast, and we know the Lorde's are financing and planning to manufacture, and we know the plan for transportation." He pushed a picture toward Devlin. "Of course, I'm going to get you on murder in the first degree."

I angled my neck to see better, and it was an autopsy picture of the flat-faced guy.

Aiden didn't even look down at it. "Is that a fact?"

"Yeah, and even better, since this kill wasn't part of your job, I'm sure you made a mistake." Pierce pushed another autopsy picture toward Aiden. "This was heated, and this was emotional, and this was because of pretty Annabella Fiona Albertini."

I blinked. Pierce knew my whole name?

"You said her name," Aiden said quietly, pushing away from the table and standing. "I gave you one warning."

Pierce slapped the table. "Sit back down."

"No. You brought me in here on arrest, in cuffs, and you read me my rights. You're fishing, asshole, and it isn't going to work." Aiden looked toward the window and directly at me, his gaze heated. "I *want* a *lawyer*." The way he said it was dark and deep and full of innuendo.

For me.

CHAPTER 34

Something was nagging at me, and I couldn't place it as I finished a late Sunday lunch at McQuirk's Deli with two cranky oversized men. Detective Pierce kept glaring at a group of teenagers over in the corner who weren't doing anything wrong, and Nick kept drifting off into silence, no doubt planning his next opening argument.

I, on the other hand, enjoyed a spinach salad and tried to filter through my brain to see what I was missing.

Various women, from college students to tourists to grandmothers did a double take as they went by. I guess Pierce and Basanelli were hot, but for now, I had set them both firmly in the colleague column. It made things so much easier.

Pierce finally focused on me. "Do you have even more bruises on your face than you did before?"

"Yeah. I thought your guy told you." I set my napkin down and told him about the naked guy in court. By the time I finished, his cheek had creased in a very appealing way.

"Interesting things happen to you," he murmured, finishing his diet coke.

Yeah. I couldn't argue that. My brain finally snapped to attention. "That's it. Oh. Okay." I gathered my thoughts. "Beast hasn't been distributed yet, has it?"

Nick swung his focus back to me.

"No," Pierce said. "Well, not really. We think there has been a test run to Los Angeles because limited amounts were found during two drug busts."

Nick nodded, taking a big bite of his pastrami sandwich. He chewed thoughtfully, smiled back at a couple of women out walking their dogs, and then cleared his throat. "It's kind of like a sample sale. They send the drugs out, get good word going, and then flood the market. Why?"

"The naked guy. He said he'd taken blue pills and Beast." Adrenaline pumped through my blood. "Where did he get Beast?"

Both men sat back in almost an identical movement. Interesting. "Go find out," Nick said.

Pierce nodded. "Yeah. If they put him under observation, he's in the hospital's psych ward for the three days."

I sipped my iced tea. "Can I just go talk to him? Without a warrant?"

"Did he ask for a lawyer?" Nick asked.

"No, but he was sent away to the psych ward," I countered. "An argument can be made that he's not able to consent."

Pierce shrugged. "Sure, but we're not after him. He might just provide a lead, and we'll worry later how we got there."

"Maybe you should go," I said, already sorry I'd opened my mouth.

"No," Nick returned. "He likes women, and it sounds like he thought you were cute. Use that."

Okay. I did not like that. At all. But it did make sense. "Fine. Lunch is on one of you." I pushed away from the table, and every bruise I had ached in protest.

"Anna?" Pierce also stood. "We're cutting both Melvin and Devlin loose. Just so you know."

246

I'd figured. There wasn't enough to hold either one, and they were more likely to make a mistake outside of custody. "Got it."

"Watch your back, and I have a cop on you." Pierce moved around the table and took my arm to head for the door. "I'll walk you to your car where he's waiting."

"Lunch is on me," Nick said wryly.

"Your expense account is much larger than mine, lawyer," Pierce returned, grinning and looking younger than usual. As soon as we had moved down the sidewalk a ways, he coughed. "I, ah, wanted to apologize if I said anything that made you uncomfortable in the interview with Devlin."

Wow. Okay. Pierce apologizing? He was much easier to keep at a distance when he was being a jerk. "I understood the strategy," I said, stepping over a winding crack in the sidewalk.

"Just be careful." We made it past my office building to the adjacent parking lot. "Whether it makes sense or not, he has feelings for you, and he obviously doesn't know what to do with them."

Aiden wasn't the only confused one in this situation. I nodded.

We reached my car, which had the top on, and I nodded at Bud, who sat in his patrol car two parking spots away. He nodded back, looking big and beefy even sitting in the car. I wasn't sure I needed protection, but I had to admit that I liked it. Just in case.

Pierce opened my door for me. "I was thinking." He angled his head to check out the back seat, probably to make sure it was empty. "I've been invited to a barbecue in Silverville tomorrow at Sheriff Franco's house. Kind of a Monday evening get together, I guess?"

"Yeah?" I looked up at him, surprised again by how bright his eyes really were. Did he need directions or something?

"Want to go with me?" he asked.

My head bobbed. "Are you asking me on a date?" I wasn't being coy. The words came out fast and curious.

He shifted his weight. "Kind of. You'll know everyone there, and I don't. We are working together."

Man, he really didn't understand small towns. "It'll be seen as a date, Pierce. Even if we spend the entire barbecue mingling around and not with each other. My grandmothers will be pulling out their wedding dresses and fighting over whose lace I'm going to wear at our nuptials." I shouldn't have taken such glee in watching the color drain from Pierce's bronze face, but hey. I'm just human.

"Oh." He glanced at Bud and then back at me. "Well then, let's make it official. It's a date."

"Why?" I asked, suspicious. Did he think this would draw Aiden out or something?

Pierce pinched the bridge of his nose as if a headache was attacking him. "Why are you such a pain?" he muttered. Then he focused on me again. "Because I want to see you outside of work. I'm interested. Why not just go to a simple picnic and find out if we have fun together?"

It probably was as close to an 'I like you' as Pierce was able to get. Warmth flushed me. He really was cute and didn't seem fifteen years older than me. I'd slept with Aiden, but we weren't dating, so why not hang out with Pierce a little? "All right," I surprised myself by saying. "Why not?"

* * *

I LEFT Bud at the door and walked through the hospital entrance toward the elevator bank, which took me swiftly to the small east wing of the third floor. I'd never visited the crisis wing, oddly enough. Pastel colors made up the floor, walls, and reception area. I smiled at the blonde behind the counter. "Hi, Cathy."

"Hey." Cathy Bacca graduated the year before I had and was on her third marriage. She had wild blonde hair, heavily made up brown eyes, and a smile that brightened all of the pastels around us. She had the shoulders of a Montana girl and could rope a steer in seconds if I remembered right. "What's up?"

"Well, I was hoping I could visit Charles Monroe, even though it's Sunday." Figured I'd just go the direct path.

Cathy typed into her computer. "What happened to your face? I have a bat if you need to borrow it."

I grinned. "No, I'm good. It has been a serious of incidents one after the other. I did fall out of a tree."

"Nice." She leaned forward. "Did I hear that Nick Basanelli was back in town?"

"Yes," I murmured. Was she looking for husband number four? "And yes, he looks even better than in high school."

Her grin reminded me of a cat my cousin Lacey had saved years ago. Then Cathy read her screen. "It looks like Monroe can have visitors. Go through the light green door to the left, which leads to the rec area. I'll have him brought in."

"Thanks." I paused near the door. "Basanelli likes to eat lunch at McQuirk's most days."

Cathy's eyes gleamed. "Thanks. Appreciate it."

"Any time." If anybody needed some fun, it was Basanelli. Plus, if he was seeing somebody else, he was off the table for me, and I was wimp enough to admit it. The guy was tempting, and I had too much temptation going on around me at the moment. I pushed through the door and stopped short. It was just like on television. Patients watched movies in an area sporting a sofa and chairs, while others played checkers or board games at tables scattered throughout. One elderly lady in a housecoat stood at a window and just looked outside.

I scouted the room for a good place to chat just as Charles entered from the far peach-colored doors. He zeroed in on me and danced my way, shimmying his butt in the thick robe as he arrived. They'd let him keep on his slippers, and I swear, they winked at me.

"Hiya cutie," he said, stopping right in front of me and

reaching for the belt at his robe. "Come for a second look?"

"No." I waved the air. "I just wanted to visit you and talk. You undo that robe, and I'm out of here."

His bottom lip pouted out, and since he had to be late seventies, he looked kind of adorable. "You're no fun." He dropped his hand and pointed to a vacant table to the right. "Wanna sit?"

"Yes." Relief coursed through me as I walked over and pulled out a chair, sitting as he did.

He looked my face over. "Is that from me? I'm sorry." His long fingers played with the tie of his robe.

"Just one is from you. The rest are from ducking from bullets and then falling out of a tree."

His face crinkled. "You have an interesting life."

I nodded. "Yeah, so, I was wondering if you'd talk to me a bit. Maybe tell me where you got the blue pills and the other ones. The white ones?"

"Beast?" he asked, cocking his head. He'd slicked his thin hair back, and his eyes were clearer today than they had been.

"Yes," I said, lowering my voice. "If you don't mind. Where in the world did you get that pill?"

He grinned, showing a gap in his lower teeth. "At Bingo night. We do it right, baby." He leaned forward. "Maybe you could come with me after I get sprung from here. Like a date."

Man, I was popular today. "Maybe. Where do you play Bingo?" I was on to something. I could just feel it.

"At the rec center in the middle of the houses." He looked around. "It has brighter colors than this place. I like it."

"What houses?" I fought to keep the excitement out of my voice. Maybe I should go into investigative work.

He frowned. "Where I live. The Sunnyside Retirement Community."

Oh. Wow. "Do you know Melvin Whitaker?" I murmured.

"Of course. I play Bingo with him every Thursday." Charles' expression dropped. "You like him? Everyone likes him. He's not as young as he looks, you know. There's something to say about experience."

What. Whoa. Okay. "Right. Did Melvin give you the pills?"

"Yeah. I drove him to his work one day, and in exchange he gave me the pills. Beast and some edibles. His car wasn't working." Charles smoothed his greasy hair back. "Good stuff, too. Beast took all the pain away, even in my leg joints. Really good stuff."

I tried to keep my expression mildly curious, but my heart was galloping. "You took him to his lab in Washington?'

"No. Not that one. The other one near the mountain closer to town." Charles shook his head. "I don't want to talk about another man. Let's talk about you. What's your favorite flower?"

"Tulips," I said absently. "Can you at least tell me a little about where the lab is?"

"No," he shouted. "Ask again, and I leave. Now. What is your favorite color?"

I bit my lip. "Green but I like pink a lot, too. What kind of car do you own?"

His eyes lit up. "A new Buick. Real fancy. You like fancy cars?"

"I truly do." A newer car would have GPS in it, right? Oh, I had to get out of there.

Charles paused. "Wait a minute. If you don't know where I live, how have you taken care of Snuffles?"

"Snuffles?" I frowned. "Who?"

"My baby." His voice rose. "Oh God. Who has fed her? Oh no. You have to go let her out. She's been in the house this whole, time? Oh, my baby." He stood, his voice getting even louder. An orderly built like a building pushed off the far wall.

I held up my hand. "I'll go right now. Give me your address and tell me how to get into your house."

He calmed. Slightly. "Use the key under the pot by the front door." Then he gave his address. His home was across the street from Thelma and Georgiana's.

This case was finally coming together.

CHAPTER 35

I called Nick as I drove toward the retirement community.

"Basanelli." He answered on the third ring.

"Hey. It's Anna. I have permission to enter Charles Monroe's apartment and feed his animal, who I'm assuming is a dog since it needs to be let out. Monroe seemed lucid when he asked me. Can I do this without a warrant?" I thought I could but needed to double check.

Nick was quiet for a second. "Yeah, there are exigent circumstances with an animal that has been left alone. You have valid concerns about its safety, and you do have permission from its owner."

I didn't like that I was thinking like a lawyer and not somebody concerned solely about the animal, so I sat with that for a moment. If we got the drugs off the streets, it'd save lives. Still, I wished for the luxury of just worrying about the pooch and not about evidence admissibility in trial. "If I check the GPS on his car, I might be able to find where the Beast lab is." I filled Nick in on everything Monroe had said.

The pause was longer this time. "You will need a warrant for the GPS information. I'll have Celeste type up the application and affidavit for you first thing tomorrow morning. You'll have to take it to a judge since I'm heading up to Boundary county to handle several arraignments we can't put off any longer."

"Which judge should I ask?" I asked.

He exhaled. "Judge Hallenback is the easiest since he's gone off the deep end, but you can only use him if he's in the office. Since there might be some question as to your getting the information from a guy in the psych ward, I'd go for him. Anybody else might deny the warrant, and we really need to find that lab."

Nick was right, but this felt kind of shady. Was the end result justified if it kept a dangerous drug off the street, or is that just how we lived with our decisions? "Okay," I murmured. "I'll check out the dog before heading home tonight."

"Is the cop still on you?" Nick asked.

I looked in my rearview mirror to see Bud right behind me. "Yep."

"Good. Devlin is back on the street. Pierce had a tail on him, but he lost the guy within five minutes."

I swallowed. "I'm in no danger from Aiden."

"Until you are," Nick returned. "Don't forget that Devlin has had more than his share of assault charges. Two with deadly weapons."

I rubbed my aching temple. "That goes against everything I know about him."

"That's just it. You haven't seen the guy in twelve years. You don't know a thing about him." Nick hissed out a breath.

I drove into the retirement community, impressed again by the organized landscaping. "I know." I felt like I knew Aiden. Did I? "Let's fight about that later."

"Fine. By the way, I've finished interviewing all of the prosecuting attorneys and have now fired them. They can re-apply if they want. The DEA is still conducting interviews with former staff, and you're up next. They want to talk to you about Scot, of course," Nick said.

He'd fired everybody on a Sunday? What a butthead. "Of course."

"Crap. I have to go. The paperwork will be ready for you first thing tomorrow morning because I'll leave a note for Celeste before I take off tonight. Check in with me after you get a warrant, would you?"

"Sure," I said, winding around and parking in the driveway of a light green single-family home across from Thelma and Georgiana's duplex. "Bye." I clicked off and stepped out of my car. The sound of night crickets droned in the distance, and the smell of freshly cut grass was all around. It'd be nice to live in a place where lawn and garden maintenance were included with the association fees.

I shivered and looked around carefully at the darkened night. Last time I'd been in the neighborhood, two men with guns had chased me up a tree. Of course, those two men were now dead.

Charles' lawn was perfectly groomed, and I found the key under an overflowing flowerpot on the front porch, just like he'd said. His porch light was on, which meant it was probably set with a timer. "Snuffles, I'm coming in," I called out, unlocking the door and gingerly pushing it inward.

Snuffles hit me full force with a happy bark, knocking me back several steps. I yelped, my arms windmilling, and fell down the stairs, landing hard on my butt. The dog jumped over my head, and I ducked, turning. *"Hey!"*

The dog was huge. Maybe part mountain dog and part mutt. His thick fur shaking, he ran for the nearest hydrangea bush and emptied his bladder, somehow wagging his tail the entire time. His fur was a light gray and his eyes a deep blue. Well, one was blue. The other looked green.

My entire body aching, I turned and stood to see Bud leaning against his patrol car, illuminated by the moon. He shook his head.

"Whatever," I muttered, brushing grass cuttings off. The dog probably weighed as much as Bud. "Please keep an eye on him," I said.

"My job is to keep an eye on you," Bud returned, not moving.

I gave him a look and walked up the steps again, wincing as my ankle protested. The same one that had been burned by a bullet. Maybe being a lawyer was just too dangerous for me. I shook off the unease and pushed into Charles' house, turned on the lights, and stopped short. Apparently, Snuffles hadn't liked being left alone. Tuffs of fabric stuffing littered the entire floor, torn out of what looked like had been a nice leather sofa and chair set. The dog had chewed down to the steel frame.

Stepping gingerly over the mess, I turned right into the kitchen. Ah. The dog had figured out how to get into the pantry. Cornflakes, spaghetti noodles, and cookie wrappers covered the worn tile. A half-eaten dish rag was still on the counter surrounded by dog hair.

At least the puppy hadn't gone hungry.

A smell caught me from the back of the house, and I winced, walking over the faux wood floor and turning on lights until I reached a neatly made up bedroom. The stench came from the other side of the bed.

If I was a really nice person, I mean super nice, I'd probably clean up the dog poop.

But I wasn't feeling all that kind at the moment. Instead, I looked around. Charles was a neat freak. The pictures were neatly lined up on his dresser, and I looked them over, not recognizing anybody. A photo of him in a navy uniform caught me, and I picked it up, studying it. He'd looked young and sure and brave.

I headed for the kitchen to find garbage bags, wood cleaner, and hopefully gloves. I couldn't let a veteran come home to this kind of mess. Man, I was ready for bed. It took about an hour, but I cleaned up the house.

After disposing of the garbage in the bins, I'd just finished checking the pristine garage to see the new blue Buick. The inside was clean, and I couldn't see anything that would give me a reason to open a door. Yeah, I'd definitely need a warrant to access the GPS data.

I whistled for Snuffles, who came bounding inside happily. After petting him, I locked the door and kept the key before striding down to Bud. "Are you watching me all night?" I asked, trying not to yawn.

"Nope. We already have a car at your place. I'll follow you there and then leave." He smiled.

The man sounded way too happy to be dropping me off.

Then he frowned. "I'll be there first thing in the morning to follow you to the office." He sighed.

That made me smile for some reason. "Fine, but we have to come by here and feed Snuffles in the morning." With that last thought, I all but skipped to my car, more than ready for a good night's sleep.

MONDAY MORNING ARRIVED with a soft breeze and a lovely blue sky. Sure enough, Bud was waiting for me as I pulled out of my driveway and drove to the retirement community again, this time singing along with Taylor Swift on the radio.

I pulled into Charles' driveway and waited until Bud had parked behind me before striding up the walkway and unlocking the door.

This time, I knew to jump out of the way to let Snuffles bound out for his hydrangea bush.

I peeked inside. "Darn it, Snuffles." He'd torn up the living room carpet. Now I had to clean that? "I'll be a few minutes,

Bud," I called out, happy I'd worn slacks and a light sweater today.

It only took a half hour of cleaning until I was happy. Sighing, I turned back to the now clean kitchen and opened the sliding door to let in some fresh air. The small backyard was full of weeds, showing the association only worked on the front of the homes. About ten hummingbird feeders, all red, hung from the gutters along the back of the house.

I carefully shut and locked the sliding glass door and walked through the now clean house and out the front door to see Bud petting the dog. He straightened immediately, flushing as if being caught eating off somebody else's plate. "It's okay. He is cute," I teased. Bud's darkening cheekbones cheered me considerably. I patted my knees. "Come here, Snuffles. Time to go back inside."

Snuffles sat near Bud and wagged his tail. "I have food and fresh water," I said, trying to reason with a canine.

"Anna? What are you doing here?" Thelma came out of her garage dressed in a brightly flowered sundress complete with a wide and floppy pink hat. Her knobby knees were bare over flip flops covered with colorful fish drawings.

"Anna?" Georgiana came next, her hair in a bun held together with chopsticks as she hustled across the road to us. She held a cute white kitten with big blue eyes against her denim shirt. "Look what we—"

Before she could get the words out, I saw the disaster to come. Snuffles barked. The cat hissed and escaped from Georgiana's hands before she could stop it, twisting high in the air and landing on the police car to skid across the hood toward Bud.

He made a grab for it, but the little animal found purchase with the windshield wiper and scrambled up the window to the top of the car.

Snuffles barked enthusiastically and knocked into Bud, throwing the cop against the car. Then the dog leaped up onto the hood, its nails skidding and its legs sliding out from under it.

"Betty White," Thelma called, her voice panicked. "You come back here right now."

The kitten howled in protest as the dog tried to lever up the front windshield. Its front paws hit the roof, and the cat wailed, jumping over Bud's head and straight for me. I yelped and made a grab for the cat, but it zipped by me, followed by the dog.

I jumped for Snuffles, hitting the canine mid-center and locking my arms around his body. We tumbled to the ground and rolled right into the hydrangea bush, fur shoving up my nose. The dog kicked against me, fighting hard, his sloppy tongue against my neck. I held tight, my body heaving. "Knock it off," I snapped.

The dog struggled.

Then Bud was there, grabbing the dog by the neck and yanking it away from me. "You okay?"

I sat up and picked flowers out of my hair. "No." Everything hurt. My clothes were once again ruined.

Thelma walked around the corner of the house, the kitten safely in her arms. "Snuffles only goes in the fenced back yard unless he's on a leash," she said, rather helpfully.

The dog saw the kitten, yipped, and bunched its back legs. Bud lifted the canine against his chest and strode for the front door, setting the dog down gently and shutting the door. Then he came back to me and lifted me by the armpits, much like he'd handled the dog.

I slapped his hands. "Don't even think of kissing me." Nick and Aiden were enough for one week. Now I had a date with Pierce later.

Bud reared back. "I don't even like you. Not at all."

Huh. I pushed bark off my pants, wincing as slivers dug into my already scratched palms. "Why not?"

"Seriously?" Bud gingerly reached out to tug a full blossom from my hair. "You're a disaster. Every time I see you. It's lucky I haven't been shot somehow."

I'd take umbrage or at least be a little irritated if he wasn't a hundred percent correct. Still. Lately it seemed like most of the men around me were a mite interested. Not that it mattered. I wasn't looking for romance at the moment, especially since I was a disaster, as Bud so kindly put it.

Thelma reached out her bony hand to pinch Bud's bicep. "What about me? You have such nice arms."

"I'm taken," he croaked, his eyes nearly bugging out. "Nice girl. Been together forever."

Bud really wasn't a very good liar.

"Well." Thelma fluttered her thick eyelashes. "In case things don't work out, keep in mind that I used to be a gymnast. I'm very bendy."

My phone buzzed, and I reached for it, but it wasn't in my back pocket.

Bud shoved branches of the plant out of the way and drew it out. "Here."

"Thanks." I took it. "Albertini."

"Hi, Anna. It's Celeste. Your documents are ready, and Judge Hallenback is in his chambers, so you can catch him for the next hour or so. He usually works a few hours before heading off to parts unknown."

"Thanks." I clicked off just as a rumble of motorcycle pipes ripped through the peaceful community. Several bikes drove by, and I recognized Spider as well as Aiden. My chin lifted, and my body flared wide awake, even with the new bruises. How had they found me? Were they following me, or were they looking for Melvin?

Bud edged his way between me and the bikers, setting his stance wide and his hand on the butt of his gun.

Aiden grinned and opened the throttle, disappearing around the corner.

My lungs seized. I gestured toward Thelma. "Were you two going somewhere?"

She nodded. "Yes. We're going to the vet and then shopping for a bed and food for Betty White. We'll check on Snuffles and feed him dinner tonight."

Good. "Okay. I'll see you later." I'd waited until the ladies had gotten into their car and driven away before looking at Bud. "Don't argue with me, but you need to stay here and guard Charles' car. I'll have Detective Pierce execute the warrant as soon as I get it."

Bud shook his head. "I go with you."

"No. I'll go straight to the office and then the courthouse, I promise." I couldn't let Spider get his hands on the car, if that's why he had just ridden through the neighborhood. Were he and Aiden trying to tie off loose ends? "Trust me."

Bud crossed his arms. "Fine, but you call me the second you get to the office. If you don't, I'm coming after you."

The sound of the motorcycles faded into the distance. "No problem."

I had to hurry.

CHAPTER 36

The warrant and affidavit were on my desk the second I arrived at the office. I signed, had the receptionist notarize it, and then hustled back into the nice spring day.

The smell of flowers followed me from my office to the courthouse, and the sunshine helped my mood, even though fresh bruises were making themselves known. Soon I was going to be one big purple blob. I'd called Bud the second I'd arrived safely at my office, and he'd reported that the Lordes hadn't driven by again. For now, I dodged up the stairs to the third floor, taking a left for the office area. Then I knocked on Judge Hallenback's door. Hopefully he was in the office this morning.

"What?" he bellowed.

That was probably an invitation to enter. I nudged the door open and peeked around it to see him behind his desk. "Hey, Judge. I have a warrant for you to sign."

"Alberto. Come in. Happy Monday to you." He gestured me inside a spacious office with manila files and papers stacked around. The wall behind him was windows, while the two on the side were bookshelves stuffed full of legal periodicals. Today his gray hair was slicked back, and his eyes were sharp. He wore a

'Hallenback' Used Car lot shirt in a very mellow yellow along with what looked like tan-colored jeans. "What do you want?" He reached for a pair of reading glasses.

I set the papers in front of him and on top of several court briefs before taking a seat in a thick leather chair across from him. "A warrant to search a car and follow up on the GPS in order to maybe find a drug lab." Then I waited.

He read through the application as well as my affidavit. "Did you walk over here?" he mused, looking over the top of the papers.

I blinked. "Yes. It's a nice day."

He shook his head. "I saw you in your convertible the other day. Thing doesn't have airbags. You should get a new car." He scrambled through the stack of papers and then handed over a business card for his brother. "We own a car lot, you know."

"I do know that." I really needed him to concentrate. "I like my car, Judge."

"You can't drive that vehicle in the winter." He slapped the papers down.

I looked for a pen so he could sign. "No, your Honor. I have a SUV for the winter." As did most people in the town. "Would you please sign the warrant for me?"

"What warrant?" he muttered, looking toward the bookshelf. "I have books. Do you have books?"

An executive style silver pen was on the floor, and I pounced on it, sliding it toward him. "How are you feeling, Judge? Maybe you should have a check-up or something?" I didn't want to insult him, but the guy needed help. Maybe I could help him.

He lifted one fit shoulder. "Yeah, maybe. Sometimes I forget things." He took the pen and signed the bottom of the warrant. "Though it has been pretty stressful lately. I miss seeing some of the older guys in the courtroom. The rest of you are just so young."

"Sometimes I don't feel young. Especially this week." My

whole body was one big bruise. I took the papers. "I could make an appointment with a doctor for you, if you'd like. My cousin, Wanda, might be a good place to start."

He shook his head. "That's okay. I have a doctor, and I have to see her every year for the insurance."

Even so, I needed to follow up with him. If all the family he had was his brother, and his brother wasn't helping any, then I would. "Okay. Thanks for this." I backed toward the door, wanting to help him somehow. I felt like I was taking advantage of him with the warrant, and I really didn't like that, but we needed to find that drug lab.

"Good luck, Alberto," he said, kicking back in his chair and planting his bright green tennis shoes on the desk.

"You can call me Anna, Judge," I said, opening the door and smiling when he nodded. Then I turned and all but ran down the stairs and outside, angling around the park for the police station to find Pierce. It was his job to execute the warrant, but I was going to be involved on this one.

We were close. I could just feel it.

* * *

I SAT in the passenger side of Detective Pierce's car, surrounded by his salty ocean-breeze scent as he parked across the street from Charles' house. My gun was at the back of my waist, while his was strapped to his thigh. His looked way cooler.

Two patrol cars flanked the driveway, which still held Bud's car.

I cranked my head to see. "Where's Bud?"

Pierce peered out the front window. "Not at post." He jumped out of the blue Buick. "Stay here." The door slammed, and he jogged across the road to meet the two uniformed officers. One of them said something into the radio attached to his shoulder, waited, and then shook his head.

My stomach rolled over. Where was Bud? I looked toward the ladies' home, but it was dark with the curtains drawn. They probably wouldn't be home for hours. No movement showed at Melvin's, either.

Pierce made hand gestures like they did on television and then drew his weapon. He went toward the front door and disappeared inside the house while the other two officers headed for the sides, their guns also out.

The curtains at Melvin's rustled, and I turned to see better. He peeked out, caught sight of me, and quickly shoved the material back into place. My heart beat even faster and I shifted my weight, careful to grab my gun if I needed it. The curtains settled and then there was no movement.

Just then, Charles' garage door opened slowly, and Pierce stood over Bud's prone body. The car was gone.

"Bud," I breathed, opening the door and jumping from the car to run across the road and driveway. Oh God. Was he dead? Was it my fault? I reached him, dropping to my knees.

"He's breathing. Just out cold," Pierce said, standing and scouting the area behind me.

Bud lay face up, his body relaxed, his breathing easy. Red marks marred his big neck. I nudged his arm. "Is he wounded?"

"Nope. Looks like he was choked out," Pierce said as one of the uniformed officers came around the side of the house, shaking his head. "Call this in, would you?"

Bud groaned and then flailed, swinging out and rolling to the side. His knuckles caught me on the chin, and I flew back into the wall, my head hitting hard enough that lights flashed behind my closed lids. I grabbed my chin, and tears welled. I forced my eyelids open.

Bud blinked several times and caught sight of me. "Ah, nuts," he muttered.

I wanted to laugh but wasn't sure if he'd broken my jaw or not.

Pierce moved for me and held out a hand. I took it to stand, wobbling only a little. "You okay?" he asked, his gaze narrowing on me.

I released my chin and worked my jaw. It hurt, but nothing cracked. "Yeah. I'm fine." Compared with most of my recent injuries, this was no big deal.

Bud shoved to his feet. "Sorry about that."

Pierce pivoted. "What happened?"

"Dunno." Bud rubbed the back of his neck beneath the buzz cut. "Guy came out of nowhere, from behind, and put me in a hold." He shook his head and then winced. "Knew what he was doing. Strong arm, male, bare."

"No leather jacket?" I asked.

"No," Bud said. "Could've killed me but didn't."

Pierce looked around the empty garage. "Killing a cop carries a much harsher sentence than assault and grand theft." His gaze then pinned me.

I nodded. Yeah. I was fully aware that Aiden had been charged with both at some point. "We did see the Lordes' drive by earlier today." They couldn't have known we were getting a warrant for the car. Although, if they knew about Melvin getting a ride from Charles to the hidden lab, then it wouldn't be too hard to figure out. Especially if the door was suddenly guarded by a uniformed police officer.

Pierce looked around. "All right. With this, we have grounds to search the entire house, closets and all. Everyone put on gloves."

I rubbed my pounding jaw. "I'm going to go take another crack at Charles. Maybe he's better medicated now, or perhaps he'll be happy with me for feeding his dog. Hopefully he'll remember how to get to that lab." Once the hospital released him, something told me I wouldn't be able to find him again.

Pierce nodded. "Bud? Drop her at her vehicle before you go to the hospital, would you?"

"I don't need the hospital," Bud growled.

"Too bad. It's procedure, and you know it. You're off duty until you're cleared." Pierce moved for me, tugging my jacket shut. "I don't have a guy to put on you until next shift. Keep your weapon. Go to the hospital and then home, and I'll send a car out around nine tonight. Tell me you'll just go to those places."

I nodded. Considering the bad guys, most likely the Lordes, had confiscated Charles Monroe's car, I wasn't feeling too vulnerable. Well, any more than usual. Jareth Davey had been close at one point to send that card, but he'd been sending me cards for years. "Got it."

Pierce released me. "We'll have to take a raincheck on the barbecue tonight. Another time?"

"Of course." Was I relieved or bummed I wasn't going on a date with Pierce? I'd have to figure it out later.

He nodded. "Call me if Monroe gives up an address for the hidden lab." He sighed and studied my jaw. "You need to put ice on that."

"I will." For now, I had to get to Charles before visiting hours were over.

CHAPTER 37

*U*nfortunately, Charles had experienced some sort of breakdown and wouldn't see me that afternoon. So I headed back to my car after checking in with Detective Pierce and promising him I was going to try again the next morning, if Charles hadn't been released. Maybe it was a good thing our date had been canceled. Was it a mistake to go out with Pierce? More than likely. It was almost five, so I didn't see a reason to go back to the office. At the moment, all I needed was a hot bath and a stiff drink.

Until Tessa called, saying she and Donna were meeting at Vassallo's for a drink.

I swung a U-Turn in the middle of the street and headed for the ancient bar while reaching for my bag and the concealer in it. After parking, I liberally piled it on along with lip-gloss before walking slowly across the darkened sidewalk and inside the bar in a useless attempt to hide my newest limp.

Vassallo's was at the older end of town and had been there forever. The floor and bottom half of the walls were red shag carpet, and the tables were dingy and wooden. But the food was fantastic and the patrons local. I moved toward a tall table in the back.

"What happened to you now?" Tess asked, reaching over to check my jaw.

"Rough day." I hopped up on the red leather stool and reached for the bowl of peanuts. "What's going on?"

Donna, her dark hair curled around her face, motioned for the waitress and pointed at me. "We're celebrating. I closed on the McGilley place across the lake."

I grinned and then winced as pain shot through my skull in response. "That's awesome." It'd be a fantastic commission. Her brown eyes sparkled, and in her white business suit, she looked all professional and grown up. If I wore a white suit, it'd be brown and bloody and covered in mud by now.

The waitress set a large wine glass in front of me, and Donna poured immediately from the bottle.

I leaned in to read it. Blue Oak Cabernet. Nice. "You're obviously paying," I murmured, taking the glass.

"Obviously," Tessa agreed, shoving her titian hair away from her face. She wore a white shirt and dark jeans, obviously just off work.

My sisters had both found jobs where nobody shot at them. They were definitely smarter than I was, at least at the moment.

"Cheers," Tessa said, holding up her glass.

We cheered, clanked, and then I drank down half of my glass. Man, it was good. Spicy and oaky and delicious. I reached for more peanuts. "What's new?"

Donna tugged the peanuts her way. "Tess has a date with a preacher."

I coughed out a nut and then took a sip of wine. "What?"

Tessa rolled her eyes. "He's a nice guy. A preacher at that nondenominational church out on the prairie. Name is Dan Teskey, and he comes into the restaurant a lot."

Donna snorted. "Tessa and Teskey. Could it get any cuter?"

I tried not to laugh. But a nondenominational church? "We're Catholic." Like seriously Catholic on both sides.

"God and I are tight," Tess returned, stealing the peanut bowl from Donna. "I don't think He'd mind if I dated somebody who preached His word and knew how to drink. This guy drinks Scotch. I like that in a preacher."

It would be nice for the family to worry about Tessa instead of me for a while. "Is he cute?"

"Over six-foot, dark brown hair, really green eyes. He's seriously cute and nice and built like a linebacker." Tess leaned closer. "He brought me flowers when he asked me out."

Now that was just sweet.

She lifted an eyebrow. "You?"

There was a lot to say, but I wasn't ready to share about Aiden. "I did have a date with Detective Pierce to Sheriff Franco's in Silverville tonight, but he got caught at work and had to reschedule."

"Silverville?" Donna breathed, her eyes sparkling. "Oh, dude. That would've been a mistake."

"Did you just say dude?" Tessa snorted. "As funny as that is, she's right. You do not want to go on a date in Silverville. You would have been married by sundown."

I nodded. "I know." Enough about me. "Donna?"

She shrugged. "No date. Dry spell."

"Now that's just a pity." Nick Basanelli suddenly appeared at the table, his shirt sleeves rolled up and his collar loosened. He looked long and lean, and the hard angle of his jaw showed his Italian heritage, as did his dark hair and very bourbon colored eyes. Right now, they surveyed us, sparkling. "Hey, Donna."

"Nick." She grinned and leaned over for a hug. "Good to see you. It's been years. Since graduation?"

He nodded. "Yeah. I've made it home a few times but spent it with family. Well, you know." He said hi to Tessa and then to me. "Mind if I borrow your sister for a moment?"

"Keep her as long as you want," Tessa said, a dimple flashing in her left cheek.

I cut her a look and hopped off the stool, careful to grab my wineglass as I went. I followed him toward a low table near the door, where we sat. "What's up?"

He looked over the bruise on my jaw. "As your boss, I'm making it very clear you are no longer participating in the execution of either search or arrest warrants. Do you understand me?"

I blinked. His throat looked strong and fit above the unbuttoned shirt, and his gaze was direct. "No."

"That's a direct order, Albertini." He rested his fit hands on the table. "Got it?"

"No." I leaned toward him. "That's sexist. You wouldn't give me that order if I weren't a woman."

"Bull." He leaned just as far toward me, leaving only about six inches between our faces. "Man or woman, anybody who ended up bruised and battered like you are right now would be on desk duty. I'm letting you remain on this case because you've worked hard, and well, because I've fired everybody else."

I should just kiss him. Take him off guard for once. "Did my grandmother call you?"

"No. Mine did, but that's irrelevant." He sighed, and his minty breath brushed my face. "This case has gotten too dangerous, and your personal connection to Devlin puts you in the crosshairs. Participating in the execution of warrants isn't normally a part of our job. Finally, you're new at this. It's time to step back."

All of those were good points. Why was I mad? My job was in the courtroom. "You do make sense," I acknowledged.

"Good." He sat back before I did. "We both need time off. Let's forget about this case for a few hours, all right? At least one night without you getting bruised." He moved from the booth and stood, turning to look at me. For several seconds, he stood there, obviously debating something. "Night, Anna." Then he strode out the door, and I'm not ashamed to admit, I watched him go. The guy moved like an athlete.

My phone buzzed just as I was about to stand. "Albertini."

"Where the hell are you?" Detective Pierce snapped.

I winced, and then my temper took over. "None of your business." Who did he think he was?

"I have a man at your cabin, and you're not there. You're supposed to be there," he said. "Did I, or did I not, tell you to go right home after you tried to see Charles the crazy bastard?"

"You know, Pierce?" I stood. "I don't work for you. Frankly, I don't need a police escort. The bad guys got the car and GPS data."

"I still want a guy on you," he said. "Where are you?"

Sighing, I gave him the address and then promised to wait until my escort showed before I left. Then I hung up and grumbled all the way back to my sisters.

"What?" Donna asked.

I reached for the bottle to pour more wine into my glass. "I'm getting really tired of men telling me what to do."

"Amen, sister." Tessa held her glass up.

I did the same and drank. We ordered appetizers, ate, and basically enjoyed just being us. Soon a shadow fell across the table, and I looked up to see Bud. He'd changed into a fresh uniform and appeared all pressed and put together again. With his buzz cut, he looked like a tough guy. "Hey. How's the head?" I asked.

"Fine. All checked out with the doc. I'm on your house tonight." He smiled at Donna and looked like a whole different guy. "I'm Bud Orlov." He held out a hand.

I blinked. "Is that Russian?"

Bud kept his gaze on Donna. "Yes. It means *Eagle*," he said.

I bit back amusement and then introduced him to Tessa, who was clearly trying not to smile.

Donna blushed all pretty and gave him the flirty smile I'd tried for years to learn how to do. I never came close. They made kind of a cute couple, though I didn't know much about Bud.

We finished the bottle and headed out.

I had to admit that knowing Bud was behind me in the police car did provide comfort, considering the world was scary right now. Both of my sisters had offered to stay the night, but it was time for me to be a grownup.

I pulled into my driveway and waited for Bud to park before heading toward my cottage.

A package by the door caught my eye, and I grabbed it, unlocking the door and moving inside. Interesting. The postal guy often left packages, but I didn't remember shopping online lately. Of course, that didn't mean I hadn't. I set the keys in the bowl and turned on lights as I went.

Then I yelped.

Aiden Devlin sprawled on my sofa, his shoes off, his eyes closed. He opened them and that blue was a dark bottom of a riverbed in the height of fall. "Hey."

"What are you doing here?" I looked wildly around. How had he gotten in?

He yawned, looking all mussed with his hair and wrinkled T-shirt over what appeared to be very hard muscles. "Wanted to check on you. So much has been going on."

"There's a cop outside." Why I told him that, I wasn't sure. "I could have you arrested right now for trespass." I faltered, truly not sure what to do.

"You could," he agreed, swinging his legs so he was more sitting than sprawling. "But why would you?"

I licked my lips and tasted wine. "Did you steal Charles Monroe's car today?"

"Nope, but if I did, I wouldn't tell you." His gaze dropped to the package. "What's that?"

I shrugged and turned it over. No return address, and it had been processed in Spokane. Blood rushed through my veins and I set it down, ripping open the sides. Probably a neighbor had left me goodies? The back of a frame showed, and I pulled it out, flipping it over to see the picture. It was the newspaper photograph of Nick and me after the shooting. A folded note had been tucked into the corner.

"What the hell?" Aiden stood and moved for me.

I unfolded the note to read:

Dearest Anna,

This is not appropriate. Please act like a wife. You always have, and I'd hate to change things. XO Your Loving Husband.

Aiden read over my shoulder. "Fuck."

Yeah, that summed it up. I swayed. "He's never contacted me like this. Never even signed a note." The picture with Nick had done it? It was that simple. "I always figured he'd be back, but now?" I looked up at Aiden's concerned gaze. "Of course, you're here now, too."

He shook his head. "Things always come full circle, now don't they?"

I nodded. "Yeah. But they change, too. I'm calling the Silverville sheriff about this and then I'm calling Detective Pierce. You're not going to want to be here, Aiden." I couldn't change the decisions everyone else made in their lives, but I could sure make the right ones for me. But I had something to say first. Words that needed to be expressed. "Thank you for saving me years ago. If I could save you, I would. Until you tell me everything, it's impossible." I faced him as squarely as I could, letting go of any childhood dreams I'd had of him. It was time.

He studied me, looking big and bad and so sexy it hurt to look back. But I did, and I fought the insane urge to jump him and take him down to the ground with a hard kiss.

Then he nodded. "Bye, Angel."

$\mathcal{T}$uesday morning dawned with a crackle of thunder and a zing of lightning. I rolled over in my bed and tucked the pillow over my head. Where had the decent weather gone? Oh, in Idaho we could have rain, snow, hail, sun, and too much heat all in one day. Spring was for volatile weather, so why it was ticking me off was beyond me.

Grunting, I rolled over and tossed the pillow across the room before glancing at the clock. It was only seven. The local cops had been at my house until about midnight, gathering the picture frame and scouting the area for any other signs of a person. They found nothing. I appreciated that Sheriff Franco and Detective Pierce opened an investigation together, using all of the old anniversary and Christmas cards as well as the new evidence. Pierce had even called Nick for an update from his investigators, who hadn't found Davey yet.

Those investigators also hadn't requested my casefile from Franco after saying they were federal investigators. That left Jareth Davey. He'd had the balls to contact Franco and ask for the file. It was the only explanation. That wasn't good.

I'd finally gone to bed with Bud at the front door making me feel all safe. Except, of course, that Aiden had gotten in the night before. I hadn't mentioned that to anybody.

Today I needed to try and talk to Charles again, if he was up to a visit. First, I'd pop by his house and feed his dog again. Maybe if I took a couple of pictures of Snuffles, Charles would talk to me and tell me where that stupid lab was located. I really needed to finish this case.

I showered and dressed in light jeans and a peach-colored sweater before taking a cup of coffee and bagel out to Bud, who was parked beneath the eve of the garage. "Why are you still here?"

"I'm off duty at ten," he said, his face lighting up at the coffee. "Thanks."

"Sure." I handed over the bagel and told him my plan of hitting Charles' house and then the hospital. "After that, I'll just be at the office for the rest of the day."

"Good." Bud leaned back and stretched his neck. "I could use a break." Then he took a couple more drinks of the pumpkin flavored brew. His gaze tracked the area around the garage. "Is your sister Donna single?"

"Yep." I turned for my car. "You can ask me questions at Monroe's place." I had plenty of questions to ask him if he wanted to date Donna. While he seemed like a pretty nice guy, that didn't mean he was, although Donna had appeared interested, and she had far better taste in men than either Tessa or I did. For sure.

I kept the top on the car out of respect for the darn storm waging around me, driving toward the retirement community. Once I parked in Charles' driveway, I dashed inside with Bud on my heels. "Why are you coming?" I asked.

"Last time I was here I got attacked. Let me clear the house." He did so with Snuffles jumping around him, trying to get attention. "All good."

I let the dog out back and replenished his food and water before taking several pictures of the pooch. Maybe those would appease Charles. "All right. Let's go." I led the way outside after locking the door. The rain continued to fall, while the wind had increased in force and blew my hair back. When would summer arrive? I walked along the house to the driveway, where I stopped short.

Pauley was jumping out of a tall red truck in Melvin's driveway, his notebook in his hands.

"Pauley?" I called. Wait a minute. Pierce had ordered a uniform to watch him until he went to the library this morning. Right now, Pauley was supposed to be safe at the college before his mom drove him over the hill to take some pictures of the river this afternoon. What was he doing there? I turned to yell for Bud just as he walked down the stairs.

A man wearing a Lorde's cut came around the side of Charles' house, firing a big black gun three times toward Bud's back. The sound was deafening. Bud's eyes widened, and he flew face first into the hydrangeas, landing hard and not moving. "Bud!" I moved for him, flattening my hand over his lower back.

Something hard. Oh. Bullet proof vest? Was he alive?

"Get up." The guy pointed his gun at me. I squinted, trying to breathe, my chest hurting. I stood and turned to face him, blinking through the rain. The man was vaguely familiar. He'd been one of the guys in the Lordes' garage the other day when we'd executed the warrant. Then he gestured toward the driveway.

I took one last look at Bud and then walked around the house. God, I hoped Aiden was in that truck. Pauley stood on the other side, his gaze darting around, his head bobbing.

Spider stepped out of the driver's side. "What is going on?"

Panic tried to grab me, and I sucked deep to stay calm. I searched the back of the truck. Nope. No Aiden.

The guy behind me nudged me in the ribs. "I saw the cop car and investigated. Had to shoot him." He prodded me across the grass and over to Thelma and Georgiana's half of the driveway toward the truck. "Look who I found."

Spider's eyes widened. "You shot a cop? Are you crazy?"

"Didn't have a choice."

"Unbelievable." Spider snarled, his gold tooth gleaming as he took out his phone and pressed it to his ear. "Devlin? We have a problem. You can return to base. I've got your girl."

Devlin? I frowned.

Spider nodded. "Yep. He was on the way to fetch you, anyway. It was nice of you to make this convenient."

"Why?" I asked, trying to look for a way around him.

"Oh, we'll talk about that inside," Spider muttered. Then he ran a hand through his dark hair. "Shit, Grease. You shot a cop?"

I coughed, trying to get Pauley's attention. His gaze remained fixed on the hood of the truck.

"The cop didn't see him—or you." I said. How could I get Pauley out of there?

"But you've seen me," the guy behind me said, shoving the gun between my ribs.

I reacted then. Exactly as I'd learned in my one self-defense class last year. Pivoting, I pushed the gun away from my body and grabbed it, bringing my knee up as hard as I could to the guy's groin. He howled and bent over. I stepped back with the gun and turned to point it at Spider.

Melvin Whitaker stood at the edge of the sidewalk to his house with a shotgun pointed at my cousin's head. My entire body jolted, and my chest expanded in a need to fight or flee.

"Nice move," Spider said, appraisal in his gaze.

"My cousin. She is my cousin. She can kick. Used to play kick-ball at the river." Pauley's eyes widened, and he rocked in place again. "My cousin kicks. My cousin. She is my cousin."

"It's okay, Pauley," I said, lowering the gun. He wasn't even looking toward Melvin. "There has to be a decent way out of this mess."

Thelma's garage door started to open. I turned, but the guy behind me grabbed me fast, his hand slapping over my mouth and his arm banding around my waist. He carried me to the other side of the truck, near Pauley, and Spider joined us, yanking the gun out of my hand.

This could not be happening. I eyed Melvin sideways, and his hands stayed steady on his weapon. He slowly backed toward his house so the elderly ladies couldn't see him.

Thelma came out first, carrying a stack of plastic paper. "I tell you; they don't use enough of this stuff to protect the plants. This storm is gonna kill them. For what we pay, we shouldn't have to take care of the garden, too." Her hair was in a high ponytail, and she wore bright red shorts with a polka dot shirt beneath a see-through rain slicker. Her rain boots were a muted tan, oddly enough.

"I agree, but you do like to garden," Georgiana said soothingly, her head protected from the rain with a large bucket hat. She walked behind Thelma, holding a bag of what looked like garden tools.

Both women turned toward us in unison.

Thelma paused. "Anna?" She looked at the three men with me on the other side of the truck. "Are you having a party at Melvin's?"

Georgiana looked us all over and then took a step back. "Yeah. Looks like a fun party. Singing in the rain and all of that." Her voice shook just enough. "I'll go get everyone some hot chocolate. It's getting cold."

"Freeze." Spider lifted his gun to point at the ladies. "Now walk over here."

Thelma looked toward her friend and then gulped loudly. "I don't understand. Is this about the pot?"

"Interfering women." Melvin stomped down the stairs, his bony knees shaking beneath his denim shorts. Rain poured down his face. "If you hadn't tried to get into my house, we wouldn't be in this mess."

"Probably not true," I whispered. "But we are in this mess. How about we all just go our separate ways?"

"Can't." Spider gestured toward the elderly ladies. "Get in the backseat of the truck. Right now."

My knees started to shake. They'd shot a cop. Maybe killed him. They wouldn't want to leave witnesses. Our only chance was for one of us to get free.

As if he'd read my mind, Spider pressed the gun barrel right above my ear. "Pauley? Get in the rear seat from this side, or I'll shoot your cousin in the head."

"But, but, but. I'm here to do math. Not go. Not go. Here to do math." Pauley's voice rose. He didn't like getting wet, and I was surprised he was managing to stay so calm.

Melvin turned his gun toward Pauley.

"No," I said, my voice high. I cleared it. "Pauley? You're here to do math. Let's get in the truck, out of the rain, and we can do math somewhere else. It doesn't have to be here."

Pauley looked up and saw the gun at my head. He ducked his and then walked around us to get in the truck. "Do not shoot my cousin."

Spider shoved me across the front bench seat. "Any of you move back there, and I shoot her." He jumped in beside me and rolled down the window. "Whitaker? Get your ass in the backseat of the truck. We have to figure out a better route system before we distribute later today." He glanced over his shoulder. "Pauley will do more math for us."

"Let Anna go," Pauley said, kicking the back of the seat. "Let go. Anna go. Going is good. Birds go. Let Anna go."

Melvin hesitated. "I need to check on the lab. Haven't heard from my techs, and there was a power outage last night. We don't want to lose any product."

A power outage in the secret lab? Where had power outages been in town? Or in the county? I had to find out.

Spider shook his head. "Now, Whitaker. We'll worry about your lab later."

Melvin gave him a look and then walked around the other side to sit next to Thelma, his shotgun now pointed at the floor.

"No. My cousin goes. Now. No," Pauley continued his litany, rocking back and forth.

"I'm okay, P," I lied, considering Spider now had the gun in my ribs. Grease opened the driver's door, sat, and ignited the engine. My gaze darted around the quiet subdivision. How was it possible to kidnap four people without anybody seeing? There was nobody in sight. Just stubborn rain, perfectly manicured lawns, and a lot of bright flowers getting really wet.

That quickly, we drove out of the retirement community and onto the road, heading toward I-90. "Where are you taking us?" I asked, my voice shaking. I needed to throw up.

"We don't have a lot of choices here," Grease said, pressing harder on the gas pedal.

"You're a fucking idiot," Spider muttered. "Shooting a cop."

Grease hunched his shoulders. "I didn't have a choice."

"Yeah, you did," I countered. Could I get these two fighting? There had to be a way to save Pauley and the women. Thelma cried softly in the backseat, while Georgiana remained silent, eyeing the doors. Good. She'd be ready to go if I made a move.

Pauley kicked my seat, his body hunched over, his gaze on his notebook.

We drove onto I-90 toward Washington state, and my hope of anybody seeing us leave disappeared. We were on our own.

CHAPTER 39

$\mathcal{I}$ was a little relieved when Grease took the exit nearest the border and wound through the residential area toward the Lorde's apartment complex, remaining in Idaho. At least they weren't taking us out in the woods somewhere to shoot. Yet. For now, they seemed to need Pauley. "I saw your map," I said to Spider. "How are you transporting the drugs?"

"You talk too much." He shoved the gun harder into my ribs.

I lowered my voice. "You can't seriously be considering hurting Pauley and these two nice ladies." It was unthinkable.

"I've done worse," he said, his voice grim. "So has your boyfriend."

Aiden wouldn't hurt me. It went against everything I knew about his pathology. Spider, on the other hand, obviously had no problem with the idea.

We pulled into the parking area of the complex, which was deserted in the heavy rain. The garage doors were closed.

"We should do this somewhere else," Grease said. "Away from our base."

Icicles pricked up along my skin, and I trembled. He was serious. I started to panic when the sound of motorcycle pipes echoed

281

against the building. Aiden roared up, swinging his bike around to park. He strode for the truck and yanked open the driver's door, grabbing Grease by the neckline and jerking him from the truck. "What did you do?" he growled.

Grease swung out, and Aiden caught his fist with one hand, the sound harsh, even over the loud purring of the truck engine.

I gulped.

Rain matted Aiden's wet hair to his head, and his eyes blazed an avenging blue. In his leather cut, with the storm waging around him, he looked furious. Hell, he *was* furious. "Get out, Whitaker."

Melvin audibly gulped and stepped out of the truck; the shotgun pointed down but still looking deadly. "I don't want any part of this. I'm a chemist. That's all. I'm not a murderer."

"Shut that door," Aiden ordered.

Whitaker obeyed, his beady gaze darting all around.

Spider opened his door and dragged me out, keeping the gun to my side. "Devlin? "We have to talk about this."

In a move that was as fast as it was shocking, Aiden pulled a gun from the back of his waist and smashed the butt against Grease's temple. Grease's eyelids actually fluttered shut, and he dropped to the ground with a harsh thud. Aiden turned and kicked the shotgun out of Melvin's hands, and it clipped across the wet cement and under the truck.

Man, he was fast.

He then slammed the driver's door, lifted his gun and pointed it at Spider, walking around the front of the truck with an animal's grace.

Spider backed away from the truck, pulling me with him.

Keeping us in his sights, Aiden kicked the passenger door closed. "Ladies? Get Pauley and yourselves out of here," he ordered, over the pounding rain.

Georgiana launched into motion, diving over the front seat and scrambling, arms and legs flying, for the driver's seat. She punched the gas, and the truck roared down the drive toward safety.

Spider started to remove the gun from my side. No doubt about to shoot at the truck.

Aiden tensed, and Spider stopped. Melvin hovered in place, rain soaking through his thin clothing.

"What the hell are you doing, Devlin?" Spider bellowed.

Aiden shook his head. "Not letting you kill a kid and two old ladies. Are you crazy?"

"It's too late. Grease killed a cop." Spider had a strong hold on my arm, and I tried to control my mind enough to think of the right move. My body shook, from cold and fear, and my legs felt frozen. Pauley and the ladies were safe, and they'd call for help as soon as possible. So I had to think.

Spider coughed. "You're in this deep, Devlin." He partially turned toward me, keeping Aiden in sight. "Aiden here is the one who stole Charles Monroe's car the other day. After choking out your cop buddy."

I blinked in the rain. Aiden had choked out Bud? My legs wanted to give out.

Aiden's expression didn't change. "I didn't kill him, now did I? You moron."

Spider's lips peeled back. "I knew you weren't a true brother. Look at you. Choosing a woman over your brothers. What really happened with the Diablo Riders?"

"Choosing *my* woman. I told you I would," Aiden countered, his voice a low growl. "I told you to leave her alone and we'd be fine."

His woman. He couldn't mean that. What was going on? None of this was making sense, unless it really was that simple. Aiden was a bad guy who just couldn't let me get hurt. Had that moment in time, the one he'd talked about, shaped him as much as me? Maybe so. I cleared my throat. "Just let me go. Neither of you want a prosecutor's death on your hands. That leads directly to the death penalty."

"Oh, we're already there," Spider snapped. "Or did you forget about Scot Peterson?"

My stomach cramped. "You killed Scot?"

"Yeah. The asshole was having second thoughts about the deal, even though his retirement fund sucked, and I think he was planning to talk. So I took care of him." Spider glared at Aiden. "I also found and burned his trial notebook on you, dickhead, which slowed your case down considerably."

Aiden shook his head. "I didn't ask for your help."

The center apartment door burst open, and a man rushed out, shooting an automatic weapon at us. Spider jumped and turned, lifting the gun from my ribs.

I smashed his hand and punched his face, turning to run. The gun dropped to the ground.

Aiden grabbed my arm and Melvin's hair, running full bore for the far side of the garage. Spider ducked out of the way, reaching for his gun and running the opposite way.

We reached the garage and Aiden threw Melvin against the metal siding. I slid down, my hands shaking. "Anybody hit?"

"He wasn't aiming to harm," Aiden said grimly, crouching near the edge. "Hit the cement. Obviously not sure who to shoot."

Yelling voices echoed through the rain.

"Now they know who to shoot." I wiped rain off my head.

"No shit." Aiden angled around the corner, and bullets pinged up from the cement. "Keep low." He knocked the back of his head against the siding. Then he took a deep breath, pivoted, and fired several times. A cry of pain rippled through the morning.

"How many are there?" I asked, gulping as Melvin shivered next to me.

"Too many." Aiden looked down at me. "Your only chance is to run for the woods. I'll keep them busy while you get free."

I tried to concentrate, but my mind was fuzzy with fear. Or

adrenaline. If I left him, he'd die. I looked frantically around. "There has to be another gun around here."

Aiden reached in his boot and drew out a nine-millimeter. "Here. Take this and go."

A Lorde's member slid around the back side of the garage, gun out. I reacted instantly, lifting the gun and squeezing the trigger. The bullets hit him in the shoulder and the leg, and he went down with a harsh cry.

Melvin shook wildly next to me and buried his face in his hands. "I'm just a chemist. That's all."

Aiden leaned his head back, his body one long line of tension. "You know how to shoot?"

I breathed out, trying to keep in the moment and not freak out. "I've been stalked by a psychopath most of my life. Yeah. I know how to shoot."

His grin was short and unexpected. "Should've guessed that." Then he turned and fired rapidly.

"We're outnumbered," I hissed. "Should we run for the woods?"

"Yes." Melvin levered up.

In that moment, I decided to do my job. Kind of. Well, not really. I pointed the gun at Melvin's forehead. "Where's the lab, asshole?"

Melvin blinked rapidly. "Kill me, and you'll never find it. My people have orders to destroy the entire facility if I don't show back up." He tried to cringe away from the gun, but I kept it pressed against his skin. "Go ahead. Kill me and you'll never find any of it."

I blinked at looked at Aiden. "Do you know where his lab is?"

Aiden shook his head. "No clue."

Did I believe him?

A body came around the back again, and Aiden pivoted, shooting quickly.

More shots volleyed from the other side.

"We have to run," I said, grabbing his arm, keeping my weapon up and ready to shoot.

Something crashed through the woods.

"You'll never make it," Melvin said, blowing out a snot bubble. "You've turned against your club, Devlin. They're going to kill you. Keep me alive, get us out of here together, and I'll cut you in on the rest of the drugs. I'll take you right to my hidden lab, now that the power is back on."

A helicopter suddenly careened into place above us, and the sound of sirens pummeled off the mountains. Hope filled me. "Thelma, Georgina, and Pauley got to help."

A motorcycle roared to life on the other side of the garage.

Aiden stood, angling to the side. "There's a back road. Spider is on the run."

Red and blue swirled through the misty rain.

Melvin bunched his legs to run, and Aiden grabbed him by the neck and threw him face first into the metal wall. Blood spurted in a dark arc. Melvin slumped to the ground, not moving.

"He'll be okay," Aiden said, looking around. "It's fine. Point your gun down now."

"I have to know, Aiden," I said, letting the rain pummel me at this point. "Why did you do this? Why save me?"

He scouted the area, his gaze alert. "I promised you I wouldn't let anything happen to you. Asked you to trust me. That matters, Angel."

His words warmed my chilled body, but what the hell? I mean, just what the hell? Why did he have to be a criminal? There was a good guy in there. "Come in with me. Let me find you a deal. You just saved me, and we can use that." I was almost pleading, but who cared?

He flicked his head, and rain sprayed off his thick hair. "It's too late for that."

Guys with guns came out of the forest in several directions, all wearing combat gear and carrying heavy weapons. God. They wouldn't shoot Aiden, would they? I tried to angle slightly in front of him, and he shoved me to the side, covering me with his body. My strength was no match with his. Not even close. His muscles vibrated down his back and side.

"Don't do anything stupid," I warned him. Seeing him get shot would destroy me.

The oncoming force wore jackets ranging from DEA to ATF to FBI. The local cops came from the front, their sirens so loud I winced. There was a quick skirmish on the other side of the garage, but soon the gunfire abated.

How had this force been amassed so quickly? Even if the ladies had found a phone right away, there was no way. "What is going on?" I asked.

One guy with a buzzcut and scarred jaw, wearing a DEA jacket, headed our way from behind a tree, and I set my gun down. My hand trembled so hard, I was afraid for a second that I'd accidentally squeeze the trigger. He led with his weapon, pointing it to each side as he scouted the area and kept advancing. The agent reached us, looking us over, face to face with Aiden at about the same tall height.

I tensed. "Don't hurt him. He saved me."

The DEA agent didn't twitch. He glanced down at the unconscious Melvin on the ground and then focused back up at Aiden.

Aiden dropped his gun and lifted his hands.

Thank God. He was giving up peacefully. Just as my breath finally calmed, he pivoted and punched the DEA guy so hard it sounded like a boulder had been split in two.

"Aiden!" I cried out.

The agent went down, and Aiden leaped over him, running full bore for the trees. "No," the agent grunted, rolling onto his stomach and firing toward the forest. His bullets pinged off trees and threw bark in the air. He kept shooting, but Aiden was long gone. I'd never seen anybody move as quickly as Aiden just had.

Had that just happened?

CHAPTER 40

I paced the conference room at the police station as Nick watched impassively. "I just don't understand. Any of it." After spending most of the day being questioned by every federal agency in the world, and then the state agencies, my head hurt, and my bruises pounded. "Aiden saved me. Then he hit that DEA agent." I stopped moving. "Did you make the phone call?

Nick eyed the wall screen of areas that had experienced the power outage the other night. "Yep. Called my contacts at the DEA, and Aiden Devlin does not work for them in any capacity. He's not an undercover agent, and he's not an informant. Get that idea out of your head right now."

He'd moved like he'd been trained, and he'd saved me. Aiden had also been careful not to really hurt any of the agents or any of the Lordes, for that matter. "That's disappointing, but something still doesn't feel right about this." I scrubbed both hands down my battered face, which had to look just fantastic after the day in the rain and then questioning. Maybe I should find some lip-gloss or something. "I heard the agent has a broken jaw?"

"No. Just cracked." Nick rolled his neck. "I checked on him when I called about Bud."

Bud had been wearing a vest, and all three bullets had impacted it. He had two broken ribs, and the doctors said he'd be okay, thank goodness.

"The question is, where has Aiden gone now?" I murmured, staring at the board.

"No. The question is, where is the hidden lab and the first shipment of these drugs?" Nick shook his head. "Forget Devlin for now. We have bigger problems."

Yeah, we surely did.

"Now run me through the entire day again," he ordered.

I glanced at my phone. Pauley was safely at home up in Silverville, and the elderly ladies had taken off to spend time in Seattle with friends after being questioned by the cops. I liked that everyone was out of town for now.

Detective Pierce crossed into the room and typed rapidly on the laptop, changing the screen to show an area out by the Timber City Airport, which was a small community strip for local planes. "I went off what you said about electrical outages, and only a small part of the county had that problem on the day Melvin complained about. I think we've found the lab." He pointed to a large metal building two blocks away from the airport that looked like a standard metal shop. "I'm running the electrical and gas usages now."

I stood. "Let's go check it out."

He looked over his shoulder, his eyes greener than normal. "We need a warrant. And then, I'm executing the warrant. You can check the place out after it's been cleared."

Irritation tickled my throat, and I coughed. "We're going."

"No. No lawyers when we take the lab. These guys are creating drugs and are probably well guarded and armed." He looked at Nick. "I'll call you in when it's cleared, and you can study the scene all you want."

Nick stood. "Fair enough. I'll get a warrant."

I hustled after him. "I'm assisting on the warrant." I brushed past cops in the hallway to the still raining dusk outside. Water splashed into my eyes and cooled my burning cheekbone. "Nick?"

"Haven't you had enough pain?" He ducked his head against the rain and increased his steps, almost jogging until reaching our offices. "You've been attacked, shot at, and now kidnapped." He unlocked the door and held it open for me.

I walked into the quiet interior and turned to face him, having to look up. Way up. I shook the water from my hair, spraying us both. "I'm in this, and I'm not going away. It's my decision."

His light brown gaze wandered over my battered face. Standing there in his dark T-shirt and even darker jeans, he looked solid. Kind of pissed. But definitely strong. "You're right. It is your decision."

Triumph filled me. I liked that about him. A lot.

We quickly drafted a search warrant with the accompanying affidavit from me about the kidnapping and discussion with Melvin about his lab losing electricity. I read it over again. "This is weak. Whitaker's statement about lost power doesn't tie to this one building out of the rest of the buildings." We needed something more.

Nick leaned over my shoulder to read the screen, his scent of smoky wood filtering around. It was comforting and something more. "I'd rather not make a deal with Melvin, if we can help it. Let's get to this place without his cooperation."

I swallowed and printed it out. "Judge Hallenback," I sighed. "We kind of suck."

Nick took the papers. "We surely do. I'll drive."

I had no problem with that. We finished the paperwork and ran back outside. The clouds had turned even darker and the rain more insistent as dinnertime passed. I dodged into his car and sighed in relief, watching him start the engine and drive. Nick had pushed his shirt sleeves up. The rhythmic sound of the windshield wipers added an intimacy to the warm car.

He followed Main Street toward the historic section. "Did Pierce ever ask you out?"

I peered out at the empty sidewalks. "Sheriff Franco in Silverville had a barbecue that we were supposed to attend, but work got in the way."

"Cops and lawyers. Never a good combination," Nick mused.

I didn't feel like reminding him that he'd kissed me. Obviously, he knew that. I sure as heck wasn't going to tell him that I'd slept with Aiden. "Jealous?" I tried to lighten the mood.

"A little." He drove quickly, heading back toward the west end of the lake and the historic homes. We reached the gate on the private drive, and he pressed a button.

"What do you want? It's after dinnertime," Judge Hallenback mumbled.

"It's Nick Basanelli. I need a warrant signed," Nick said.

I looked at the beach on the other side of the road. Whitecaps tossed waves toward the sand, which was being pelted by the rain as night strengthened and banished the day. Nobody was around for miles.

The buzzer rang and the fence lifted.

Nick drove past the other three silent mansions to the Judge's. "I hate taking advantage of him like this, but..."

I nodded. "I get it. I really do." Then I jumped from the vehicle and jogged to the safety of the porch to ring the old-fashioned bell.

The judge opened the door wearing a Hawaiian shirt, grass skirt, and combat boots. "Morning, Alberto."

I blinked. "Evening," I murmured. "I mean, good evening."

He scrunched up his gray eyebrows. "What happened to your face? It looks even worse than the other day."

"Long story. Part of it is in the affidavit," Nick said, handing over the papers and not looking at the judge's hairy legs. "We need a search warrant for a building we think is being used as a drug lab, Judge."

"Hmm." The judge gestured us inside, where it was about a thousand degrees. He led the way to a darkened study with Cherrywood desk, walls, and ceiling. He skipped around the wide desk to an executive style leather chair, reading the papers. Finally, he looked up. "You don't have enough here. An off the cuff statement about power, which could be anywhere, doesn't lead to this one building. You need a better connection in order to search it. People have privacy rights, you know."

My hopes plummeted. Worse yet, I knew he was right. "Judge? We have to get out there before these drugs are put on the street."

The judge looked over my shoulder. "Tell me the police are watching this building and waiting for a warrant."

"Of course," Nick said. "DEA, FBI, State, and even the ATF. We've got the place covered."

"Then get a proper warrant." The judge shoved the papers across the desk. "You don't want this whole thing thrown out of court or later overturned on appeal, do you?"

I sighed. The guy had probably been a pretty good judge before his brain had started to slip. Maybe there were medications he could take to regain his faculties.

Nick took his phone from his pocket. "Excuse me, Judge." He wandered toward the door. "Hey, Pierce. No warrant for this particular building." He explained the circumstances and then listened for a minute. "What do they have? You think? Okay. We'll be right there." He clicked off and turned toward me.

I was already shaking my head. "No. We can't give Melvin a deal." The guy had created opioids that could make the meth epidemic look like a minor societal inconvenience.

Nick's eye gleamed. "A couple of the biker bunnies are talking. Want deals. One will have three strikes from burglary and prostitution charges. It appears she's been to the hidden lab with Whitaker."

My breath caught. "She can lead us to the lab? She's seen it?"

"Looks like it. I just need to make her a deal," Nick said. "She wants it in writing."

The judge reared up. "Then get it in writing and acquire her affidavit to support the search warrant. With the cops on the property, they aren't going anywhere. Let's do this right." He rolled his hips, and his skirt danced. "Alberto? We need to flesh out your affidavit, as well. You need more evidence as to what Melvin Whitaker said, what you heard, and better details about the kidnapping."

I winced. We had tried to hurry it along.

The judge pounced on his keyboard. "I can't write it for you, but you can dictate. And then you sign it and so will I." His eyes got a faraway look. "I'd like to end a major drug operation while I still, you know, can." He started typing. "It'd be a nice way to go out."

Nick paused by the door. "Anna? Maybe you should come with me?"

"Oh." The judge's face fell. "Well, okay." He looked around the large and very quiet room. "You can redo the affidavit at your office and then come back. I have some good floral tea from Hawaii." He glanced down at his grass skirt as if surprised.

I faltered. We had tried to take advantage of him. "We're under a bit of a time crunch." The lab might lead us to the one shipment that had been let loose. Who knew how big it was? "The Judge and I will fix this affidavit while you get the deal and information from the bunny. You should only be an hour or so, Nick." Maybe I could talk the judge into getting some help.

Nick shook his head. "No. Devlin and that Spider are still out there."

I snorted. "Come on. Nobody followed us down this private, one-way street." I cocked my head and mouthed to him, 'I'm armed.' My gun was right back where it should be at my waist and beneath my jacket.

Nick's eyebrows lifted. "Well, all right then."

The judge danced toward Nick and the door. "If it makes you feel better, I'll engage the alarm." He pointed to what looked like a brand-new faceplate with numbers and pretty colors.

Nick nodded. "I'd appreciate that. I'll be back quickly." He opened the door and walked onto the porch, heading into the storm.

The judge shut and locked the door before engaging the alarm. He turned around and smiled through his dentures. "I'll get us some tea before we work on the affidavit." Humming, he walked out of sight and down a long hallway. "It has been a while since I worked on an affidavit other than signing one," he called out. "This might even be fun."

It seemed like the guy was really lonely. Maybe I should introduce Thelma to him. Or Georgiana. I looked around the impressive office. His diplomas, bar certificates, and judgeship certificates had been framed and hung in free areas on the walls. Law books squeezed out more law books, all looking well read.

I moved for a table by the corner that held more books along with a few framed pictures. The first was of the judge holding his diploma with a couple of older people smiling behind him. His hair had been dark brown, and he'd looked young and energetic. The next picture was of him with a very pretty blonde woman, captured probably in the early seventies, if the clothes were to be taken seriously.

A framed photo of four boys at the lake caught my eye. I pulled it out, looking them over. The judge had to have been around ten years old with scrawny arms and wild hair. He had his arm around a kid who looked like him. I brought it closer. It was Sal. His brother.

I grinned. They'd been all knees and elbows.

The kid on the far right caught my attention. He looked familiar. Hey. "Scot," I murmured. I'd seen pictures of him from summer camp in his office just a month before. The blood roared through my ears, pounding between my temples as I studied the fourth kid.

That nose was unmistakable. It was Melvin Whitaker.

I dropped the frame and turned to see Judge Hallenback at the doorway with a gun pointed at me. He'd changed into black pants beneath his Hawaiian shirt. His hold was imposingly steady on the weapon. He cleared his throat. "So. I'm not really crazy."

CHAPTER 41

I backed away until my butt hit his desk. "Judge." Wait a minute. The wind howled outside, and I shivered. "You knew each other as kids." Then it hit me. Right between the eyes. I slapped my forehead. "The car dealership. Those odd cities circled on the map are car auction cities."

He nodded. "I thought you were smart from the first time you stepped into my courtroom."

Once. I'd only been in his courtroom once. "I thought you were nuts."

He lifted a shoulder. "Yeah, that was the plan. Just in case."

"Okay." Why was it so hot in there? Sweat rolled down my back and pooled near my gun. "Melvin manufactures Beast, Scot was supposed to keep the law off you guys, Hallenback's Used Cars distributes the drug with cars at auctions, and the Lorde's do what? Deal?"

"They helped finance and have the connections to the dealers in various cities once we get the drugs there." The judge shrugged. "It's a good drug. Pain killer. Opioid made at home from yeast. Melvin has always been a genius and they were just taking advantage of him at that seed company. He was meant to do great things."

"Like start a new drug epidemic?" I tried to look scared, which wasn't hard because my knees were trembling.

"Yeah, well, nobody is perfect." The judge flashed his dentures again. "Melvin was a moron for bringing samples of pot home with him, and his even dumber nephew tried to deal that. Jackass."

"Did you kill them?" I whispered.

"No. I'm not a killer." He glanced down at the semi-automatic in his hand. "At least, I haven't been. Do what I say, and I won't have to kill you."

My stomach rolled over.

He reached for a phone on the table and dialed. "Hey. Guess who I have?" He leaned away from the phone. "We have men out looking for you, and you came right to me. Spider thought we'd have to take you from the cops, and he was geared up to do it."

"Most of Spider's gang is in custody," I retorted.

"Not all," the judge said, returning to his phone call. "All right. I'll bring her." Then he clicked off and widened his stance. "Take the gun out of your waist with two fingers and set it on the desk. I'll shoot you in the arm if I have to, and believe me when I say that I'm a crack shot."

I did believe him. He had the trophies in the corner to prove it. I gingerly removed my gun and put it on the desk, keeping him in my sights.

"Good. Now walk this way." He motioned with the gun. "Don't try anything."

Like what? I moved for him, waiting for an opening. He motioned me ahead of him down the hallway and through the fifties-styles kitchen to a garage, where he had me flip on the light. An older Chrysler waited.

"How can you be all right with Spider having killed Scot?" I asked. "You and Scot go way back."

The judge sighed. "I know, but Scot had second thoughts, and he was going to turn us in."

I looked at the car. Okay. He couldn't drive and keep that gun on me the whole time. If he made me drive, I'd smash into the nearest building when we got close to town.

He reached for a set of keys on a hook and pushed a button. The trunk opened.

"No way." I started to back away, and he lifted the gun barrel to the center of my forehead.

"Get in the car," he said. "We want you alive, so you should probably cooperate. I'd hate to kill you. I really would."

The car was older and didn't have the safety features of new cars. I wouldn't be able to kick out the lights. My legs wobbling, I moved for the trunk. He shoved me hard in the back, and I fell inside, scrambling for purchase. The lid came crashing down, and I screamed, rolling into a ball to keep from getting hit with it. The sound echoed all around, and darkness surrounded me.

I kicked and punched the sides, trying to knock out the lights. Nothing. The old car was solid. And quiet. I lost track of the time as I lay in the dark, trying to hit different points to get free. Even punching what was probably the back seat didn't help. Where was the judge?

Finally, the car roared to life. I froze. Completely.

Then we were driving.

I LOST count of how many bumps the judge hit driving, finally curling into a ball to keep from bouncing off the trunk's lid and sides. He truly sucked as a driver. The car smelled like old golf socks. I tried to pay attention to twists and turns and pauses, but my ears rang, and my entire body hurt. Where had he been while I'd been locked in the trunk?

And where were we going?

It didn't make sense that he wanted me alive. No way would the DEA give him the drugs from the lab in exchange for me. He had to know that. So why?

Finally, he slowed, and the sound of the rain increased in pitch. He drove up something, and then...silence.

I could do this. It might be my only chance. I rolled to my knees to charge when he opened the trunk. Heavy footsteps sounded, and then the trunk opened. Light flashed into my eyes, and I shut them, attacking with fists and fingernails. I hit him beneath the jaw, and we went down.

My elbow smacked concrete, and I cried out, trying to scissor my legs around his waist.

"Damn it." Fingers leeched into my hair and dragged me off him. "Quit it." Spider yanked me to my feet.

I kicked his knee hard and punched for his soft gut, impacting surprising muscles.

"Stop." He twisted and backhanded me so hard I fell to the ground. Pain exploded in my cheekbone. My good one. I leaped up, and the cocking of a gun stopped me. I turned, panting, to see Sal Hallenback in a greasy T-shirt and overalls holding a silver pistol pointed at me.

Spider grunted and half-bent over, catching his breath.

I swiveled, my hair still a wild and wet mess. We were in a well-lit empty metal shop with a couple of cars parked at the far side. One of several garage doors was open to a lot containing a few scattered wrecked vehicles. "Where are we?" I huffed.

"Storage garage outside of town," the judge said, slamming the trunk door closed. "We keep some of the wrecked vehicles here for parts if we need them."

Great. There was nobody near to hear me scream. He didn't need to say it.

Spider straightened, murder in his eyes. "I get ten minutes with this bitch before we end her."

"Original," I muttered. What a moron. "You'd better hope he

doesn't drop that gun," I threatened. Boy, would I love five minutes and a chance to kick his balls through his temples. Adrenaline left a bitter taste in my mouth while fear heightened my senses.

Spider shoved me, and I fell against the car, my ribs smashing into the trunk. Agony slashed deep inside me. I gasped and slid to the ground, my eyes wide.

"Stay down there," he hissed.

I sat, putting my back to the car and hugging my knees to my chest. Everything hurt. There wasn't a good option between Sal with the gun, Spider with the fists, and the judge with the sharp eyes. But he was my best bet. My only option. "Judge? You know the lab is blanketed by cops. The techs there, the workers there, the drugs there…are all out of your reach." It hurt to breathe. "Melvin Whitaker is probably giving up all three of you right this second."

"No. He won't give me up." The judge stood right inside the garage and out of the rain, which splashed across his boots. "I'm his best chance of getting out of the system."

Only if he didn't get caught with me. I felt the heat slide out of my face. Panic tried to grab me, and I dug deep. There had to be a way to reach him with the law. "You kidnapped me. If I'm dead, you'll be charged with murder. This is bad enough."

"I wrecked my place but good. Looks like we gave up quite the fight." The judge's chin lifted, and he looked almost regal.

It would appear like we both had been kidnapped.

I wiped blood off my cheek that I hadn't realized was there. Had Spider cut me? That jerk. "You haven't killed anybody. Your only option is to let me go."

Spider chuckled, and his beard moved. "I have killed people, so it's too late for me."

I struggled to breathe out without wincing. "You've killed a lot lately. Randy and Cheryl." At the thought of those two young kids being murdered, anger took me. Along with a healthy dose of fear.

"Didn't have a choice," he muttered, not looking sorry in the least.

"What about the two guys from the van? The ones horning in on your drug business?" It was obvious now why he'd killed them.

"Don't forget that they tried to hurt you. Said they made you climb a tree." Spider looked down, a smirk darkening his face. "I shot them for you, and yeah, you owe me. You're gonna pay me back real good."

"Not a chance," I spit out.

Spider pulled a gun out from behind his waist. "You know what I don't get? How did Devlin get free the other day? As well as from the Diablo raid years ago?" He shook his head.

I'd been wondering the same thing. Plus, during the gunfight, Aiden moved like every trained guy I'd ever seen. Sure, he could've trained on the streets, but it hadn't seemed that way. Not at all. Also, he'd taken out a trained DEA agent with one punch.

Spider twirled his gun in one hand. "I think he's a snitch. An informant."

"Based on what?" the judge asked. "Him hitting a federal agent? Has he ever informed?"

"No, but none of us have known where the lab is," Spider said. "He might've been waiting for that."

Good point. I bent my knees in more case I had to jump up quickly. "What are we waiting for?" Not that I wanted to get shot or anything. But this was weird, and it was difficult to breathe. I thought my ribs were bruised, but who knew.

The judge angled his neck. "Your boyfriend stole something of ours for leverage, and we're using you to get it back."

I blinked. "Huh?"

"Aiden stole the first load of drugs—the only batch we have that's not in the hidden lab right now. He took them right from my dealership," Sal confirmed, grease across his chin. "We called him and said you'd be in pieces if he didn't bring it all back. Right now and by himself."

My head pounded. In pieces? My skin pricked everywhere in a sharp reminder of the adrenaline rush. "What makes you think he'll come for me?"

The sound of a truck down the lane cut through the rainy night.

Spider grinned. "We might've lost our chemist and lab, but we have enough Beast coming this way to sell and set up again."

Great plan. It included both Aiden and me being dead, however. I angled more onto the heels of my feet.

The outside floodlights flicked to life. A long car hauler drove partway by with eight used cars, all different types, lined up on it. The number of pills they might contain was staggering. The hydraulics protested when the driver halted it.

The door opened, and Aiden Devlin jumped to the ground, his arms out to show he was unarmed. His gaze instantly sought mine. "You okay, Angel?"

CHAPTER 42

Fear now tasted like acid in my mouth. "I'm fine." Then I listened. Was there any way he had backup? Only the storm cut through the night. "You okay?"

"Yep." He kept his arms out as the judge rather expertly patted him down and found no weapons.

I stared at him. Light jeans, dark T-shirt, scruff over his jaw. Stress lines cut into the sides of his eyes and mouth, but his chest was wide and his gaze direct. Nobody had ever looked better to me. He'd come for me. Into certain death, he'd brought those drugs to save me. Maybe our moment years ago had shaped us both.

Sal moved toward him, gun out. "Stand over there."

Aiden stood to the side of the garage, his hands at his sides.

Sal gave the judge the gun and ran out into the rain to jump on the hauler. He lifted the trunk to an older Ford Taurus and then looked up and smiled. "Drugs are here." He slammed it shut.

Spider stayed close to me; his gun steady in his hand. "Devlin? You a cop?"

"Nope," Aiden said, sliding his left foot back so slowly it was barely discernible.

"Then you're a snitch," Spider sneered.

The judge held the gun on Aiden. "I've looked through all the case files and haven't seen your name anywhere. It's odd with your rap sheet that you're out of prison. It's almost as if your history is made up perfectly."

"Good to know," Aiden said evenly.

"Judge?" I ignored the pain in my ribs and flattened my feet beneath me. "You haven't killed anybody and can still get out of this. Heck, you've acted insane the last year or so and probably can plead insanity. That was the plan, right?"

His gaze flickered my way.

Aiden kicked for the gun. The second I saw him move, I jumped up, chin down, and charged Spider right in the gut. My head plowed into his stomach, and we flew across the cement to land hard and skid. His gun skipped farther into the garage. He threw me off him, and I landed on my arm, crying out at the shocking pain.

Then I scrambled for his gun on my hands and knees. Small rocks and cement shards sliced into my already damaged palms.

Spider grabbed me around the waist and threw me to the side. I kicked out, nailing him in the knee. It buckled, and he went down, swinging.

I moved for the gun, and he grabbed my shoulder, twisting and throwing hard. Pain shot down my arm, and I tumbled head over tail, hitting the rear tire of the car.

Spider got the gun.

Panicking, I threw myself under the car, rolling until I got to the other side. He fired, and bullets pinged off the metal. I crouched next to a tire, looking frantically around. The judge lay prone on the ground, where Aiden must've slammed him. Right now, Aiden and Sal traded punches, Aiden definitely winning.

Until a bullet shot from Spider hit him in the upper thigh.

"Aiden!" I yelled, crab-walking to the front of the car.

He slammed Sal's head into the side of the garage and then

went down, clutching his leg. Blood welled between his fingers, pumping out a dark red. He shook his head like he'd taken a blow to the temple.

The clicking of a gun echoed through the small space. Spider needed to reload.

"Run, Anna," Aiden groaned, pulling himself up to sit by Sal. He started searching the unconscious guy's pockets with the hand not plugging what looked like an artery.

I stood and looked over the hood at Spider. He was on his knees, furiously whipping through his coat to drag out a silver clip, which glinted like evil in the dim light. I could make it to the door, but Aiden was a sitting duck. There was only one option. I yelled as loud as I could and rushed Spider, reaching him and kicking him as hard as I could beneath the chin. He fell back, and I stomped on his face out of sheer panic, trying to keep his beefy arms from swinging up again.

He grabbed my left ankle, so I jumped up and nailed him in the temple with my right foot.

His hold loosened and he flopped back.

Sobbing and grunting in sheer terror, I kicked him again, right where his jaw met his temple. It cracked loudly. He clutched it, tears streaming down his face.

I ripped the gun away from him and threw it, turning to see it smack Aiden in the head.

"Ouch!" he howled.

Then the whole world descended upon us. Men in full tack gear dropped on ropes from a helicopter, and emergency vehicles screeched to a halt on either side of the car hauler. Black SUVs with lights, patrol cars, even nondescript cars with red and blue lights.

Pierce jumped out of a patrol car and ran for me, his vest over his dress shirt. "Anna." He reached me and paused, sucking in air. "You're okay." He planted his hands on his thighs, partially bent over, breathing heavily. "All right." He tilted his head and looked at

Spider, who was bleeding profusely from the head and face. "Your work?"

Almost numb, I nodded.

Nick Basanelli leaped out of a still moving SUV and headed straight for me, his chin down, and his gaze seeing everything. He stopped right before touching me. "Are you all right?"

"Yes." I really needed to get out of that garage. Holding my rib cage, I staggered over to Aiden, where a paramedic was cutting away his jeans to reveal a very nice thigh...and bullet hole. Blood spilled out of it, running over his skin to land on the cement. I gagged.

The paramedic, a young woman with cool pink streaked hair, pressed against the wound. "It's a through and through. Not bad," she said, smiling at Aiden.

Aiden shook his head. "I told you to run." Pain pinched the sides of his mouth.

I nodded. "Yeah. I heard you." Maybe it had been my turn to save him. "Tag. You're it." My brain was super fuzzy. I needed to feel the rain, so I walked out of the garage, pausing as the judge shoved himself to a seated position.

His eyes were dazed. "Alberto. What happened?"

Red edged in from the sides of my vision. I kicked him in the calf. Hard. "It's Albertini, you jackass." Then I limped into the rain and lifted my face, letting nature cool me.

AT THE HOSPITAL, the doctors were thorough and finally declared that I was just one big bruise. Nothing cracked or broken. I should definitely call one of my sisters to pick me up, but at the moment, I just needed to sit. The reception area was vacant, and even the television was muted. Quiet. I could use some quiet. So I stumbled out of the examination room to a lime green chair and sat, shutting my eyes. Movement sounded, and a heavy body sat next to me.

Was it odd that I could identify Nick by smell? I opened my eyes. "Hey, boss."

"You earned your money today, now didn't you?" He kicked out his legs. "The DEA raided the building we thought was the lab out by the airport, and BINGO. We got drugs, recipes, and quite a few techs who were very happy to talk. It was a good bust." He patted his flat stomach.

"Good." I was probably too involved with the case to prosecute anybody if I was a witness. I yawned, and my jaw cracked. "I heard that Spider had to have his jaw wired." I didn't regret one kick. Not one.

Nick snorted. "Yeah. I heard that, too." He sobered and drew out his phone. "I have other news."

I sighed. "Like you hired all the attorneys back?"

"Nope." He placed the phone on his thigh. "My contacts found Jareth Davey."

I stilled, and my laziness disappeared. "What? Where? Here?"

"No." Nick patted my hand. "Right this second, he's in San Diego. My buddy has a visual on him, although it looks like he's ready to venture out to the wilderness with a lot of equipment." He tapped the phone. "Do you want to see a picture?"

I swallowed and stared at the quiet device. "No." My shoulders relaxed. "I mean, yes, I will. But not tonight."

"Got it." Nick put his phone away. "They've traced his movements. He was in Spokane for two days, and we're not sure why yet, but now he's gone. Safely away from you and from here. My guys will keep an eye on him."

For how long? I doubted they had that kind of time, but for now, I'd take the good news. "What about Aiden and the case against him for the drug running?"

Nick sighed and pinched the bridge of his nose. "That case was forced by the DEA to make Scot charge Aiden and see what shook out. There's not enough to go to trial on anything, so I'll have to drop all the charges. But he's not a good guy, Anna. You have to know that. Next time, we'll get him."

Maybe, maybe not. Something told me that Aiden was a good guy, or at least a decent one. "We'll see."

Nick nodded. "We can talk about Devlin at length later. For now, get some rest."

Fair enough. "Thanks, Nick."

"You bet." He looked at his watch. "I have to go. Take the rest of the week off." He patted my shoulder and strode toward the exit, quickly dodging into the darkened night.

Detective Pierce emerged from a room down the hallway, barking something into his phone before clicking off. He reached me in long strides. "I have enough of your statement for tonight." We'd talked while I'd waited to get x-rayed earlier. "Why don't you go get some rest?" He looked tired but his eyes were amped. A good bust would do that.

"I plan on it. Don't call me, for any case, until next week." I smiled, wondering if he'd take time off, too.

He grinned. "It's a promise."

I cleared my throat. "Nick is dropping the earlier drug charges against Aiden Devlin. Are you arresting him for his involvement in the bust tonight?" That would lead to new charges, and I'd have to recuse myself because I'd be a witness.

Pierce frowned, losing the smile. "Oddly enough, I don't have probable cause for an arrest tonight. We have no proof that Aiden held intent to be in possession of drugs, unless you know it to be true."

I shook my head. "I saw him drive the car hauler to save me, but I didn't see drugs." Even if the drugs were in those cars, Aiden could say he just used the vehicle to save me, which he did. "What about the battery charge from when he punched the DEA Agent during the bust at the Lordes?" It was a good case.

Somehow, Pierce's frown grew darker. "The DEA Agent said it

wasn't Devlin who hit him. It's your word against the agent's, and any decent defense attorney will get Devlin off."

I swallowed. Why would the agent cover for Aiden? "I thought Devlin didn't work for or with the DEA." None of this was making sense.

"He doesn't," Pierce said. "But he's got friends in high places, or he's involved somewhere and somehow. Either way, he's danger-ous, or he's in danger, and you should stay away from him." Then Pierce, too, walked out into the dark and rainy night without another word.

That was probably good advice, but I really needed to know the truth. Would Aiden finally tell me? Could he?

Just then, Aiden limped out of a closer room, wearing hospital scrubs. He eyed me from head to toe. "You broken anywhere?"

"No. Just bruised," I murmured, feeling way too affected by testosterone all of a sudden. "You?"

"Just stitches." He looked pretty good in scrubs.

I stood carefully, trying not to jostle any of my aches or pains. "I'm headed home. Want to come with me?" I wasn't trying to be coy or even seductive, since it was time we were honest with each other.

"Yeah." He took my hand, and we walked out into the rain together.

"You're going to level with me tonight," I warned him, heading toward his motorcycle.

He exhaled. "Tonight, we're going to eat some food, drink some wine, and get some sleep. If we wake up, feeling okay, we're going to fuck. But I am not talking tonight, and you're going to have to trust me. At least for a little while."

I sighed. "I'll try, but first I do need a couple of answers. Do you work for the DEA?"

"God, no." He kept walking in the rain, his hand warm around mine.

I exhaled. "Is your rap sheet accurate? Did you break all of those laws?"

He was silent for a moment. "No."

Hope crashed through me, and I waited to ask another question. "You're one of the good guys?"

His chuckle was dark. Sexy. "I'm not one of the good guys, but I'm not a criminal. Well, not really. That's all I can tell you right now. Trust me."

I could trust him. Heck, I was really trusting myself. One night to let him have his secrets was all right with me. While I'd give him this night, he needed to come clean soon.

He straddled the bike and held out an arm to help me on. I wrapped my hands around his waist and snuggled my face into his back.

Aiden Devlin was finally home.

CHAPTER 43

*J*slept most of the day on Wednesday. Aiden had, indeed, spent the night. There had been a lot of gentle kisses and rolling around in the morning, as well as a couple of intense orgasms on my part. But there hadn't been much talking. He'd taken off early, leaving me to sleep the day away.

Early afternoon, I called Pauley to make sure he was all right. His voice reassured me, and then my aunt confirmed that he was dealing well with the drama of the other day. Thank goodness. I then put in a call to Lacey, leaving a message because she was at work. She'd no doubt call the next day.

Late afternoon, I walked carefully into Bud's hospital room with a pretty bouquet of yellow daisies to place on his counter. "Hi."

He took up all of the long bed and then some more. The cop looked different out of uniform in the soft white hospital gown. More approachable and kind of goofy. Well, he'd always looked goofy. He eyed me and sighed. "Please don't get me killed today."

I swatted his foot. "Come on. You've been on protection duty before, and hey, you were wearing a vest. You're smart."

"I've never been injured. I'm zero for two with you, Albertini."

He glanced at the flowers. "You don't have a crush on me or anything, do you?" His face filled with a nice color. "You're cute, but you're not my type."

"No." I flopped into the chair, keeping my arm across my ribs as I did so. The doctors were right that it would hurt bad today. It did. Though I'd slept great knowing Jareth Davey was states away. Well, the pain killers didn't hurt, either. "You're probably the only new guy in my life I'm sure about. You and I are going to be great friends."

He rubbed his buzz cut. "That might be too dangerous."

"I'll invite you to a barbecue or something where my sister Donna is in attendance."

He sat up—and I swear—his chest puffed out. "Well, I guess that'd be okay."

Yeah. I'd figured out his type. Classic and beautiful Italian woman. Donna. "It's a plan, then." I stood and tried not to wince. "Thanks for everything, Bud."

"Sure thing." He turned back to the game on the television.

I grinned and moved carefully out of the room, before driving just as carefully home. Spring had finally arrived, again, and the sun set over a sparkling blue lake. I wandered into my quiet bungalow, feeling a little lonely for some reason.

My phone buzzed with a text from Detective Grant Pierce: *Hey. I hope you're feeling better. How about I take you to dinner tonight —a mellow one—and we make up for the date we lost? No pressure.*

Interesting. The cop was a hottie, that was for sure. I liked that he was older than me. I started to make tea.

The second text came in—this one from Nick—as the water was boiling: *Hi, Albertini. We nailed that case. How about I take you out for a nice drink to celebrate tonight since you took the day off? Just low key. Let me know.*

Hmm. Nick Basanelli. Sex on a stick of Italian ambition. Yeah, he'd be fun to date. The kettle whistled, and I poured water into the cup.

The next text came in right as I was dunking the tea bag, and of course, it was from Aiden: *Hi, Angel. I enjoyed last night and thought I should let you know that I don't share. If you're in my bed, or I'm in yours, we're solo. I know I have a lot to tell you, but I can't right now. So how about we just get together, and I bring over dinner?*

I sipped my tea and thought it over. Who'd have believed that a few weeks ago I'd be here right now? Three very different and interesting men, each one a risk in several ways to me. I wasn't a risky type of person and never had been. Although, a girl did have to live a little.

There was really only one answer for what I needed. I pulled the Bailey's cheesecake out of the freezer and dashed off several texts to people before tossing my phone aside.

Then I strode for my bedroom to put on exactly what I needed for the night.

* * *

Twenty minutes later, I arrived at Donna's cute Craftsman house in the older part of town, cheesecake in hand. I walked inside.

She looked up from laying colorful pillows in front of her cream-colored sofa and laughed. Her green silk pajamas appeared decadent, and I'd have to get myself a pair. "Tell me you did not wear your pajamas to drive over here."

I looked down at my duck-covered leggings with matching top. The penguin slippers might have been a bit much. "Yes, I did." I set the dessert on the kitchen's island and headed her way.

Tessa came out of the guest bathroom, already wearing her flannel pajamas with her hair up in a high ponytail. Knowing me, she tossed me a holder, and I yanked my hair up and out of the way.

Donna opened her credenza to reveal the big television set before pulling out the X-Box and three controllers. Mine was bright purple with unicorns across it, hers was green and sparkly, and Tessa's was a flashy yellow with a drawing of some Celtic knot. "All right," Donna said. "I ordered pizza. The first to lose this game pays."

I scooted her way and sat on the middle pillow, which was a dark blue. My pillow.

Donna gracefully sat on my left on the green pillow, while Tessa flopped down on the yellow pillow.

Tess snorted. "Your Aiden pillow. Is it still your Aiden pillow?"

I chuckled. "No. His eyes are a much lighter blue than I remembered."

Donna gently kicked my slipper. "You're sitting on Aiden's face."

Tessa snorted. "You're on a green turd."

I took my controller and drew it up closer, sitting between my sisters, which had always been my place. My fun and safe and given place. Sure, tomorrow I'd have to figure out what to do about Jareth Davey. Then I'd have to decide if I wanted to date anybody, and I wanted to figure out a heck of a lot more about Aiden. Regardless. I needed to delve deep and truly understand the feelings I had for him. Cousin Wanda the shrink would help with that.

But tonight, I was going to eat too much, laugh just enough, and play X-Box with my sisters.

"You ready?" Donna asked, pressing the button.

"Yeah," I said, meaning it on every front. "Let's do this."

BAILED OUT

THE ANNA ALBERTINI FILES BOOK 2

Bailed Out

The Past Never Stays Buried

Anna Albertini is settling into a routine while ignoring the fact that the blue-eyed Irishman she'd allowed into her bed has up and disappeared on her. Two weeks without a phone call is no big deal, but still. With her hottie Italian boss goofing up the prosecuting attorney's office, she at least has something to fix. Until she appears in court, across from her sister Tessa's dirtbag ex. Then she has a mission.

Unfortunately, Anna isn't the only person who wants the ex put behind bars...or in the ground. Which is not a problem until she and a local cop find the ex-boyfriend deader than dead...with both her sister and Aiden standing over the body.

As a prosecuting attorney, it's Anna's job to build a case against Tessa and Aiden. As a sister, it's SO her job to get Tess out of this mess. As Aiden's...what? Lover—girlfriend—friend from the past —it's Anna's job to figure out who the heck he really is. She has to dig out the truth, regardless of her ambitious boss or the cranky cop trying to thwart her every move. Sometimes a woman has to take matters into her own hands, regardless of the consequences.

PURCHASE NOW where all books are sold!

TAKE A QUICK PEEK AT THE NEXT DARK PROTECTOR BOOK!

REBEL'S KARMA

REBEL'S KARMA

Chapter 1

The smell of the earth, deep and true, centered her in the hastily created tunnel. It probably said something about Karma that she preferred darkness, muddy walls, and being underground to anywhere else. Battery operated lanterns had been dropped haphazardly along the trail, their artificial light dancing across the dirt-packed walls and highlighting minerals she couldn't name as she descended quickly, the swish of her skirt the only sound beneath ground.

She bent her head, trying to stay in the moment and not panic at the job to come. One she was no more prepared for than she had been for mating a Kurjan general nearly two centuries ago. Or was it closer to three?

Taking a deep breath, she turned the corner and faced the cell. The one and only cell that had been dug the day before, just in case it was needed.

It was.

She swallowed.

The male sprawled across the ground, so large he could probably spread his arms and reach the cement blocks on one side and the steel bars on the other. If he'd been conscious. Instead, bruises mottled his face and neck, while a wound bled freely beneath his jaw. The red ran down beyond his ear to pool on the dirt beneath him.

She couldn't breathe.

It really was him. Even with the bruises, blood, and dirt covering his face, she recognized him from more than a year ago. He'd tried to pull her into a helicopter with him after he'd attacked the Kurjan stronghold. He was bad, and he was the enemy, and yet...he'd saved several kidnapped human females from the Kurjans.

Had he thought he was saving her? Or, had he hurt those human females? Were they now in a worse position than they'd faced with the Kurjan nation?

She waited patiently, as she'd been taught through the years. The guard would get to her when he had time. The medical supplies in her pack became heavy, so she set them down, stepping closer to the bars to study the male.

Benjamin Horatio Lawrence Reese. He was a vampire-demon hybrid, large even for his kind. At about six-foot-seven, or maybe eight, he was as tall as many Kurjans. The wideness of his torso tapered down to his waist and led to long legs. His boots had to be a size eighteen, and his hands were big enough to cause colossal damage. Oh, she'd been hit before, but one punch from him, and she'd be dead.

He could never know how much she already knew about him. How she'd been training for this day for a year—since he'd tried to take her from another Kurjan holding. Her home.

The air changed, and she stiffened as the guard made his way down the tunnel, his white hair glowing as he came closer. He was a Cyst; one of the elite soldiers and spiritual leaders of the Kurjan nation. A single line of white hair bisected his light scalp, leading down to a long braid. His eyes were a deep purple tinged with red, and he spared her no attention as he unlocked the cell and then stepped back.

She took a deep breath and entered, wincing as the coppery smell of blood assaulted her nostrils. Then she dropped to her knees and reached inside the pack for the materials that would clot the bleeding wound. How injured the hybrid must've been after the skirmish to still be bleeding.

The second she touched his head, his eyes opened.

Metallic, deep, and fully alert in a second, his eyes were unreal. "Karma," he murmured.

She drew back. He remembered her name? Nobody remembered her name.

"Do you need blood?" she whispered, leaning closer, even as the guard locked the cell door and disappeared down the hallway, leaving her with the enemy. Right now, she was useless to the Kurjans, so if the prisoner killed her, they'd find a Plan B.

"No." Benjamin sat up, looked around, and put his back to the cement brick wall. He took up all the available space with his impressive size.

She shook her head, her lips trembling. "You're badly injured to have been taken captive. You need blood."

"I let them take me. I've been searching for you since last year."

God. The Kurjans had been correct. He really had been looking for her since she hadn't let him rescue her the year before. "The baby? Rose?" Karma held her breath. When Benjamin's people had attacked the Kurjan holding, she'd gone with her instincts in a brief second and forced him to take a toddler who had been kidnapped—and she'd paid for that decision. Then she'd jumped away when he'd tried to save Karma, and she'd wondered what would've happened had she gone. Would she be in a worse state than right now? Probably. "Is Rose well?"

Benjamin nodded. "Rose is fine. She's at Realm headquarters with a nice family."

Relief and fear were an odd combination in Karma's blood. "Realm Headquarters?" They were the enemy of the Kurjans. They were evil, or so she'd been taught. She'd always wondered, because lies were everywhere. She held out the materials, although the wound was already closing beneath his jaw as he obviously sent healing cells where they were needed.

"I don't need those," he murmured, studying her with an intensity that shot tremors through her abdomen.

"I don't understand why you'd come looking for me," she said, sitting back and keeping her knees covered with her dress. It had been the plan, but she hadn't believed it. The Kurjan leaders had noted that this male kept showing up in different attacks, and he took ridiculous risks for a soldier with his experience. They'd known he was coming. Why would this male put himself in danger for her? "You let them take you hostage?"

"Yes." Benjamin's voice was low and rough with a hint of the demon ancestry he no doubt held.

She rested her hands on the thin material over her knees. "I don't understand."

A bone snapped loudly into place somewhere on his body, but he didn't even flinch. "Let's start here. I'm Benny Reese." He held out a hand the size of a good frying pan as if they were meeting at a village game instead of in a cell.

She hesitated and then slid hers against his. "Karma."

His hold and shake were gentle, and he released her before the mating allergy could hurt either of them. She'd been mated centuries ago to a Kurjan, and no other male could touch her for long without both of them succumbing to deadly rashes.

"What's your last name?" he asked. Another bone popped into place.

She jerked at the sound. "I do not have a last name."

"Oh." He looked beyond her at the steel bars securing the cell. "I was out for a while. Where are we?"

"We are at a temporary holding area before you are transported to a more secure location." She coughed. "For questioning."

His smile nearly knocked her over. Even the slight tipping of his lips turned his rugged face from dangerously hard to nearly boyish with charm. Amusement, real and true, glimmered in his metallic eyes for a moment. "Darlin', I've been tortured before. You don't need to worry yourself about that."

She had bigger things to worry about than the life of this massive hybrid. She allowed herself one moment to stare into his rare eyes. Oh, many immortals had metallic silver eyes, gold eyes, even copper or purple. But his were a combination of all metallic colors, mingling into a hard-edge glint, even with the humor lurking there. In another time, she might've thought him beautiful. She'd learned long ago that beauty could mask the darkest of evils.

Vampires were bad, demons were bad, and this male was a hybrid of both. When he decided to kill her, and he would at some point, she didn't stand much of a chance at surviving. Yet she still couldn't comprehend why he'd come for her. "Why are you here?"

"For you. To rescue you since I couldn't last time." He stretched out his arms and healed a broken finger in his left hand.

That didn't make any sense. "Why?" Surely his ego wasn't such that he'd spent an entire year chasing her down and risking his life just because he'd lost the battle for her last time. She wasn't worth that.

He sighed. "I'd hoped to ease you into the truth, but here it is." He held up his right hand, showing a demon marking with a jagged R in the center. The R was a crest for his surname: Reese. Demons mated with a branding, a bite, and sex and the marking transferred from the demon to the mate during fornication.

Her mouth dropped open and she hurried to shut it. "You're mated?" Why did that one thought nauseate her? How odd.

"No. The brand appeared when I touched you a year ago." His chin lowered, and he studied her, towering over her even as he sat. "When you shoved me away and refused to get into the helicopter with me."

She snorted and then quickly recovered. "Impossible. I'm mated." Well, she had been mated a couple of centuries ago, although her Kurjan mate had died shortly thereafter. Sometimes she forgot what he had looked like, and that was fine with her. "Your brand appeared for someone else."

"No." Benjamin looked down at the dark marking. "The mark hasn't faded in a year, and it's pulsing like a live wire now that you're near."

Oh, Lord. The research on Benjamin that stated he might be insane must be true. She sighed. Dangerous and unstable? There was no way she could succeed in this mission. "Benjamin—"

"Benny. Might as well get cozy with me now." His smile held charm and a determination that warmed her in an impossible way.

For the second time in her life, she let her instincts take over. "Just leave. Take an opening and find freedom," she whispered tersely, her stomach cramping. "Forget about me."

"Not a chance." His gaze ran over her face like a physical touch.

Movement sounded down the tunnel, and she stiffened.

Benjamin tensed and his jaw set. "Get ready, darlin'. We're about to escape this place."

Hunter Advancing (2021)

The Dark Protector Series

Fated (Book 1)

Claimed (Book 2)

Tempted (2.5)

Hunted (Book 3)

Consumed (Book 4)

Provoked (Book 5)

Twisted (5.5)

Shadowed (Book 6)

Tamed (6.5)

Marked (Book 7)

Vampire's Faith (Book 8)

Demon's Mercy (Book 9)

Alpha's Promise (Book 10)

Hero's Haven (Book 11)

Guardian's Grace (Book 12)

Rebel's Karma (Book 13)

Immortal's Honor (Book 14)

Realm Enforcers (Dark Protector spinoff)

Wicked Ride

Wicked Edge

Wicked Burn

Wicked Kiss

Wicked Bite

Dark Protectors: Reese Family novellas

Teased

Tricked

Tangled

Dark Protectors: Rebels novellas

Vengeance

Vixen

Vampire

The Sin Brothers series

Forgotten Sins

Sweet Revenge

Blind Faith

Total Surrender

The Blood Brother series (Spinoff of Sin Bros)

Deadly Silence

Lethal Lies

Twisted Truths

The Maverick Montana series

Against the Wall

Under the Covers

Rising Assets

Over the Top

To keep up to date:

www.RebeccaZanetti.com

https://www.facebook.com/RebeccaZanetti.books

http://rebeccazanetti.com/rebeccas-newsletter/

READING LISTS OF SERIES IN ORDER

I know a lot of you like the exact reading order for a series, so here's the exact reading order as of the release of this book, although if you read most of them out of order, it's okay.

THE ANNA ALBERTINI FILES

1. Disorderly Conduct
2. Bailed Out
3. Adverse Possession
4. The Santa Subpoena
5. Summary Judgment
6. Rebuttal Evidence

* * *

DEEP OPS SERIES

1. Hidden (Book 1)
2. Taken Novella (On the Hunt anthology) (Book 1.5)
3. Driven (Book 2)

4. Shaken Novella (In PIVOT anthology) (Book 2.5)
5. Broken (Book 3)
6. Driven (Book 4)

Dark Protectors / Realm Enforcers / 1001 Dark Nights novellas

1. Fated (Dark Protectors Book 1)
2. Claimed (Dark Protectors Book 2)
3. Tempted novella (Dark Protectors 2.5)
4. Hunted (Dark Protectors Book 3)
5. Consumed (Dark Protectors Book 4)
6. Provoked (Dark Protectors Book 5)
7. Twisted novella (Dark Protectors 5.5)
8. Shadowed (Dark Protectors Book 6)
9. Tamed novella (Dark Protectors 6.5)
10. Marked (Dark Protectors Book 7)
11. Wicked Ride (Realm Enforcers 1)
12. Wicked Edge (Realm Enforcers 2)
13. Wicked Burn (Realm Enforcers 3)
14. Talen novella (Dark Protectors 7.5)
15. Wicked Kiss (Realm Enforcers 4)
16. Wicked Bite (Realm Enforcers 5)
17. Vampire's Faith (Dark Protectors 8). ***A great entry point for series, if you want to start here***
18. Demon's Mercy (Dark Protectors 9)
19. Vengeance (Dark Protectors/Rebels 1001 Dark Night Novella)
20. Alpha's Promise (Dark Protectors 10)
21. Hero's Haven (Dark Protectors 11)
22. Guardian's Grace (Dark Protectors 12)
23. Vixen (Dark Protectors/Rebels 1001 Dark Night Novella)
24. Rebel's Karma (Dark Protectors 13)

25. Vampire (Dark Protectors/Rebels 1001 Dark Night Novella)
26. Immortal's Honor (Dark Protectors 14)

*** The Dark Protectors/Reese Brothers 1001 Dark Nights novellas (Teased, Tricked, Tangled) can be read any time after Marked. There's no crossover.

* * *

SIN BROTHERS/BLOOD BROTHERS spinoff

1. Forgotten Sins (Sin Brothers 1)
2. Sweet Revenge (Sin Brothers 2)
3. Blind Faith (Sin Brothers 3)
4. Total Surrender (Sin Brothers 4)
5. Deadly Silence (Blood Brothers 1)
6. Lethal Lies (Blood Brothers 2)
7. Twisted Truths (Blood Brothers 3)

* * *

SCORPIUS SYNDROME SERIES
**This is technically the right timeline, but I'd always meant for the series to start with Mercury Striking.

- 1. Scorpius Rising (Prequel novella - was actually written after Mercury Striking and shows how it all started)
- 2. Blaze Erupting (Scorpius/Brigade novella, 1001 Dark Nights)
- 3. Power Surging (Scorpius/Brigade novella)
- 4. Hunter Advancing (Scorpius/Brigade novella)

Scorpius Syndrome NOVELS
(Can be read without the novellas)
1. Mercury Striking (Scorpius Syndrome 1)
2. Shadow Falling (Scorpius Syndrome 2)
3. Justice Ascending (Scorpius Syndrome 3)
4. Storm Gathering (Scorpius Syndrome 4)
5. Winter Igniting (Scorpius Syndrome 5)
6. Knight Awakening (Scorpius Synd. 6)

MAVERICK MONTANA SERIES

1. Against the Wall
2. Under the Covers
3. Rising Assets
4. Over the Top

ABOUT THE AUTHOR

New York Times and *USA Today bestselling* author Rebecca Zanetti has published more than fifty romantic-suspense and dark paranormal novels, which have been translated into several languages, with millions of copies sold world-wide. Her books have received Publisher's Weekly starred reviews, won RT Reviewer Choice awards, have been featured in Entertainment Weekly, Woman's World and Women's Day Magazines, have been included in Amazon best books of the year, and have been favorably reviewed in both the Washington Post and the New York Times Book Reviews. Rebecca has ridden in a locked Chevy trunk, has asked the unfortunate delivery guy to release her from a set of handcuffs, and has discovered the best silver mine shafts in which to bury a body...all in the name of research. Honest. Find Rebecca at: www.RebeccaZanetti.com

Made in the USA
Las Vegas, NV
03 January 2021